THE BEAUTY™

VOLUME SIX

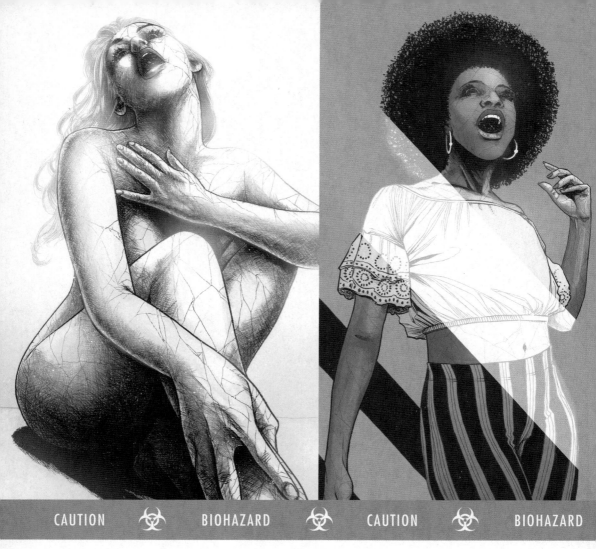

CAUTION ☣ BIOHAZARD ☣ CAUTION ☣ BIOHAZARD

IMAGE COMICS, INC.

TODD MCFARLANE President • JIM VALENTINO Vice President • MARC SILVESTRI Chief Executive Officer • ERIK LARSEN Chief Financial Officer
ROBERT KIRKMAN Chief Operating Officer • ERIC STEPHENSON Publisher / Chief Creative Officer • NICOLE LAPALME Controller
LEANNA CAUNTER Accounting Analyst • SUE KORPELA Accounting & HR Manager • MARLA EIZIK Talent Liaison • JEFF BOISON Director of
Sales & Publishing Planning • DIRK WOOD Director of International Sales & Licensing • ALEX COX Director of Direct Market Sales • CHLOE RAMOS
Book Market & Library Sales Manager • EMILIO BAUTISTA Digital Sales Coordinator • JON SCHLAFFMAN Specialty Sales Coordinator
KAT SALAZAR Director of PR & Marketing • DREW FITZGERALD Marketing Content Associate • HEATHER DOORNINK Production Director
DREW GILL Art Director • HILARY DILORETO Print Manager • TRICIA RAMOS Traffic Manager • MELISSA GIFFORD Content Manager
ERIKA SCHNATZ Senior Production Artist • RYAN BREWER Production Artist • DEANNA PHELPS Production Artist

www.imagecomics.com

THE BEAUTY, VOL. 6
ISBN: 978-1-5343-1496-2
First Printing. January 2022.

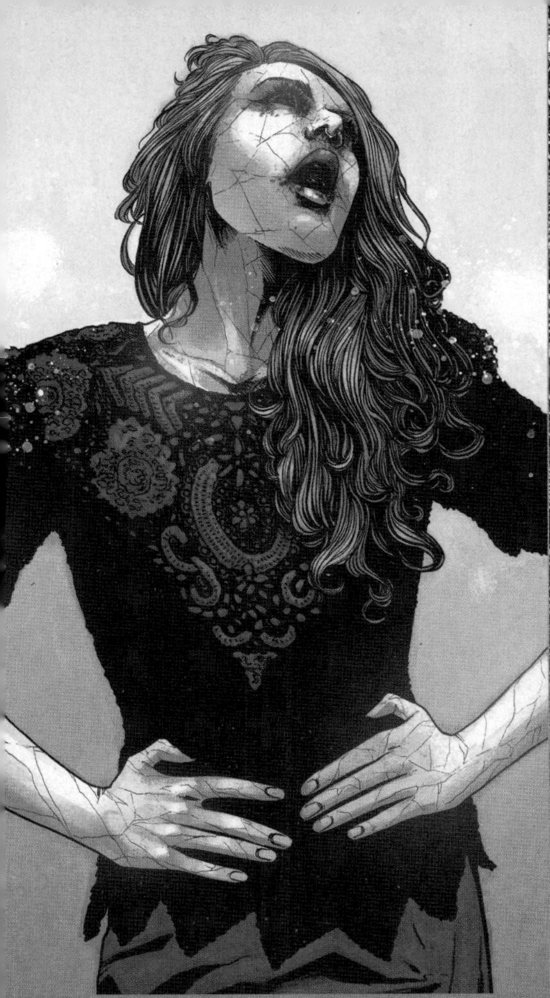

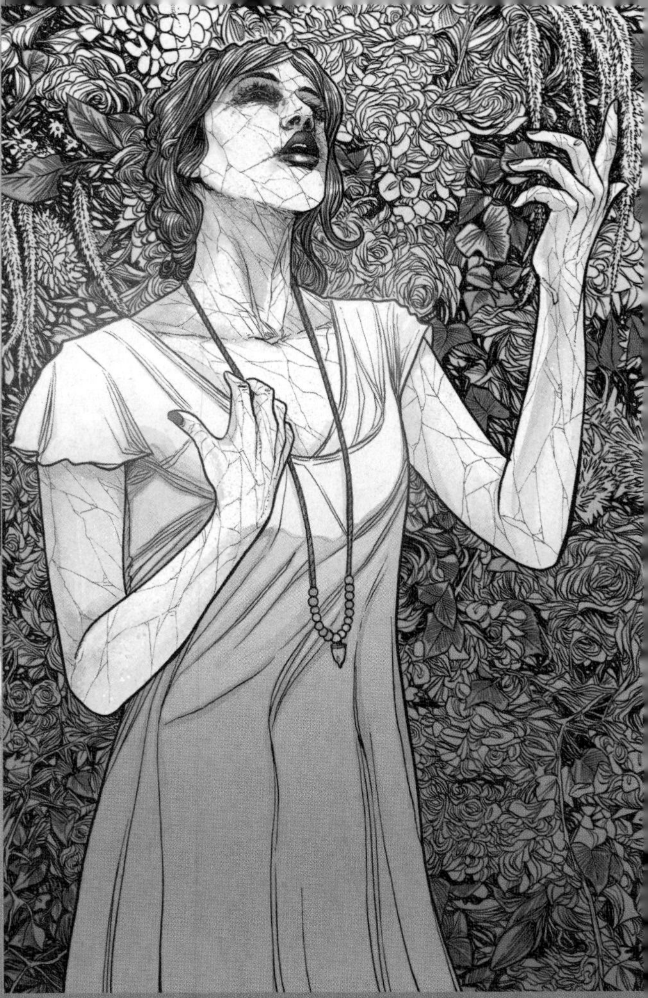

CAUTION BIOHAZARD CAUTION BIOHAZARD

JEREMY HAUN & JASON A. HURLEY
story

THOMAS NACHLIK (CHAPTERS 27-29)
MATTHEW DOW SMITH (CHAPTER 30 PART 1)
JEREMY HAUN & DANNY LUCKERT (CHAPTER 30 PART 2)
art

NAYOUNG KIM (CHAPTERS 27-29)
BRETT WELDELE (CHAPTER 30)
color

THOMAS MAUER
lettering & design

JOEL ENOS
editor

RYAN BREWER
production artist

CHAPTER

27

A WHOLE PIE

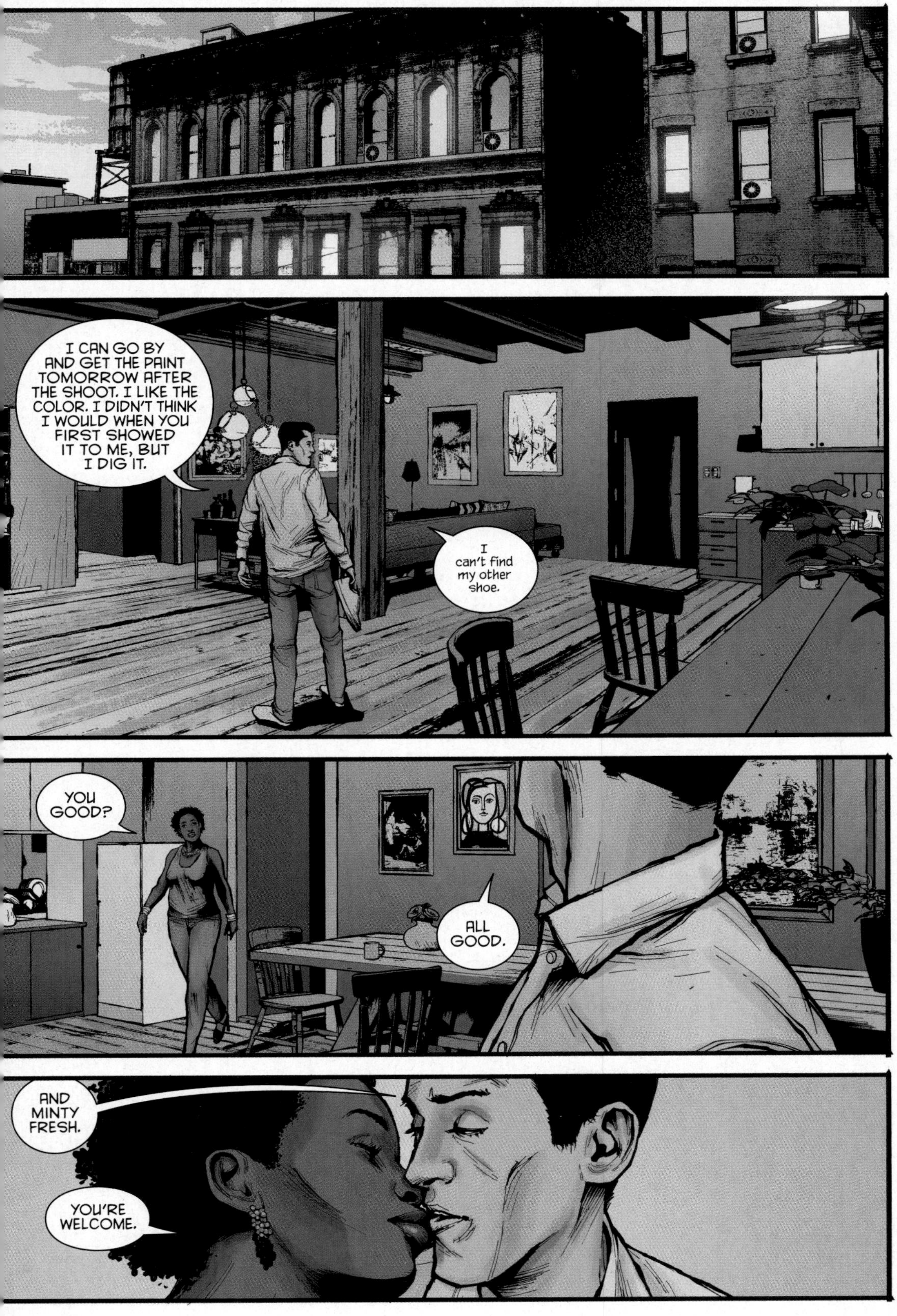
I CAN GO BY AND GET THE PAINT TOMORROW AFTER THE SHOOT. I LIKE THE COLOR. I DIDN'T THINK I WOULD WHEN YOU FIRST SHOWED IT TO ME, BUT I DIG IT.
I can't find my other shoe.
YOU GOOD?
ALL GOOD.
AND MINTY FRESH.
YOU'RE WELCOME.

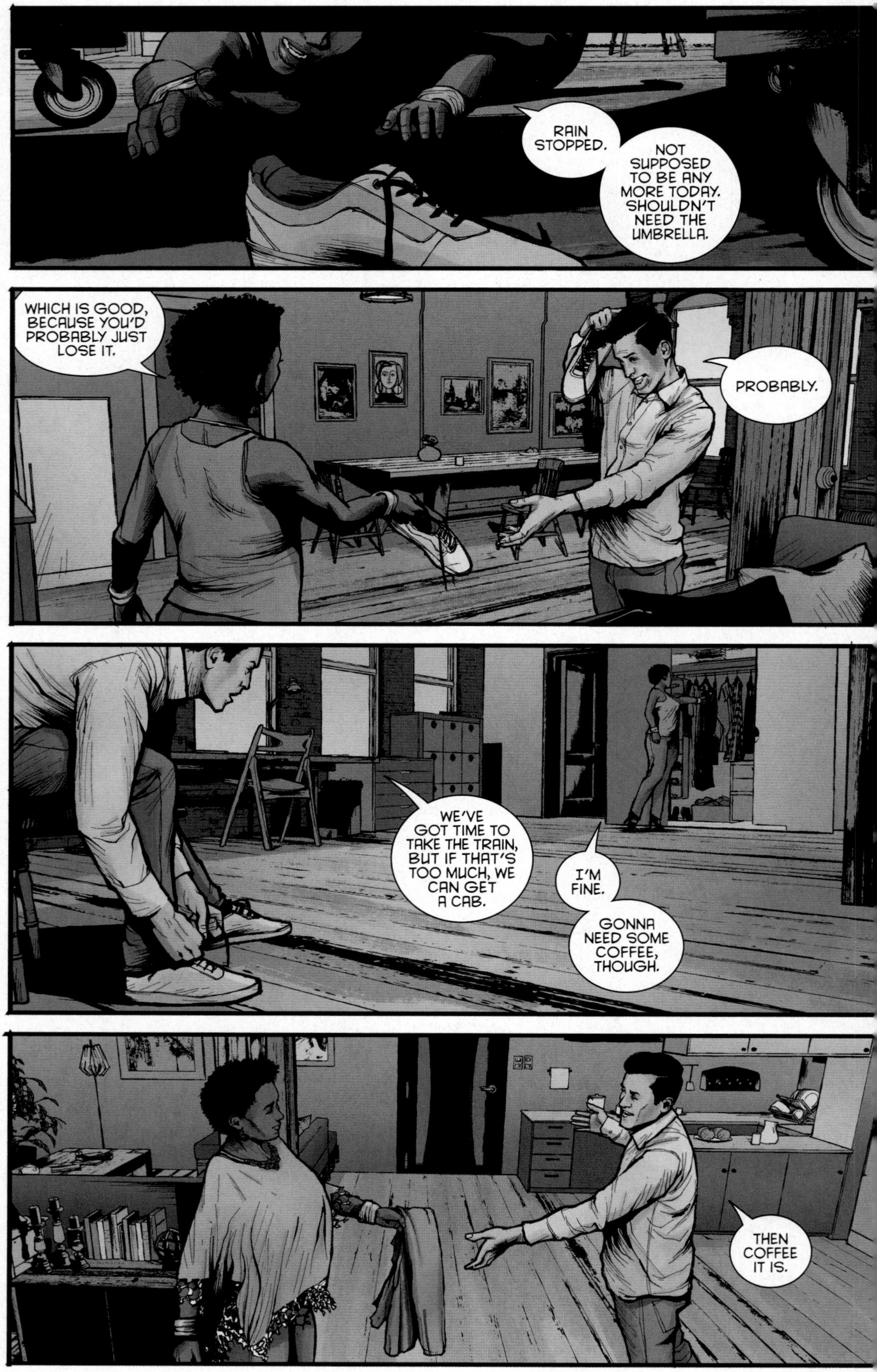
RAIN STOPPED.
NOT SUPPOSED TO BE ANY MORE TODAY. SHOULDN'T NEED THE UMBRELLA.
WHICH IS GOOD, BECAUSE YOU'D PROBABLY JUST LOSE IT.
PROBABLY.
WE'VE GOT TIME TO TAKE THE TRAIN, BUT IF THAT'S TOO MUCH, WE CAN GET A CAB.
I'M FINE.
GONNA NEED SOME COFFEE, THOUGH.
THEN COFFEE IT IS.

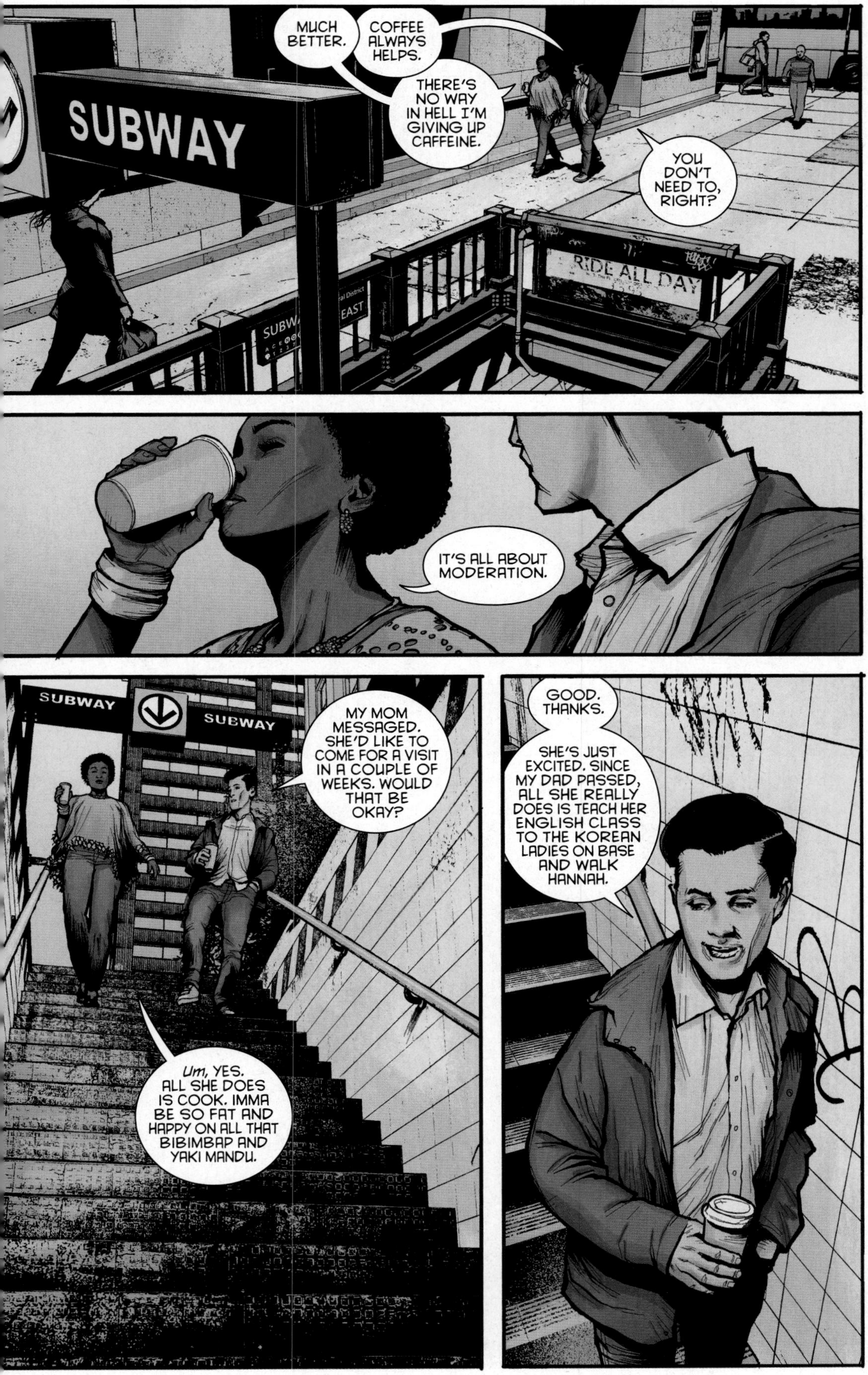
COFFEE ALWAYS HELPS.
MUCH BETTER.
THERE'S NO WAY IN HELL I'M GIVING UP CAFFEINE.
YOU DON'T NEED TO, RIGHT?
SUBWAY
RIDE ALL DAY
EAST
IT'S ALL ABOUT MODERATION.
SUBWAY
SUBWAY
MY MOM MESSAGED. SHE'D LIKE TO COME FOR A VISIT IN A COUPLE OF WEEKS. WOULD THAT BE OKAY?
Um, YES. ALL SHE DOES IS COOK. IMMA BE SO FAT AND HAPPY ON ALL THAT BIBIMBAP AND YAKI MANDU.
GOOD. THANKS.
SHE'S JUST EXCITED. SINCE MY DAD PASSED, ALL SHE REALLY DOES IS TEACH HER ENGLISH CLASS TO THE KOREAN LADIES ON BASE AND WALK HANNAH.

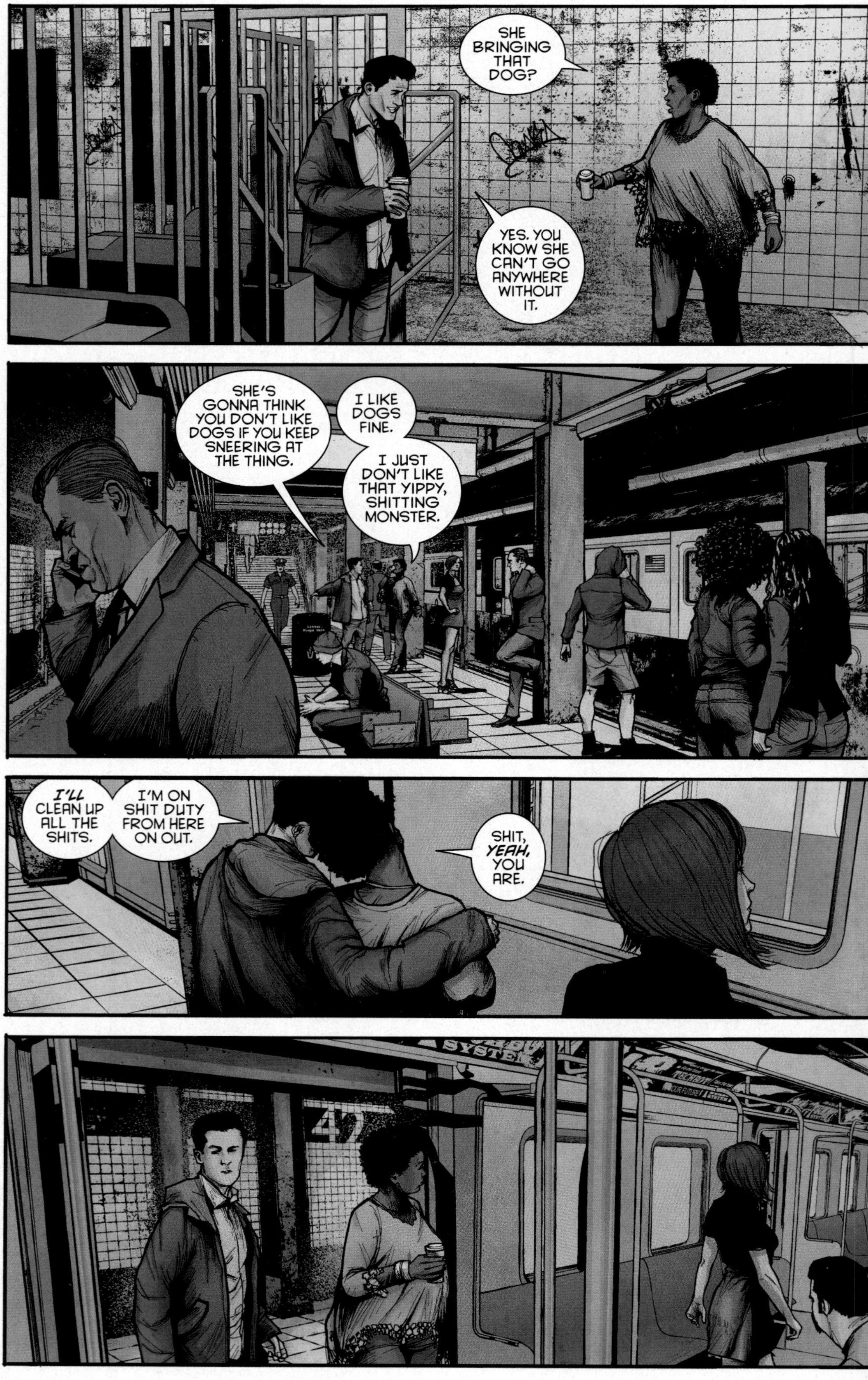
SHE BRINGING THAT DOG?
YES. YOU KNOW SHE CAN'T GO ANYWHERE WITHOUT IT.
SHE'S GONNA THINK YOU DON'T LIKE DOGS IF YOU KEEP SNEERING AT THE THING.
I LIKE DOGS FINE.
I JUST DON'T LIKE THAT YIPPY, SHITTING MONSTER.
I'LL CLEAN UP ALL THE SHITS.
I'M ON SHIT DUTY FROM HERE ON OUT.
SHIT, *YEAH,* YOU ARE.

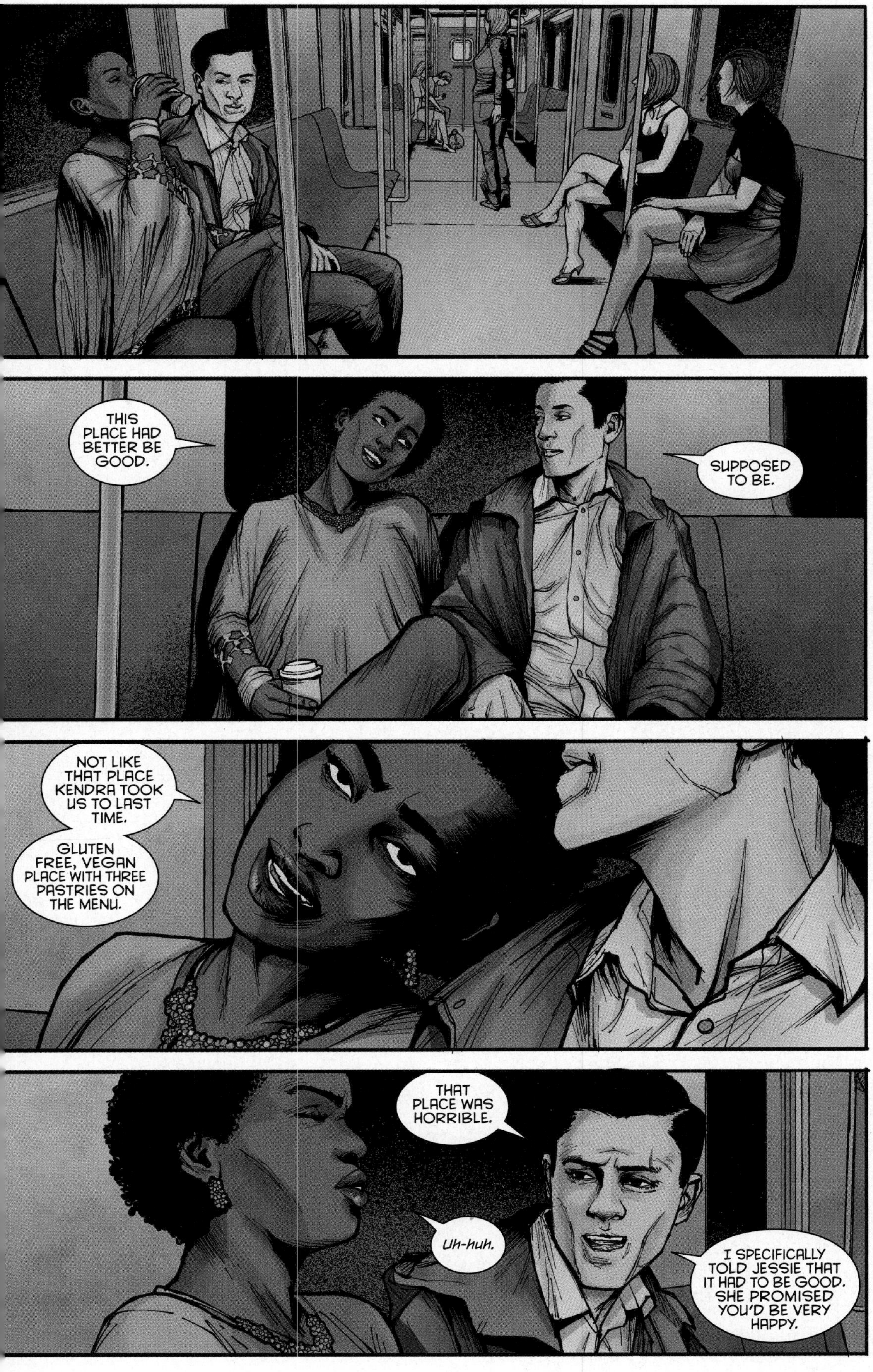
THIS PLACE HAD BETTER BE GOOD.
SUPPOSED TO BE.
NOT LIKE THAT PLACE KENDRA TOOK US TO LAST TIME.
GLUTEN FREE, VEGAN PLACE WITH THREE PASTRIES ON THE MENU.
THAT PLACE WAS HORRIBLE.
Uh-huh.
I SPECIFICALLY TOLD JESSIE THAT IT HAD TO BE GOOD. SHE PROMISED YOU'D BE VERY HAPPY.

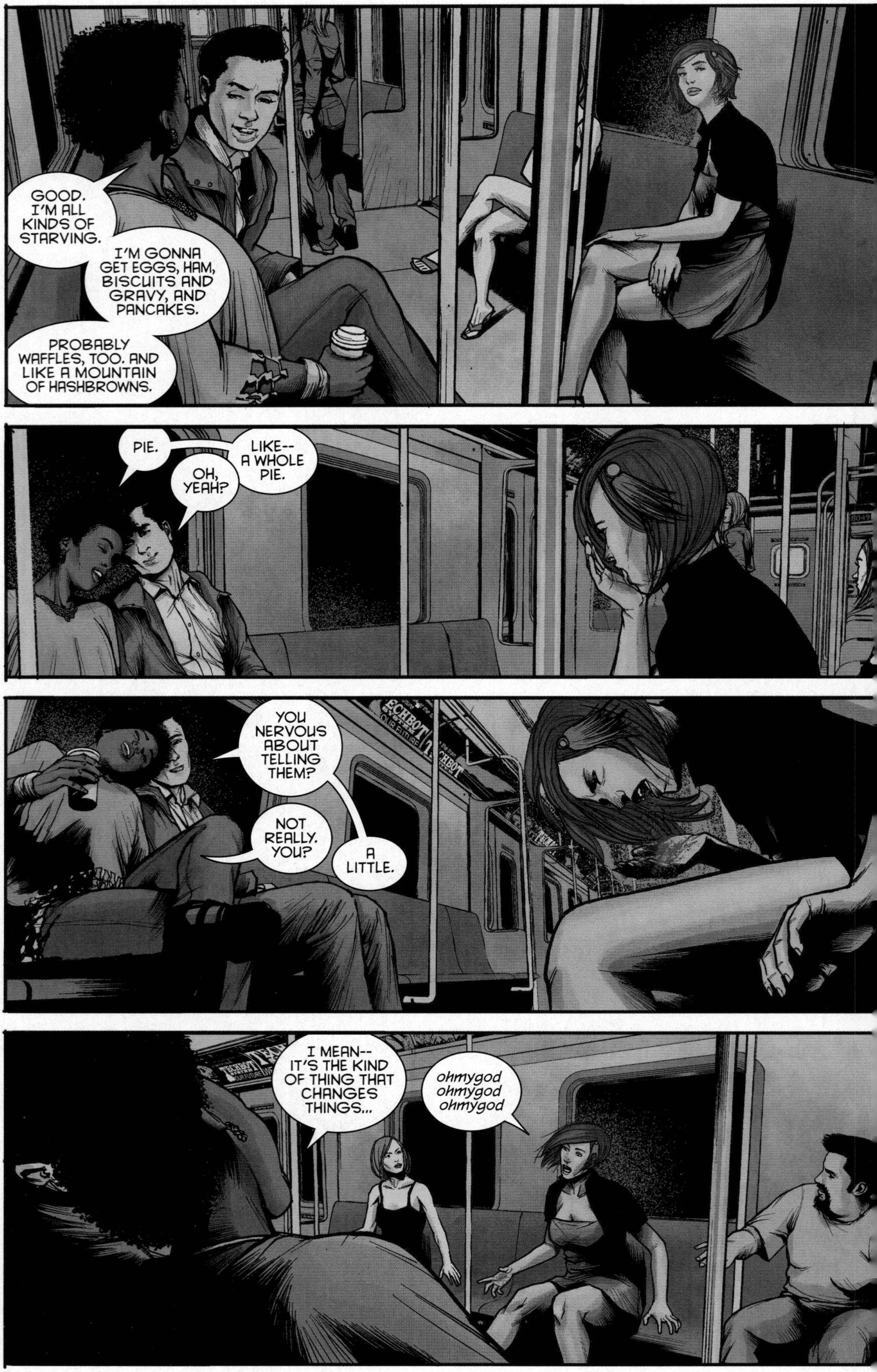
GOOD. I'M ALL KINDS OF STARVING.
I'M GONNA GET EGGS, HAM, BISCUITS AND GRAVY, AND PANCAKES.
PROBABLY WAFFLES, TOO. AND LIKE A MOUNTAIN OF HASHBROWNS.
PIE.
LIKE-- A WHOLE PIE.
OH, YEAH?
YOU NERVOUS ABOUT TELLING THEM?
NOT REALLY. YOU?
A LITTLE.
I MEAN-- IT'S THE KIND OF THING THAT CHANGES THINGS...
ohmygod ohmygod ohmygod

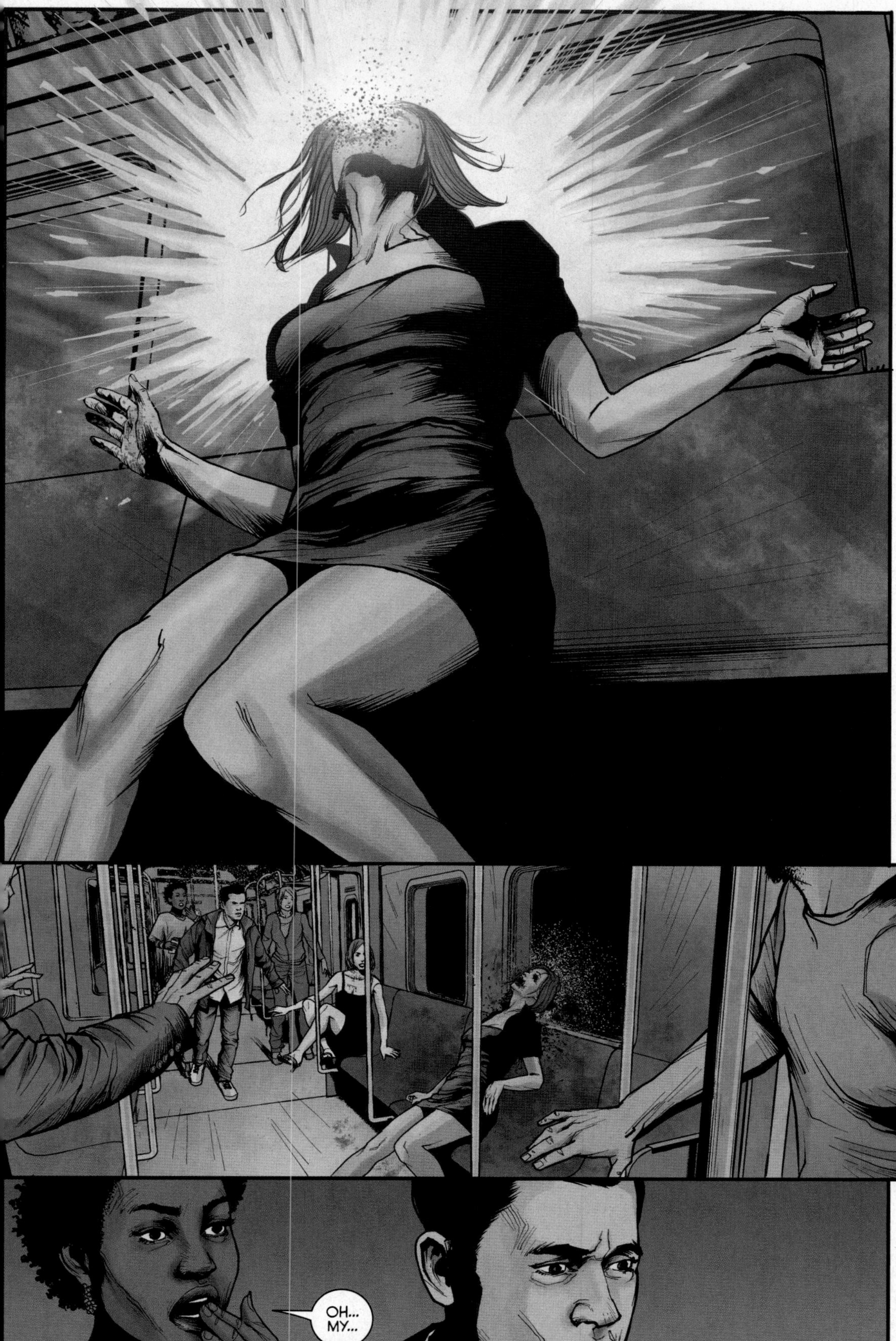
OH... MY...

PANCAKES

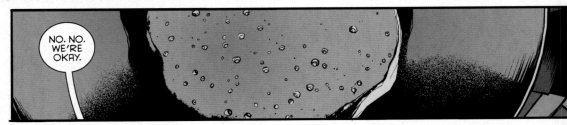

NO. NO. WE'RE OKAY.

WE JUST GOT BACK A FEW MINUTES AGO. I'M MAKING US SOMETHING TO EAT.

WE WERE THERE FOREVER. MADE A STATEMENT ABOUT WHAT HAPPENED.

SHIT.

I DON'T EVEN KNOW WHAT THE HELL HAPPENED...

YEAH. WE'LL DO THE BRUNCH THING SOON-- ONCE ADELAIDE IS BACK FROM HER TRIP. MAKE UP FOR IT.

THANKS, JESSIE.

YEAH. LOVE YOU, TOO.

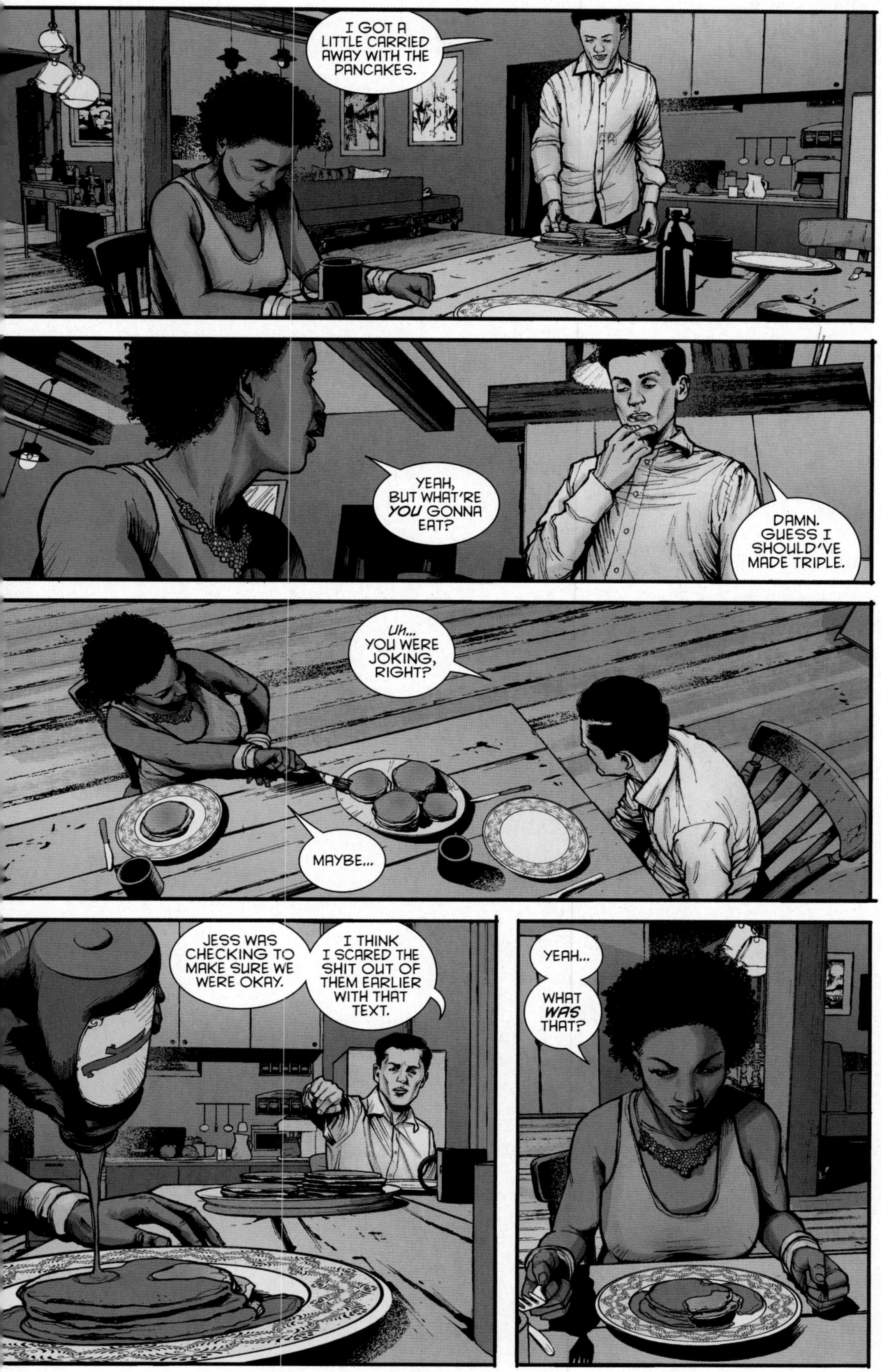
I GOT A LITTLE CARRIED AWAY WITH THE PANCAKES.
YEAH, BUT WHAT'RE *YOU* GONNA EAT?
DAMN. GUESS I SHOULD'VE MADE TRIPLE.
Uh... YOU WERE JOKING, RIGHT?
MAYBE...
JESS WAS CHECKING TO MAKE SURE WE WERE OKAY.
I THINK I SCARED THE SHIT OUT OF THEM EARLIER WITH THAT TEXT.
YEAH...
WHAT *WAS* THAT?

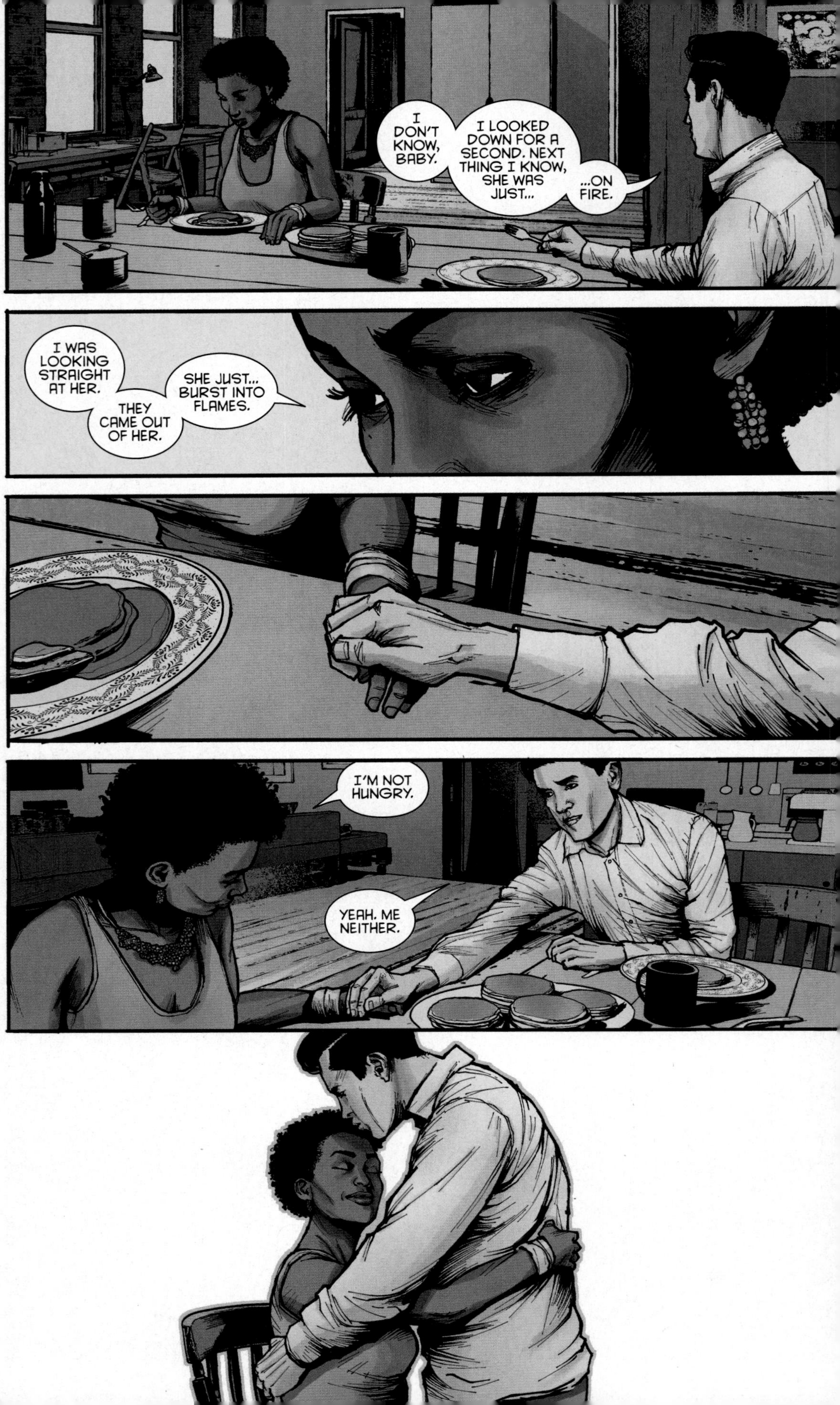
I DON'T KNOW, BABY.
I LOOKED DOWN FOR A SECOND. NEXT THING I KNOW, SHE WAS JUST...
...ON FIRE.
I WAS LOOKING STRAIGHT AT HER.
THEY CAME OUT OF HER.
SHE JUST... BURST INTO FLAMES.
I'M NOT HUNGRY.
YEAH. ME NEITHER.

THE NEWS

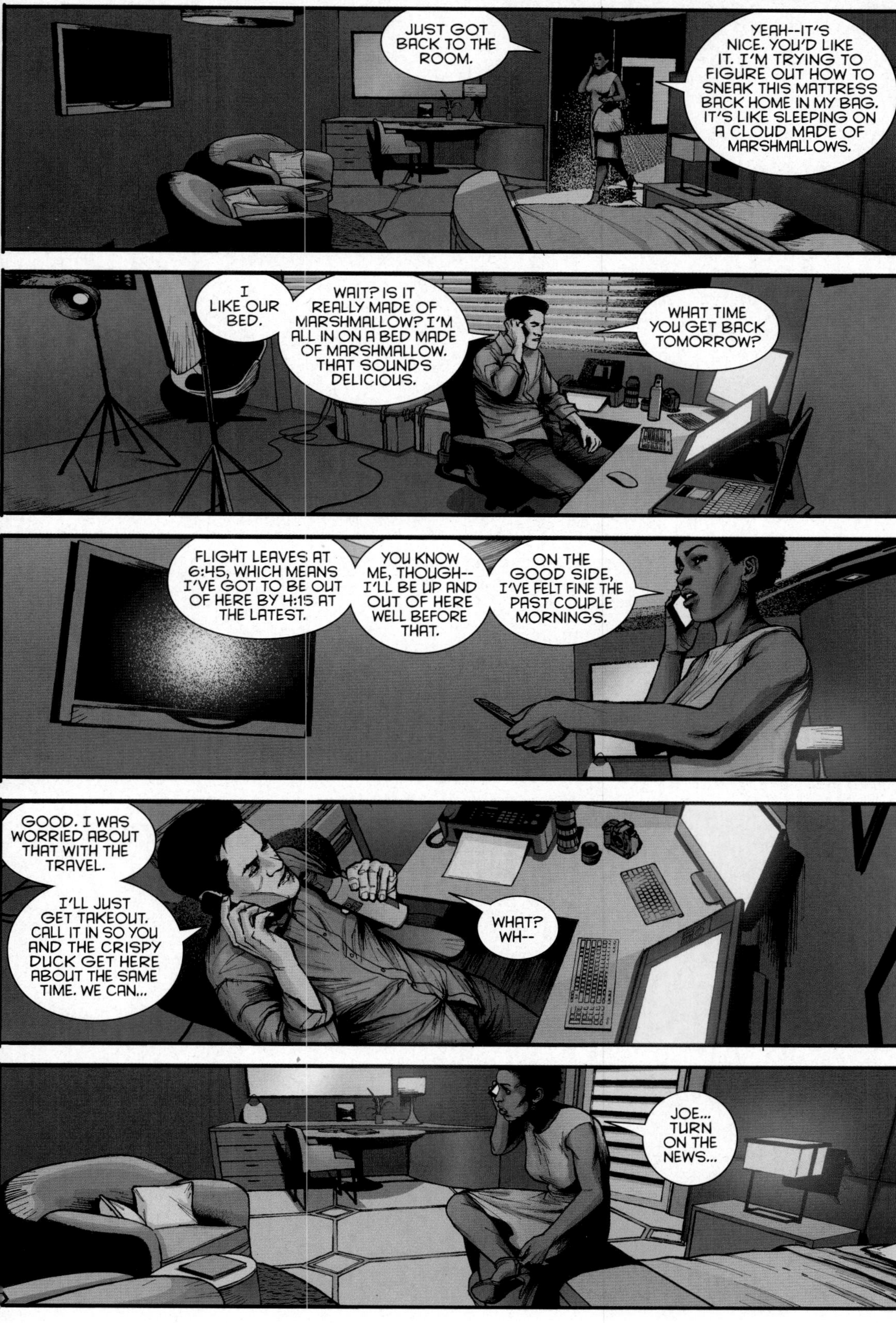
JUST GOT BACK TO THE ROOM.
YEAH--IT'S NICE. YOU'D LIKE IT. I'M TRYING TO FIGURE OUT HOW TO SNEAK THIS MATTRESS BACK HOME IN MY BAG. IT'S LIKE SLEEPING ON A CLOUD MADE OF MARSHMALLOWS.
I LIKE OUR BED.
WAIT? IS IT REALLY MADE OF MARSHMALLOW? I'M ALL IN ON A BED MADE OF MARSHMALLOW. THAT SOUNDS DELICIOUS.
WHAT TIME YOU GET BACK TOMORROW?
FLIGHT LEAVES AT 6:45, WHICH MEANS I'VE GOT TO BE OUT OF HERE BY 4:15 AT THE LATEST.
YOU KNOW ME, THOUGH-- I'LL BE UP AND OUT OF HERE WELL BEFORE THAT.
ON THE GOOD SIDE, I'VE FELT FINE THE PAST COUPLE MORNINGS.
GOOD. I WAS WORRIED ABOUT THAT WITH THE TRAVEL.
I'LL JUST GET TAKEOUT. CALL IT IN SO YOU AND THE CRISPY DUCK GET HERE ABOUT THE SAME TIME. WE CAN...
WHAT? WH--
JOE... TURN ON THE NEWS...

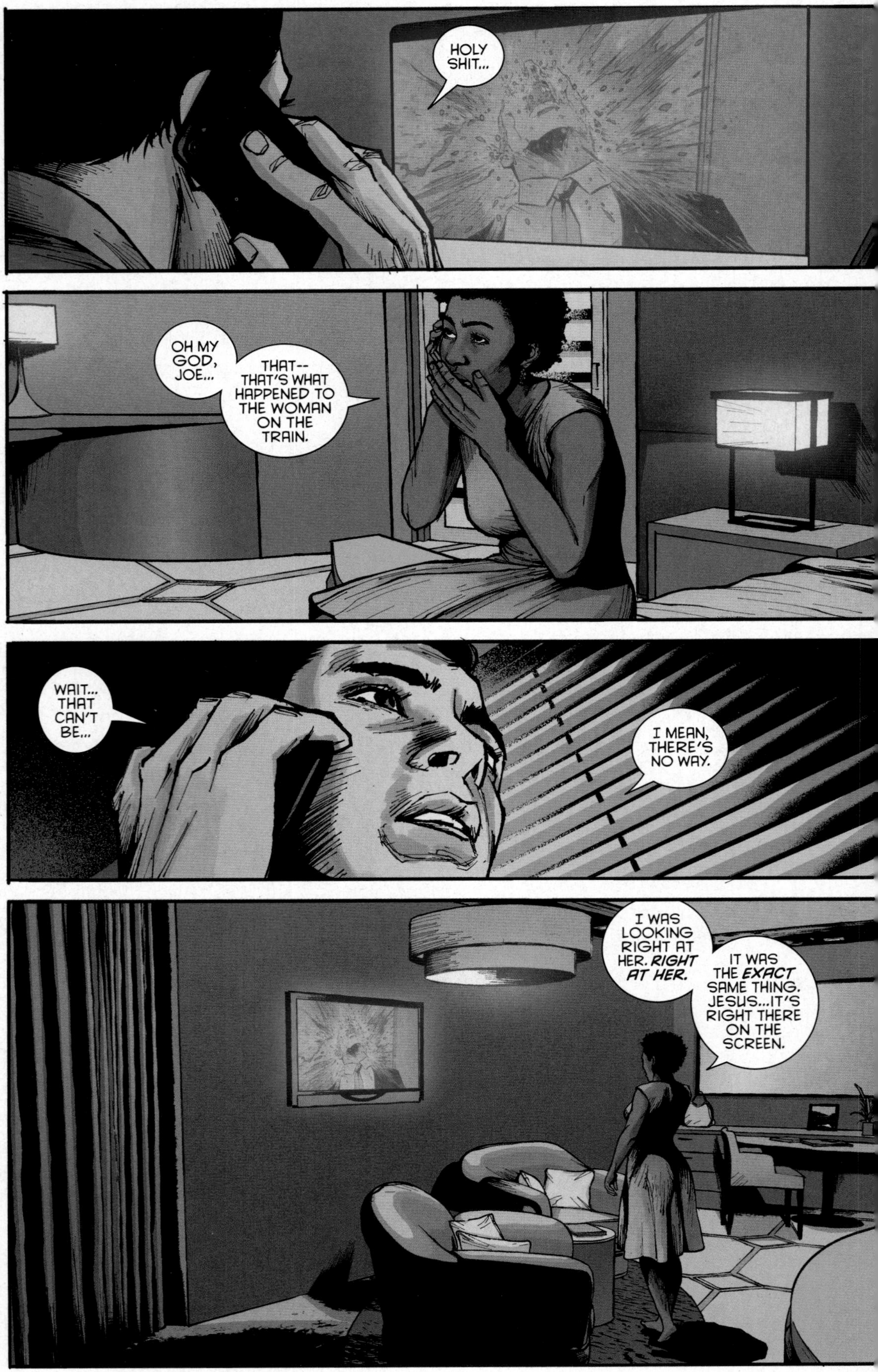
HOLY SHIT...
OH MY GOD, JOE...
THAT-- THAT'S WHAT HAPPENED TO THE WOMAN ON THE TRAIN.
WAIT... THAT CAN'T BE...
I MEAN, THERE'S NO WAY.
I WAS LOOKING RIGHT AT HER. *RIGHT AT HER.*
IT WAS THE *EXACT* SAME THING. JESUS...IT'S RIGHT THERE ON THE SCREEN.

THE RAINCHECK

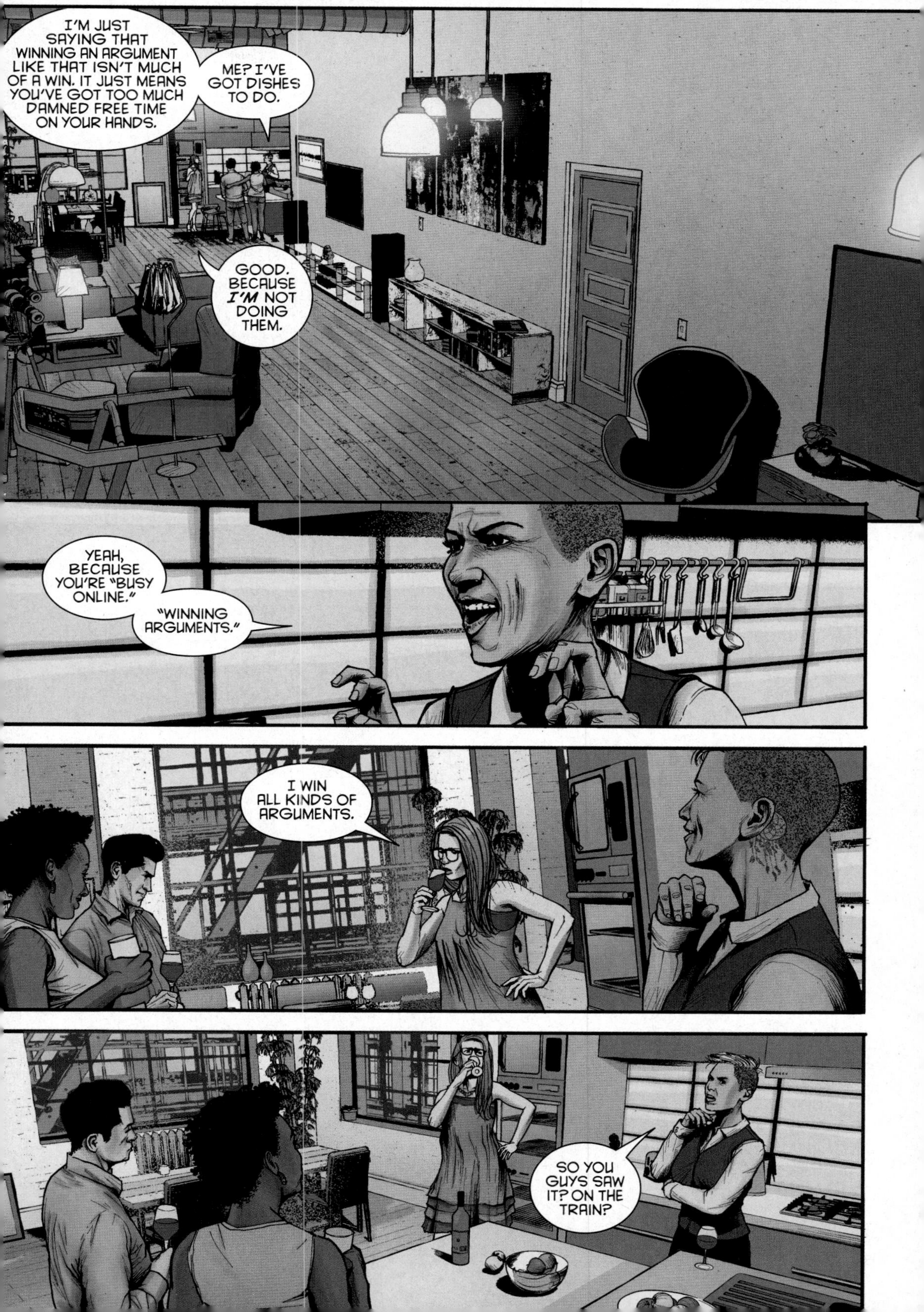

I'M JUST SAYING THAT WINNING AN ARGUMENT LIKE THAT ISN'T MUCH OF A WIN. IT JUST MEANS YOU'VE GOT TOO MUCH DAMNED FREE TIME ON YOUR HANDS.
ME? I'VE GOT DISHES TO DO.
GOOD. BECAUSE *I'M* NOT DOING THEM.
YEAH, BECAUSE YOU'RE "BUSY ONLINE."
"WINNING ARGUMENTS."
I WIN ALL KINDS OF ARGUMENTS.
SO YOU GUYS SAW IT? ON THE TRAIN?

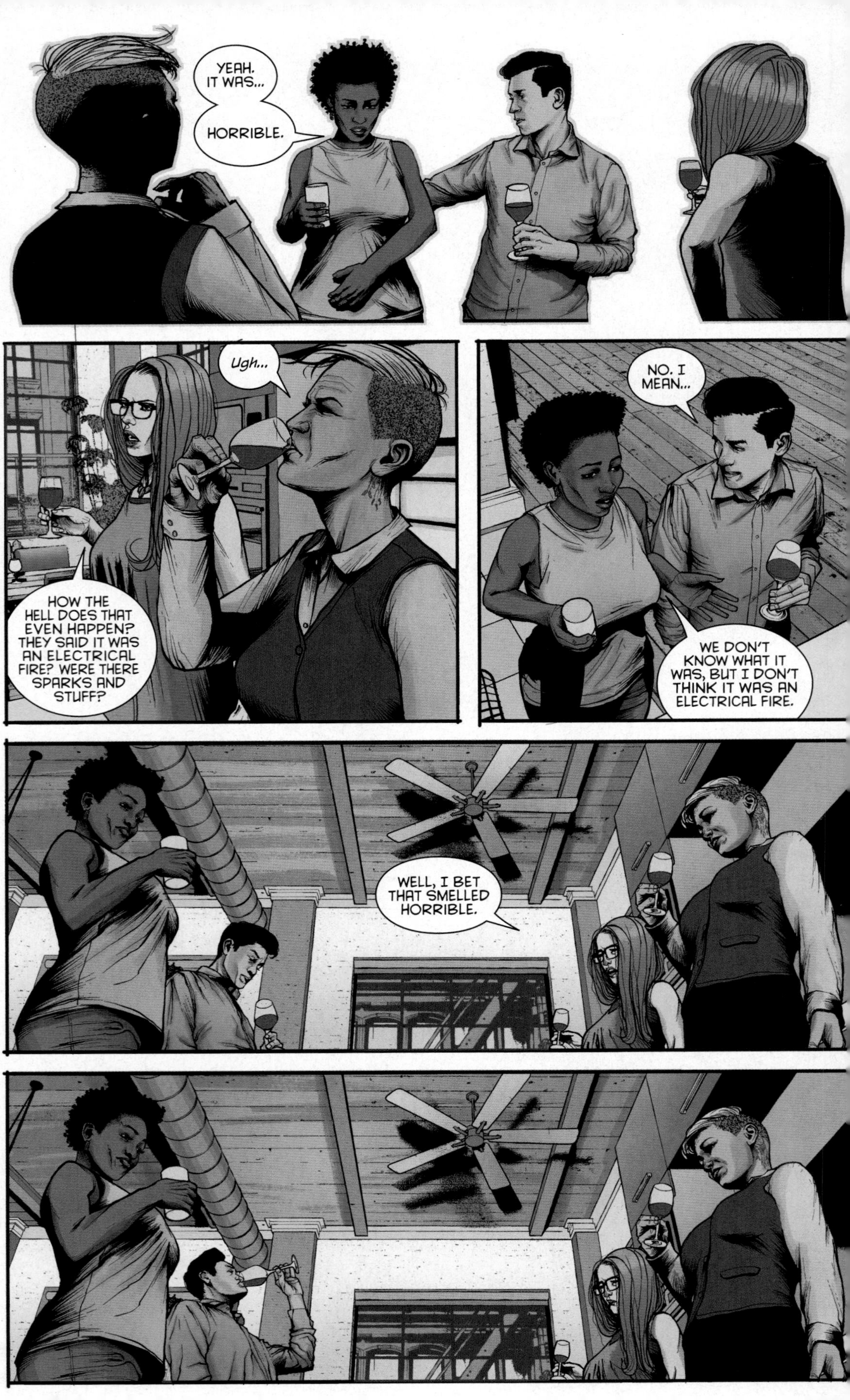
YEAH. IT WAS...
HORRIBLE.
Ugh...
HOW THE HELL DOES THAT EVEN HAPPEN? THEY SAID IT WAS AN ELECTRICAL FIRE? WERE THERE SPARKS AND STUFF?
NO. I MEAN...
WE DON'T KNOW WHAT IT WAS, BUT I DON'T THINK IT WAS AN ELECTRICAL FIRE.
WELL, I BET THAT SMELLED HORRIBLE.

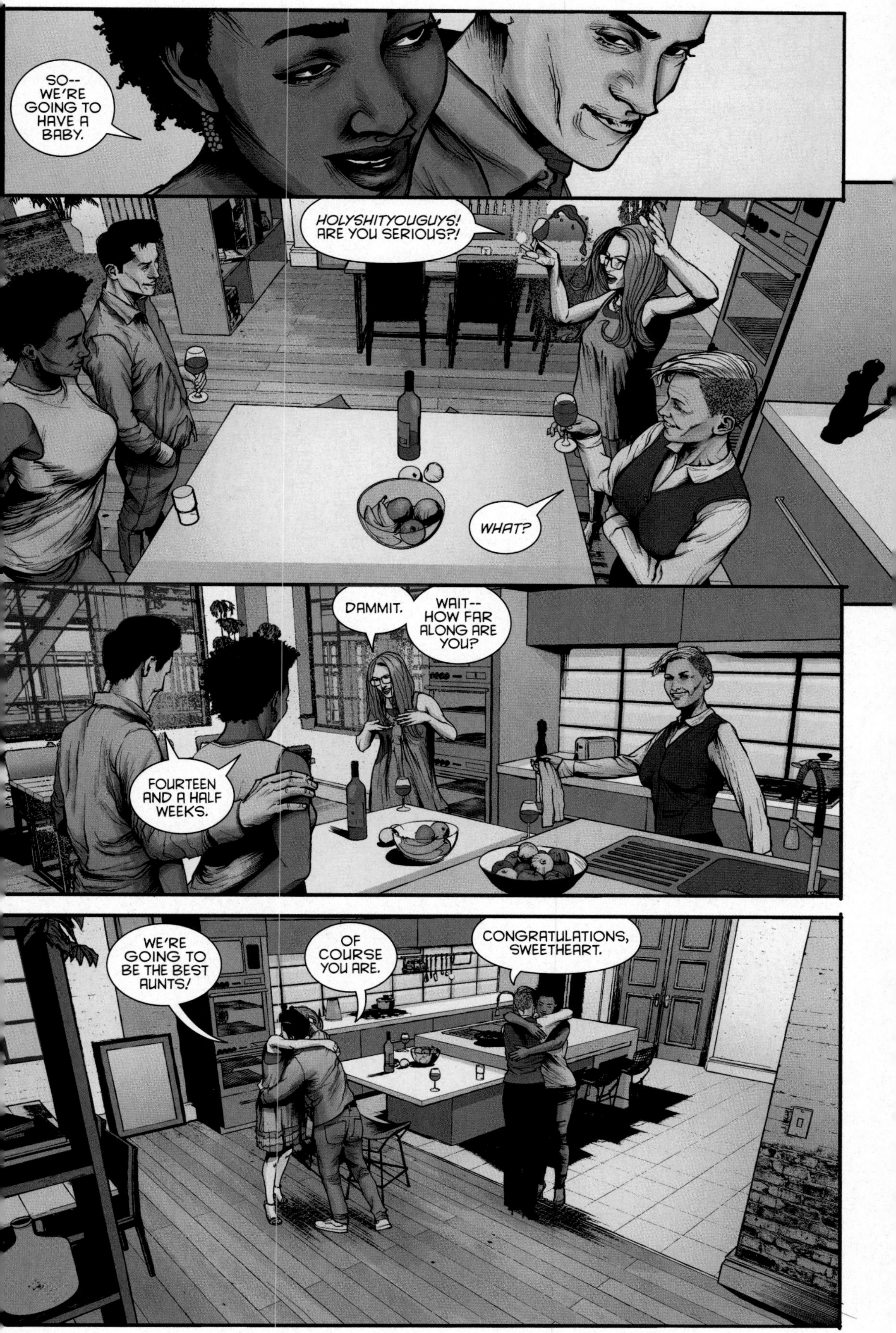
SO-- WE'RE GOING TO HAVE A BABY.
HOLYSHITYOUGUYS! ARE YOU SERIOUS?!
WHAT?
DAMMIT.
WAIT-- HOW FAR ALONG ARE YOU?
FOURTEEN AND A HALF WEEKS.
WE'RE GOING TO BE THE BEST AUNTS!
OF COURSE YOU ARE.
CONGRATULATIONS, SWEETHEART.

GOLDENROD

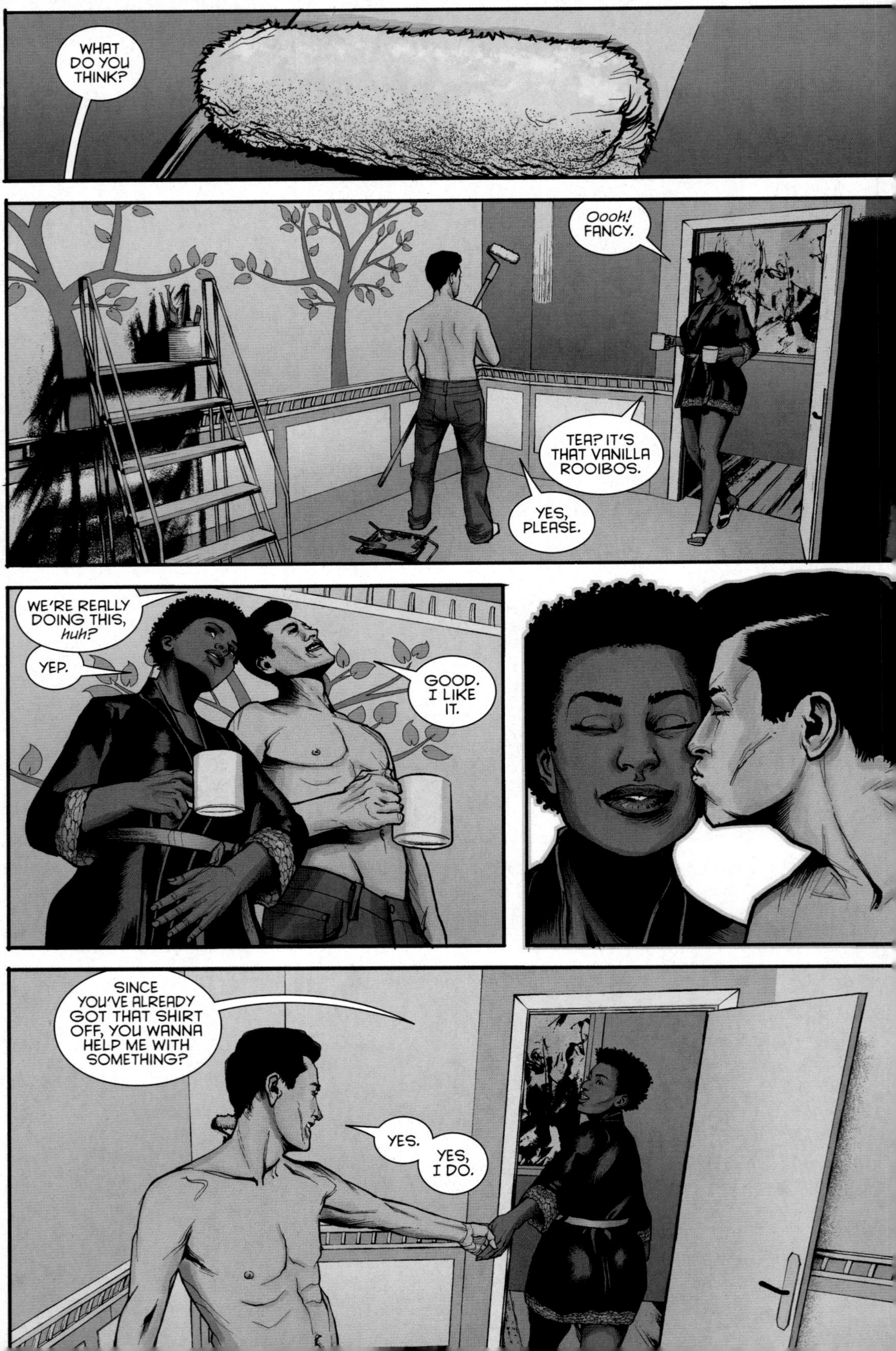
WHAT DO YOU THINK?
Oooh! FANCY.
TEA? IT'S THAT VANILLA ROOIBOS.
YES, PLEASE.
WE'RE REALLY DOING THIS, *huh?*
YEP.
GOOD. I LIKE IT.
SINCE YOU'VE ALREADY GOT THAT SHIRT OFF, YOU WANNA HELP ME WITH SOMETHING?
YES.
YES, I DO.

WHERE THERE'S SMOKE

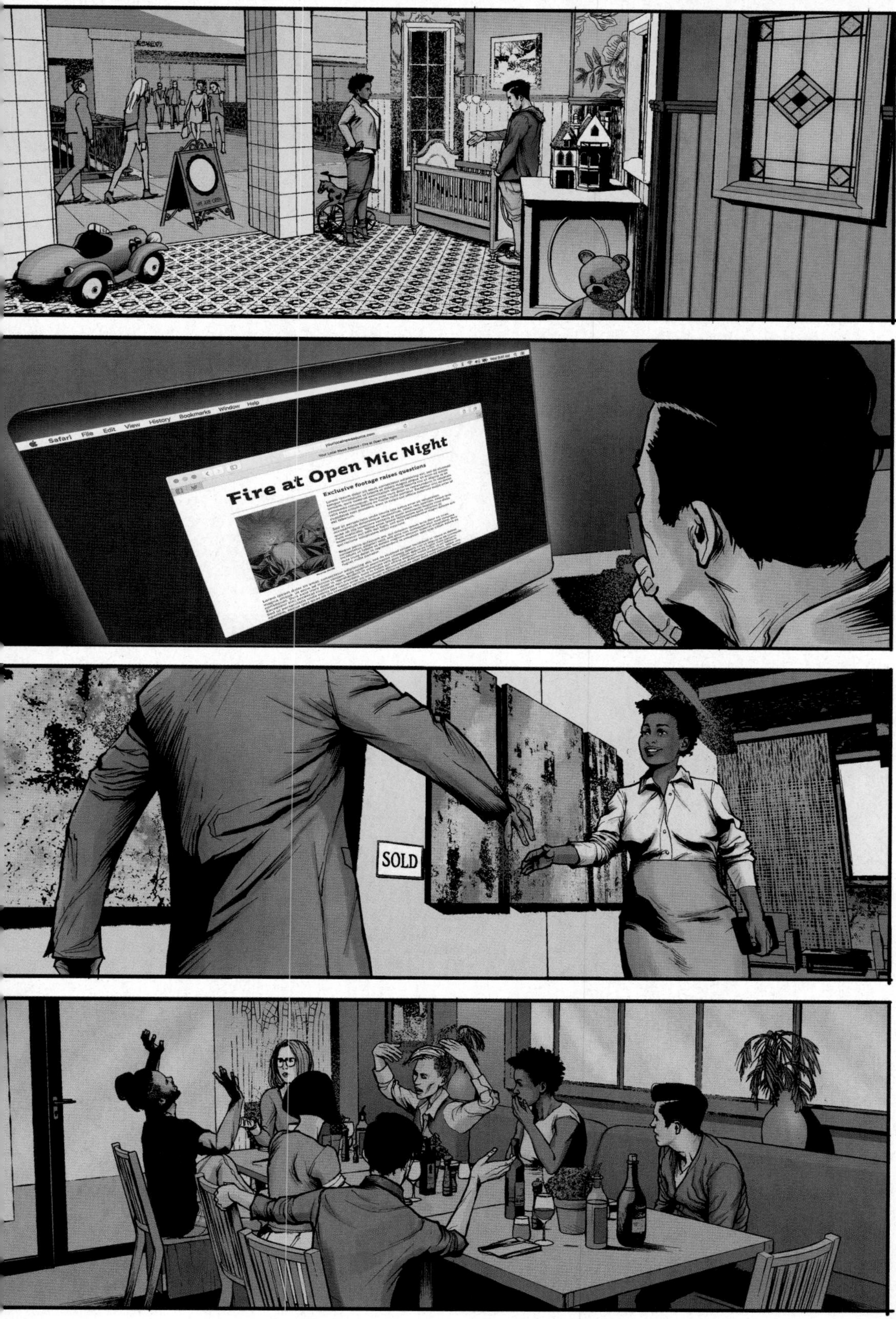
Safari File Edit View History Bookmarks Window Help
Fire at Open Mic Night
Exclusive footage raises questions
SOLD

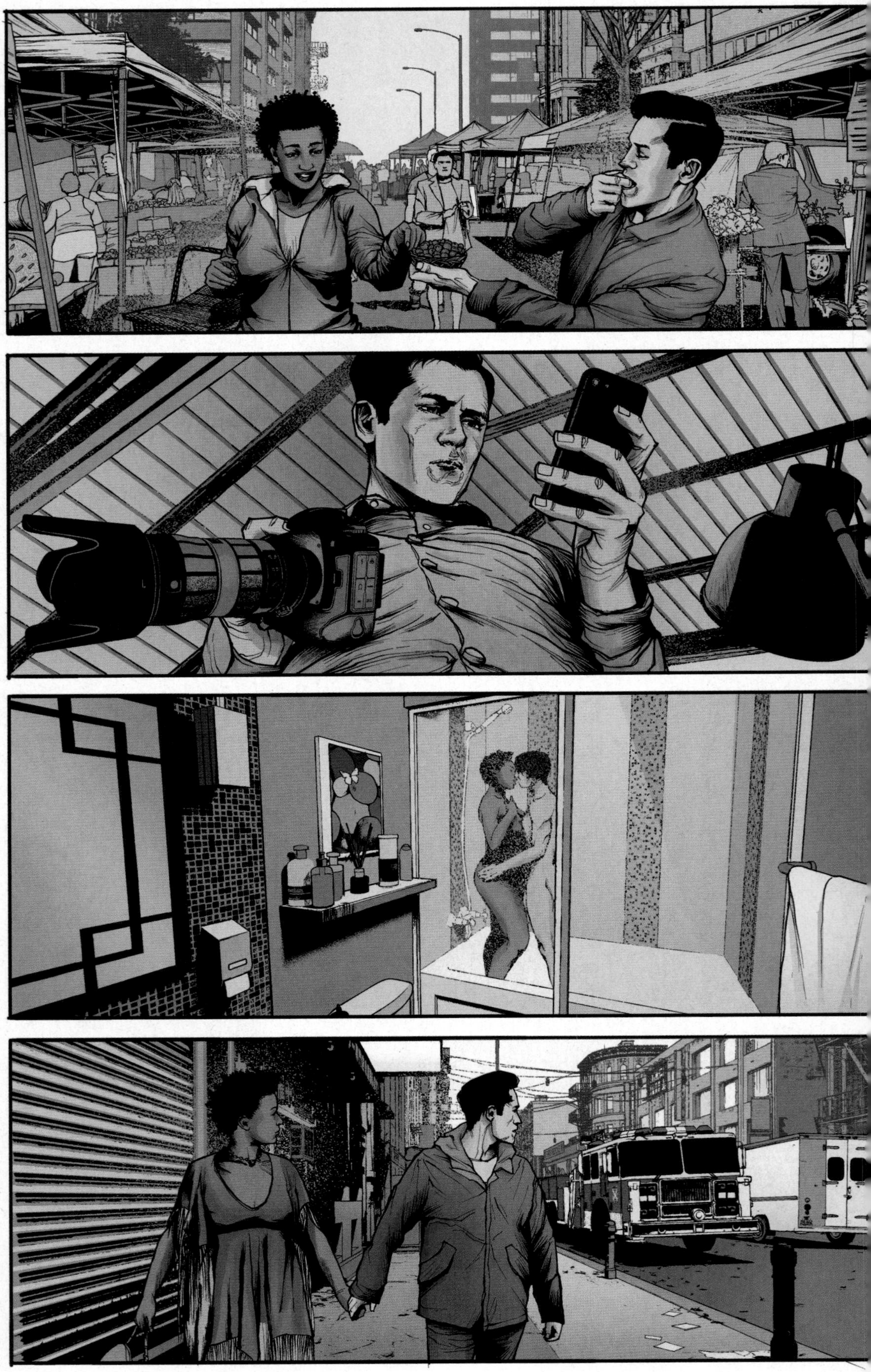

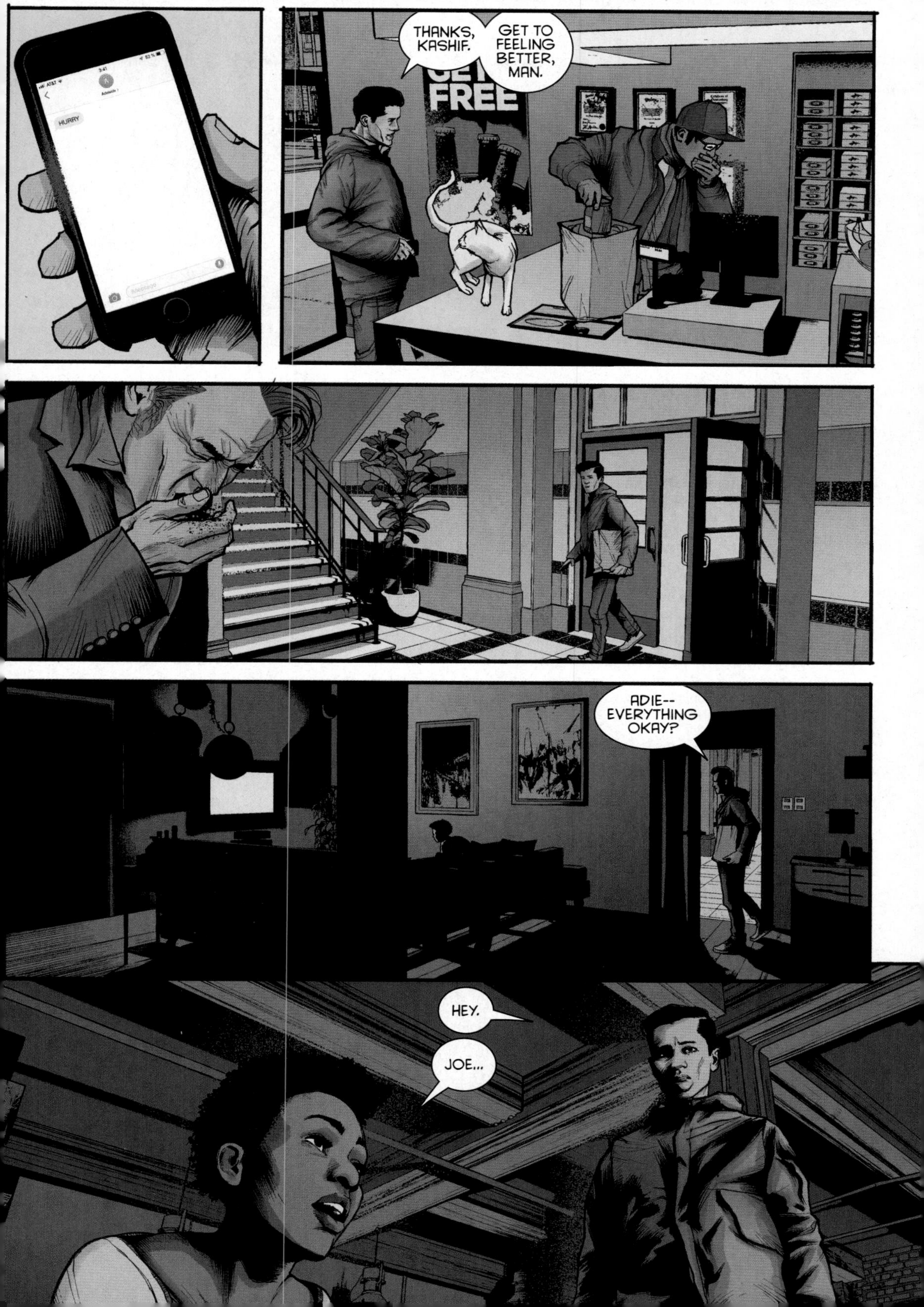
HURRY
FREE
THANKS, KASHIF.
GET TO FEELING BETTER, MAN.
ADIE-- EVERYTHING OKAY?
HEY.
JOE...

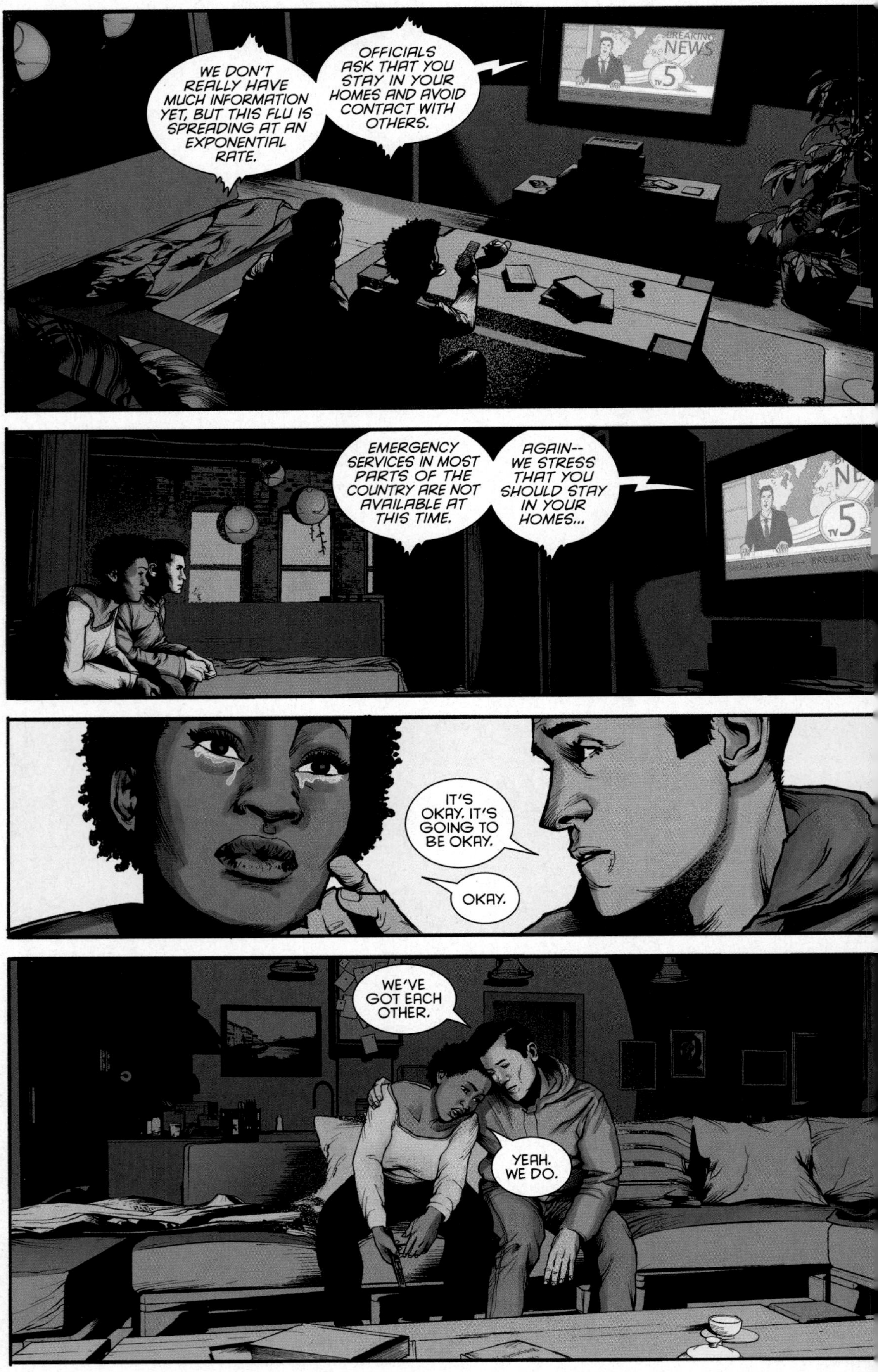
BREAKING NEWS
WE DON'T REALLY HAVE MUCH INFORMATION YET, BUT THIS FLU IS SPREADING AT AN EXPONENTIAL RATE.
OFFICIALS ASK THAT YOU STAY IN YOUR HOMES AND AVOID CONTACT WITH OTHERS.
EMERGENCY SERVICES IN MOST PARTS OF THE COUNTRY ARE NOT AVAILABLE AT THIS TIME.
AGAIN-- WE STRESS THAT YOU SHOULD STAY IN YOUR HOMES...
IT'S OKAY. IT'S GOING TO BE OKAY.
OKAY.
WE'VE GOT EACH OTHER.
YEAH. WE DO.

Unpublished cover art

Daniel Caballero

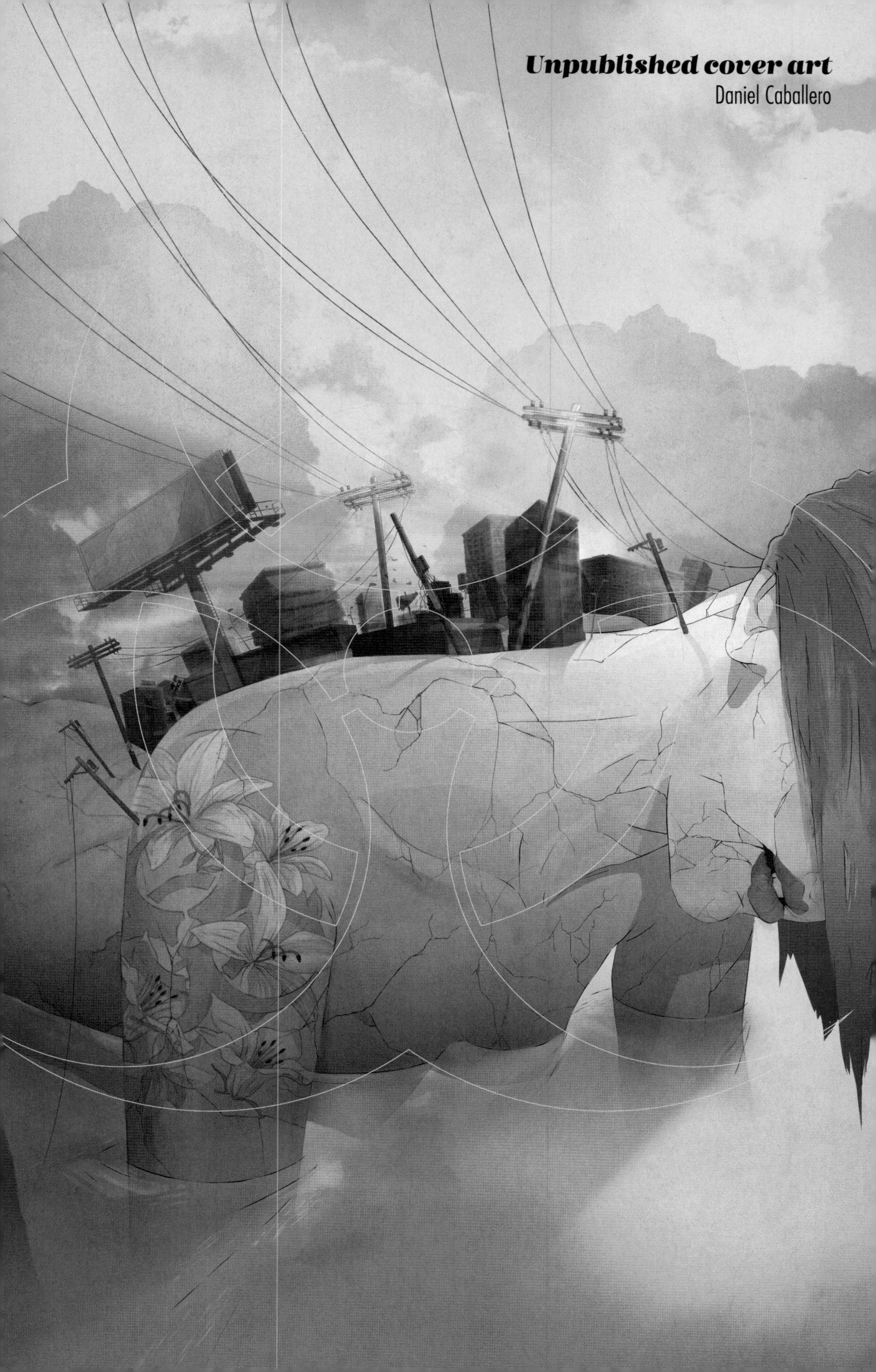

CHAPTER

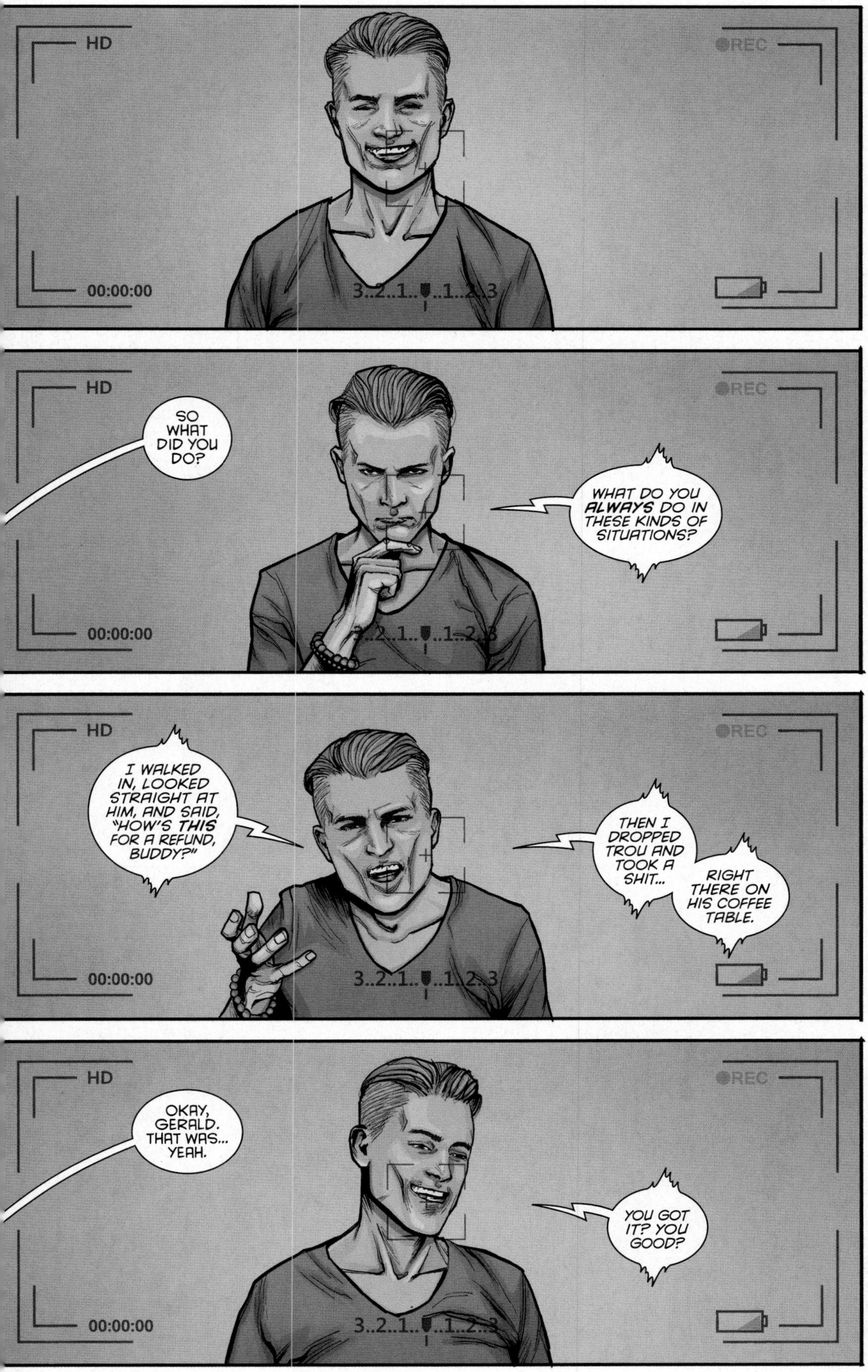
HD
●REC
00:00:00
3..2..1..▼..1..2..3
HD
●REC
SO WHAT DID YOU DO?
WHAT DO YOU **ALWAYS** DO IN THESE KINDS OF SITUATIONS?
00:00:00
3..2..1..▼..1..2..3
HD
●REC
I WALKED IN, LOOKED STRAIGHT AT HIM, AND SAID, "HOW'S **THIS** FOR A REFUND, BUDDY?"
THEN I DROPPED TROU AND TOOK A SHIT...
RIGHT THERE ON HIS COFFEE TABLE.
00:00:00
3..2..1..▼..1..2..3
HD
●REC
OKAY, GERALD. THAT WAS... YEAH.
YOU GOT IT? YOU GOOD?
00:00:00
3..2..1..▼..1..2..3

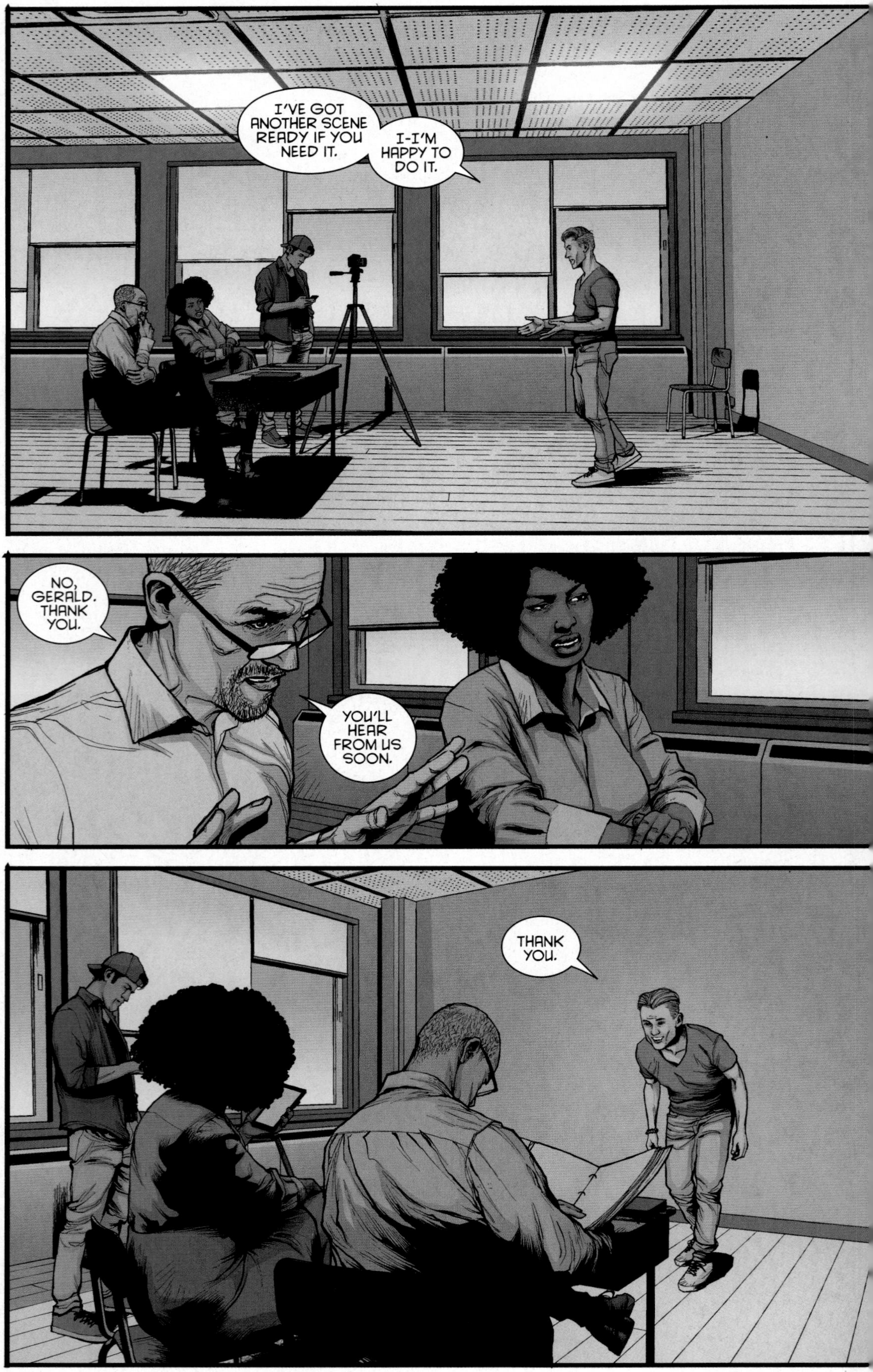
I'VE GOT ANOTHER SCENE READY IF YOU NEED IT.
I-I'M HAPPY TO DO IT.
NO, GERALD. THANK YOU.
YOU'LL HEAR FROM US SOON.
THANK YOU.

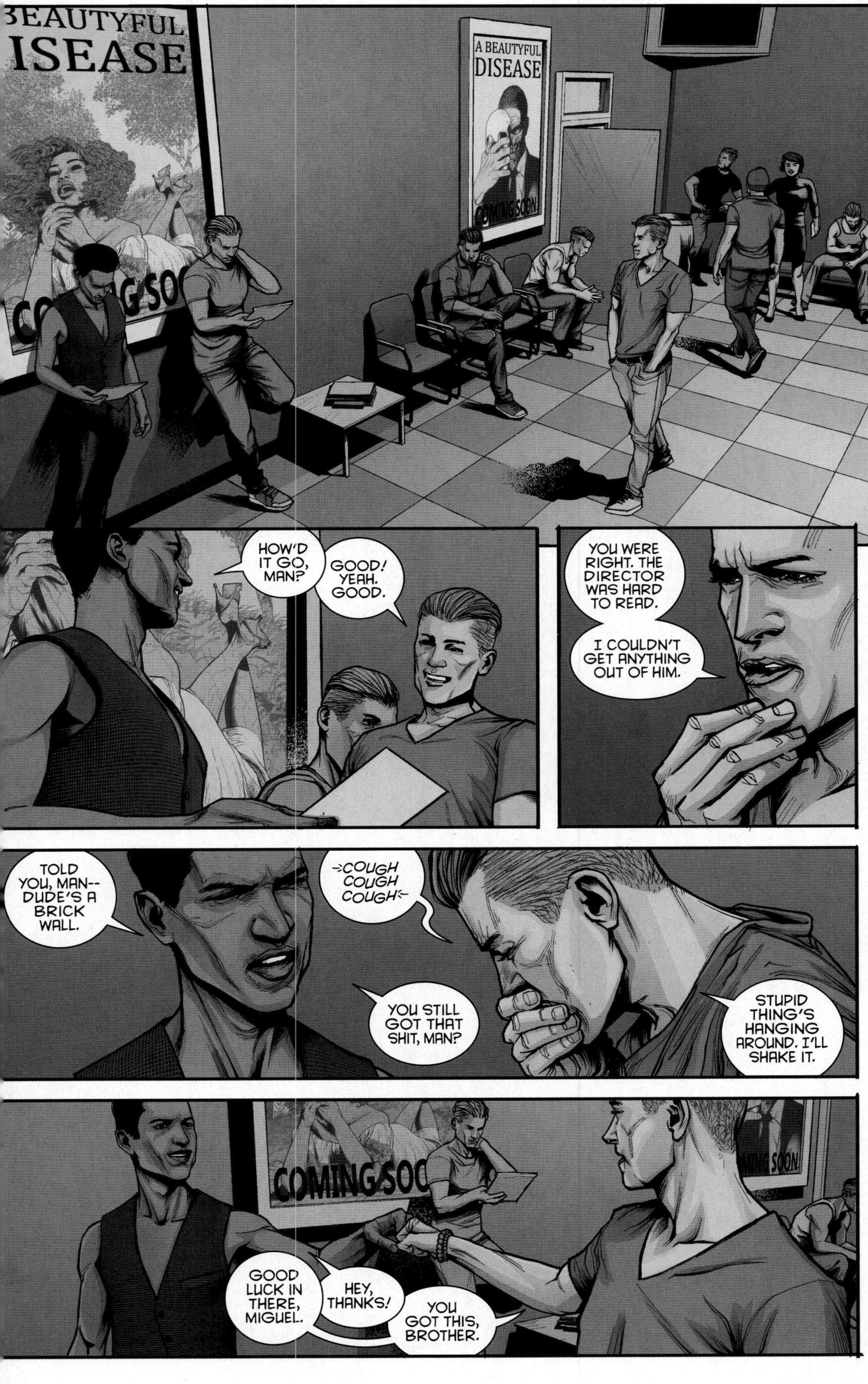
A BEAUTYFUL DISEASE
A BEAUTYFUL DISEASE
COMING SOON
HOW'D IT GO, MAN?
GOOD! YEAH. GOOD.
YOU WERE RIGHT. THE DIRECTOR WAS HARD TO READ.
I COULDN'T GET ANYTHING OUT OF HIM.
TOLD YOU, MAN-- DUDE'S A BRICK WALL.
COUGH COUGH COUGH
YOU STILL GOT THAT SHIT, MAN?
STUPID THING'S HANGING AROUND. I'LL SHAKE IT.
COMING SOO
GOOD LUCK IN THERE, MIGUEL.
HEY, THANKS!
YOU GOT THIS, BROTHER.

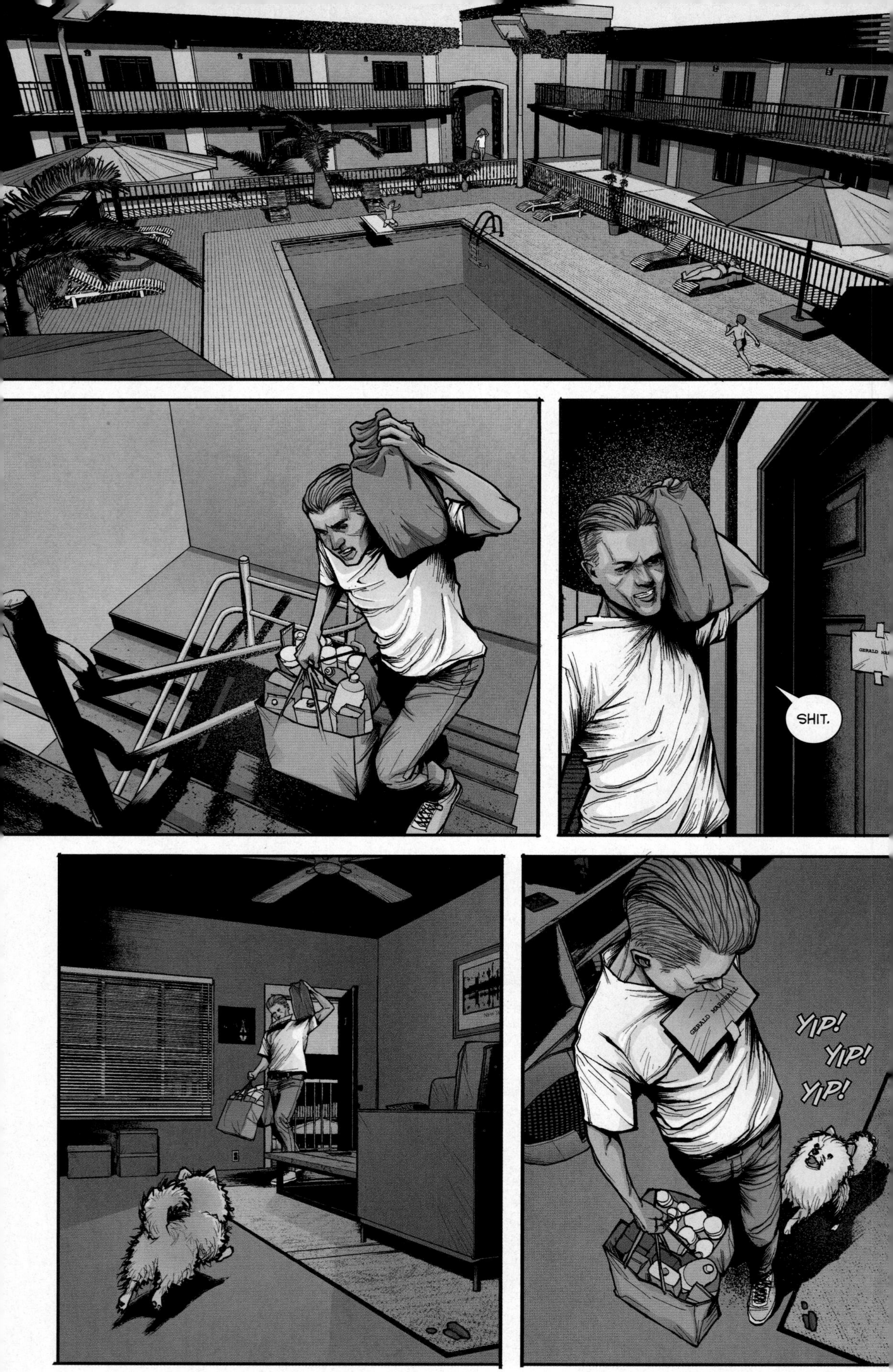
SHIT.
GERALD MARSHALL
YIP!
YIP!
YIP!

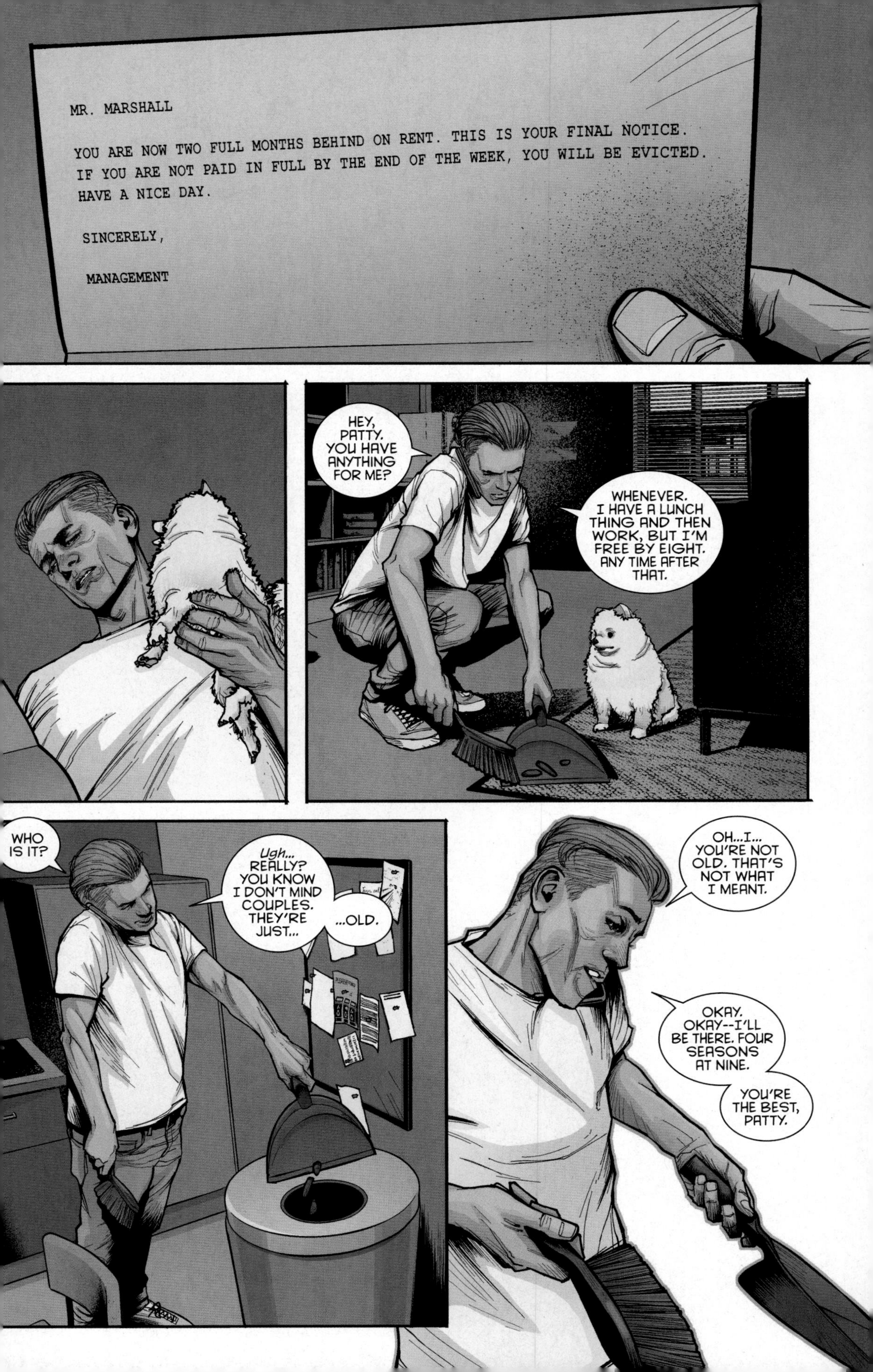
MR. MARSHALL
YOU ARE NOW TWO FULL MONTHS BEHIND ON RENT. THIS IS YOUR FINAL NOTICE. IF YOU ARE NOT PAID IN FULL BY THE END OF THE WEEK, YOU WILL BE EVICTED. HAVE A NICE DAY.
SINCERELY,
MANAGEMENT
HEY, PATTY. YOU HAVE ANYTHING FOR ME?
WHENEVER. I HAVE A LUNCH THING AND THEN WORK, BUT I'M FREE BY EIGHT. ANY TIME AFTER THAT.
WHO IS IT?
Ugh... REALLY? YOU KNOW I DON'T MIND COUPLES. THEY'RE JUST...
...OLD.
OH...I... YOU'RE NOT OLD. THAT'S NOT WHAT I MEANT.
OKAY. OKAY--I'LL BE THERE. FOUR SEASONS AT NINE.
YOU'RE THE BEST, PATTY.

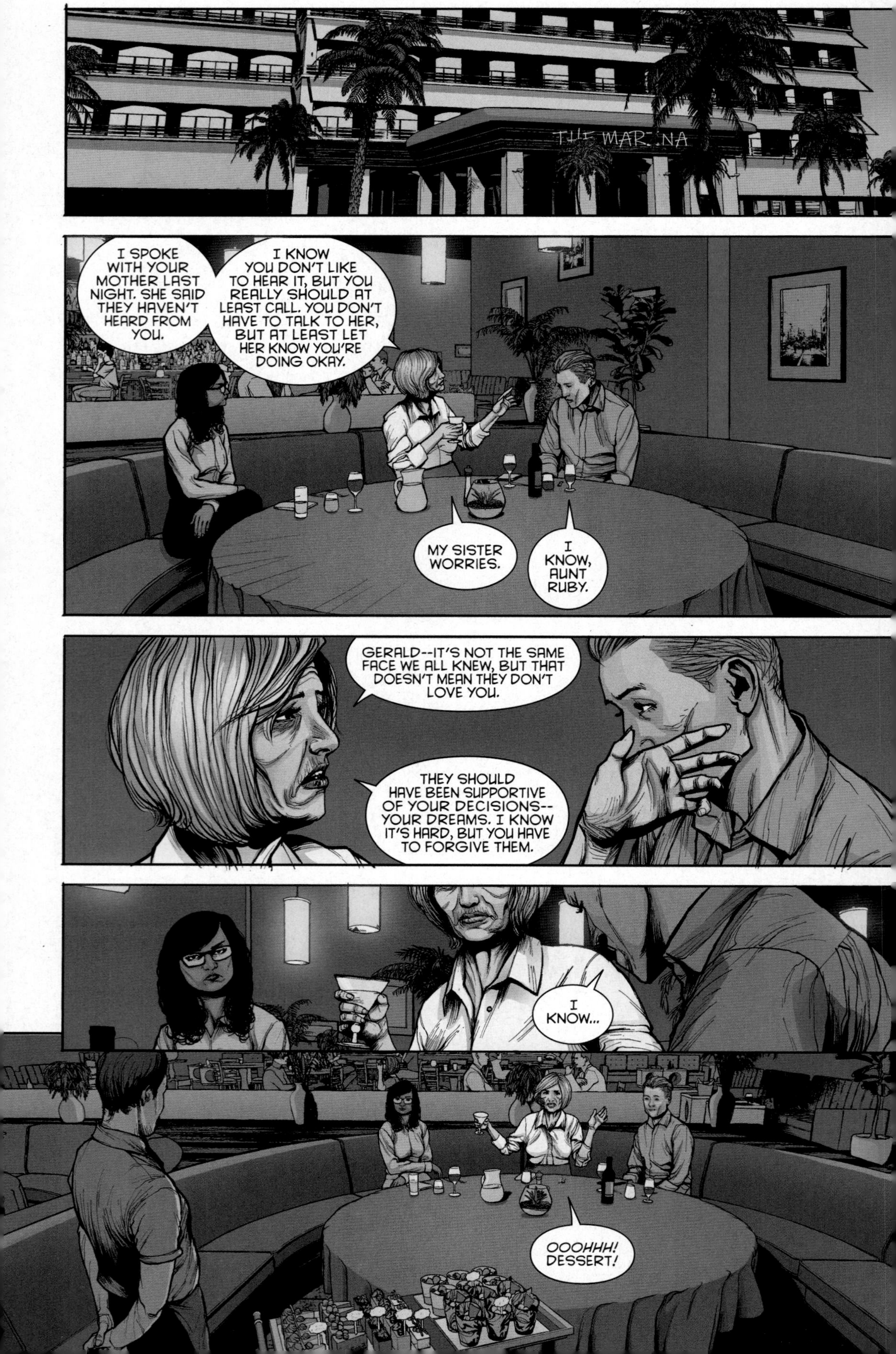
THE MAR NA
I SPOKE WITH YOUR MOTHER LAST NIGHT. SHE SAID THEY HAVEN'T HEARD FROM YOU.
I KNOW YOU DON'T LIKE TO HEAR IT, BUT YOU REALLY SHOULD AT LEAST CALL. YOU DON'T HAVE TO TALK TO HER, BUT AT LEAST LET HER KNOW YOU'RE DOING OKAY.
MY SISTER WORRIES.
I KNOW, AUNT RUBY.
GERALD--IT'S NOT THE SAME FACE WE ALL KNEW, BUT THAT DOESN'T MEAN THEY DON'T LOVE YOU.
THEY SHOULD HAVE BEEN SUPPORTIVE OF YOUR DECISIONS-- YOUR DREAMS. I KNOW IT'S HARD, BUT YOU HAVE TO FORGIVE THEM.
I KNOW...
OOOHHH! DESSERT!

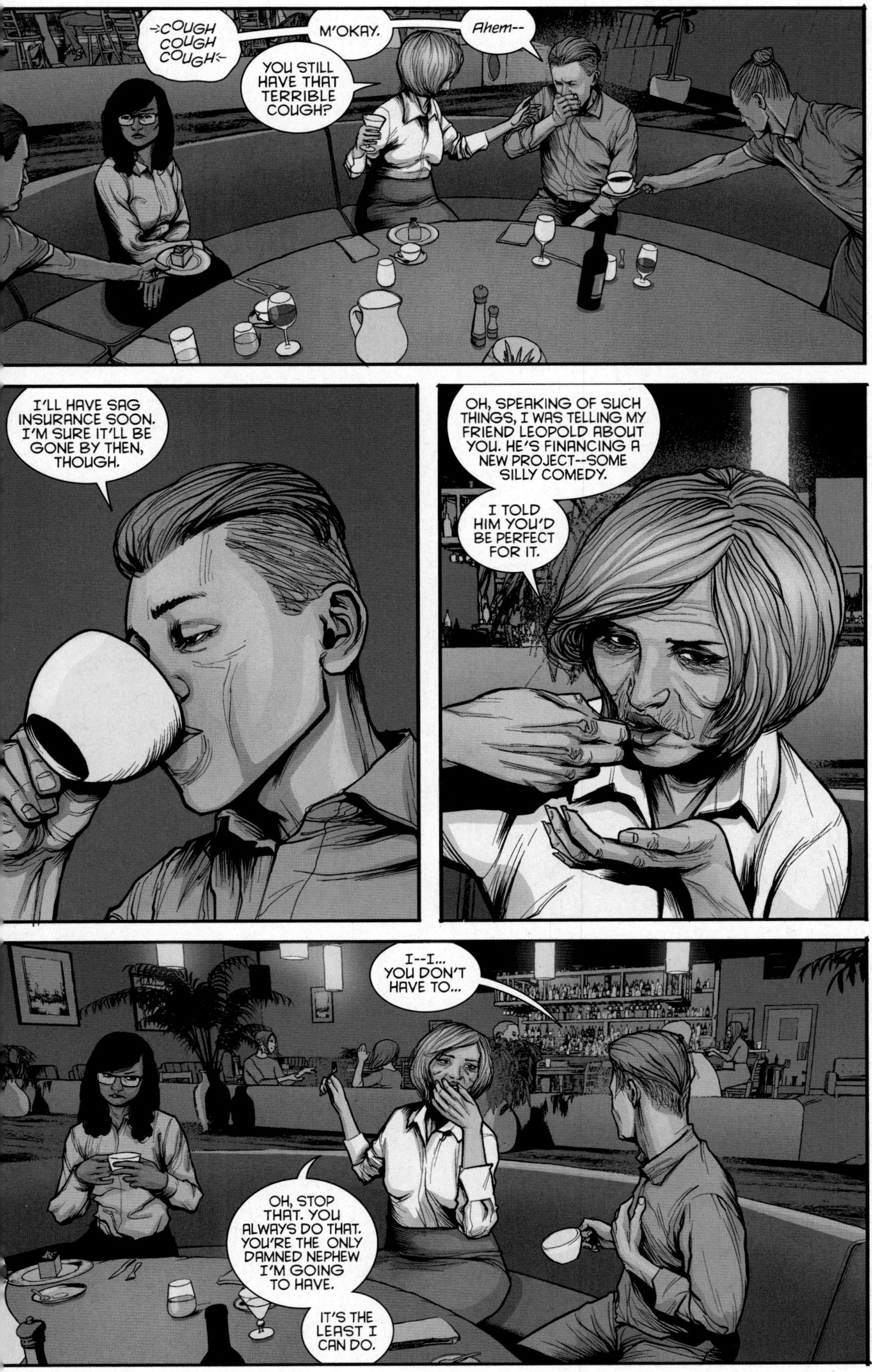

>COUGH COUGH COUGH<
M'OKAY.
YOU STILL HAVE THAT TERRIBLE COUGH?
Ahem--
I'LL HAVE SAG INSURANCE SOON. I'M SURE IT'LL BE GONE BY THEN, THOUGH.
OH, SPEAKING OF SUCH THINGS, I WAS TELLING MY FRIEND LEOPOLD ABOUT YOU. HE'S FINANCING A NEW PROJECT--SOME SILLY COMEDY.
I TOLD HIM YOU'D BE PERFECT FOR IT.
I--I... YOU DON'T HAVE TO...
OH, STOP THAT. YOU ALWAYS DO THAT. YOU'RE THE ONLY DAMNED NEPHEW I'M GOING TO HAVE.
IT'S THE LEAST I CAN DO.

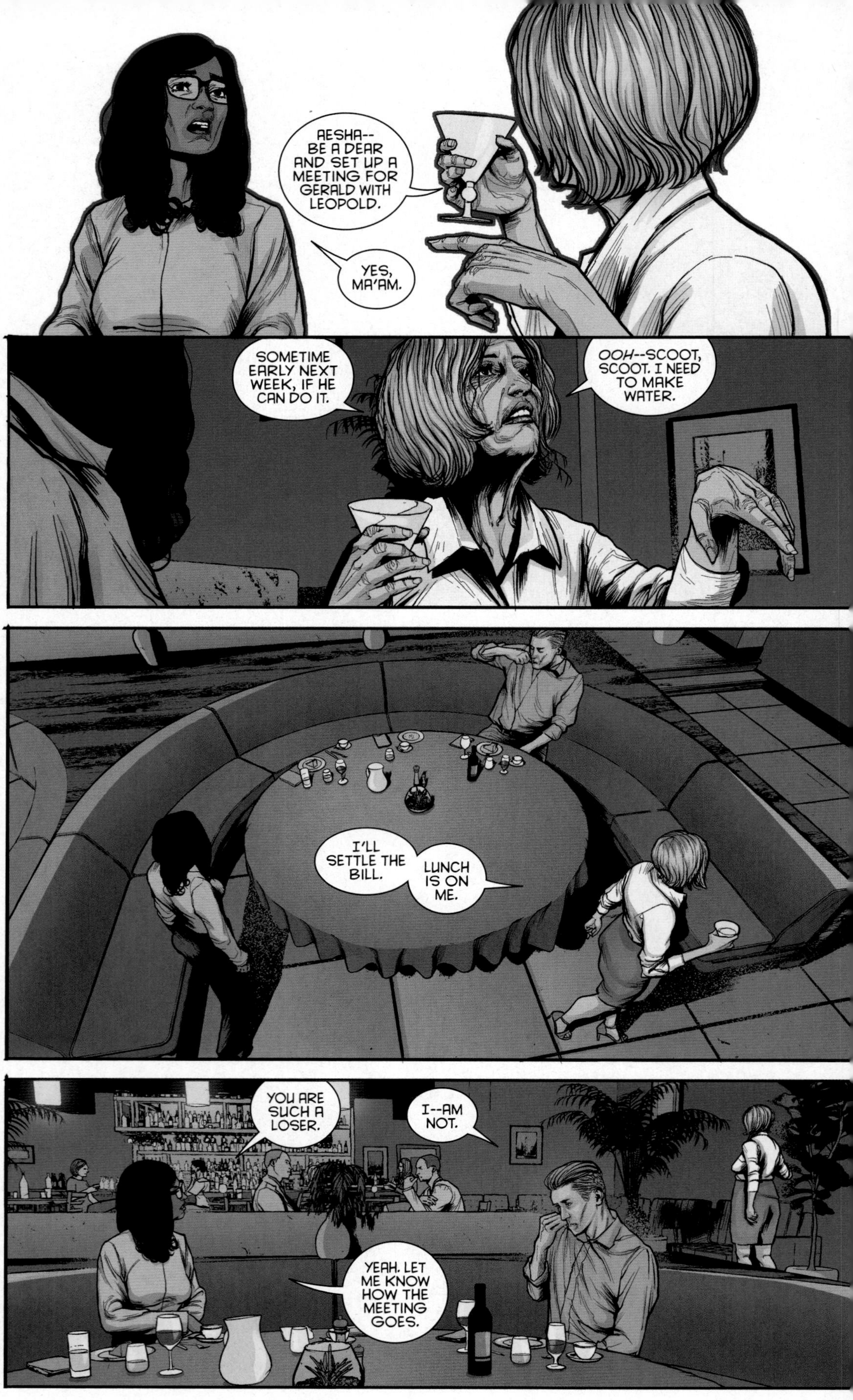
AESHA--
BE A DEAR AND SET UP A MEETING FOR GERALD WITH LEOPOLD.
YES, MA'AM.
SOMETIME EARLY NEXT WEEK, IF HE CAN DO IT.
OOH--SCOOT, SCOOT. I NEED TO MAKE WATER.
I'LL SETTLE THE BILL.
LUNCH IS ON ME.
YOU ARE SUCH A LOSER.
I--AM NOT.
YEAH. LET ME KNOW HOW THE MEETING GOES.

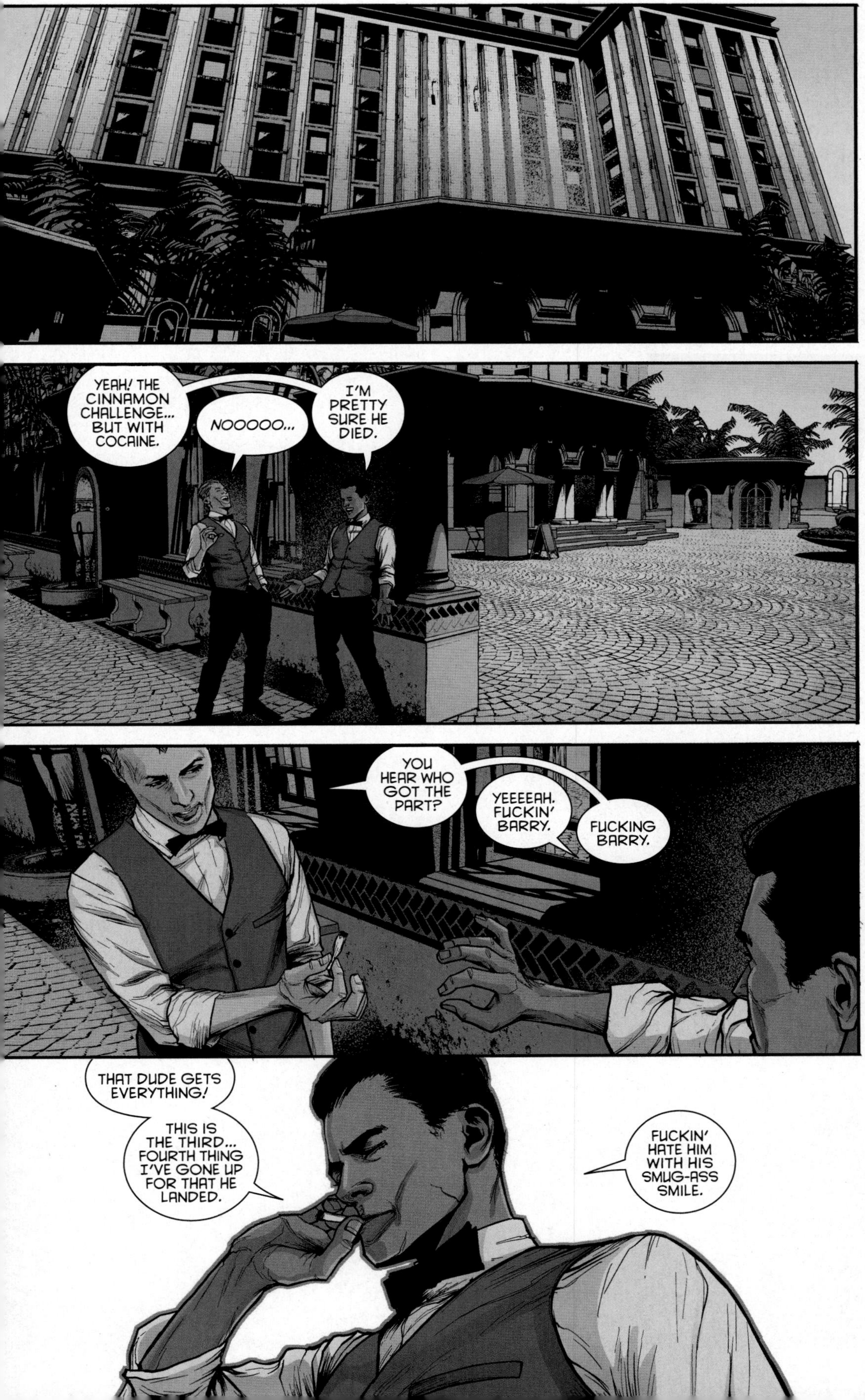
YEAH! THE CINNAMON CHALLENGE... BUT WITH COCAINE.
NOOOOO...
I'M PRETTY SURE HE DIED.
YOU HEAR WHO GOT THE PART?
YEEEEAH. FUCKIN' BARRY.
FUCKING BARRY.
THAT DUDE GETS EVERYTHING!
THIS IS THE THIRD... FOURTH THING I'VE GONE UP FOR THAT HE LANDED.
FUCKIN' HATE HIM WITH HIS SMUG-ASS SMILE.

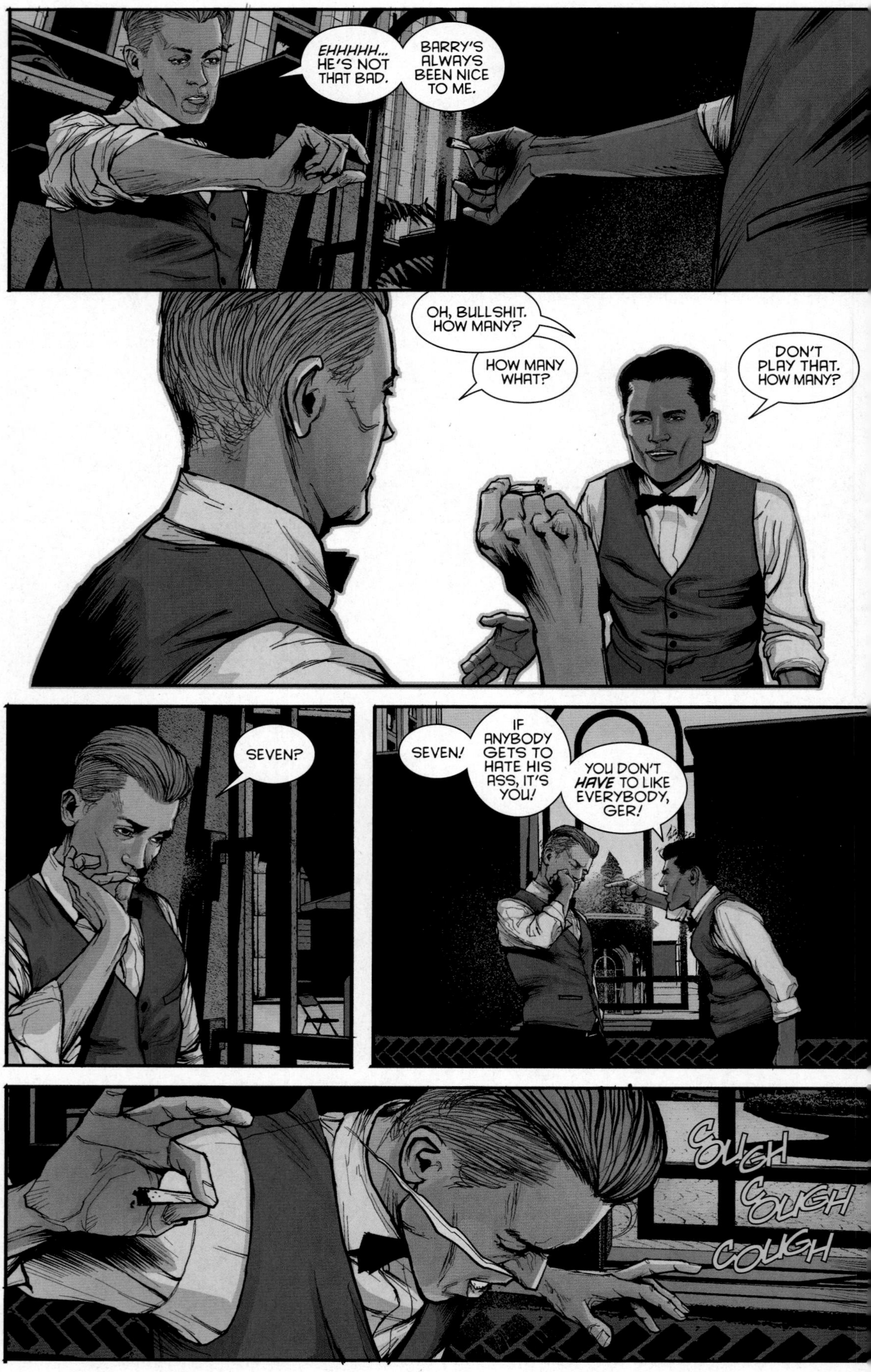
EHHHHH... HE'S NOT THAT BAD.
BARRY'S ALWAYS BEEN NICE TO ME.
OH, BULLSHIT. HOW MANY?
HOW MANY WHAT?
DON'T PLAY THAT. HOW MANY?
SEVEN?
SEVEN!
IF ANYBODY GETS TO HATE HIS ASS, IT'S YOU!
YOU DON'T HAVE TO LIKE EVERYBODY, GER!
COUGH
COUGH
COUGH

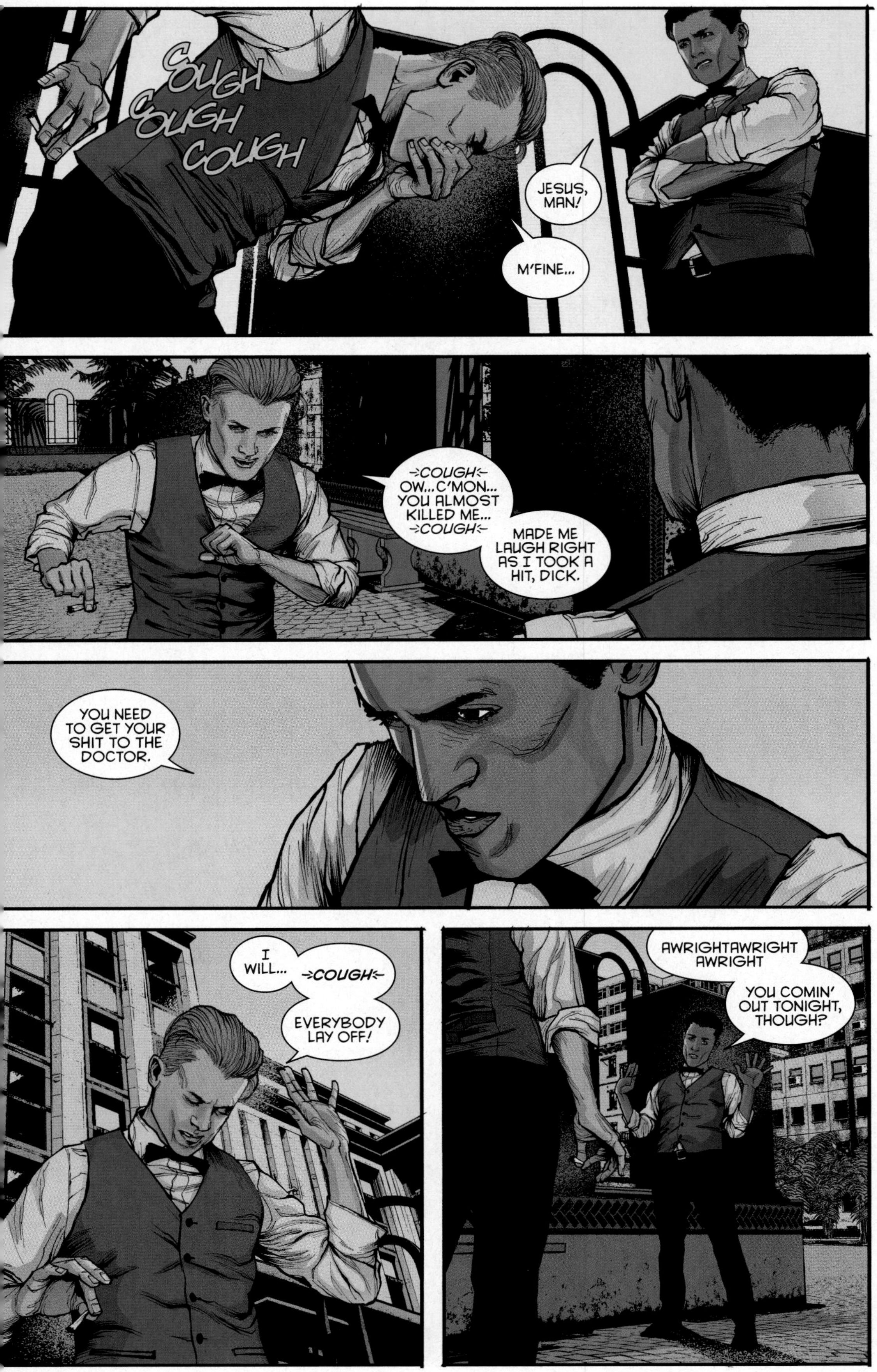
COUGH COUGH COUGH
JESUS, MAN!
M'FINE...
COUGH OW...C'MON... YOU ALMOST KILLED ME... COUGH
MADE ME LAUGH RIGHT AS I TOOK A HIT, DICK.
YOU NEED TO GET YOUR SHIT TO THE DOCTOR.
I WILL...
COUGH
EVERYBODY LAY OFF!
AWRIGHTAWRIGHT AWRIGHT
YOU COMIN' OUT TONIGHT, THOUGH?

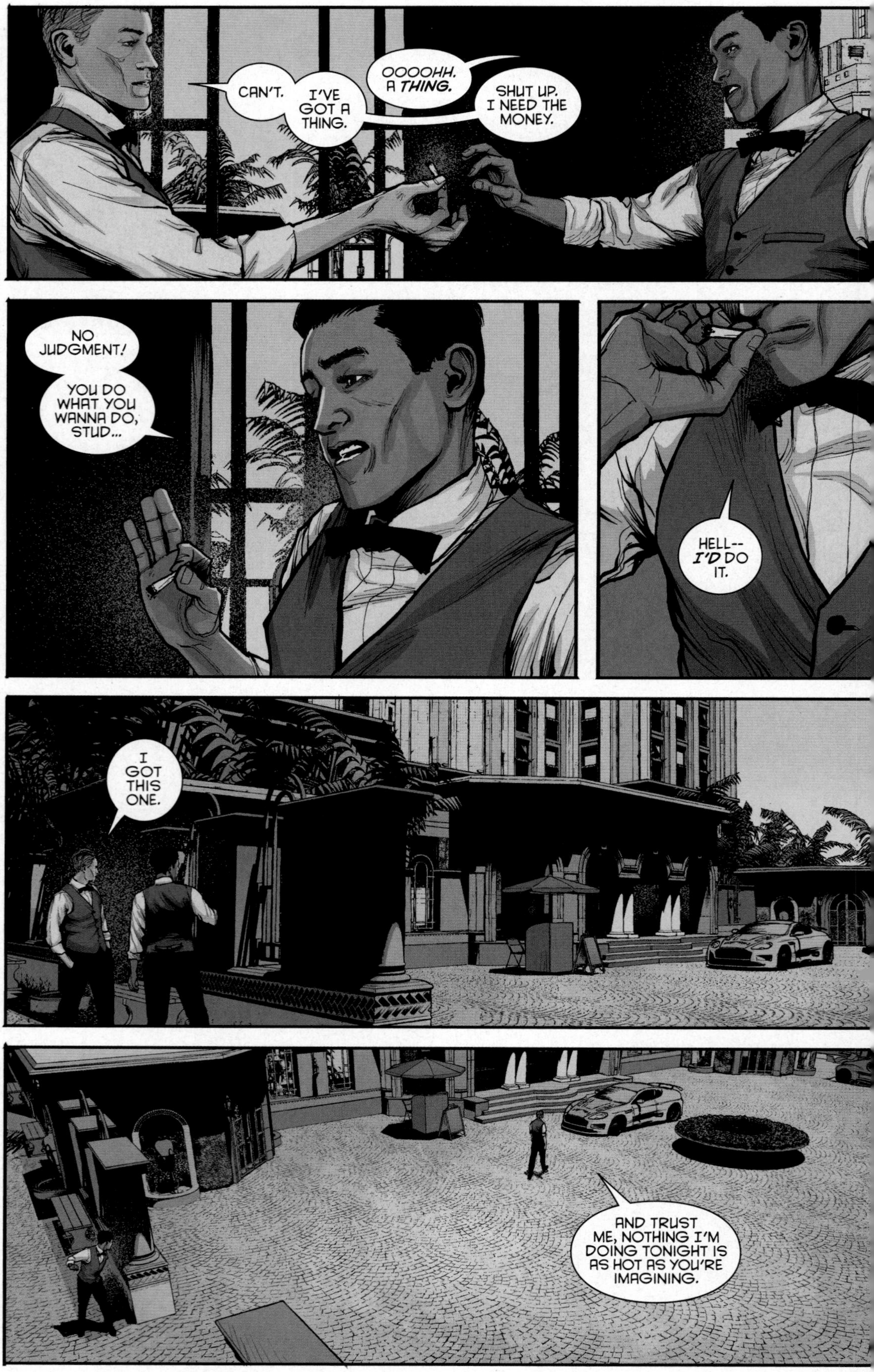
CAN'T.
I'VE GOT A THING.
OOOOHH. A THING.
SHUT UP. I NEED THE MONEY.
NO JUDGMENT!
YOU DO WHAT YOU WANNA DO, STUD...
HELL-- I'D DO IT.
I GOT THIS ONE.
AND TRUST ME, NOTHING I'M DOING TONIGHT IS AS HOT AS YOU'RE IMAGINING.

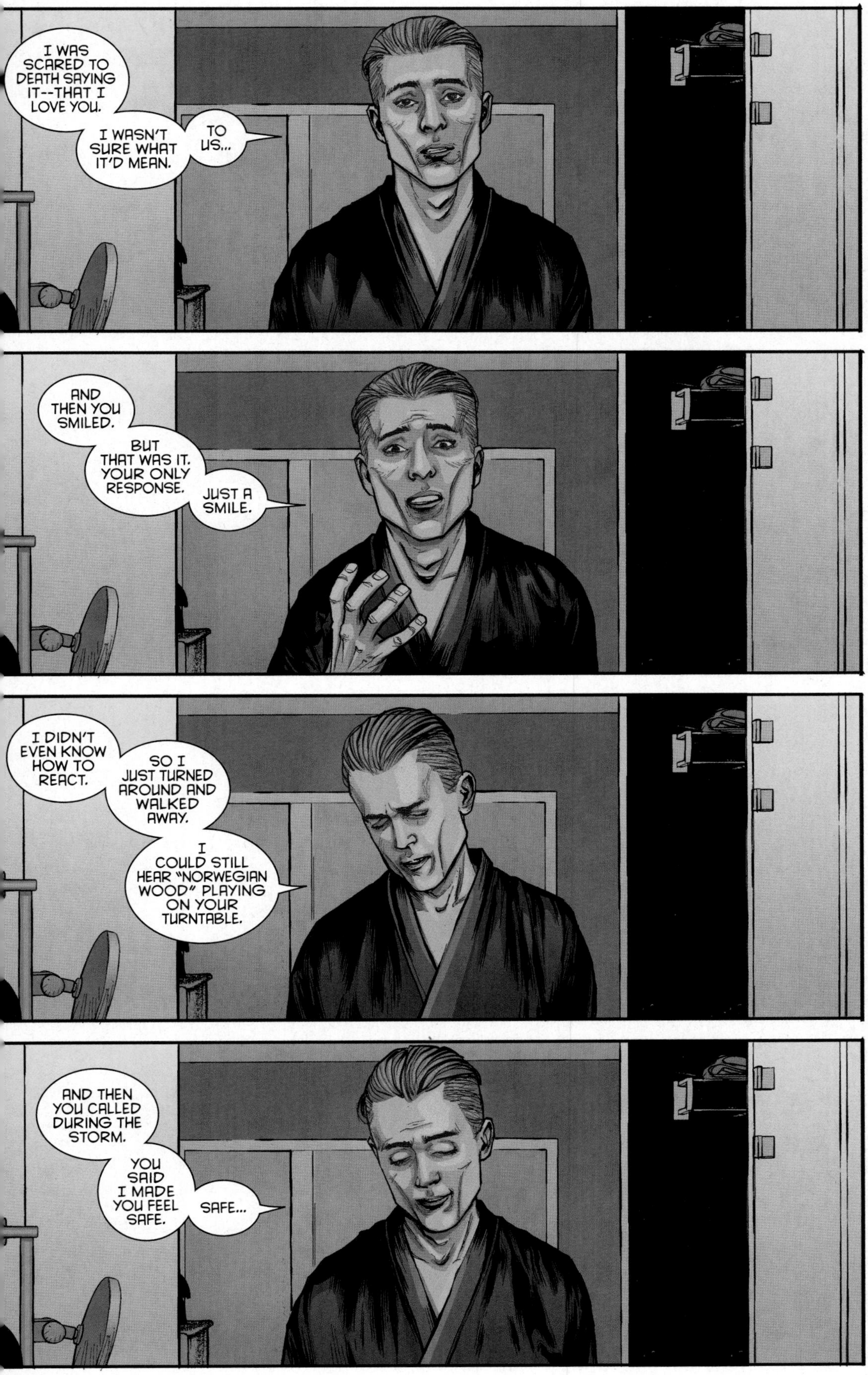
I WAS SCARED TO DEATH SAYING IT--THAT I LOVE YOU.
I WASN'T SURE WHAT IT'D MEAN.
TO US...
AND THEN YOU SMILED.
BUT THAT WAS IT. YOUR ONLY RESPONSE.
JUST A SMILE.
I DIDN'T EVEN KNOW HOW TO REACT.
SO I JUST TURNED AROUND AND WALKED AWAY.
I COULD STILL HEAR "NORWEGIAN WOOD" PLAYING ON YOUR TURNTABLE.
AND THEN YOU CALLED DURING THE STORM.
YOU SAID I MADE YOU FEEL SAFE.
SAFE...

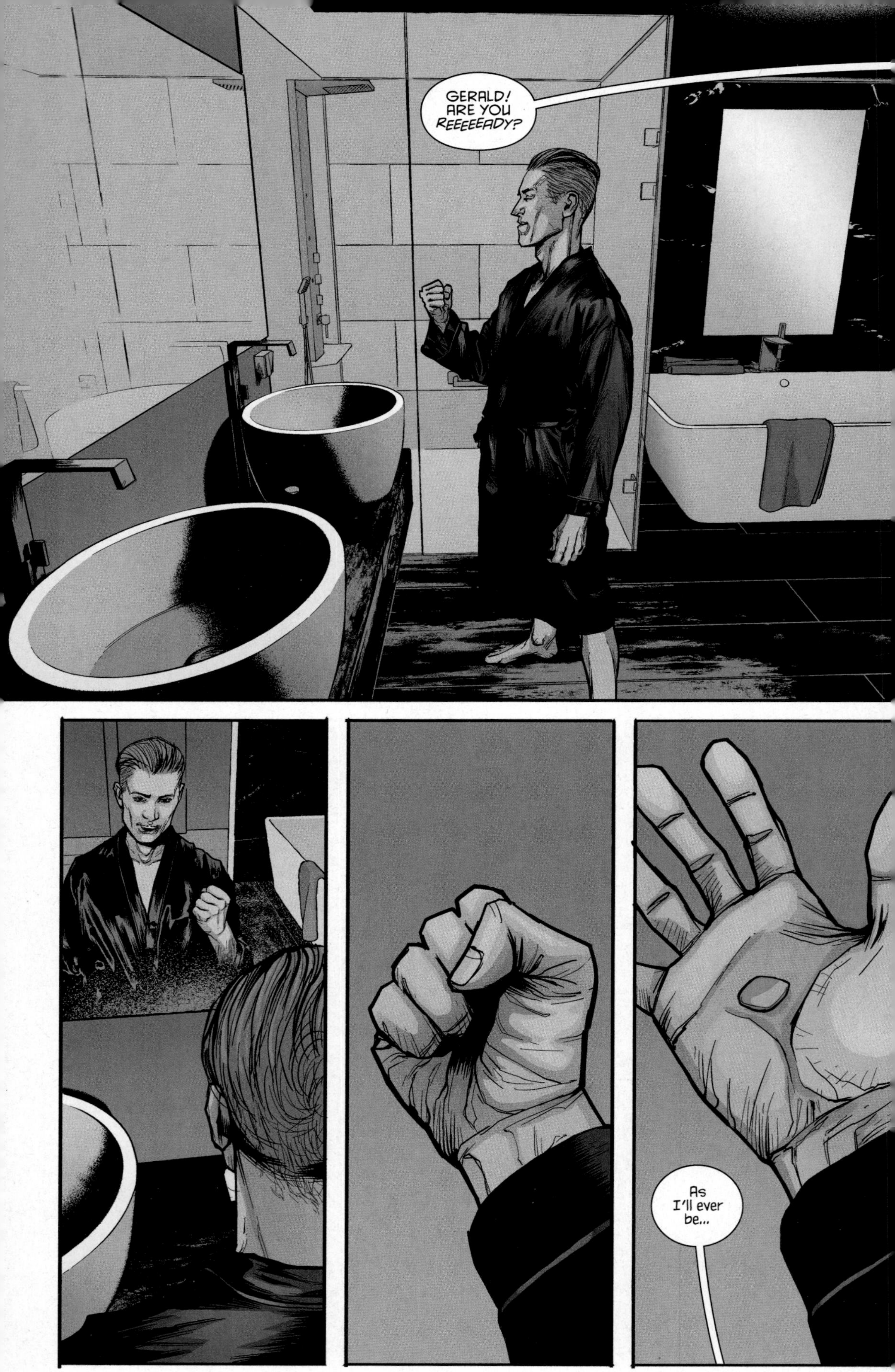
GERALD! ARE YOU REEEEEADY?
As I'll ever be...

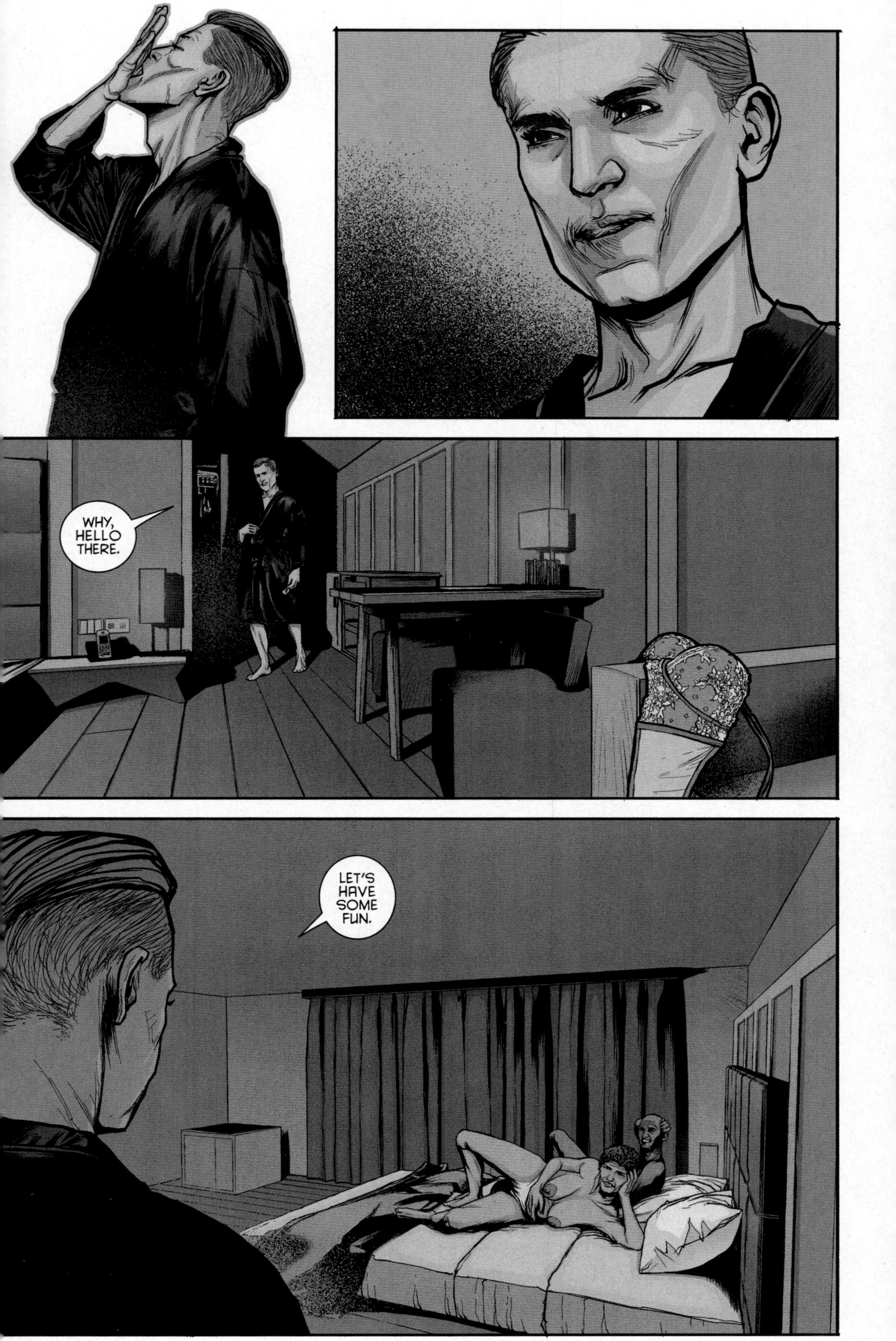
WHY, HELLO THERE.
LET'S HAVE SOME FUN.

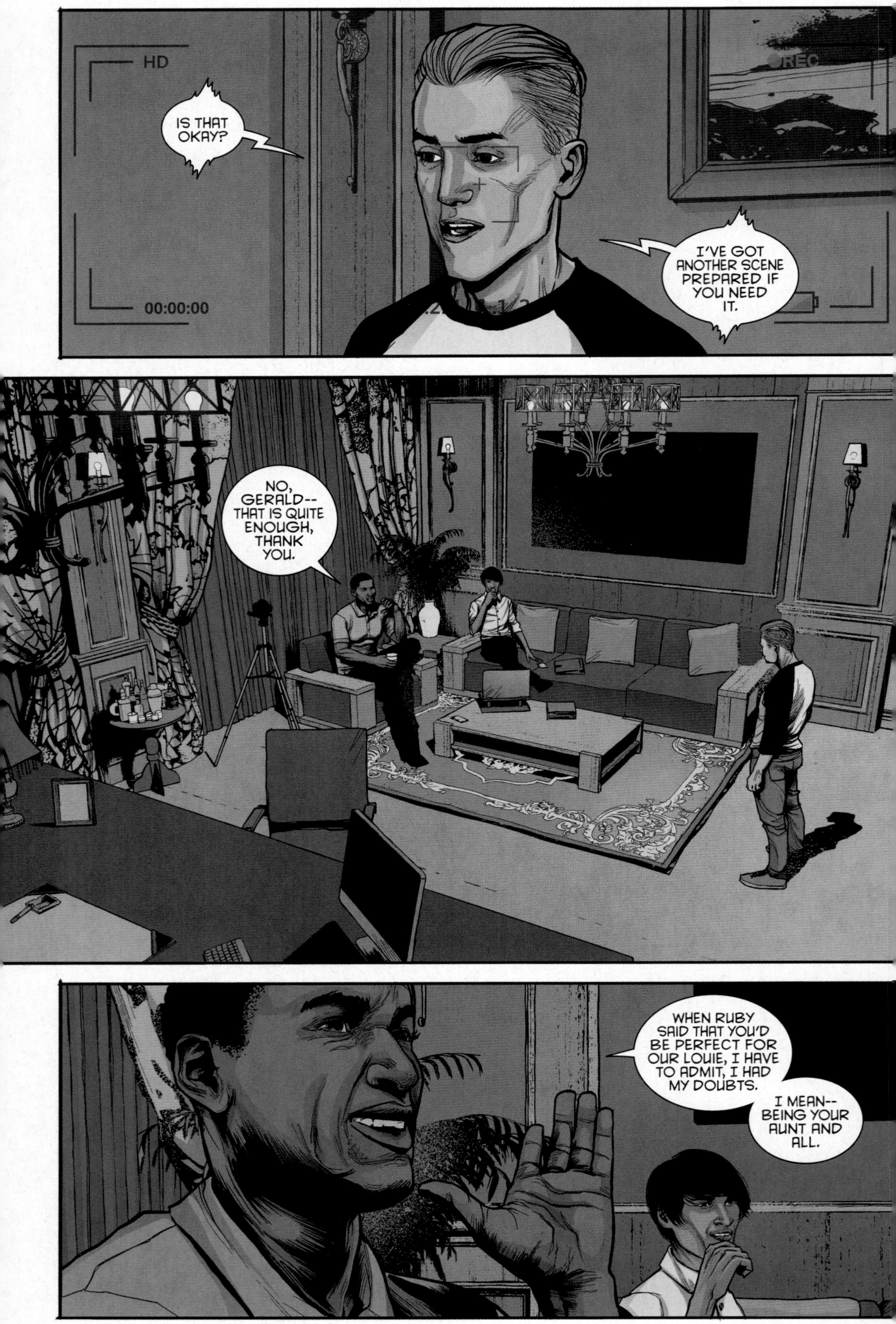
HD
REC
00:00:00
IS THAT OKAY?
I'VE GOT ANOTHER SCENE PREPARED IF YOU NEED IT.
NO, GERALD-- THAT IS QUITE ENOUGH, THANK YOU.
WHEN RUBY SAID THAT YOU'D BE PERFECT FOR OUR LOUIE, I HAVE TO ADMIT, I HAD MY DOUBTS.
I MEAN-- BEING YOUR AUNT AND ALL.

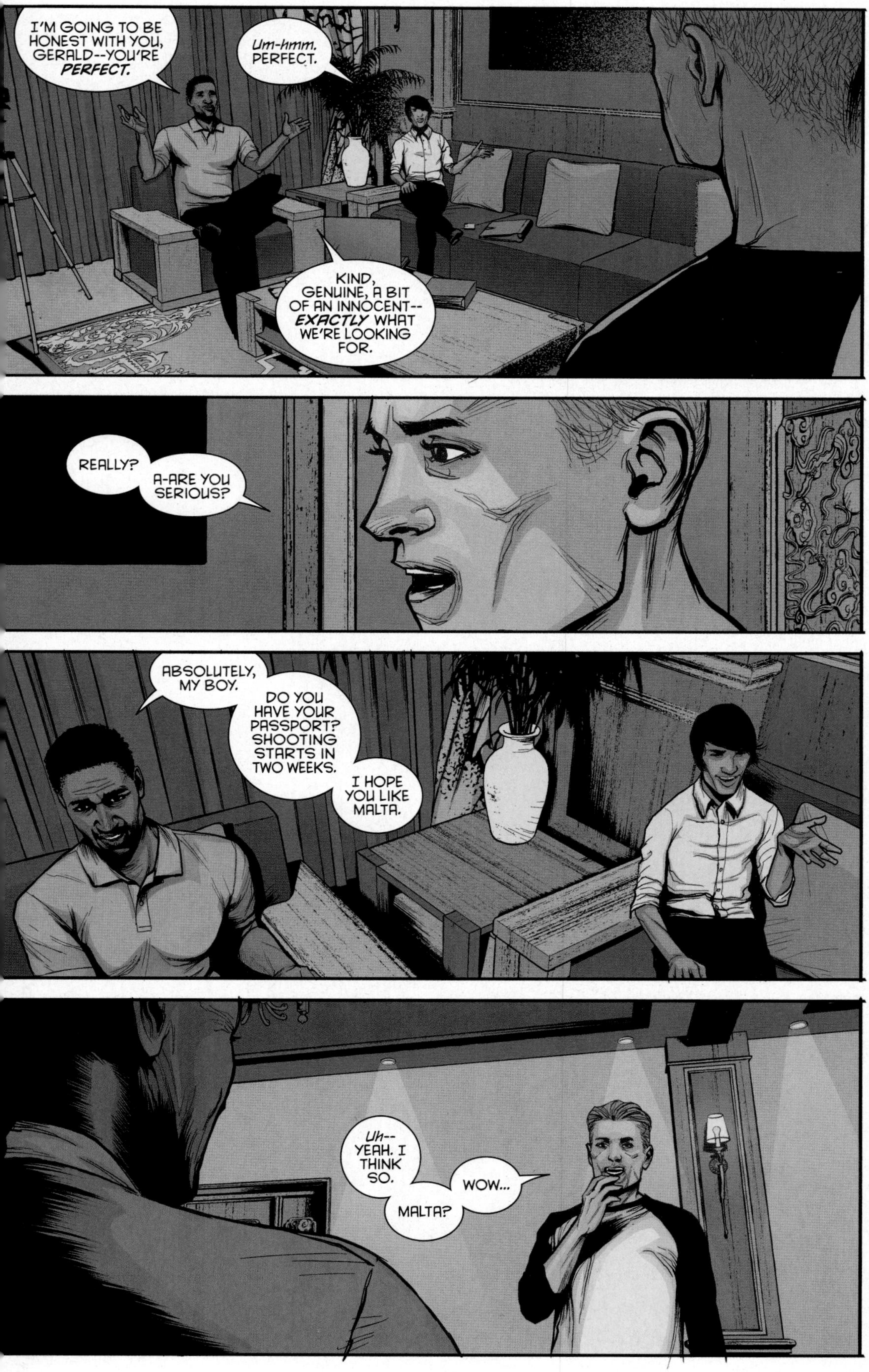
I'M GOING TO BE HONEST WITH YOU, GERALD--YOU'RE *PERFECT.*
Um-hmm. PERFECT.
KIND, GENUINE, A BIT OF AN INNOCENT-- *EXACTLY* WHAT WE'RE LOOKING FOR.
REALLY?
A-ARE YOU SERIOUS?
ABSOLUTELY, MY BOY.
DO YOU HAVE YOUR PASSPORT? SHOOTING STARTS IN TWO WEEKS.
I HOPE YOU LIKE MALTA.
Uh-- YEAH. I THINK SO.
WOW...
MALTA?

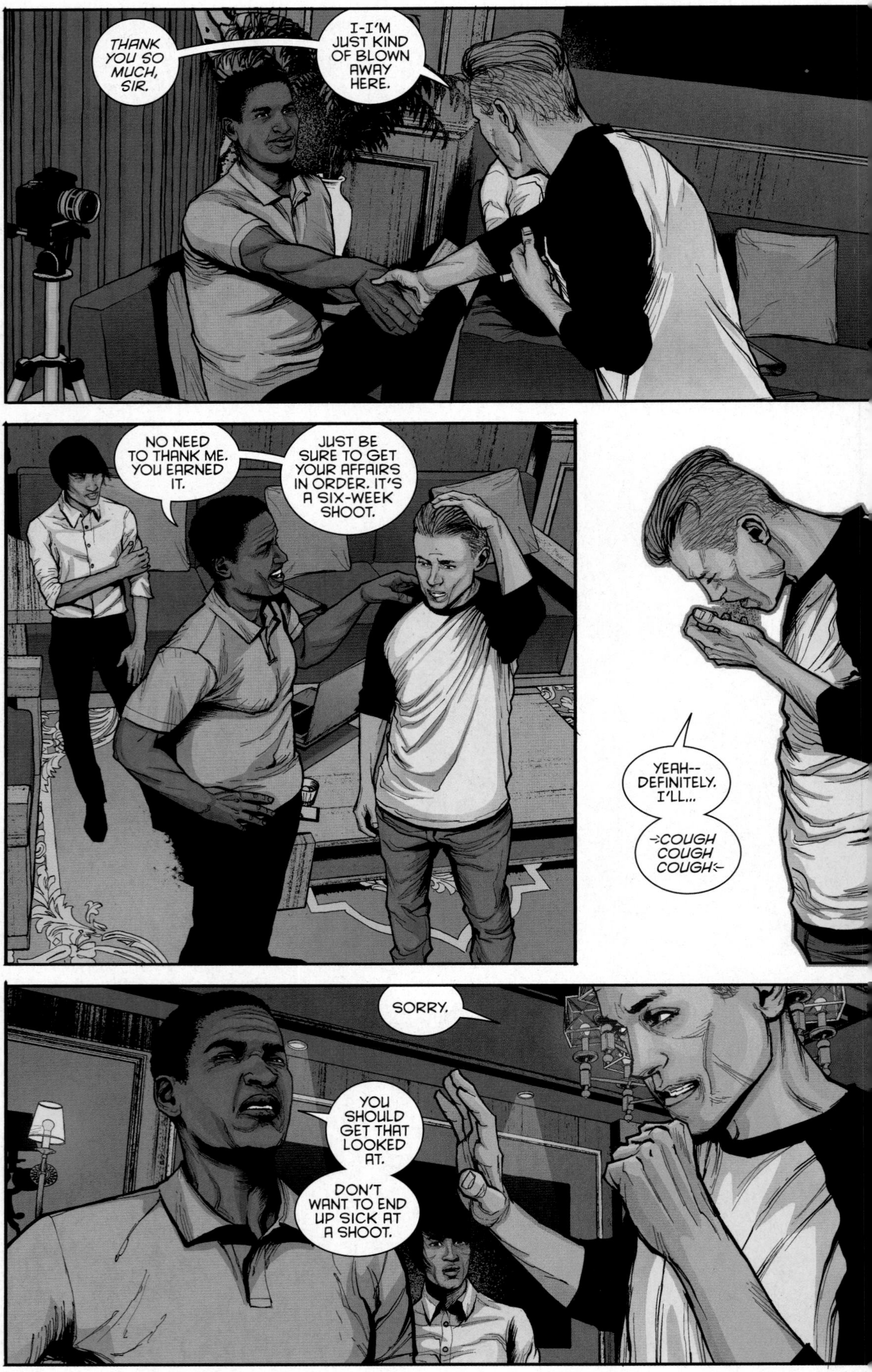
THANK YOU SO MUCH, SIR.
I-I'M JUST KIND OF BLOWN AWAY HERE.
NO NEED TO THANK ME. YOU EARNED IT.
JUST BE SURE TO GET YOUR AFFAIRS IN ORDER. IT'S A SIX-WEEK SHOOT.
YEAH-- DEFINITELY. I'LL...
COUGH COUGH COUGH
SORRY.
YOU SHOULD GET THAT LOOKED AT.
DON'T WANT TO END UP SICK AT A SHOOT.

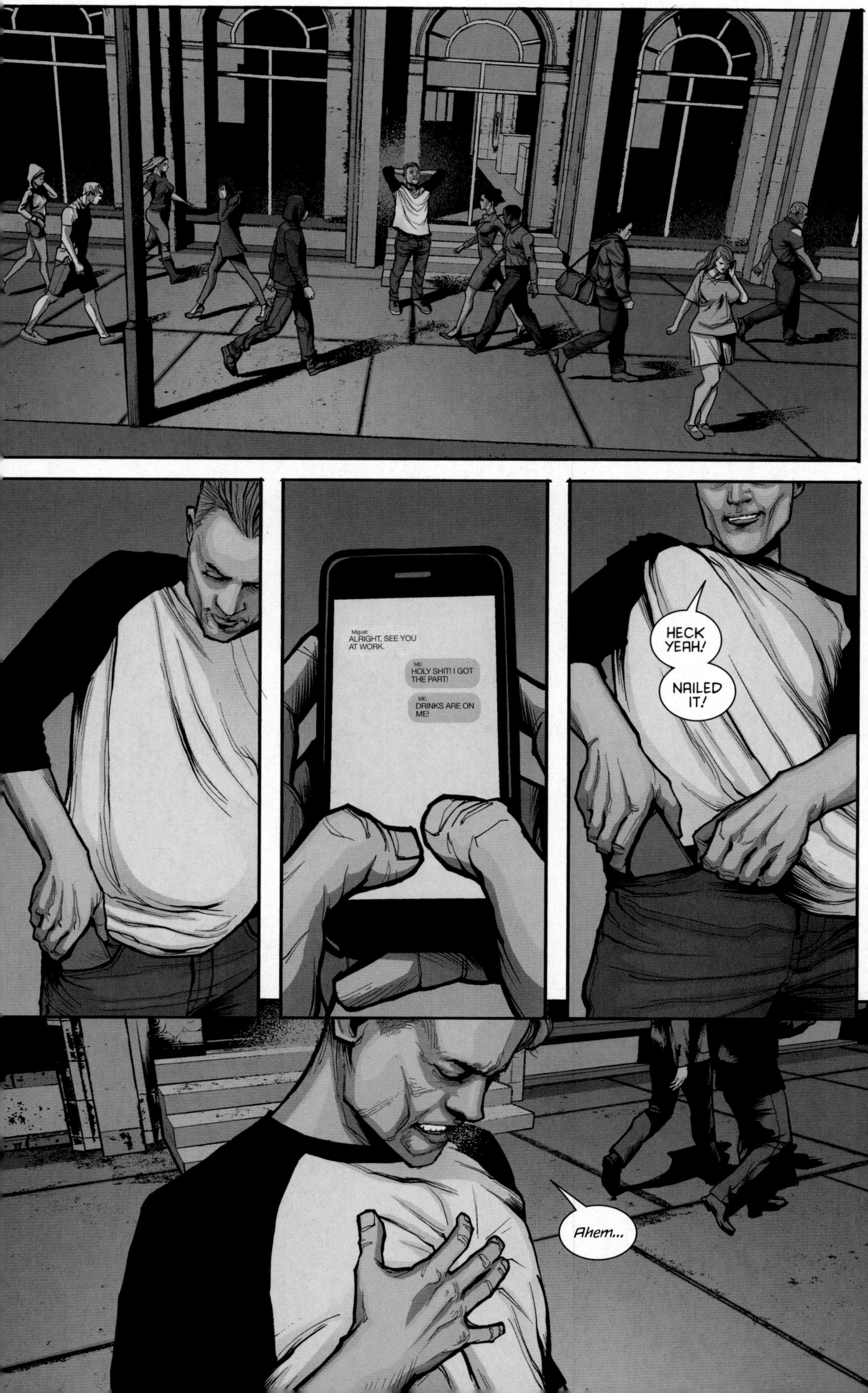
Miguel:
ALRIGHT, SEE YOU AT WORK.
ME:
HOLY SHIT! I GOT THE PART!
ME:
DRINKS ARE ON ME!
HECK YEAH!
NAILED IT!
Ahem...

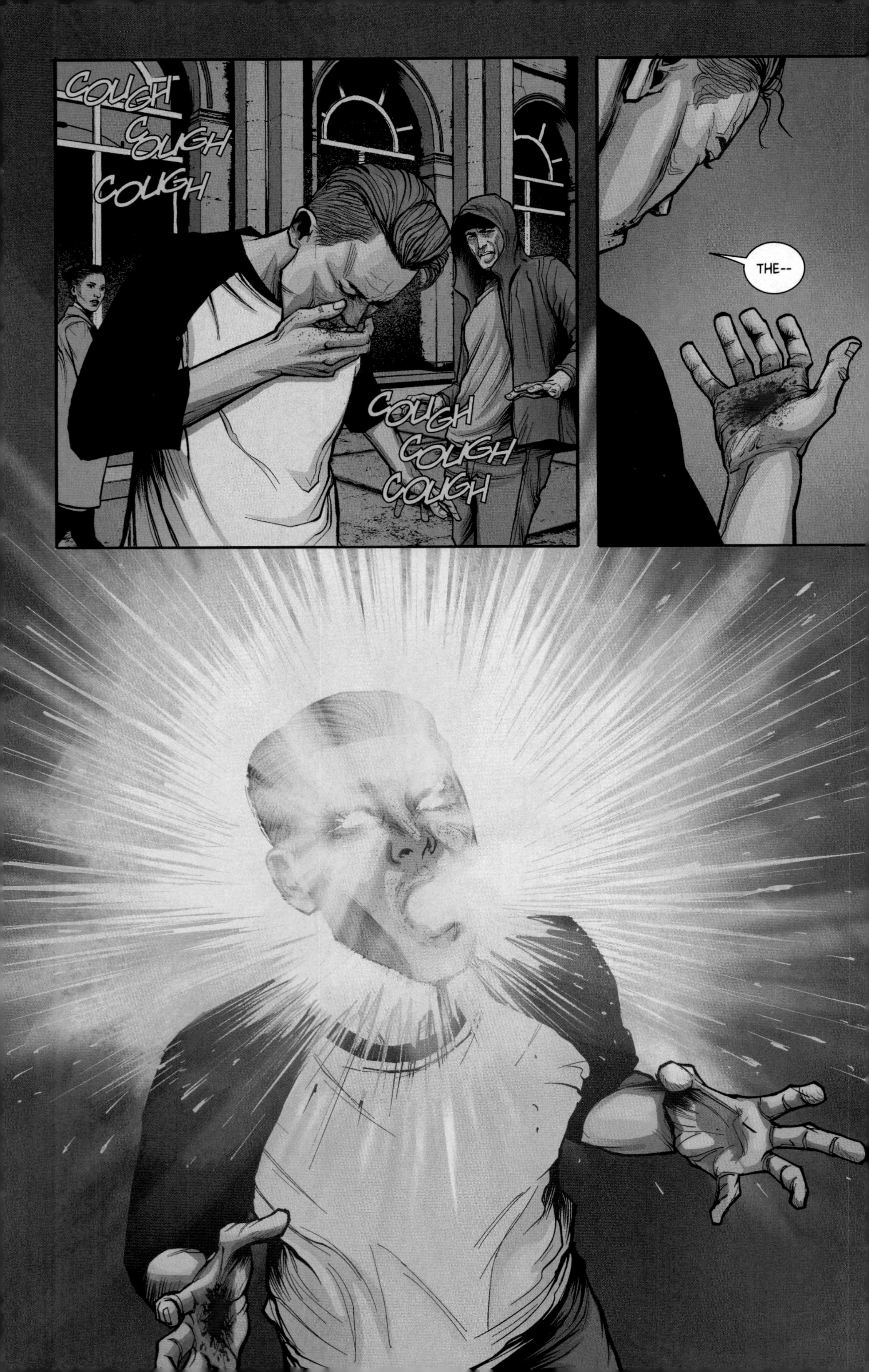
COUGH
COUGH
COUGH
COUGH
COUGH
COUGH
THE--

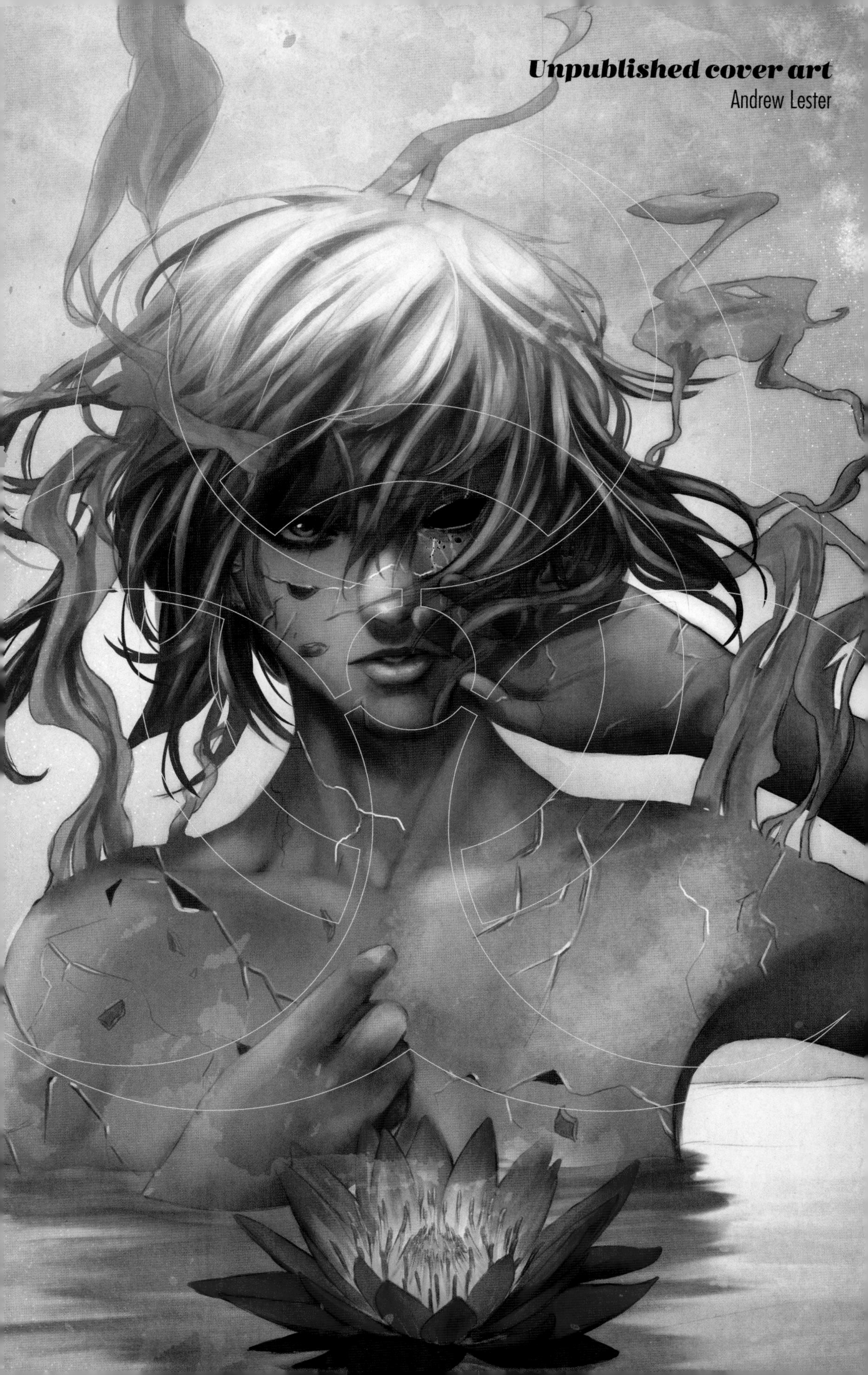

Unpublished cover art
Andrew Lester

CHAPTER

29

"OKAY. SURE...

"SO PARKS CALLS ME. IT'D BEEN A LITTLE WHILE SINCE I'D HEARD FROM HIM. MAYBE A MONTH OR TWO.

"HE SAYS HE'S GOT A JOB.

"SAYS IT'S IMPORTANT. HE NEEDS SOMEONE HE CAN REALLY TRUST.

"OF COURSE I'M IN. I'M ALWAYS IN.

"WE GET TO THE SPOT-- ROLL UP ON THIS TRUCK, THING'S PRACTICALLY A TANK. I FIGURE THEY GOTTA BE RUNNING DIAMONDS.

"I YANK THE DRIVER OUT AND PARKS GOES AROUND BACK. I THINK HE'S GONNA HAVE TO BLOW THE LOCK OR SOMETHING.

"NOPE.

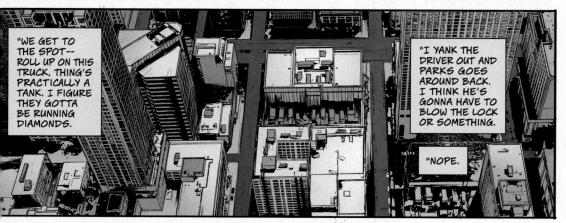

"A COUPLE MINUTES LATER, HE COMES AROUND CARRYING THIS BOX--ABOUT THE SIZE OF A CAKE.

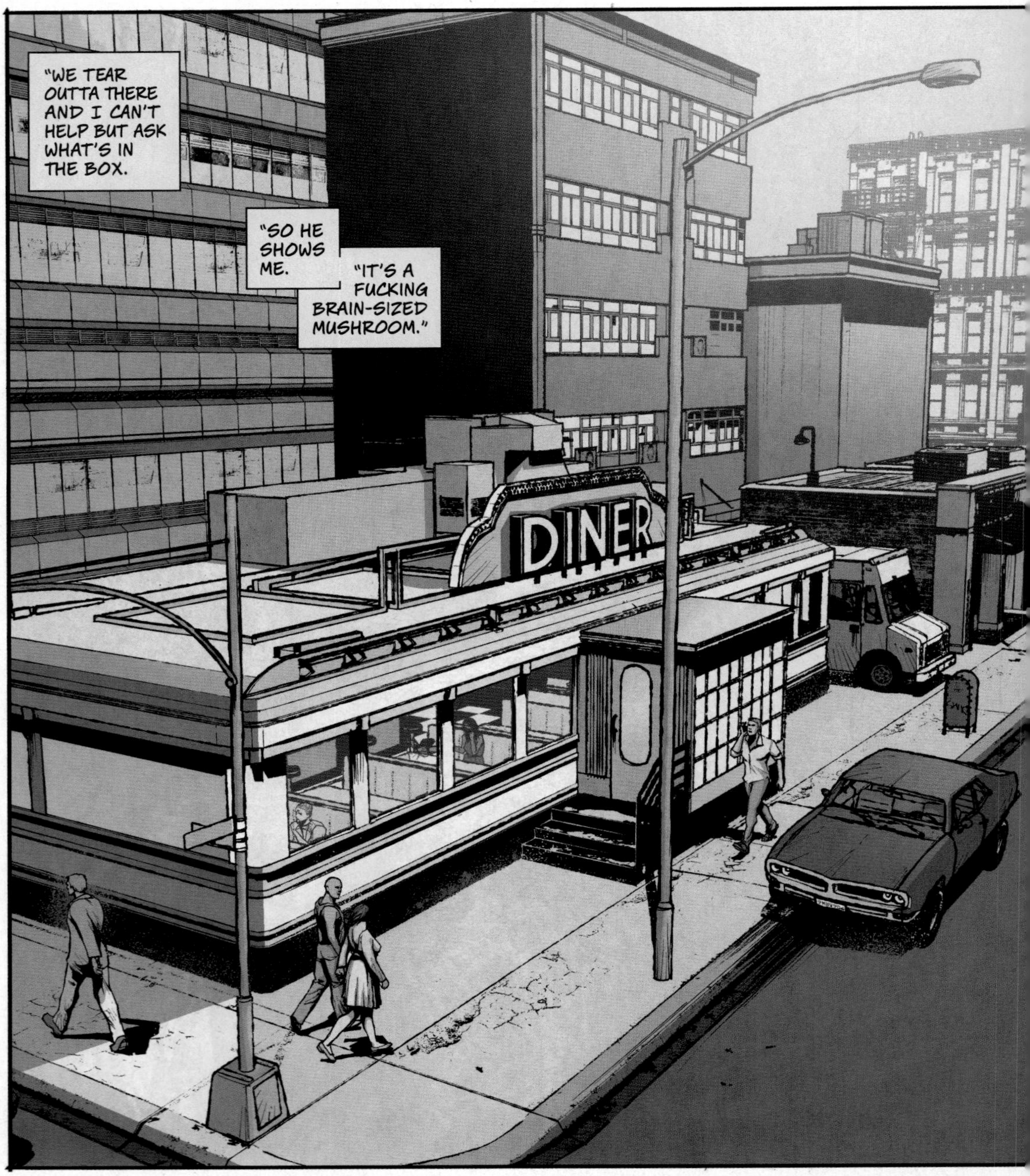
"WE TEAR OUTTA THERE AND I CAN'T HELP BUT ASK WHAT'S IN THE BOX.
"SO HE SHOWS ME.
"IT'S A FUCKING BRAIN-SIZED MUSHROOM."
DINER

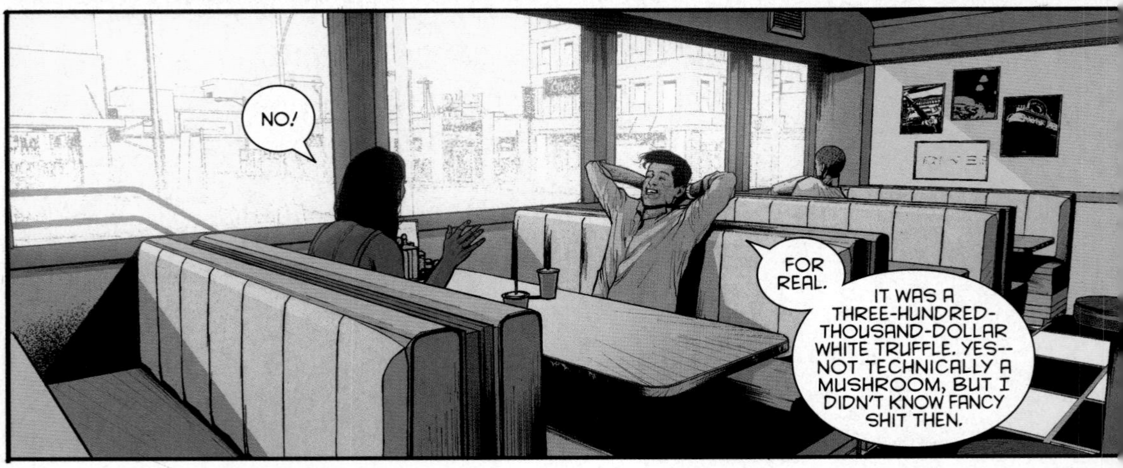
NO!
FOR REAL.
IT WAS A THREE-HUNDRED-THOUSAND-DOLLAR WHITE TRUFFLE. YES--NOT TECHNICALLY A MUSHROOM, BUT I DIDN'T KNOW FANCY SHIT THEN.

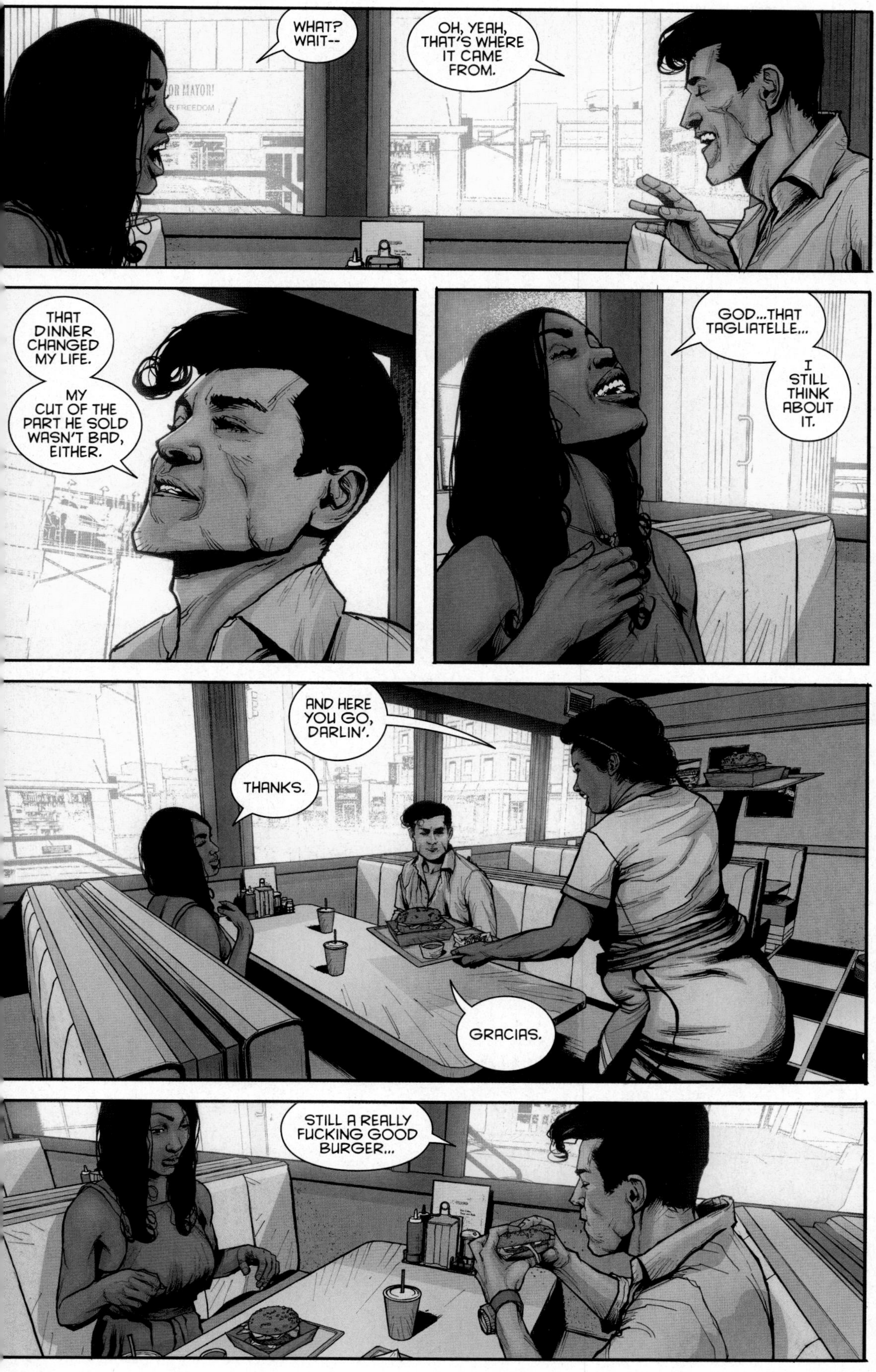

WHAT? WAIT--
OH, YEAH, THAT'S WHERE IT CAME FROM.
THAT DINNER CHANGED MY LIFE.
MY CUT OF THE PART HE SOLD WASN'T BAD, EITHER.
GOD...THAT TAGLIATELLE...
I STILL THINK ABOUT IT.
AND HERE YOU GO, DARLIN'.
THANKS.
GRACIAS.
STILL A REALLY FUCKING GOOD BURGER...

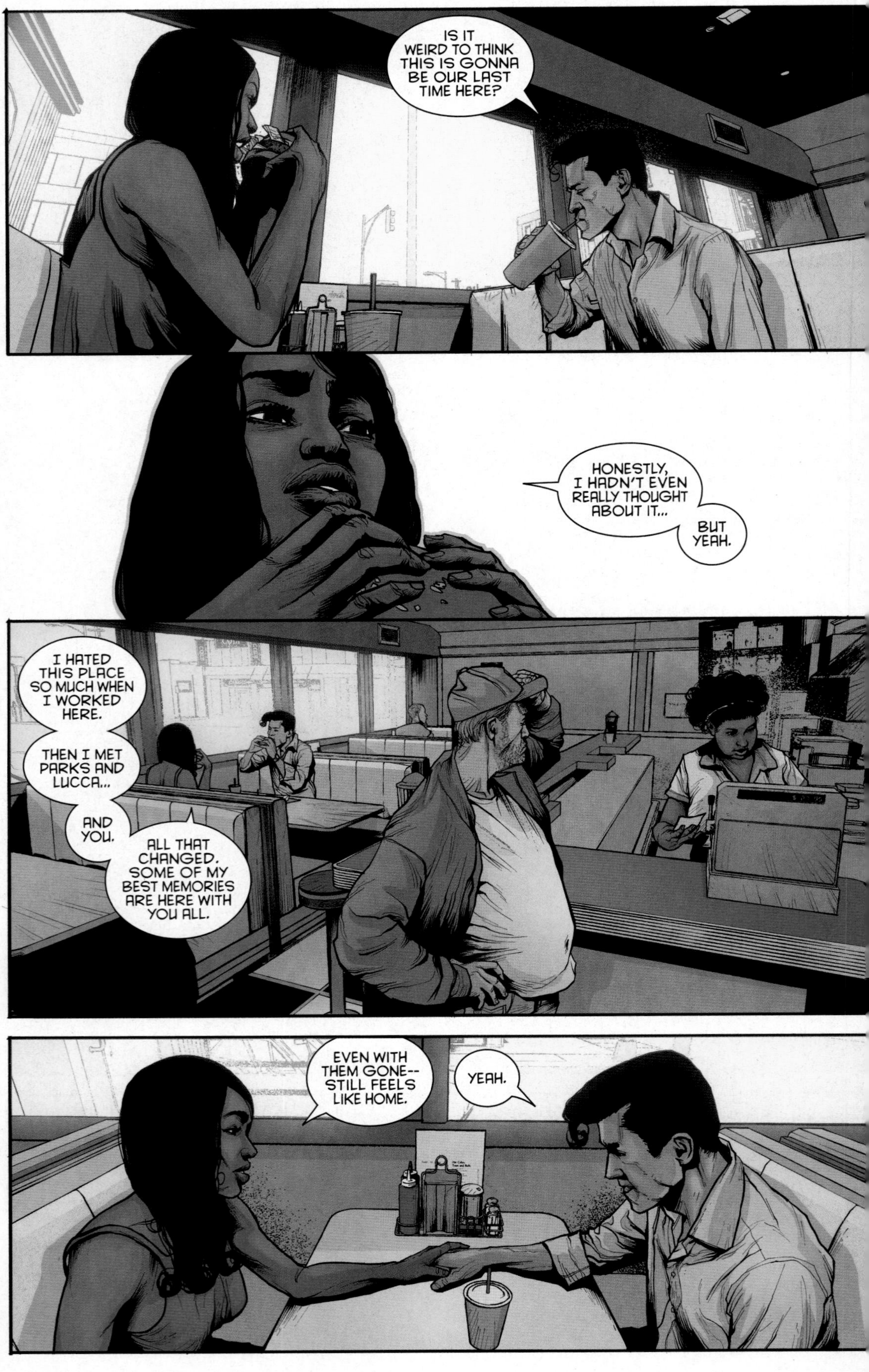
IS IT WEIRD TO THINK THIS IS GONNA BE OUR LAST TIME HERE?
HONESTLY, I HADN'T EVEN REALLY THOUGHT ABOUT IT...
BUT YEAH.
I HATED THIS PLACE SO MUCH WHEN I WORKED HERE.
THEN I MET PARKS AND LUCCA...
AND YOU.
ALL THAT CHANGED. SOME OF MY BEST MEMORIES ARE HERE WITH YOU ALL.
EVEN WITH THEM GONE-- STILL FEELS LIKE HOME.
YEAH.

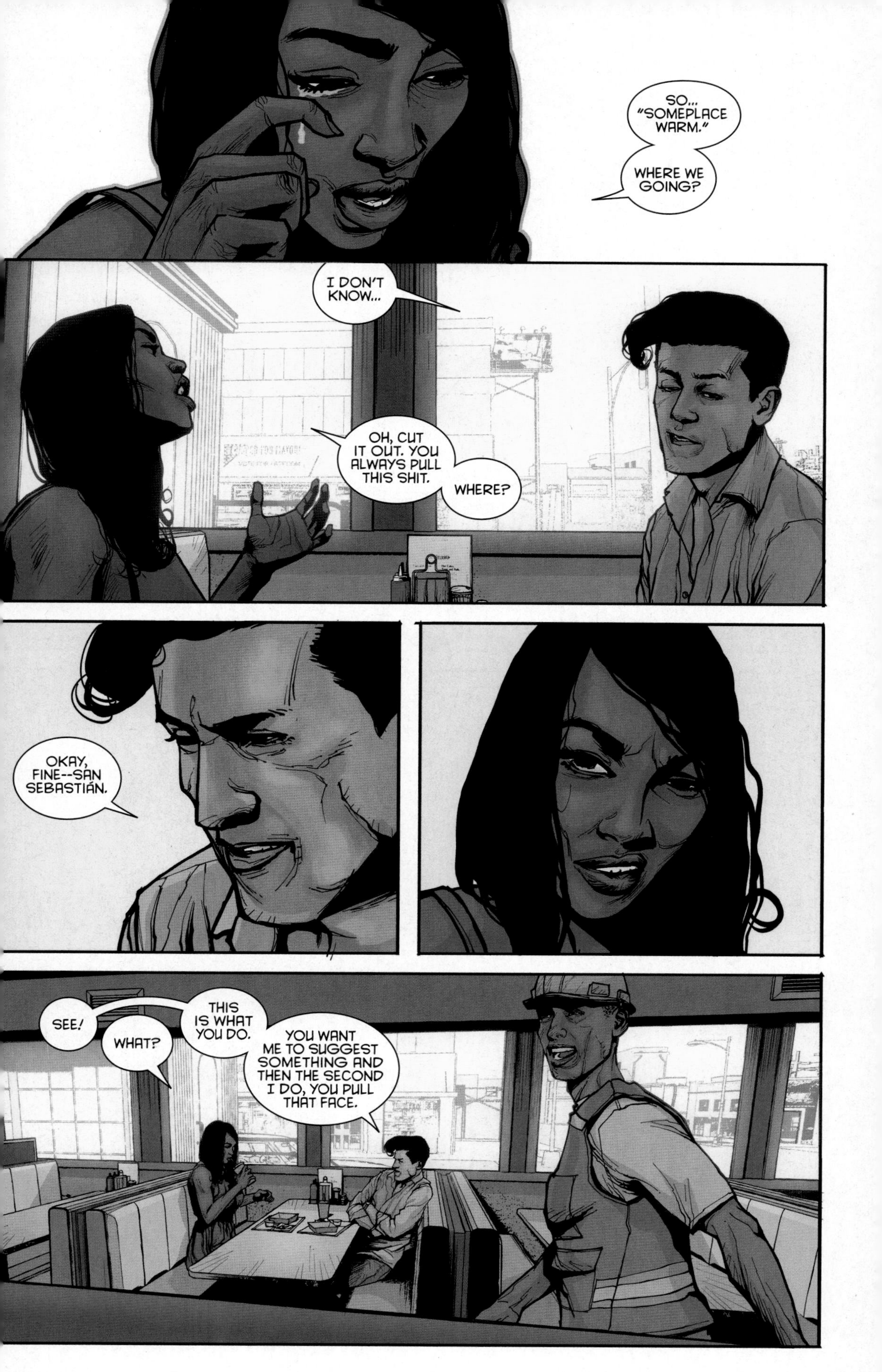
SO... "SOMEPLACE WARM."
WHERE WE GOING?
I DON'T KNOW...
OH, CUT IT OUT. YOU ALWAYS PULL THIS SHIT.
WHERE?
OKAY, FINE--SAN SEBASTIÁN.
SEE!
WHAT?
THIS IS WHAT YOU DO.
YOU WANT ME TO SUGGEST SOMETHING AND THEN THE SECOND I DO, YOU PULL THAT FACE.

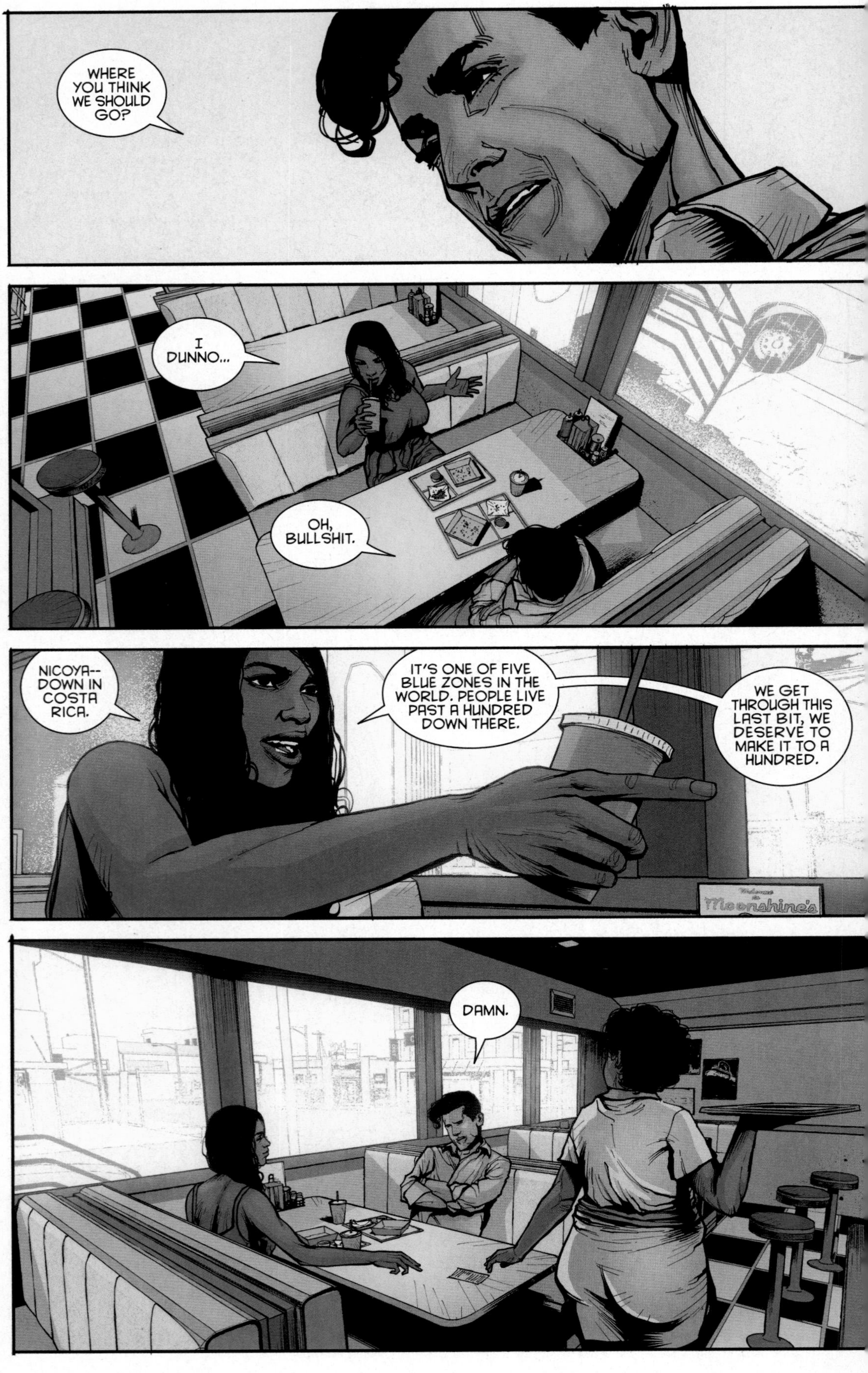
WHERE YOU THINK WE SHOULD GO?
I DUNNO...
OH, BULLSHIT.
NICOYA-- DOWN IN COSTA RICA.
IT'S ONE OF FIVE BLUE ZONES IN THE WORLD. PEOPLE LIVE PAST A HUNDRED DOWN THERE.
WE GET THROUGH THIS LAST BIT, WE DESERVE TO MAKE IT TO A HUNDRED.
Moonshine's
DAMN.

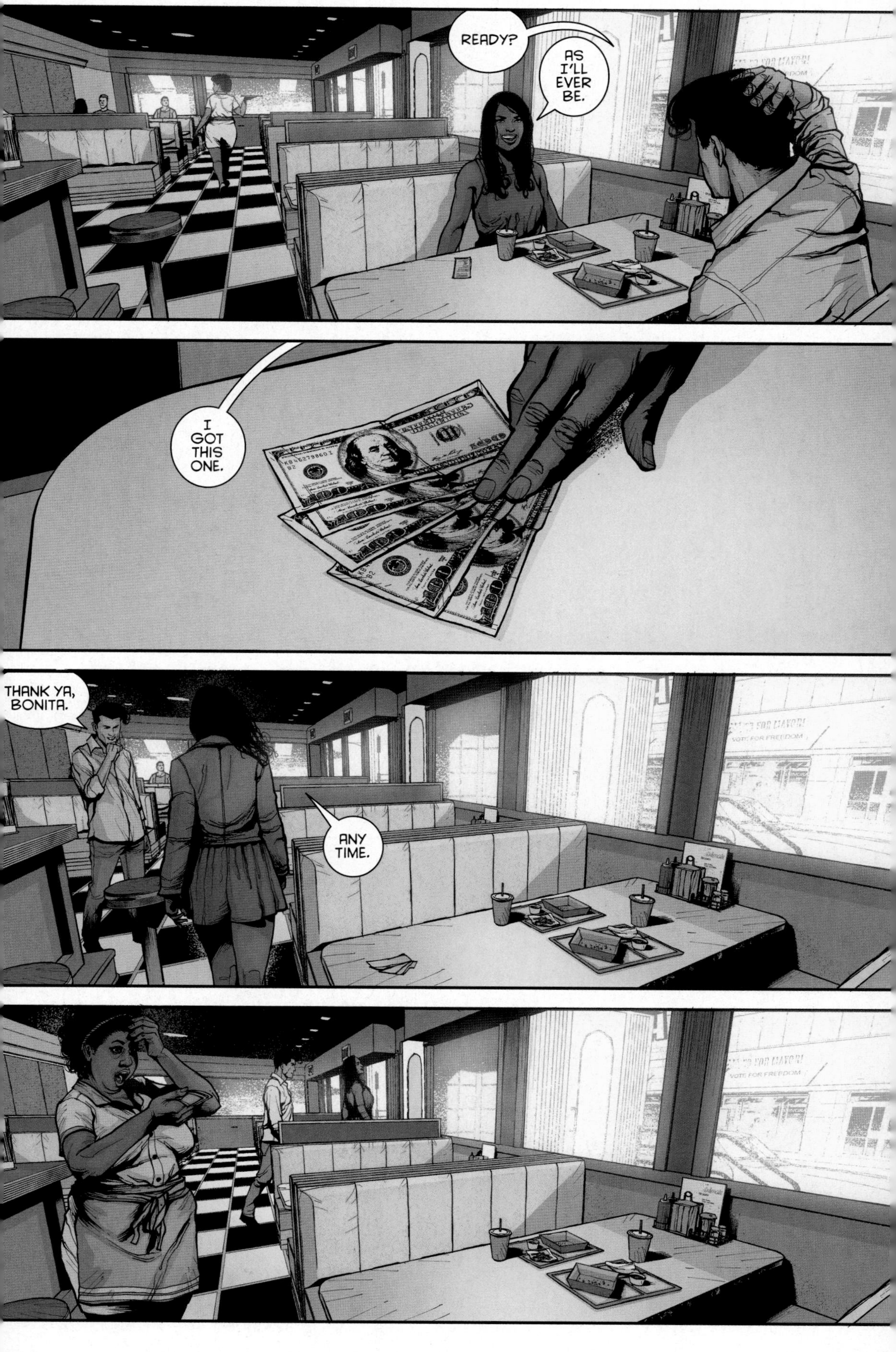
READY?
AS I'LL EVER BE.
I GOT THIS ONE.
THANK YA, BONITA.
ANY TIME.
VOTE FOR FREEDOM

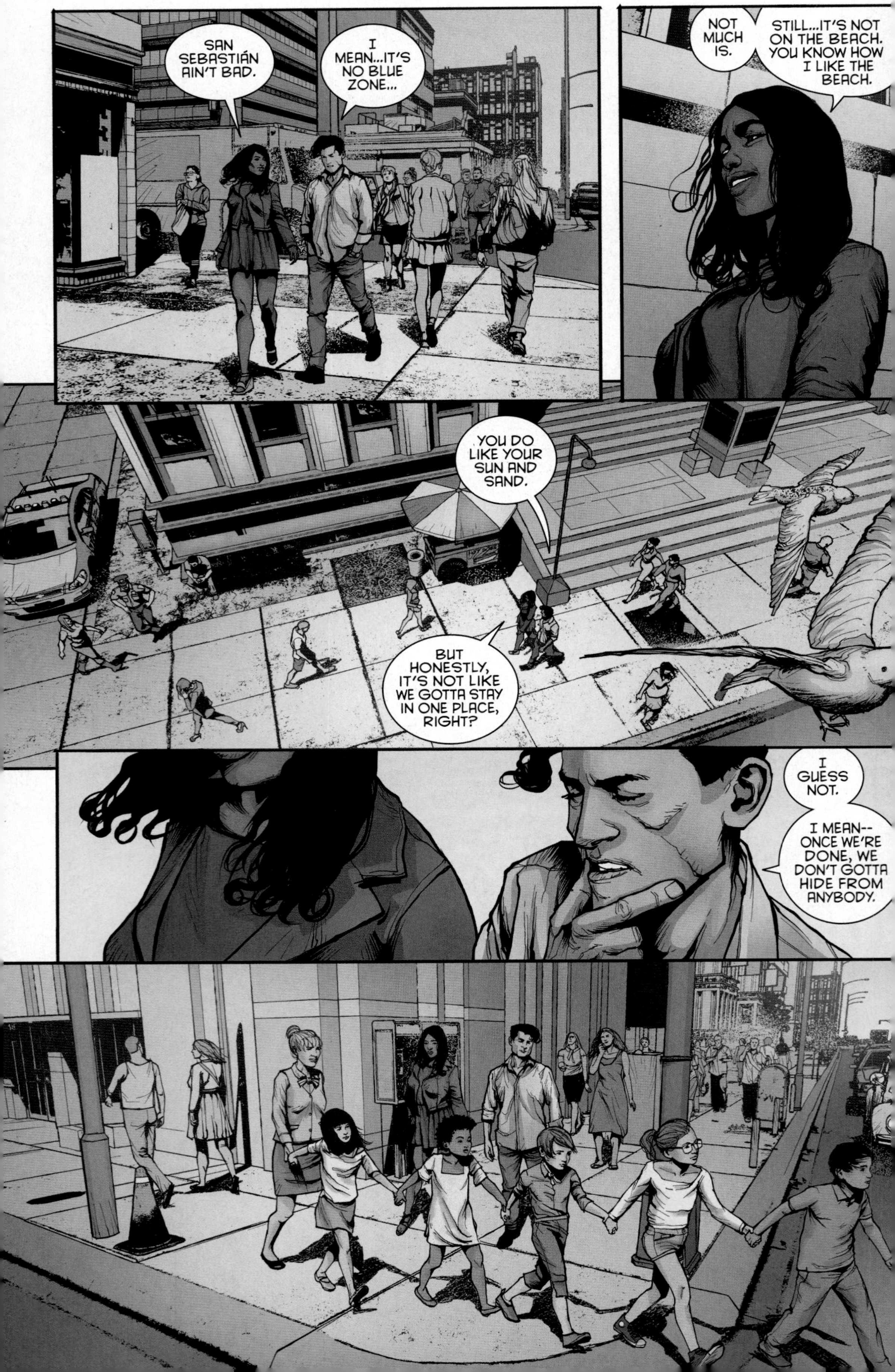
SAN SEBASTIÁN AIN'T BAD.
I MEAN...IT'S NO BLUE ZONE...
NOT MUCH IS.
STILL...IT'S NOT ON THE BEACH. YOU KNOW HOW I LIKE THE BEACH.
YOU DO LIKE YOUR SUN AND SAND.
BUT HONESTLY, IT'S NOT LIKE WE GOTTA STAY IN ONE PLACE, RIGHT?
I GUESS NOT.
I MEAN-- ONCE WE'RE DONE, WE DON'T GOTTA HIDE FROM ANYBODY.

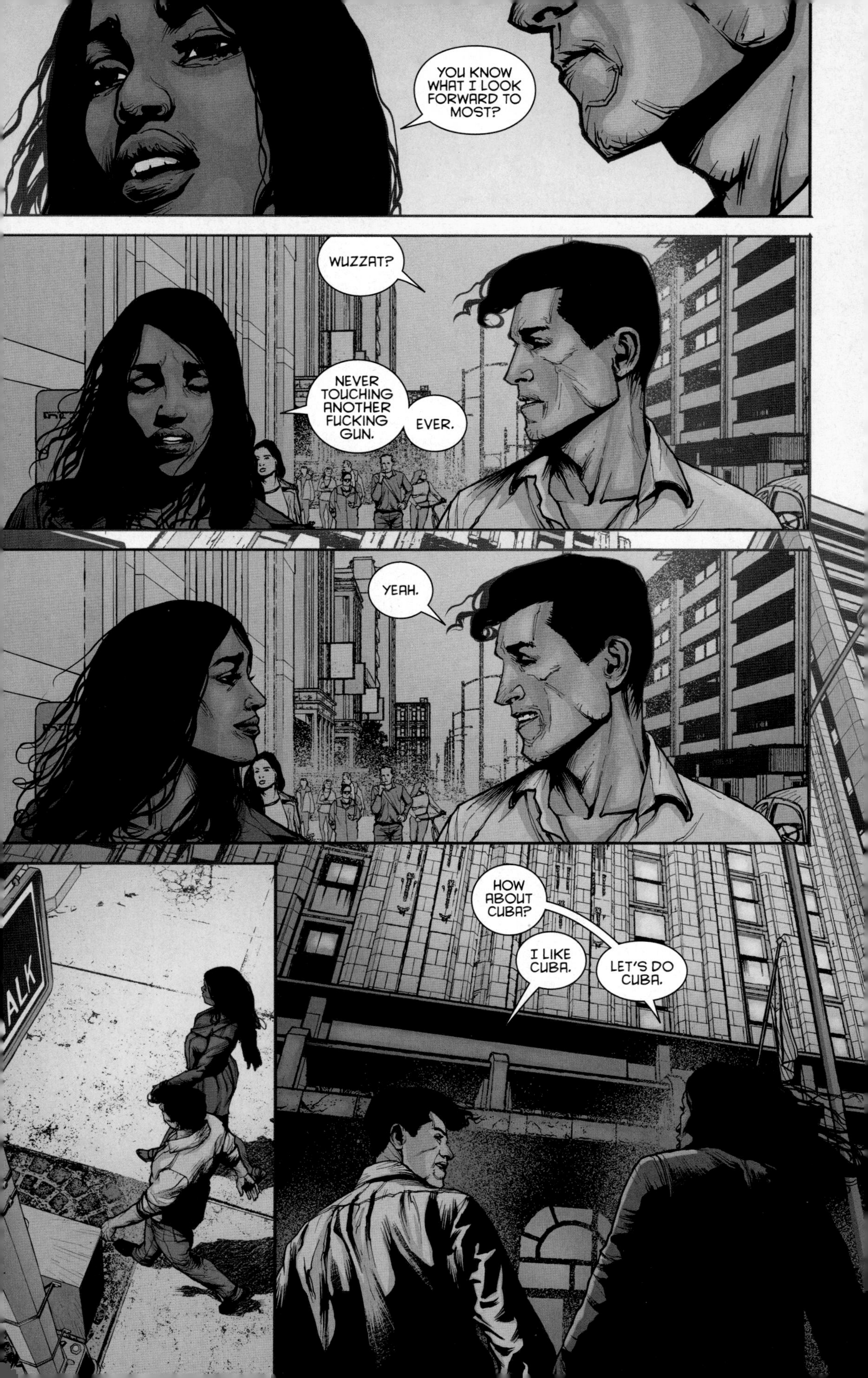
YOU KNOW WHAT I LOOK FORWARD TO MOST?
WUZZAT?
NEVER TOUCHING ANOTHER FUCKING GUN.
EVER.
YEAH.
ALK
HOW ABOUT CUBA?
I LIKE CUBA.
LET'S DO CUBA.

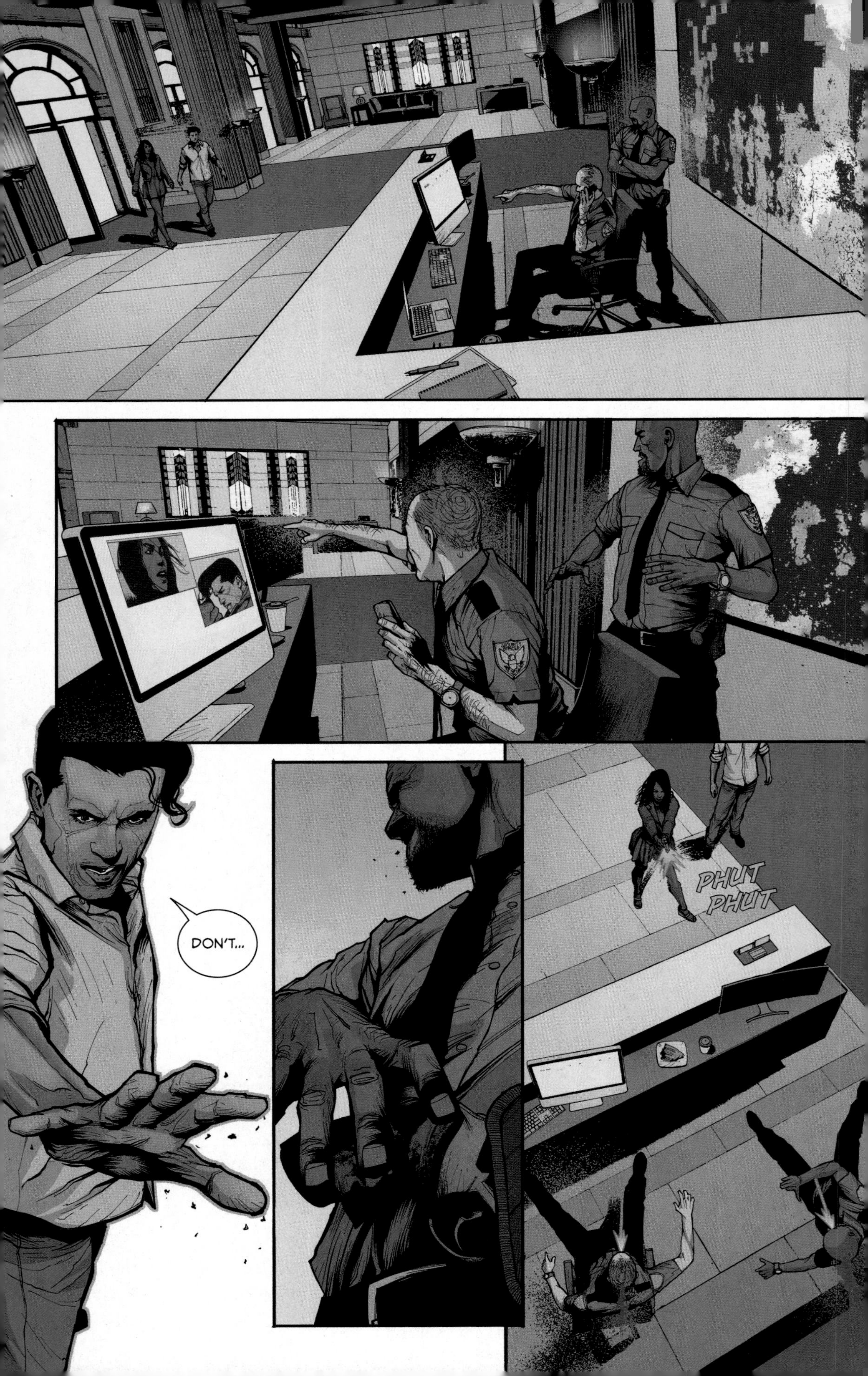
DON'T...
PHUT
PHUT

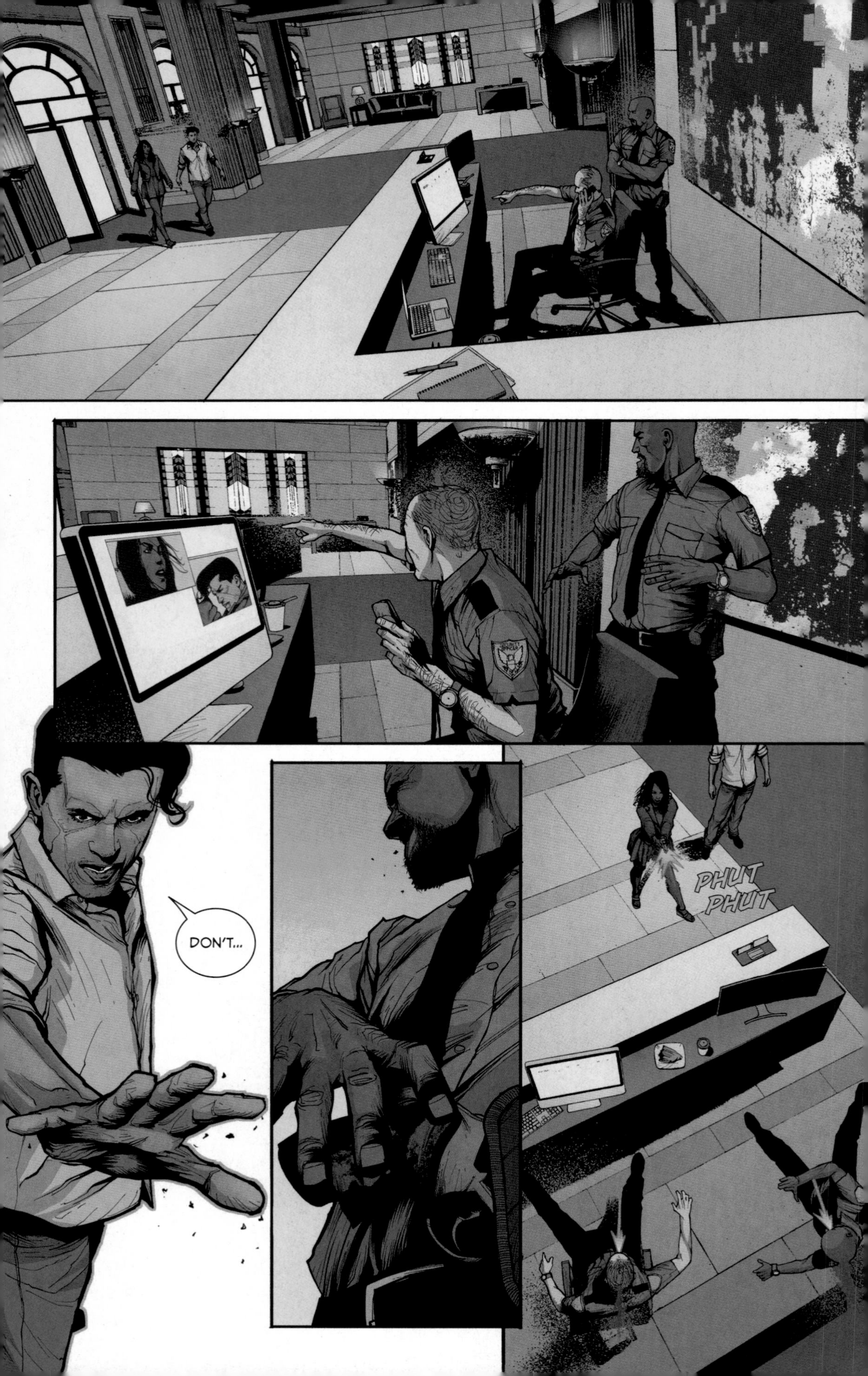
DON'T...
PHUT
PHUT

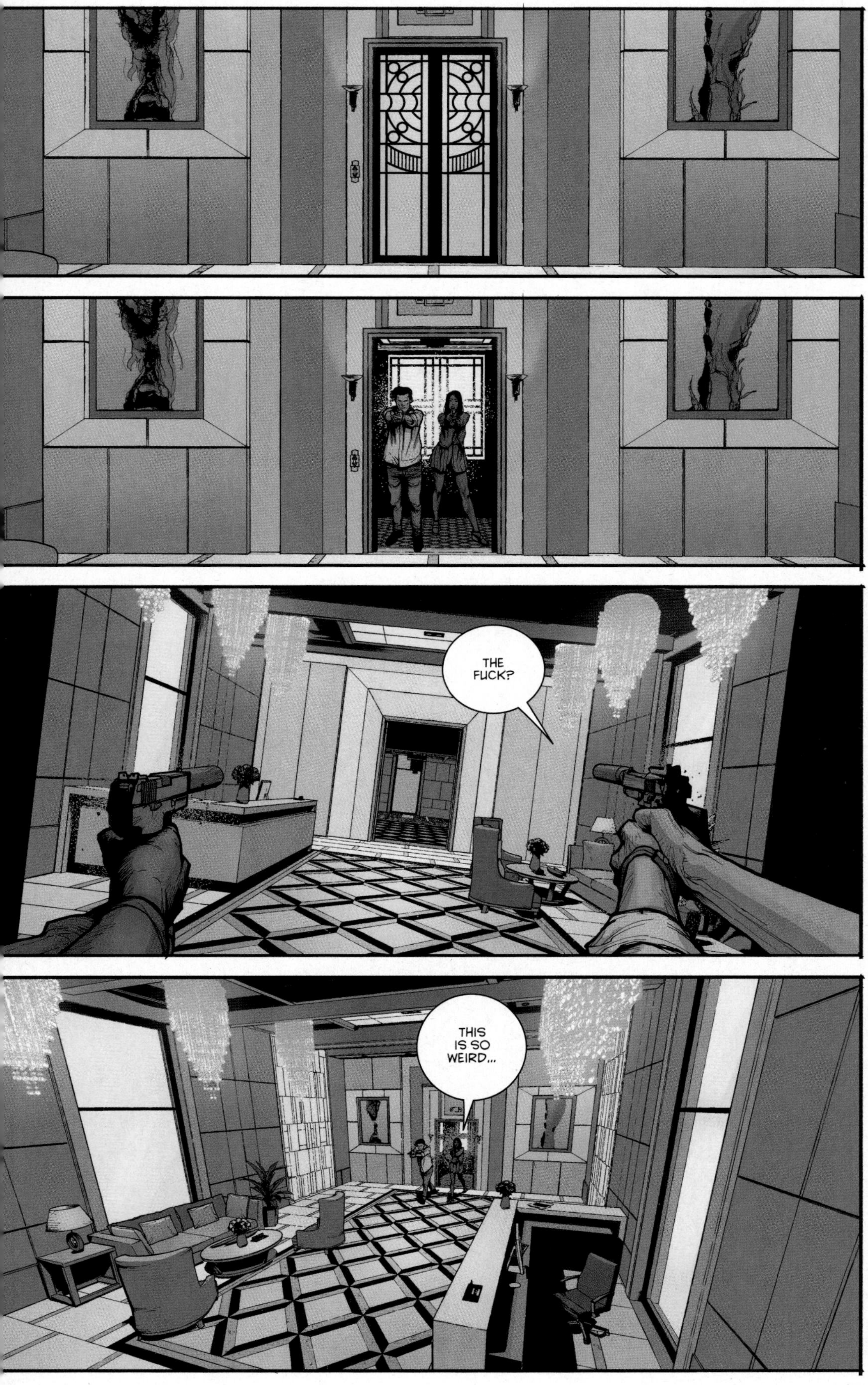
THE FUCK?
THIS IS SO WEIRD...

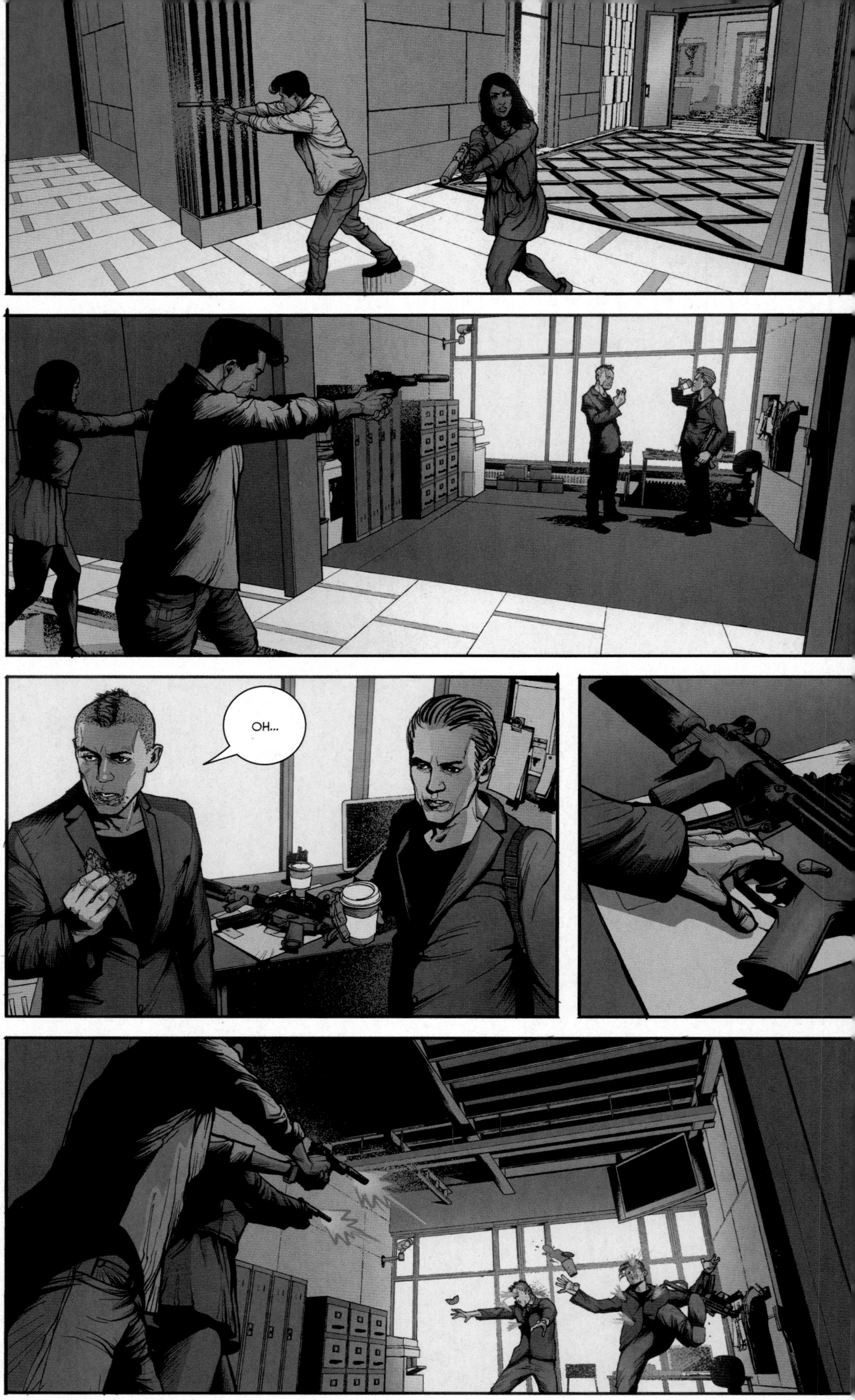
OH...

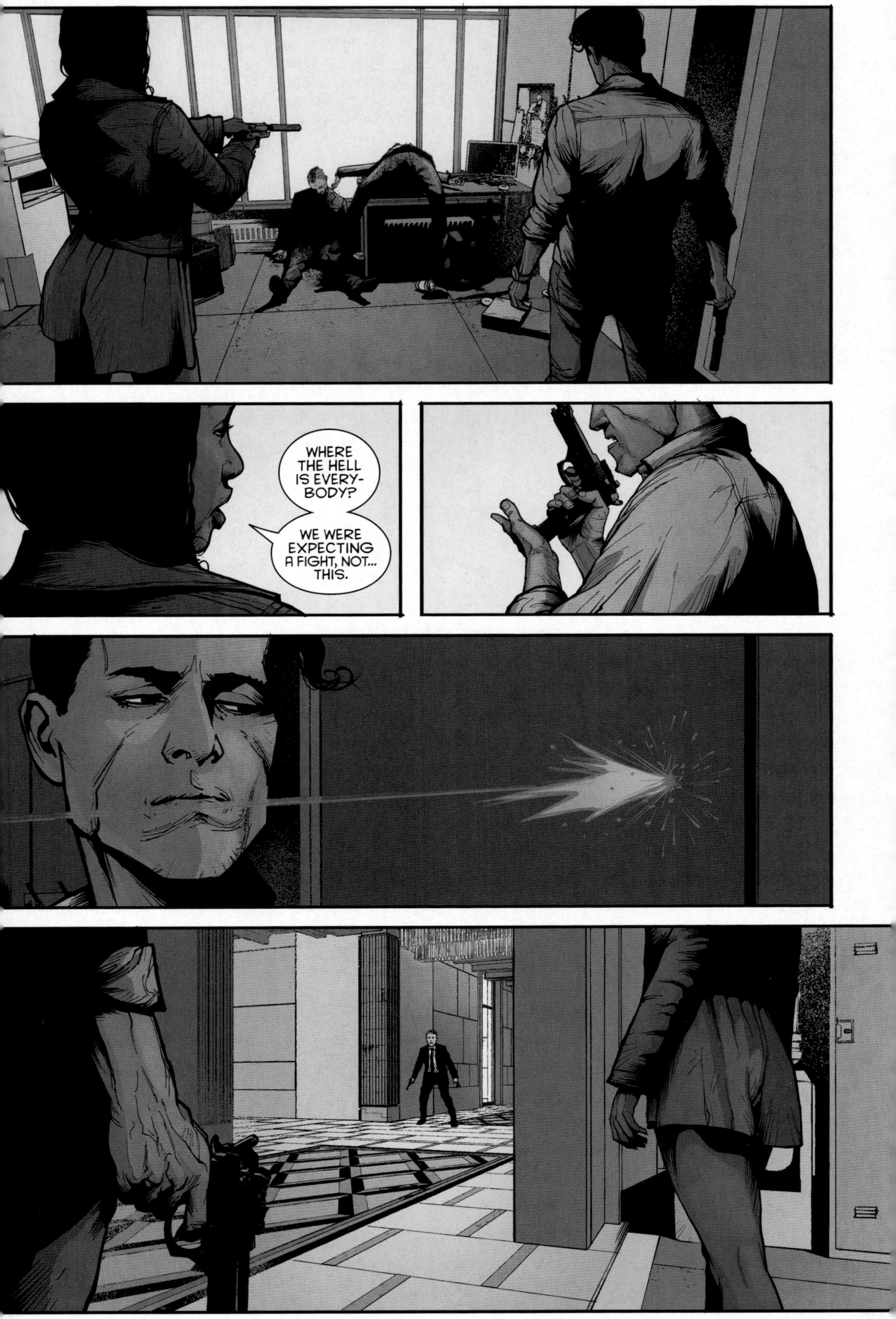
WHERE THE HELL IS EVERY-BODY?
WE WERE EXPECTING A FIGHT, NOT... THIS.

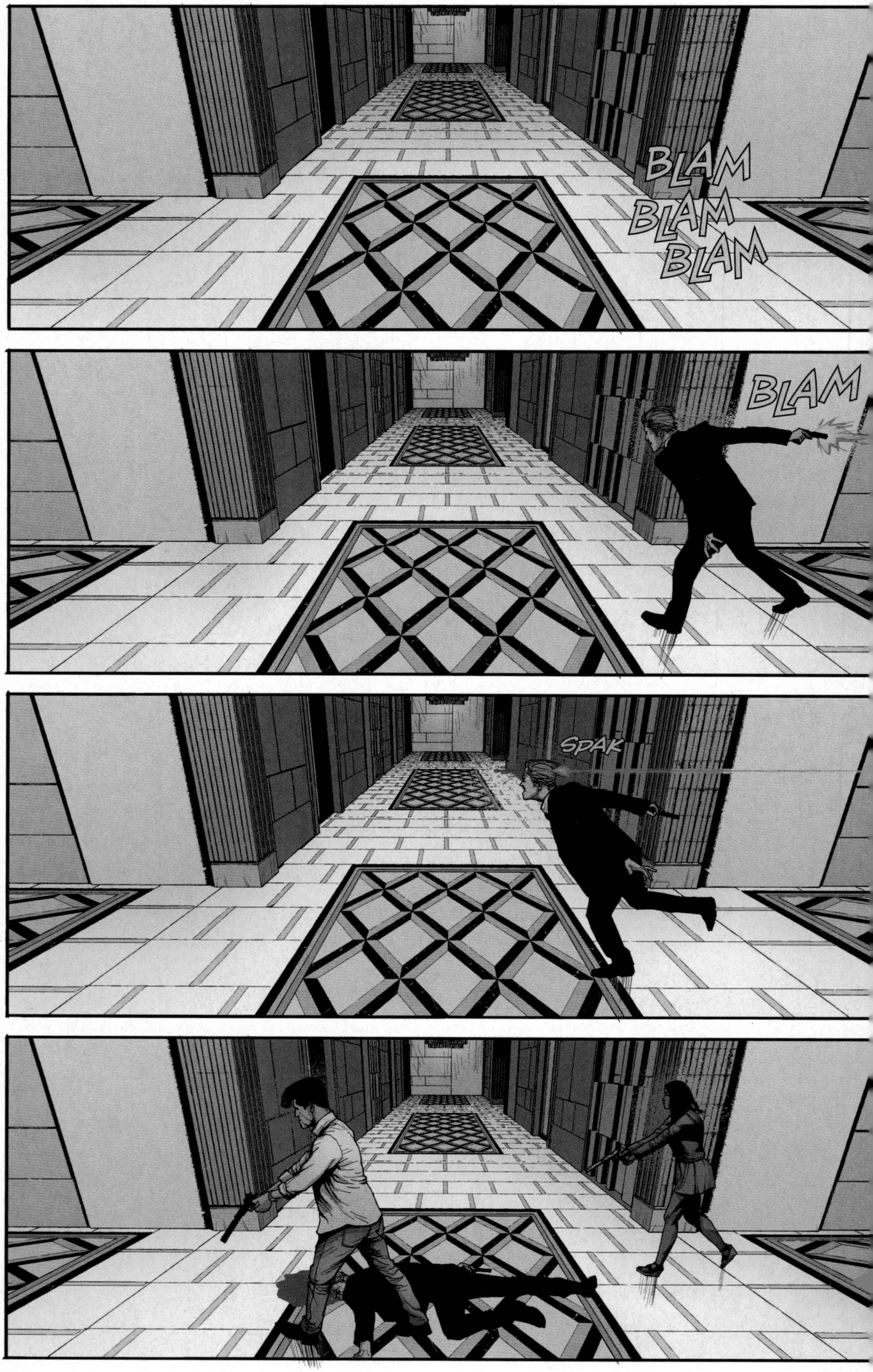
BLAM
BLAM
BLAM
BLAM
SPAK

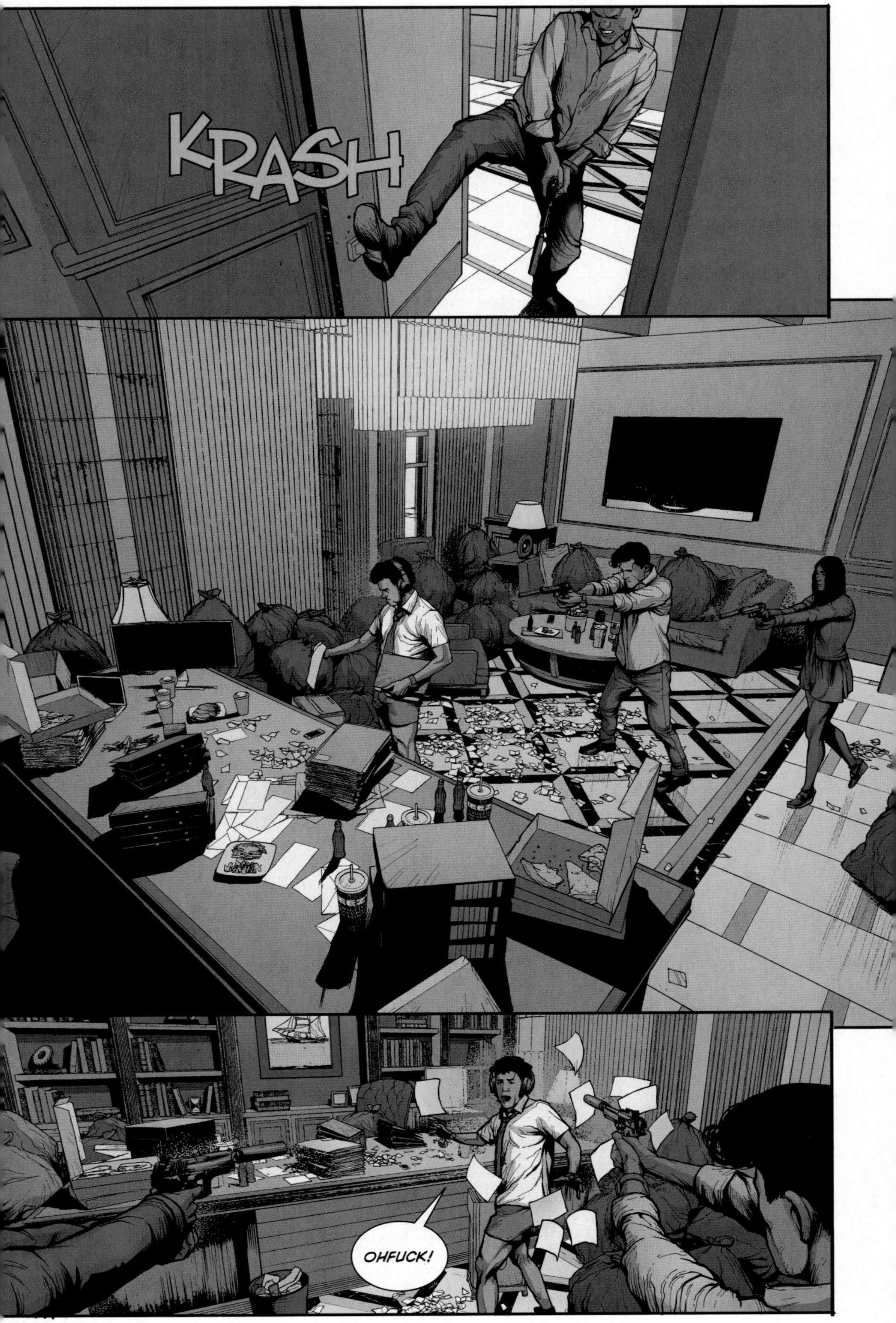
KRASH
OHFUCK!

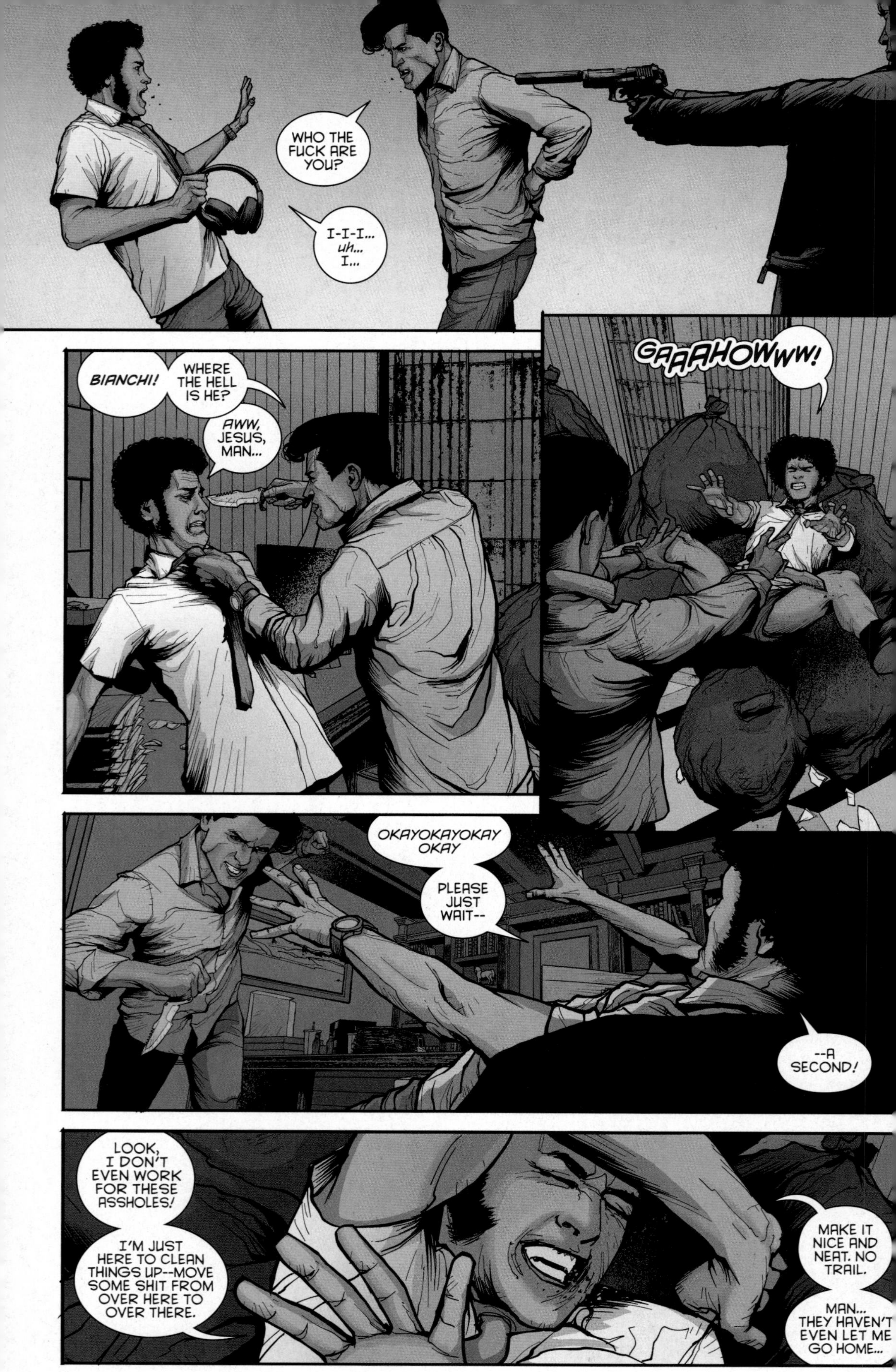
WHO THE FUCK ARE YOU?
I-I-I... uh... I...
BIANCHI!
WHERE THE HELL IS HE?
AWW, JESUS, MAN...
GAAAHOWWW!
OKAYOKAYOKAY OKAY
PLEASE JUST WAIT--
--A SECOND!
LOOK, I DON'T EVEN WORK FOR THESE ASSHOLES!
I'M JUST HERE TO CLEAN THINGS UP--MOVE SOME SHIT FROM OVER HERE TO OVER THERE.
MAKE IT NICE AND NEAT. NO TRAIL.
MAN... THEY HAVEN'T EVEN LET ME GO HOME...

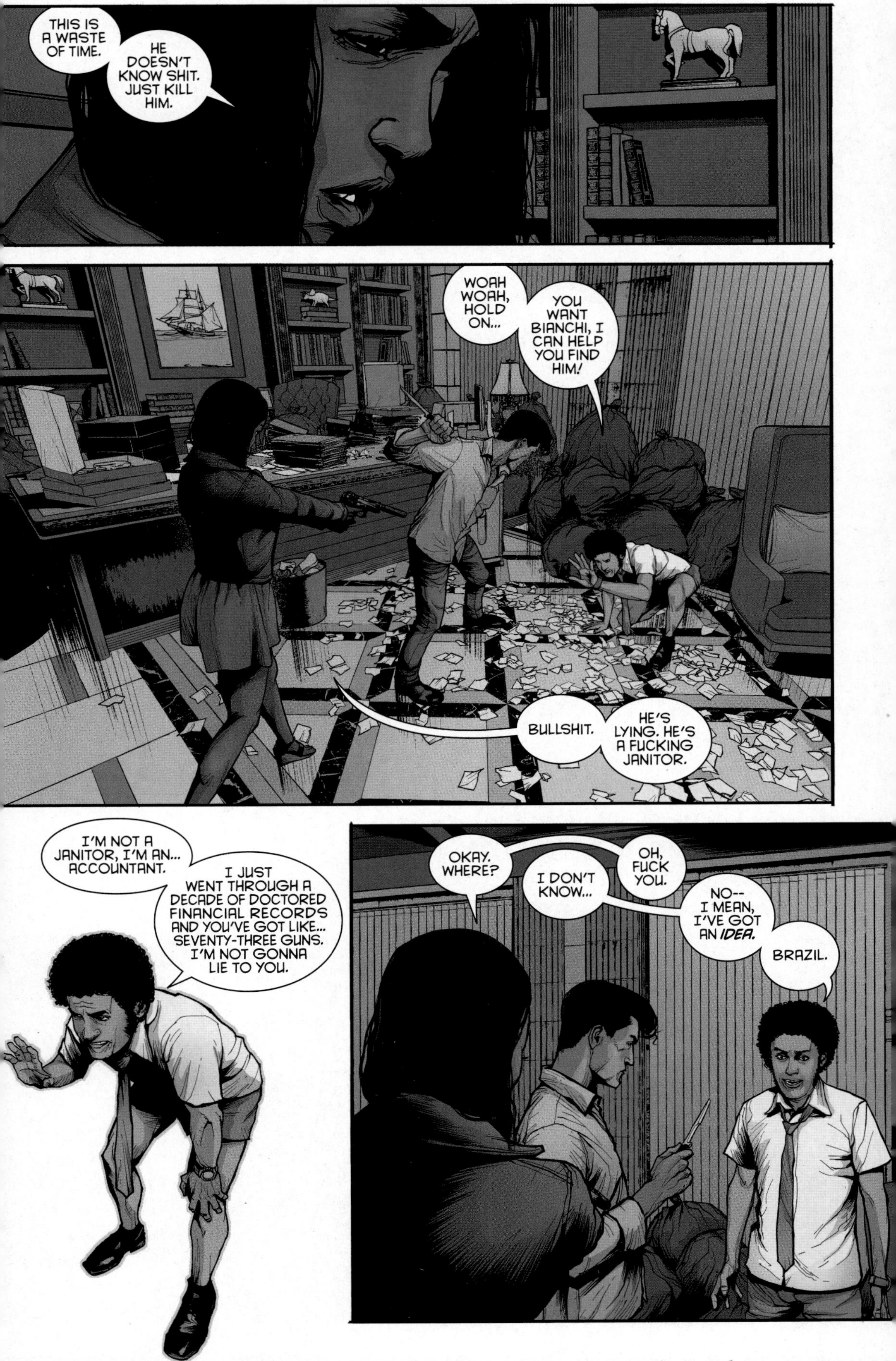
THIS IS A WASTE OF TIME.
HE DOESN'T KNOW SHIT. JUST KILL HIM.
WOAH WOAH, HOLD ON...
YOU WANT BIANCHI, I CAN HELP YOU FIND HIM!
BULLSHIT.
HE'S LYING. HE'S A FUCKING JANITOR.
I'M NOT A JANITOR, I'M AN... ACCOUNTANT.
I JUST WENT THROUGH A DECADE OF DOCTORED FINANCIAL RECORDS AND YOU'VE GOT LIKE... SEVENTY-THREE GUNS. I'M NOT GONNA LIE TO YOU.
OKAY. WHERE?
I DON'T KNOW...
OH, FUCK YOU.
NO-- I MEAN, I'VE GOT AN *IDEA.*
BRAZIL.

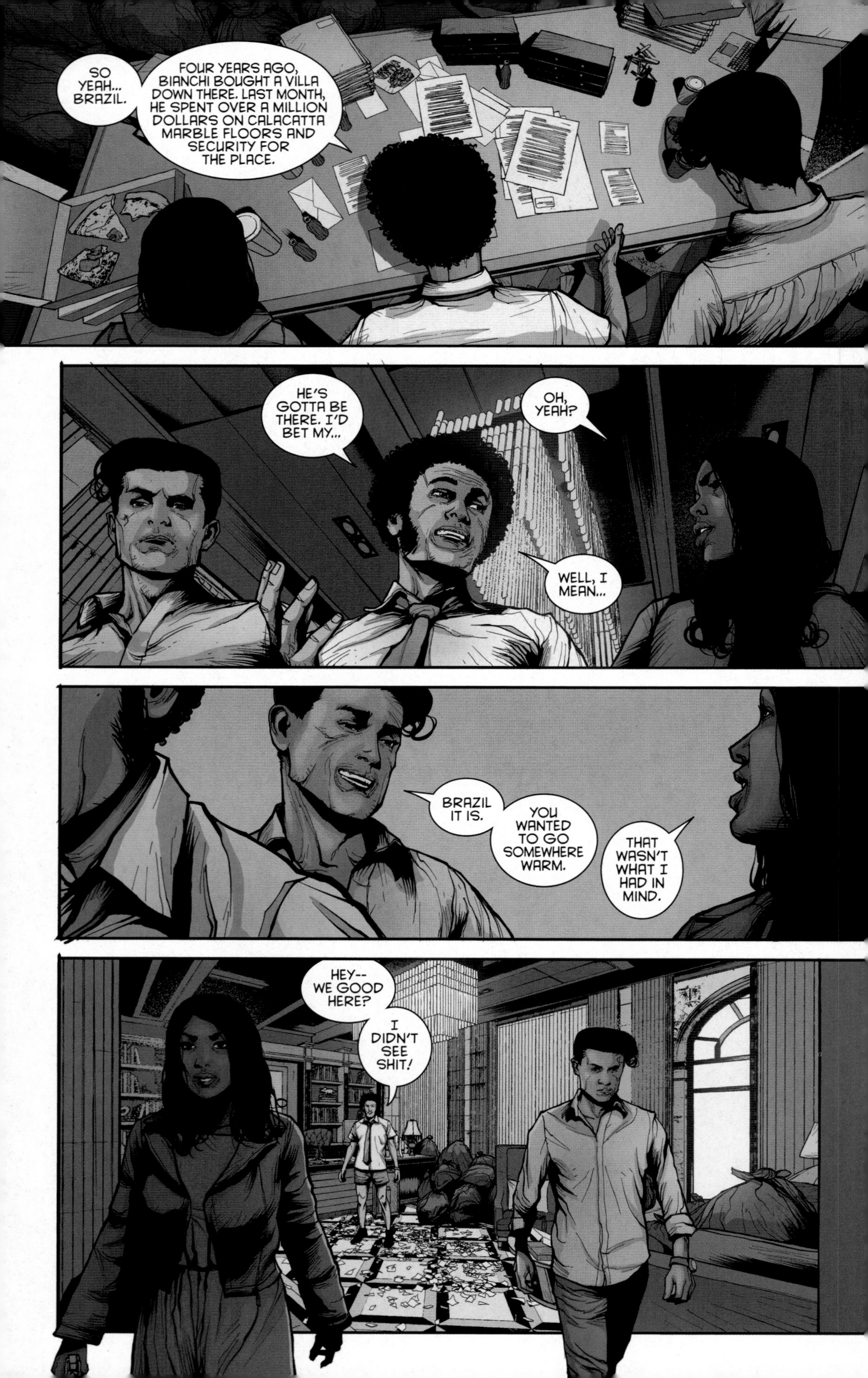
SO YEAH... BRAZIL.
FOUR YEARS AGO, BIANCHI BOUGHT A VILLA DOWN THERE. LAST MONTH, HE SPENT OVER A MILLION DOLLARS ON CALACATTA MARBLE FLOORS AND SECURITY FOR THE PLACE.
HE'S GOTTA BE THERE. I'D BET MY...
OH, YEAH?
WELL, I MEAN...
BRAZIL IT IS.
YOU WANTED TO GO SOMEWHERE WARM.
THAT WASN'T WHAT I HAD IN MIND.
HEY-- WE GOOD HERE?
I DIDN'T SEE SHIT!

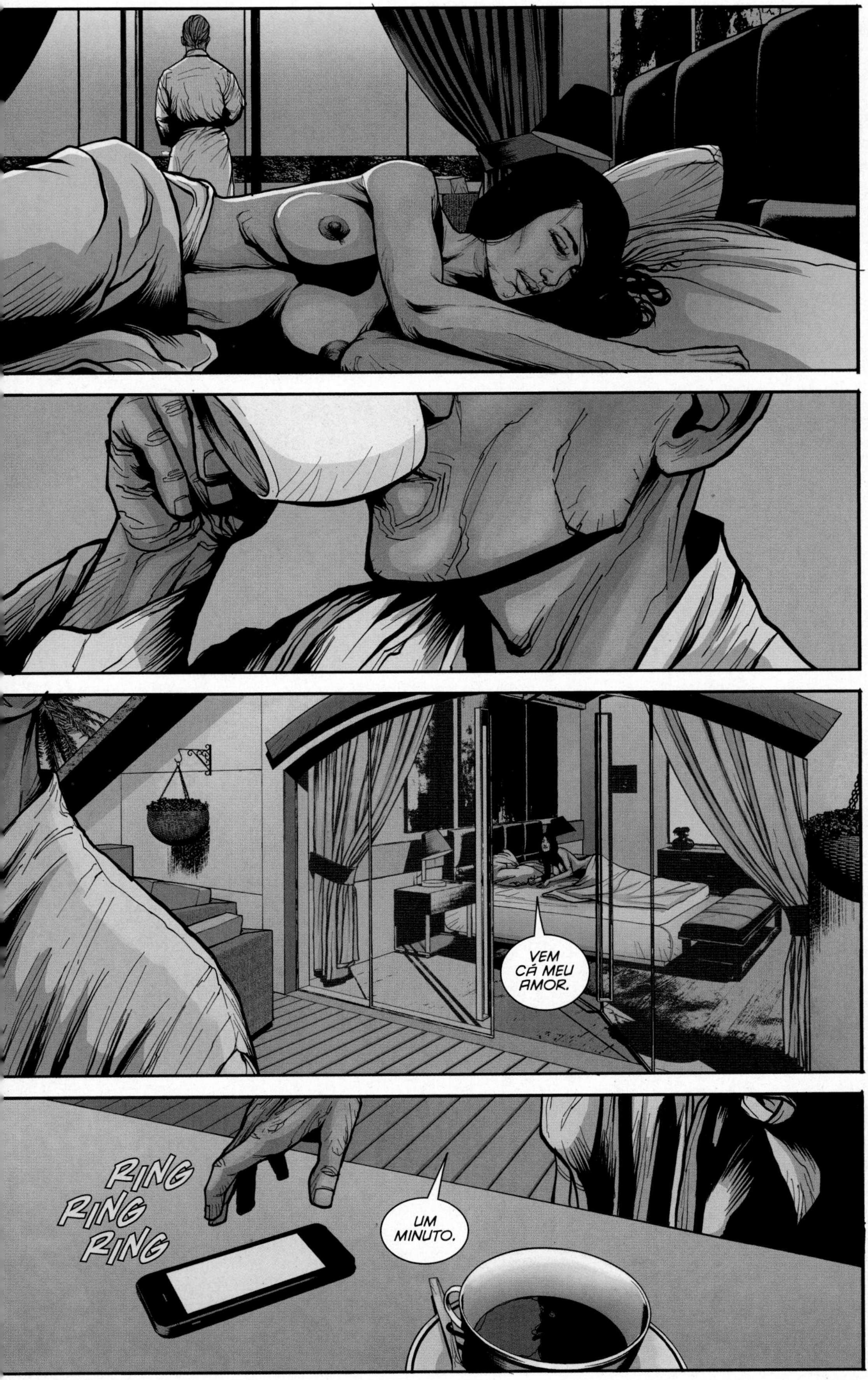
VEM CÁ MEU AMOR.
RING RING RING
UM MINUTO.

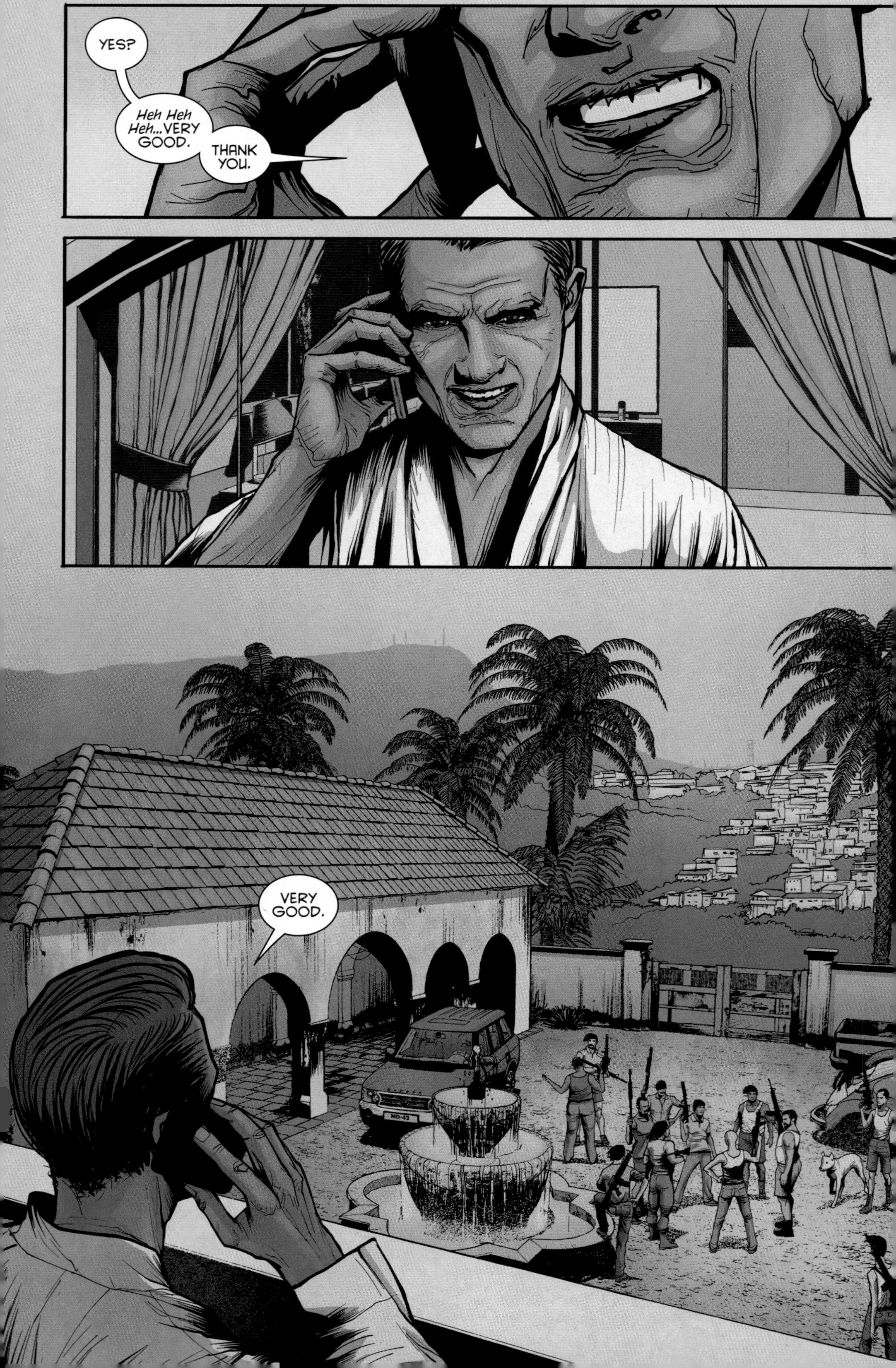
YES?
Heh Heh Heh...VERY GOOD.
THANK YOU.
VERY GOOD.

CHAPTER 30

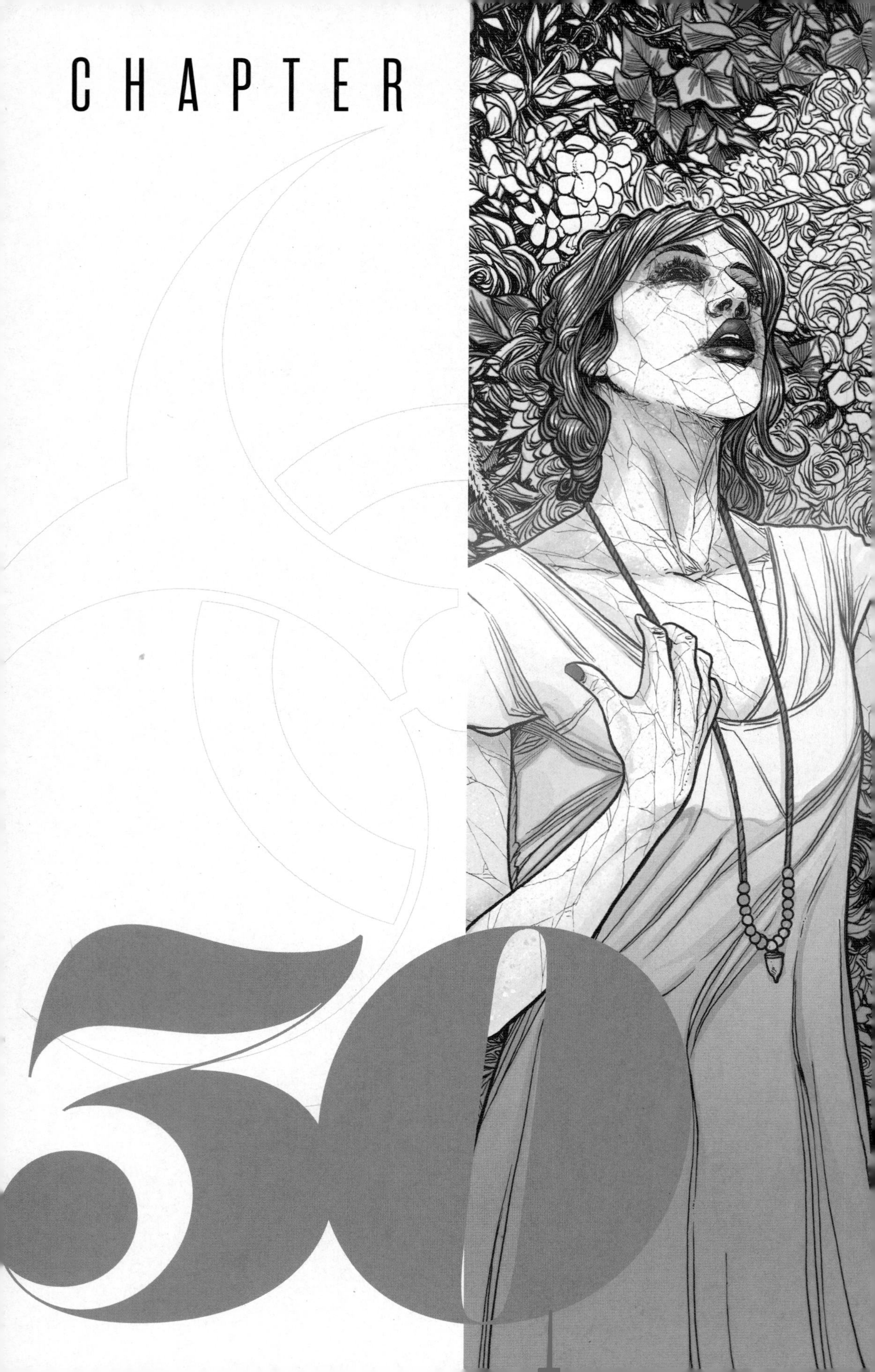

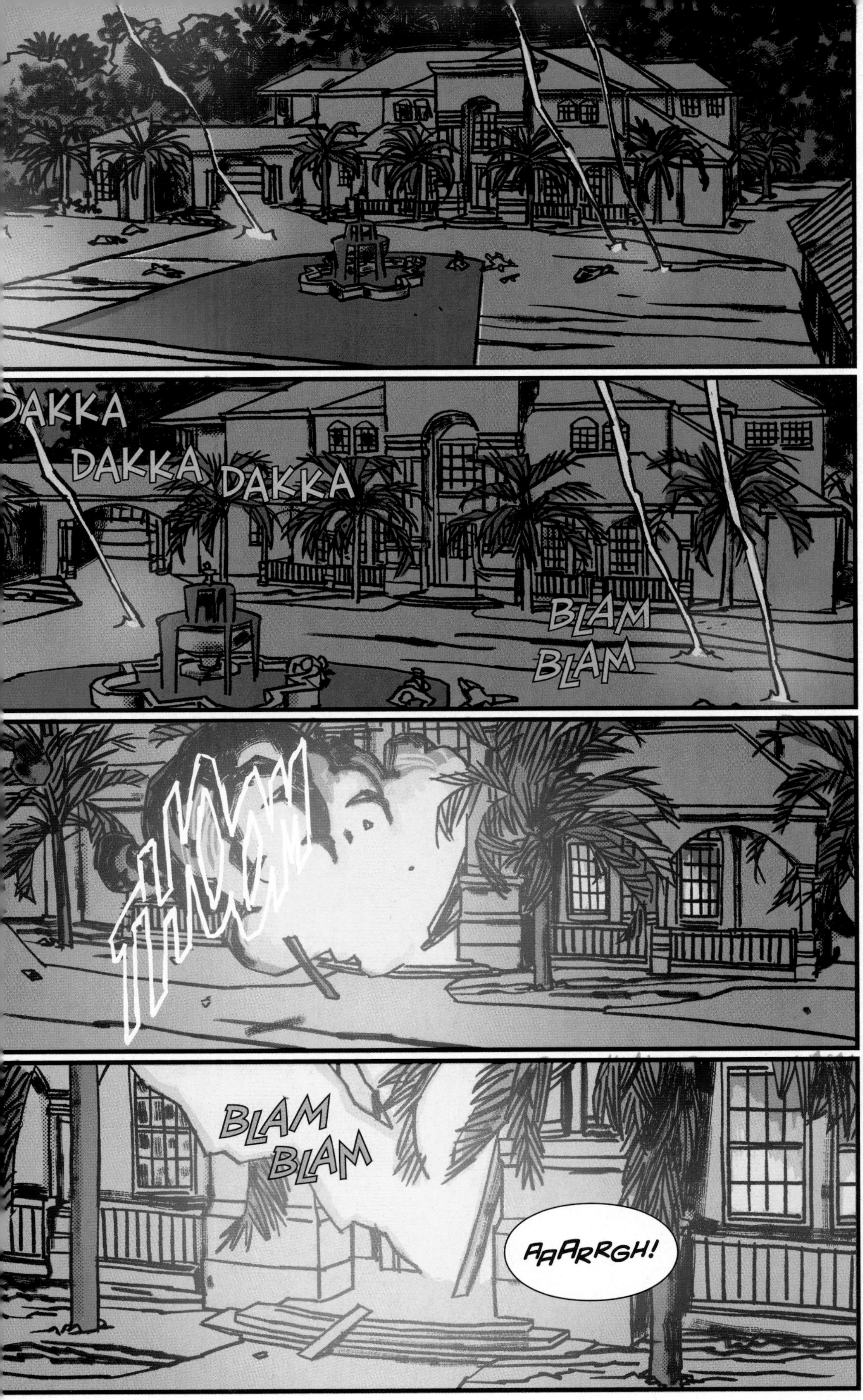
DAKKA
DAKKA
DAKKA
BLAM
BLAM
THOOM
BLAM
BLAM
AAARRGH!

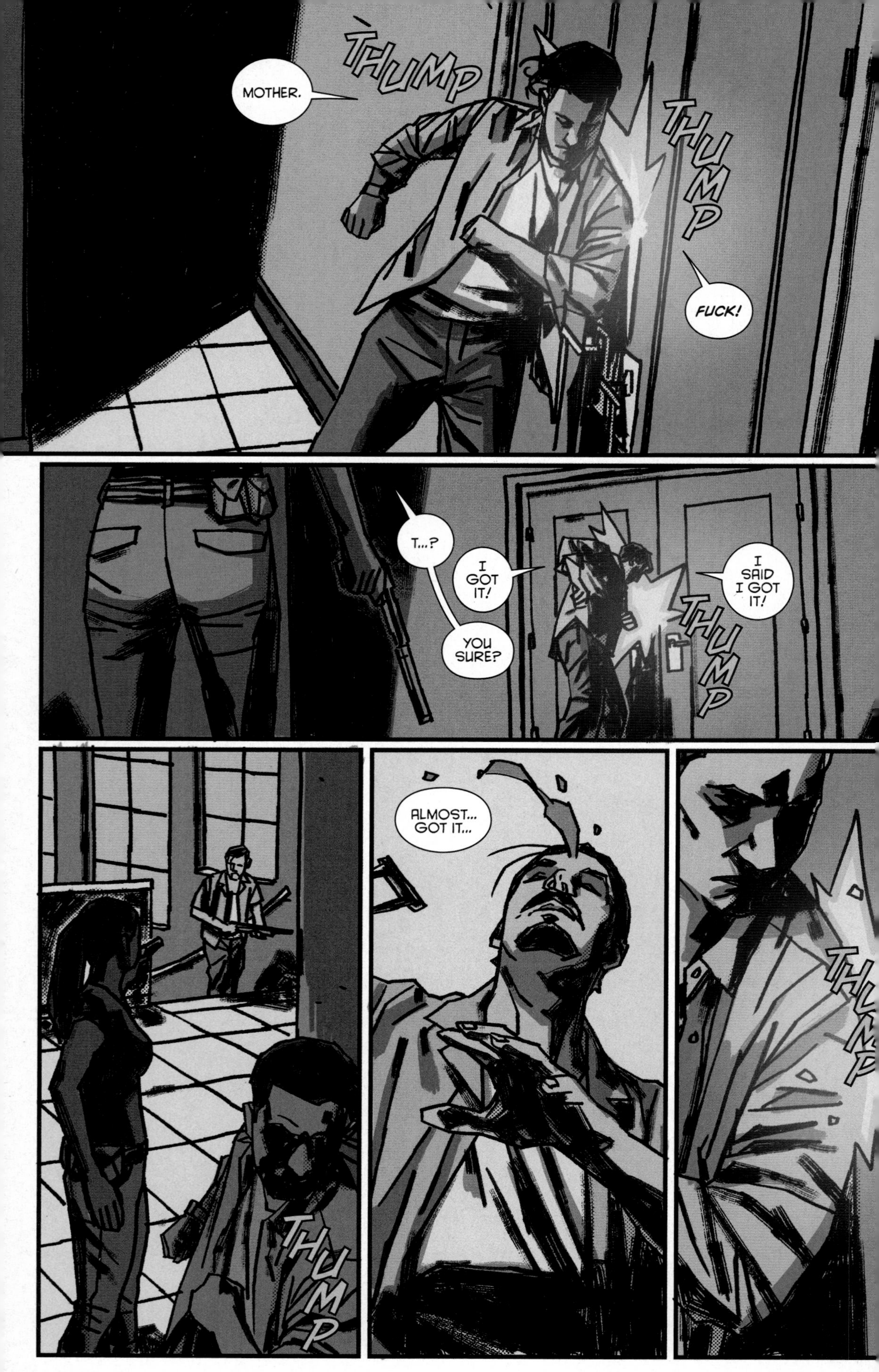
THUMP
MOTHER.
THUMP
FUCK!
T...?
I GOT IT!
YOU SURE?
I SAID I GOT IT!
THUMP
ALMOST... GOT IT...
THUMP
THUMP

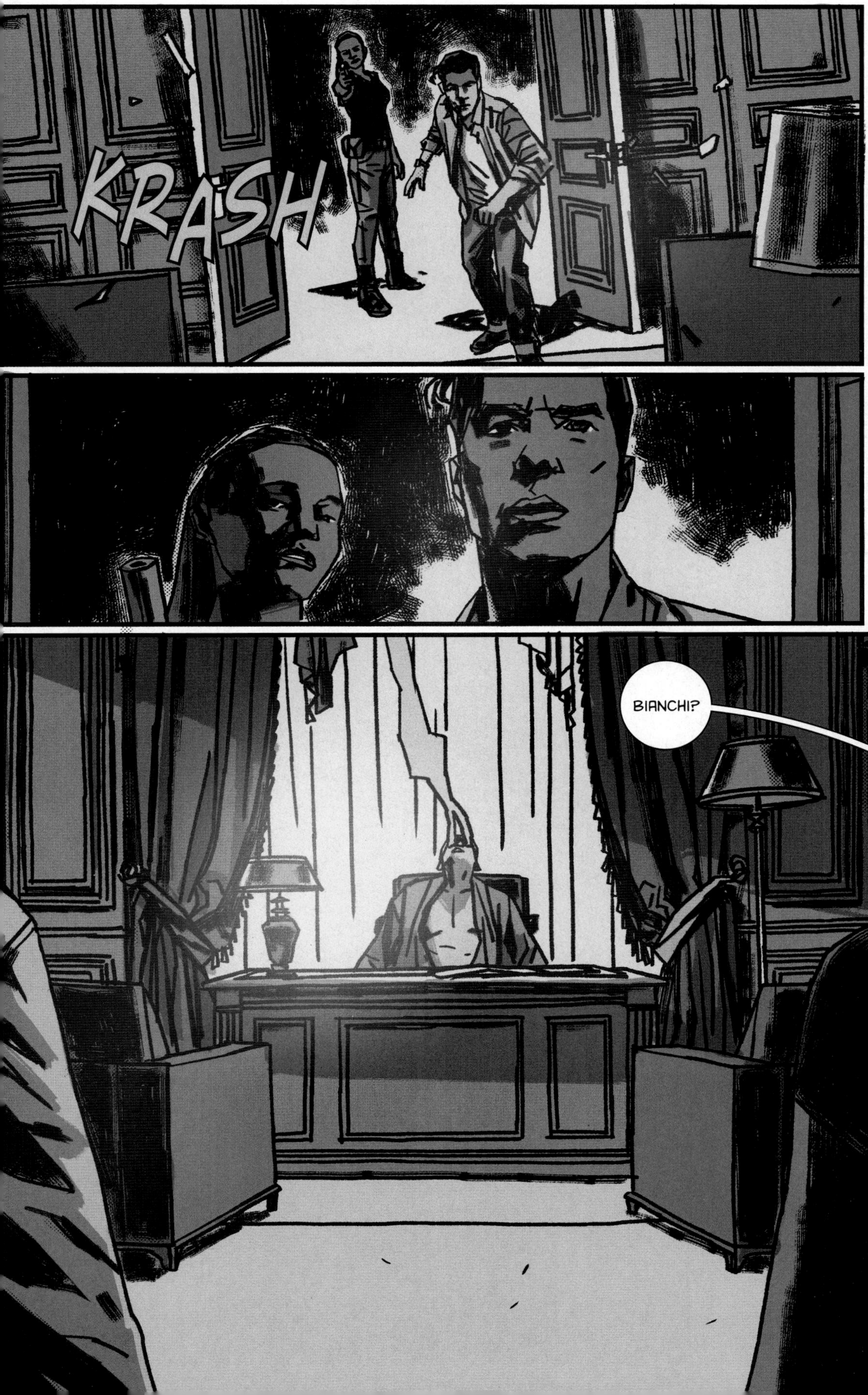
KRASH
BIANCHI?

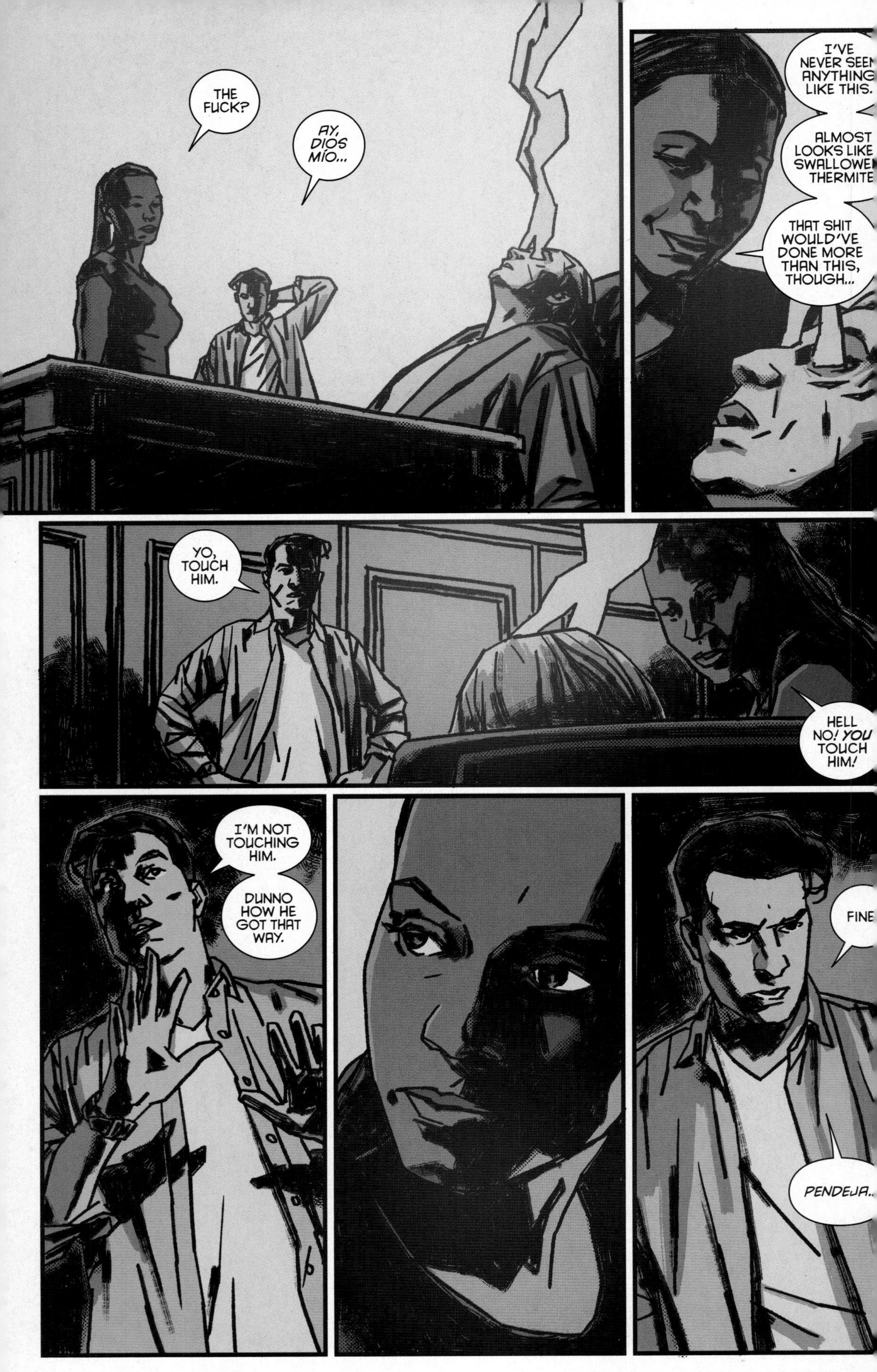
THE FUCK?
AY, DIOS MÍO...
I'VE NEVER SEEN ANYTHING LIKE THIS.
ALMOST LOOKS LIKE SWALLOWE THERMITE
THAT SHIT WOULD'VE DONE MORE THAN THIS, THOUGH...
YO, TOUCH HIM.
HELL NO! YOU TOUCH HIM!
I'M NOT TOUCHING HIM.
DUNNO HOW HE GOT THAT WAY.
FINE
PENDEJA...

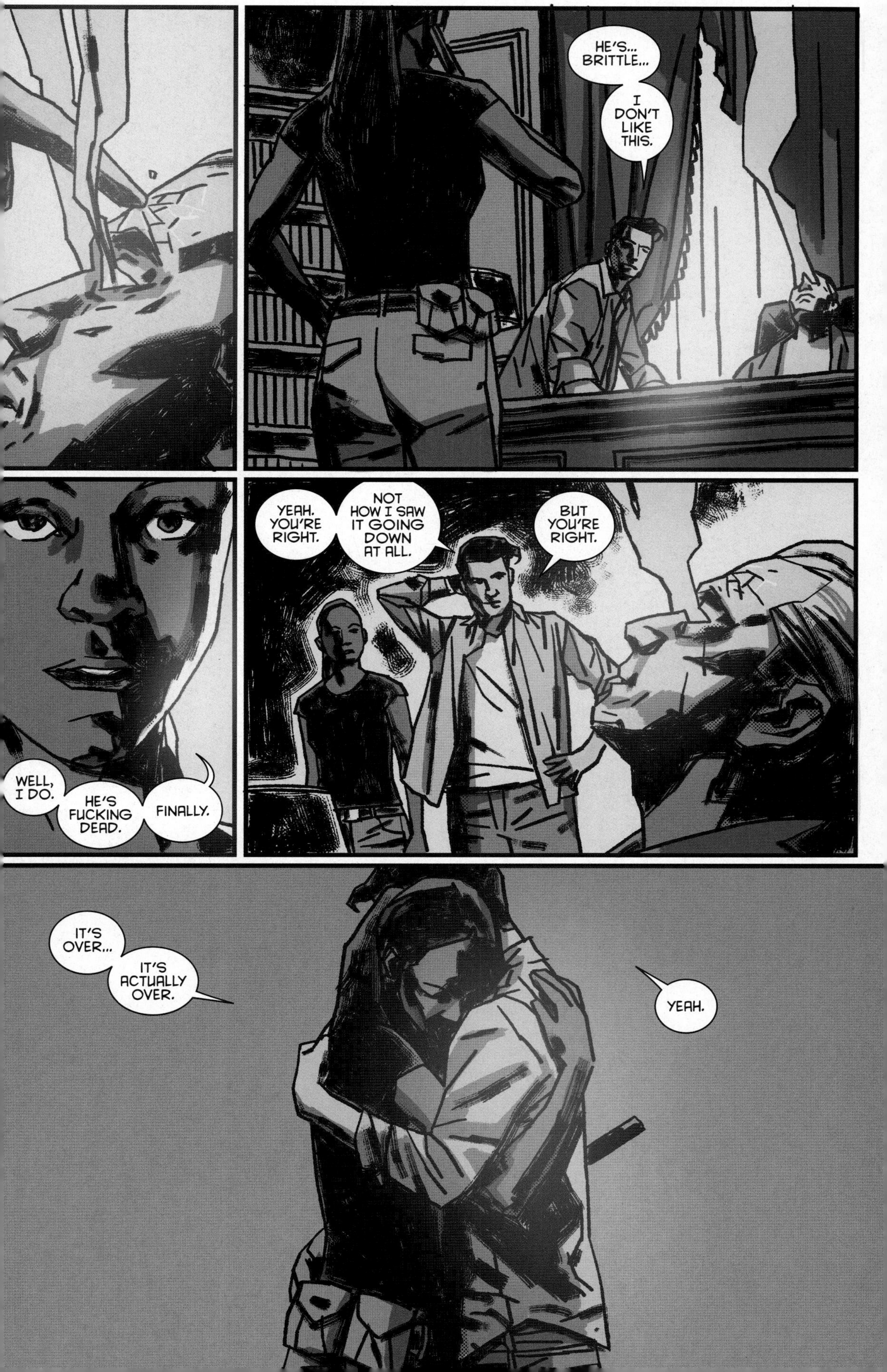
HE'S... BRITTLE...
I DON'T LIKE THIS.
WELL, I DO.
HE'S FUCKING DEAD.
FINALLY.
YEAH. YOU'RE RIGHT.
NOT HOW I SAW IT GOING DOWN AT ALL.
BUT YOU'RE RIGHT.
IT'S OVER...
IT'S ACTUALLY OVER.
YEAH.

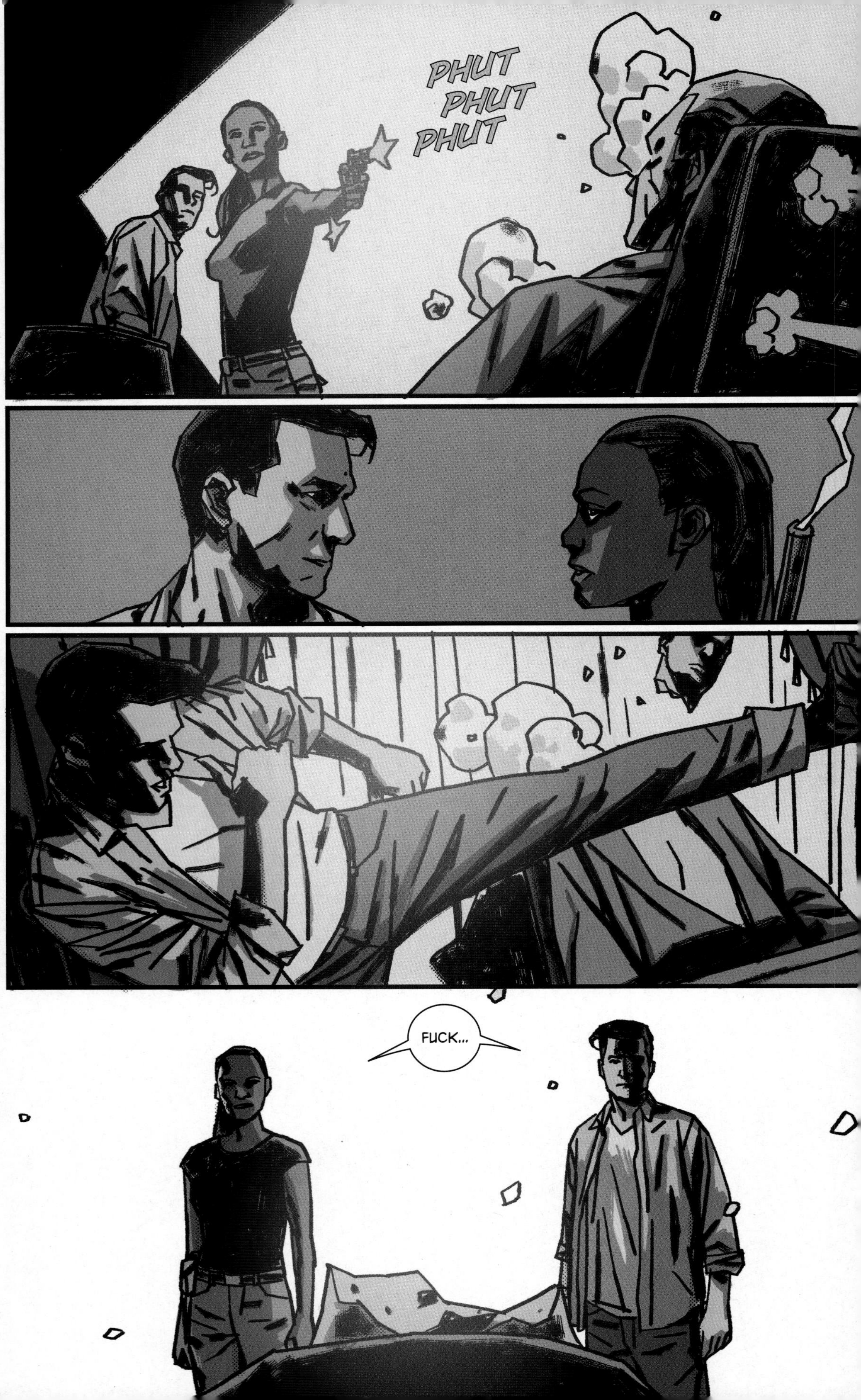
PHUT
PHUT
PHUT
FUCK...

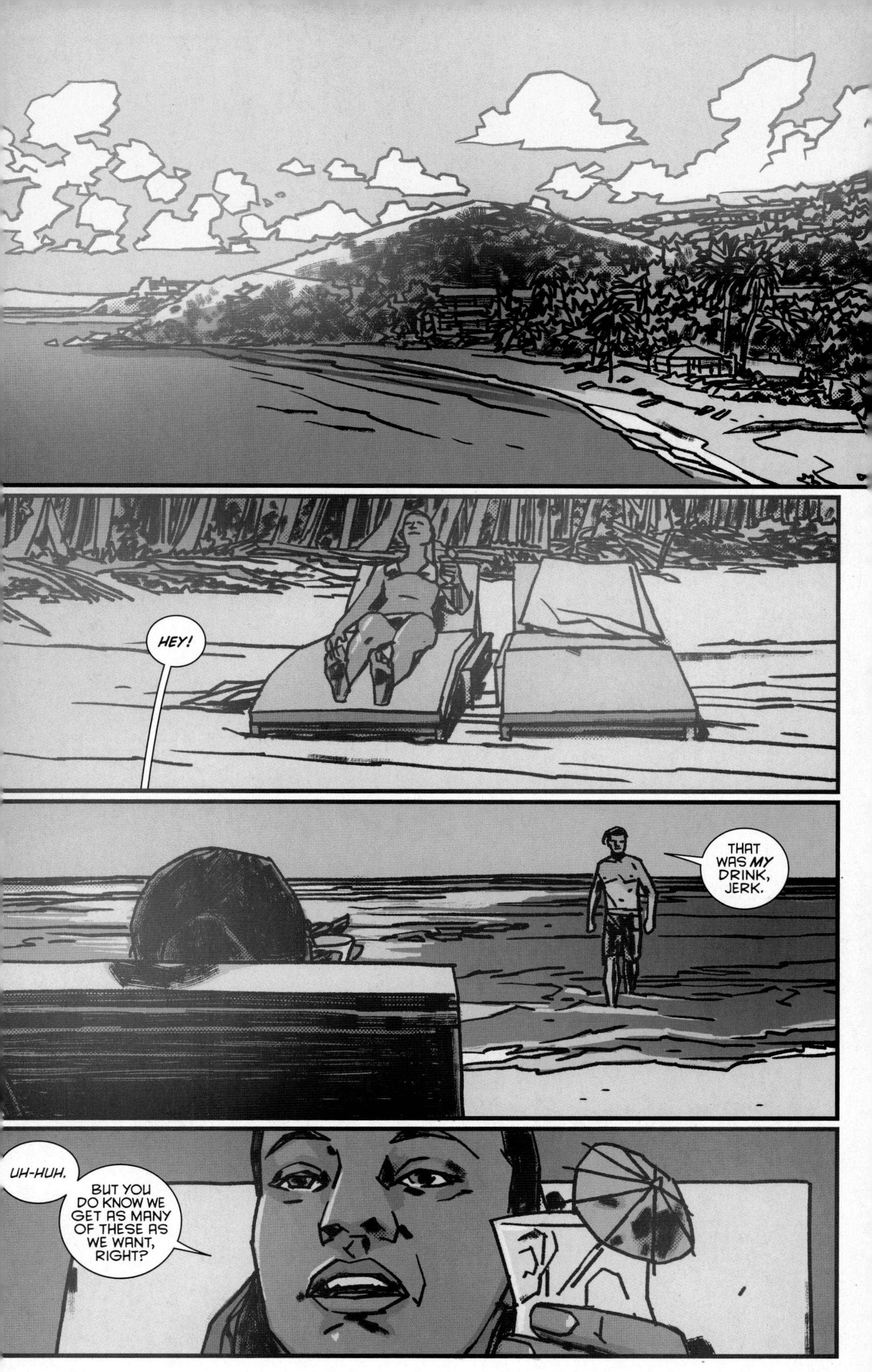
HEY!
THAT WAS *MY* DRINK, JERK.
UH-HUH.
BUT YOU DO KNOW WE GET AS MANY OF THESE AS WE WANT, RIGHT?

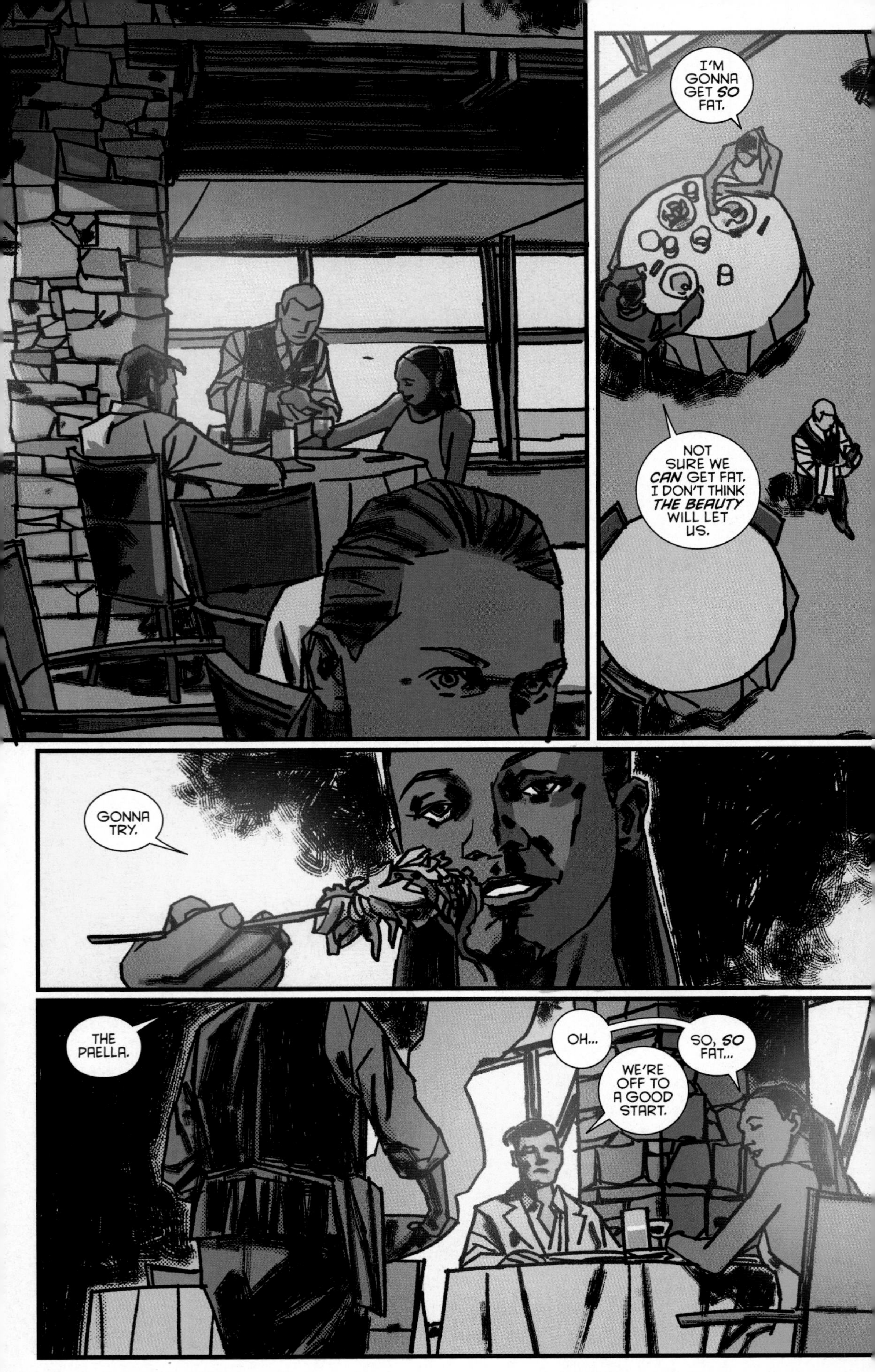
I'M GONNA GET SO FAT.
NOT SURE WE CAN GET FAT. I DON'T THINK THE BEAUTY WILL LET US.
GONNA TRY.
THE PAELLA.
OH...
SO, SO FAT...
WE'RE OFF TO A GOOD START.

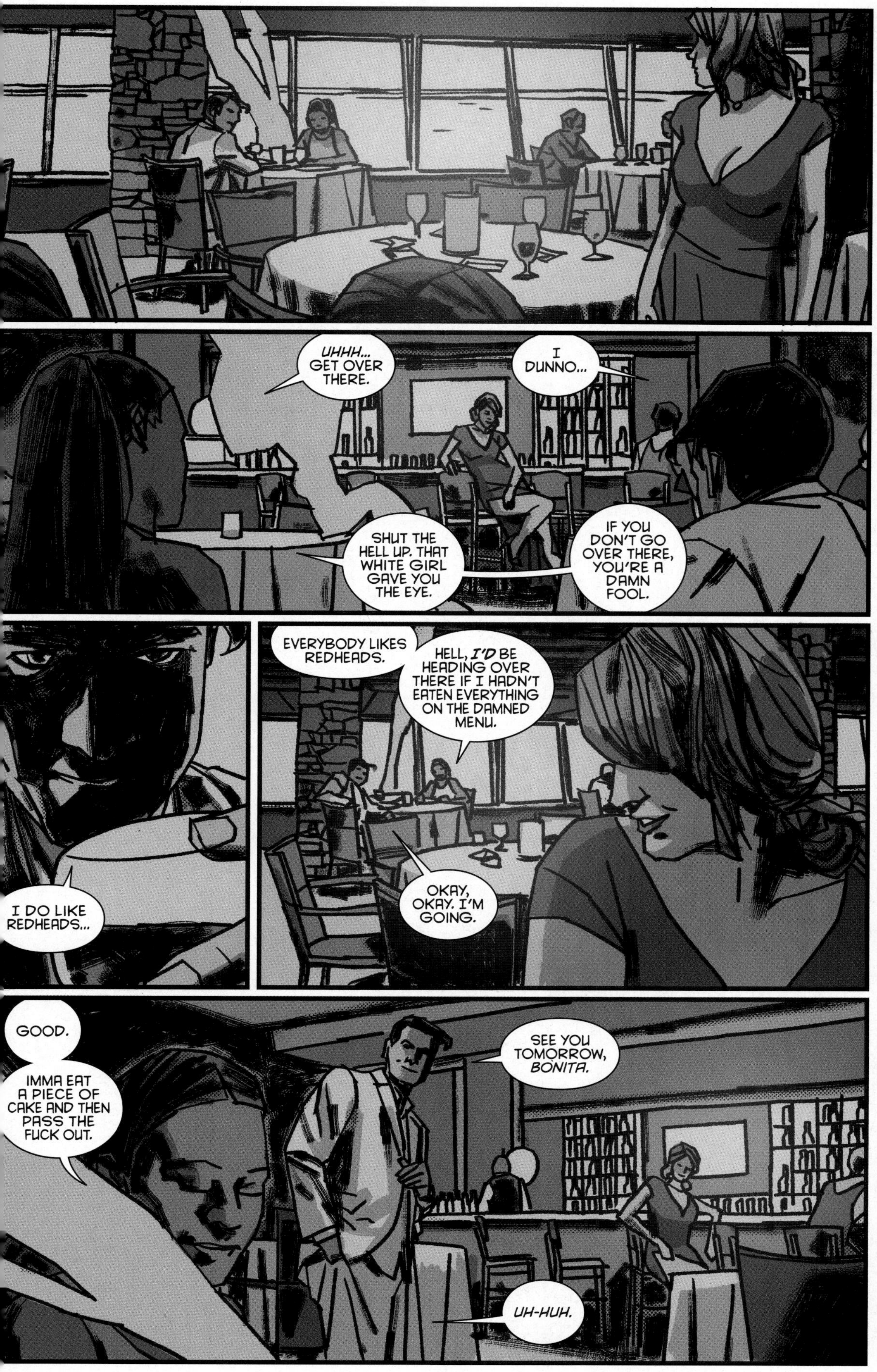
UHHH... GET OVER THERE.
I DUNNO...
SHUT THE HELL UP. THAT WHITE GIRL GAVE YOU THE EYE.
IF YOU DON'T GO OVER THERE, YOU'RE A DAMN FOOL.
I DO LIKE REDHEADS...
EVERYBODY LIKES REDHEADS.
HELL, *I'D* BE HEADING OVER THERE IF I HADN'T EATEN EVERYTHING ON THE DAMNED MENU.
OKAY, OKAY. I'M GOING.
GOOD.
IMMA EAT A PIECE OF CAKE AND THEN PASS THE FUCK OUT.
SEE YOU TOMORROW, *BONITA.*
UH-HUH.

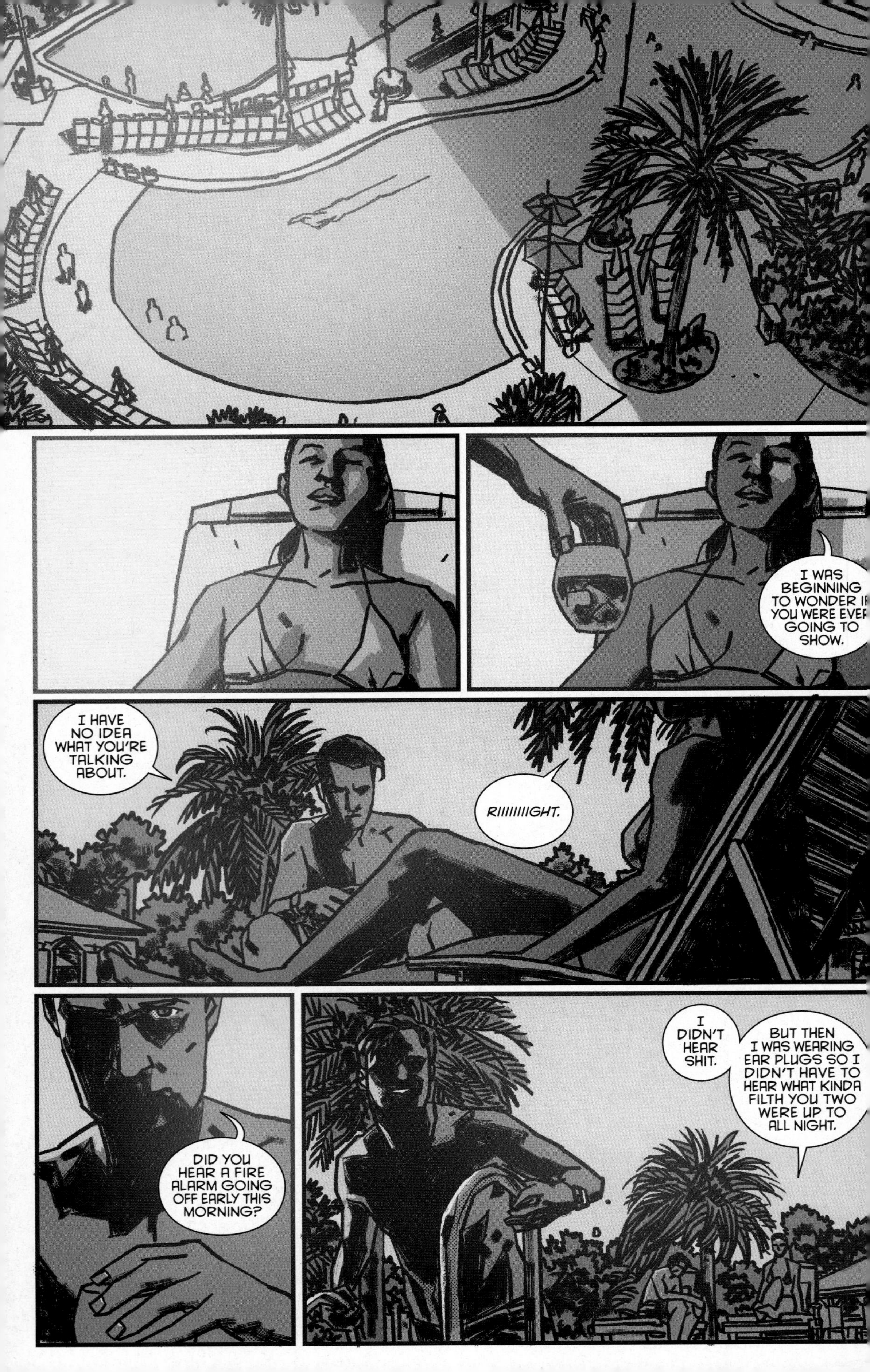
I WAS BEGINNING TO WONDER IF YOU WERE EVER GOING TO SHOW.
I HAVE NO IDEA WHAT YOU'RE TALKING ABOUT.
RIIIIIIIGHT.
DID YOU HEAR A FIRE ALARM GOING OFF EARLY THIS MORNING?
I DIDN'T HEAR SHIT.
BUT THEN I WAS WEARING EAR PLUGS SO I DIDN'T HAVE TO HEAR WHAT KINDA FILTH YOU TWO WERE UP TO ALL NIGHT.

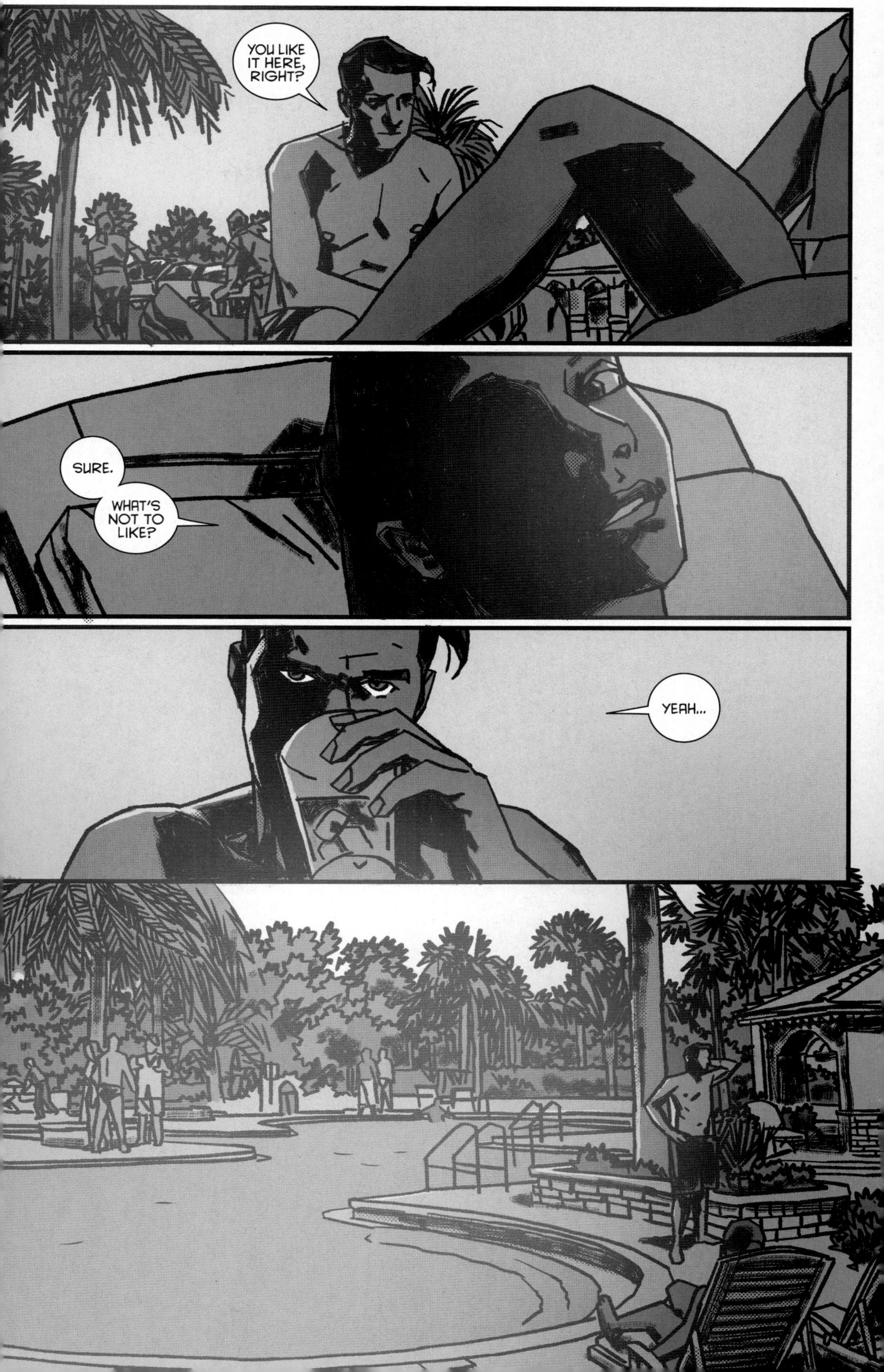
YOU LIKE IT HERE, RIGHT?
SURE.
WHAT'S NOT TO LIKE?
YEAH...

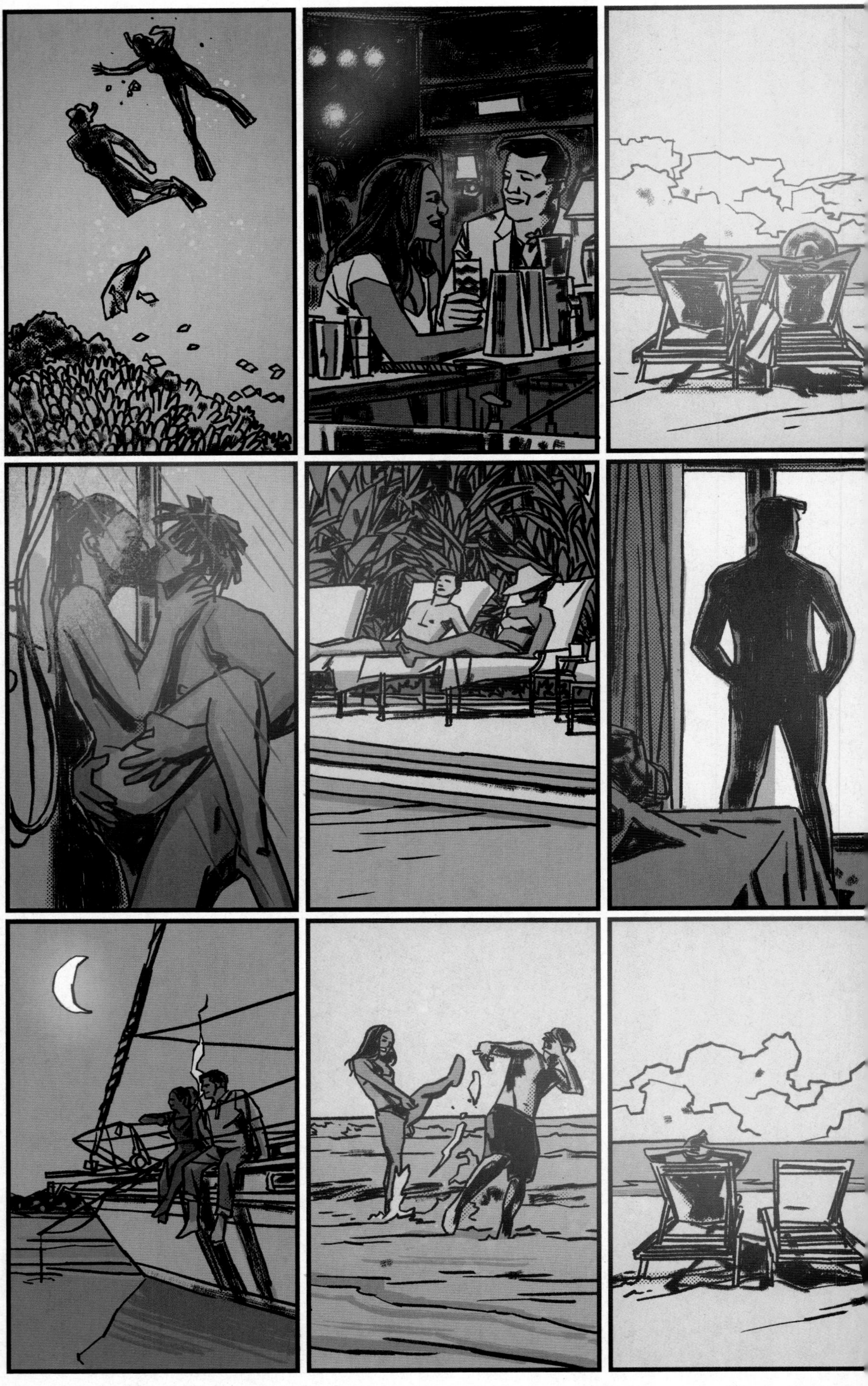

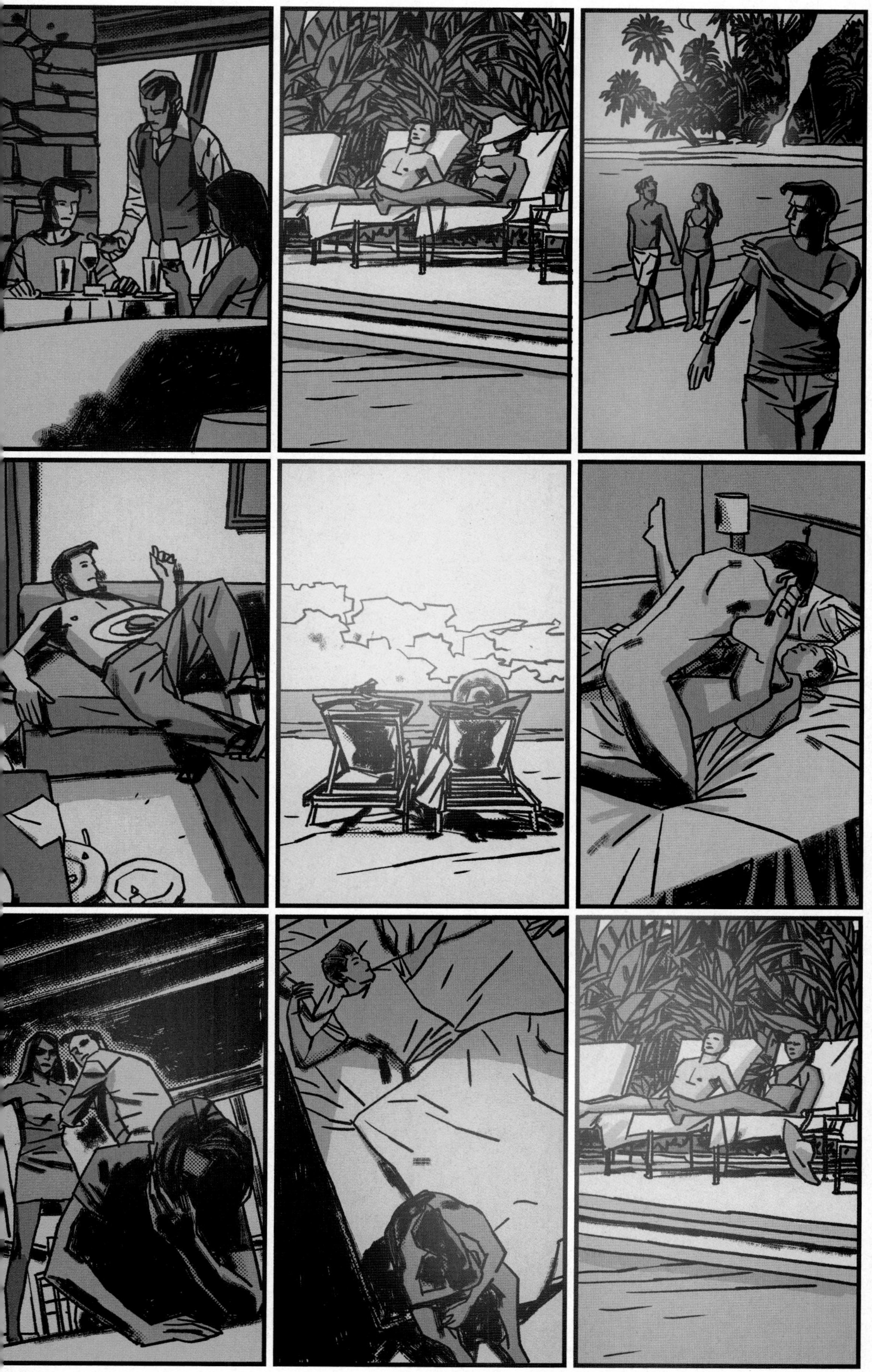

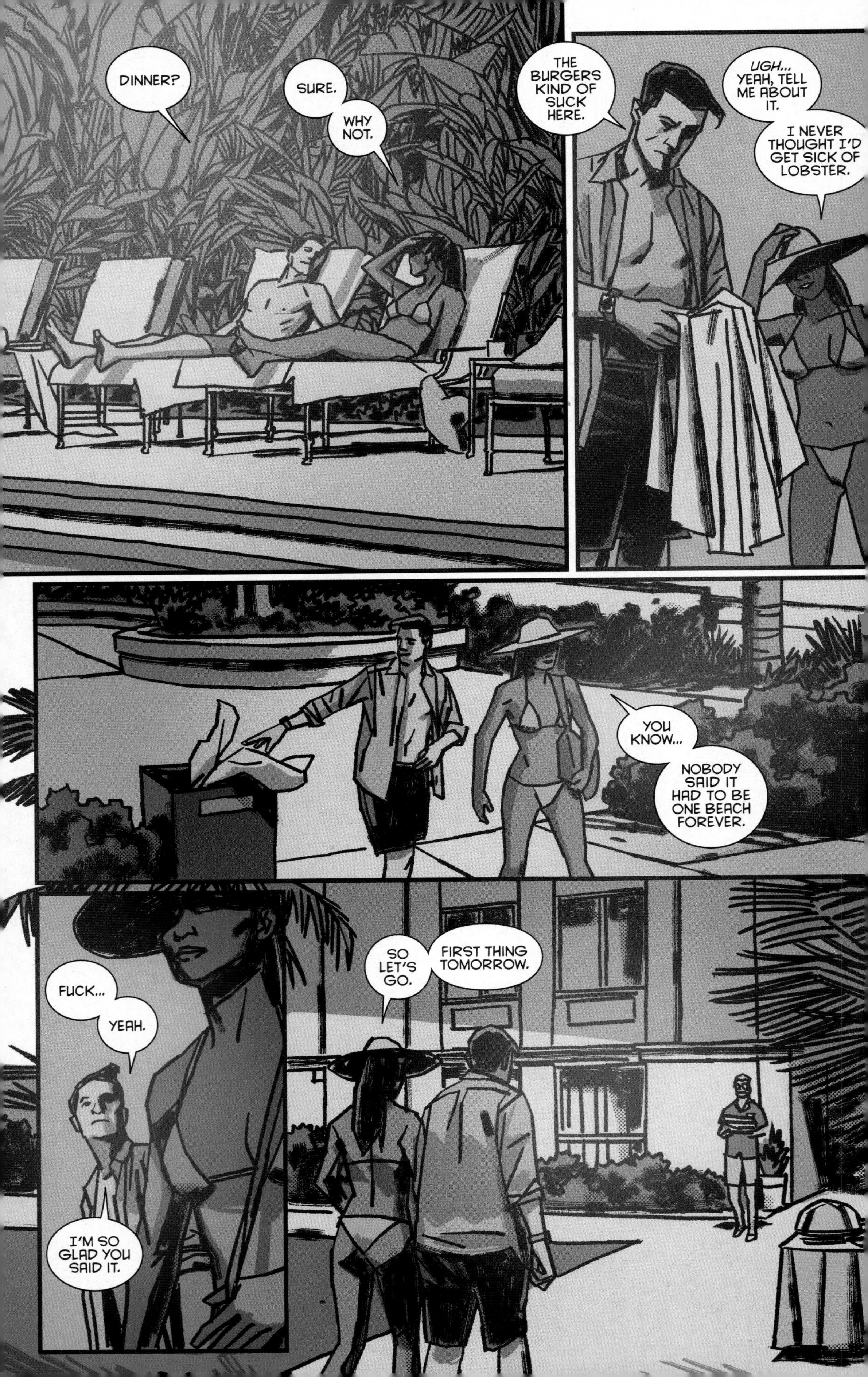
DINNER?
SURE.
WHY NOT.
THE BURGERS KIND OF SUCK HERE.
UGH... YEAH, TELL ME ABOUT IT.
I NEVER THOUGHT I'D GET SICK OF LOBSTER.
YOU KNOW...
NOBODY SAID IT HAD TO BE ONE BEACH FOREVER.
FUCK...
YEAH.
I'M SO GLAD YOU SAID IT.
SO LET'S GO.
FIRST THING TOMORROW.

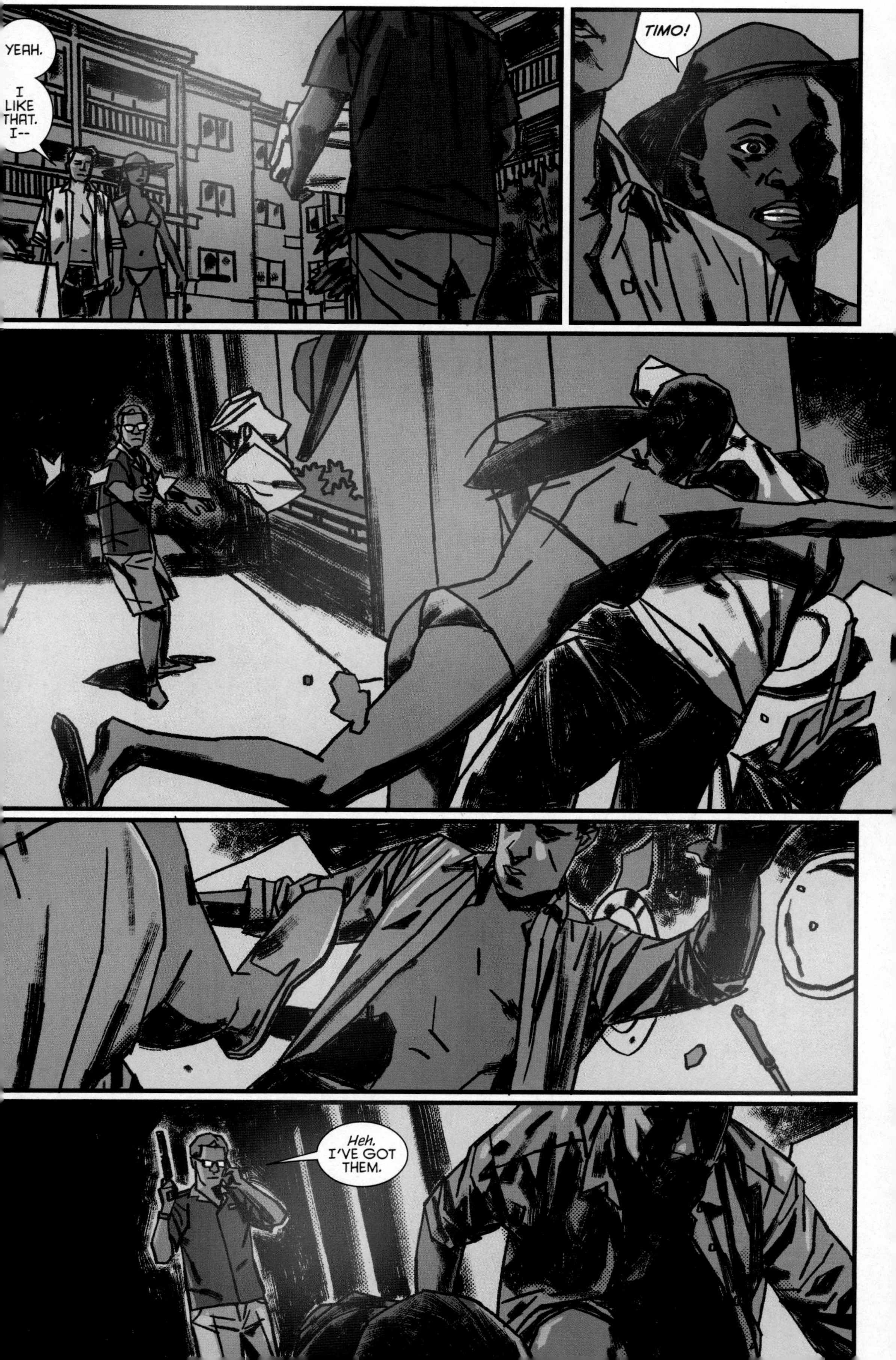
YEAH.
I LIKE THAT. I--
TIMO!
Heh. I'VE GOT THEM.

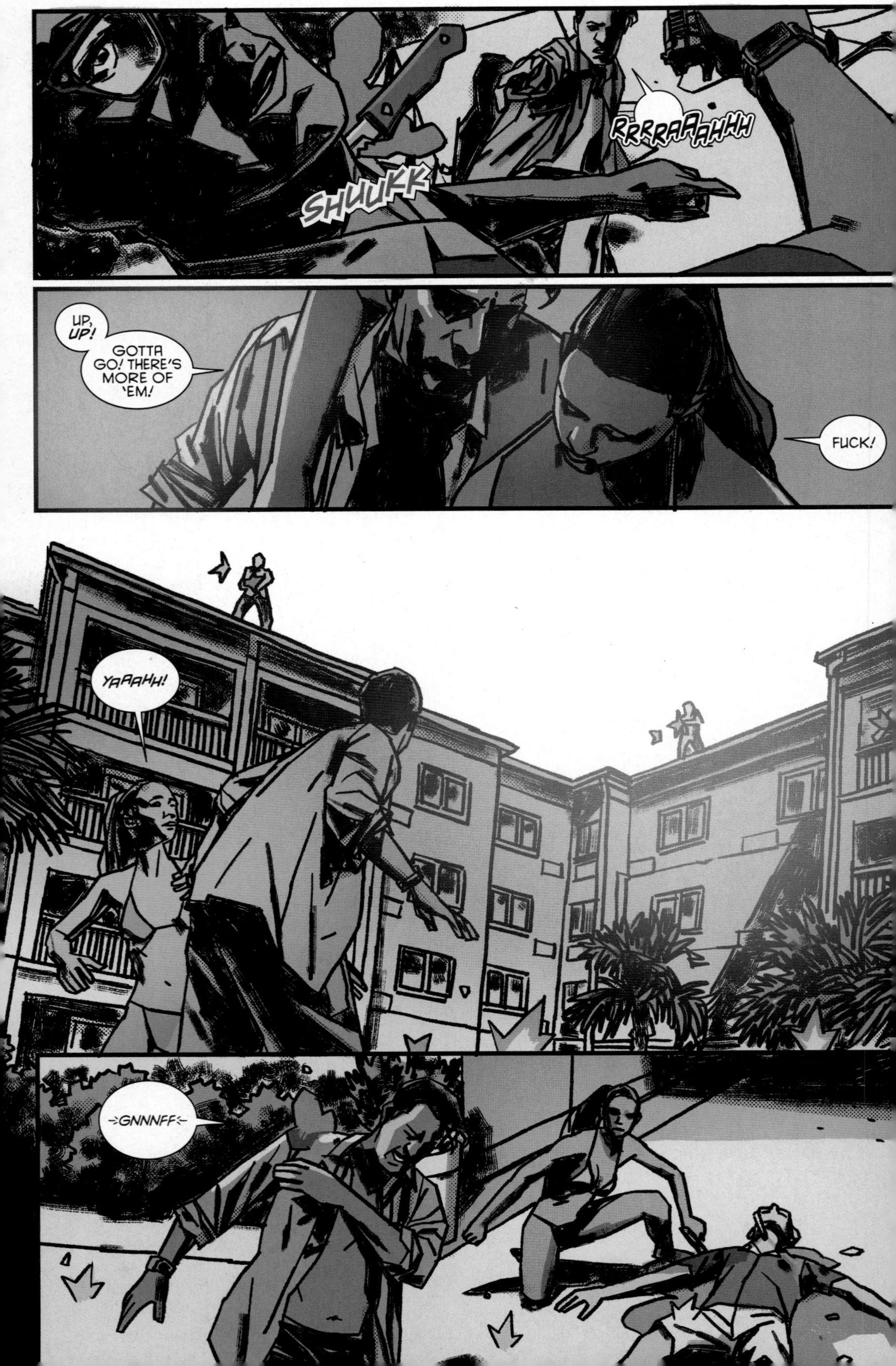
RRRRAAAHHH
SHUUKK
UP, UP!
GOTTA GO! THERE'S MORE OF 'EM!
FUCK!
YAAAHH!
-GNNNFF-

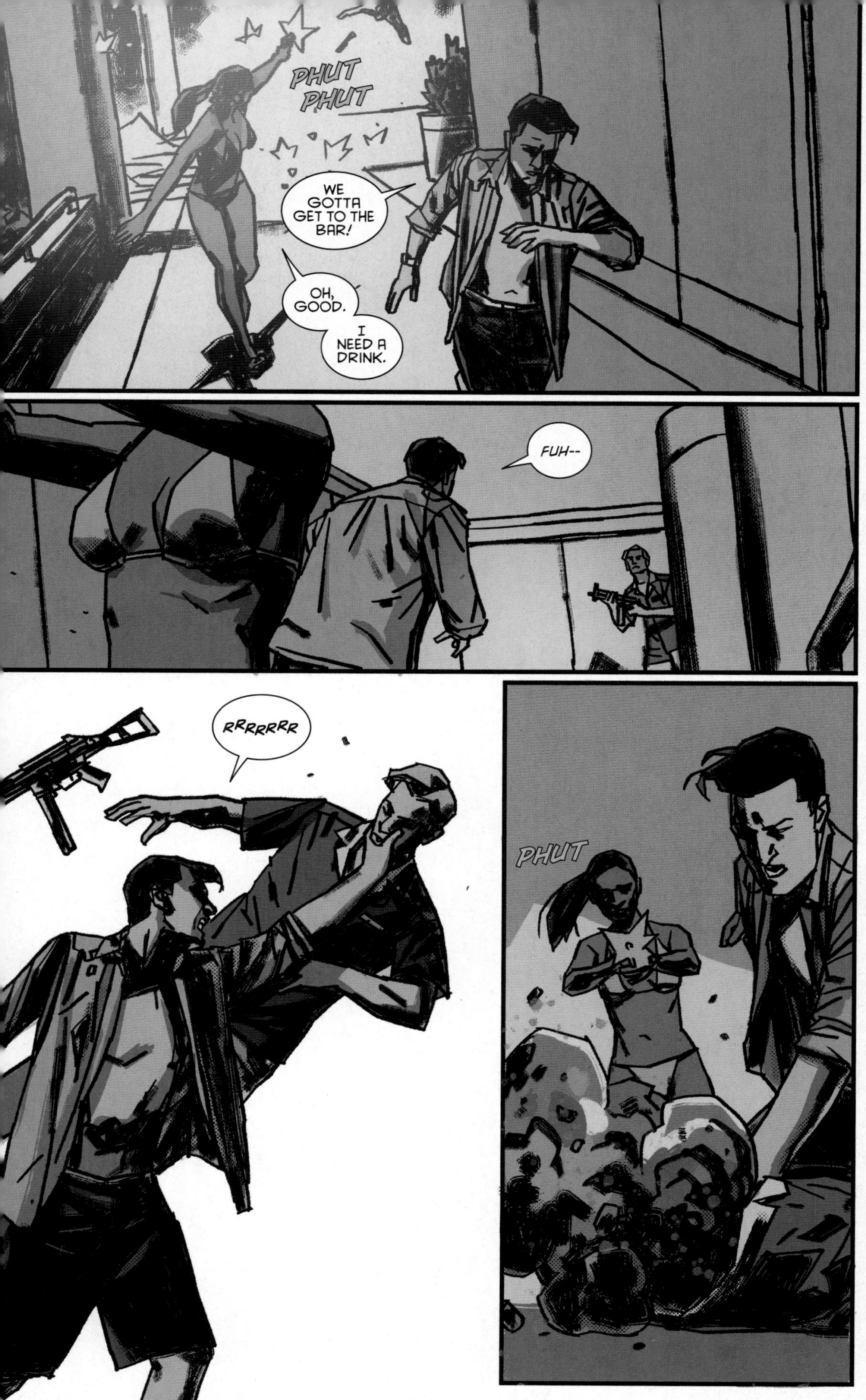
PHUT
PHUT
WE GOTTA GET TO THE BAR!
OH, GOOD.
I NEED A DRINK.
FUH--
RRRRRRR
PHUT

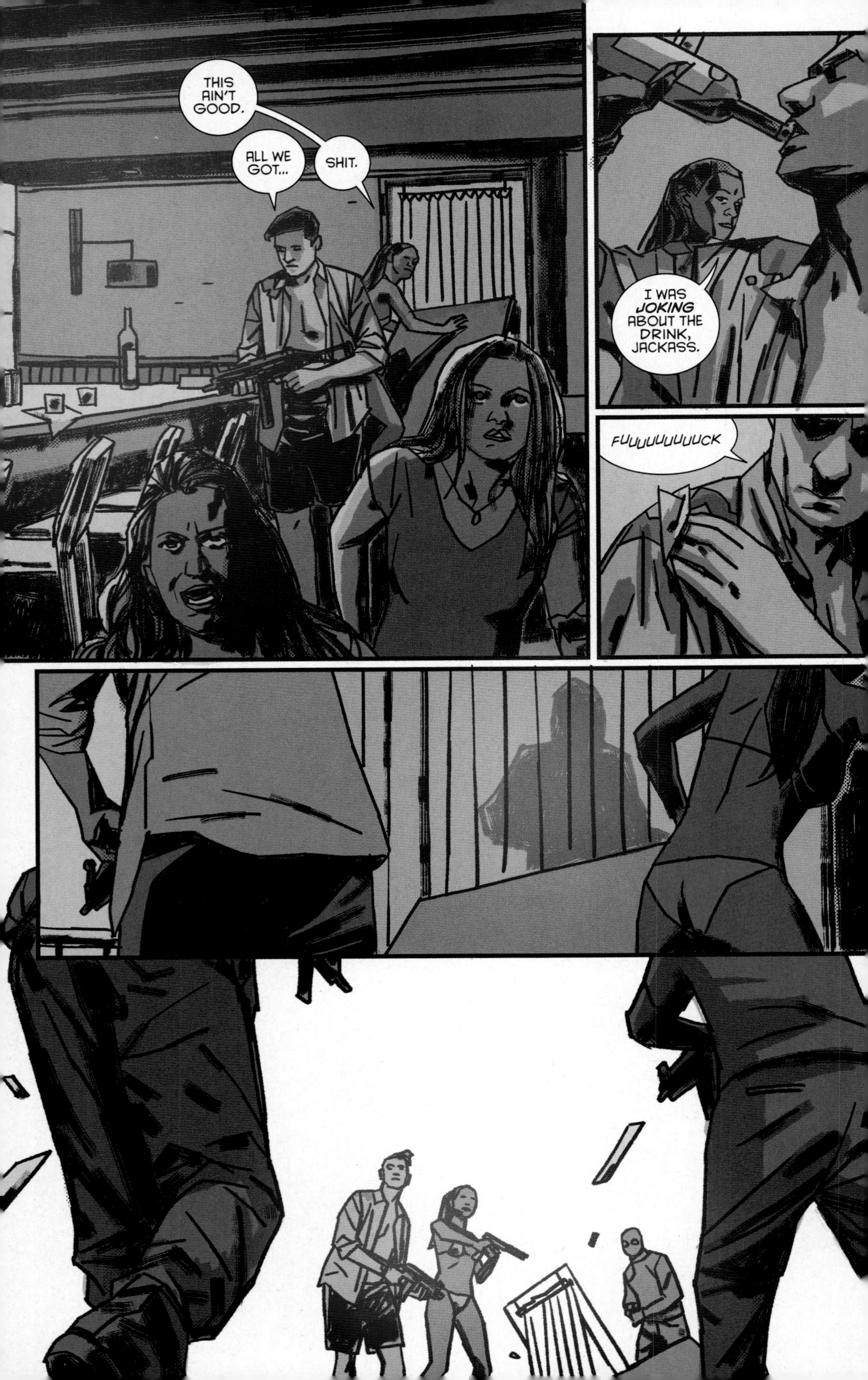
THIS AIN'T GOOD.
ALL WE GOT...
SHIT.
I WAS JOKING ABOUT THE DRINK, JACKASS.
FUUUUUUUUUCK

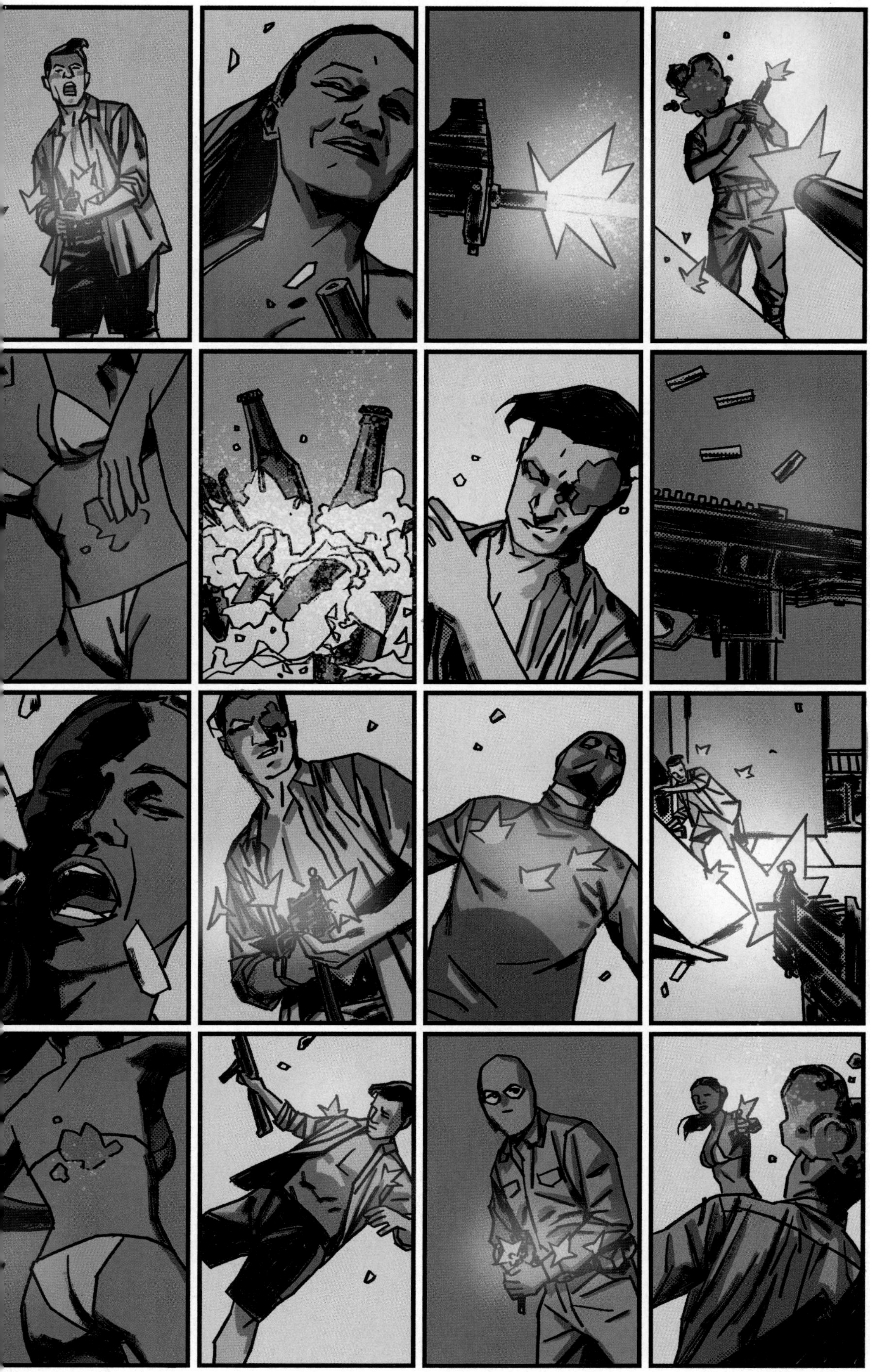

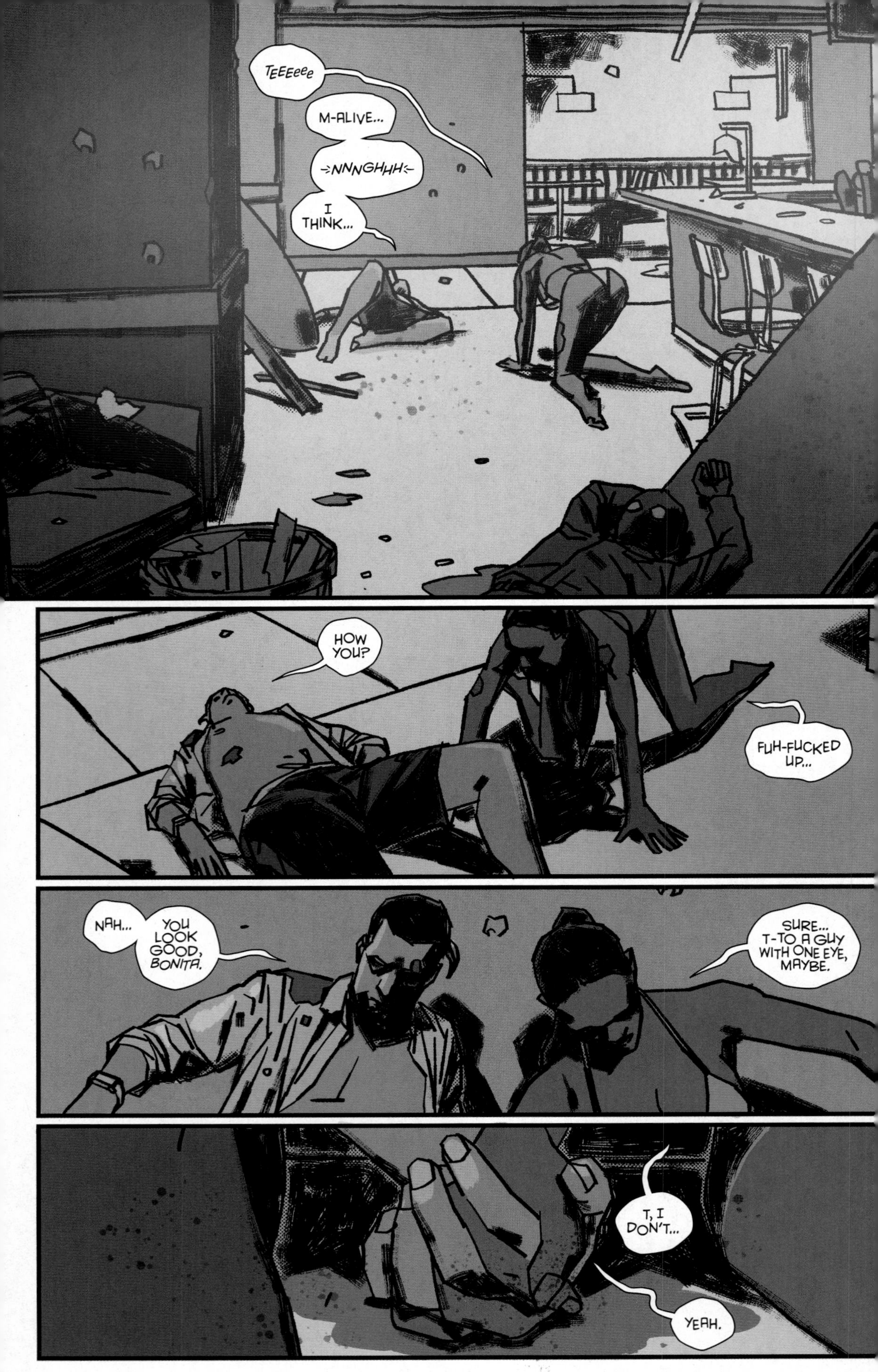
TEEEeee
M-ALIVE...
NNNGHHH
I THINK...
HOW YOU?
FUH-FUCKED UP...
NAH...
YOU LOOK GOOD, BONITA.
SURE... T-TO A GUY WITH ONE EYE, MAYBE.
T, I DON'T...
YEAH.

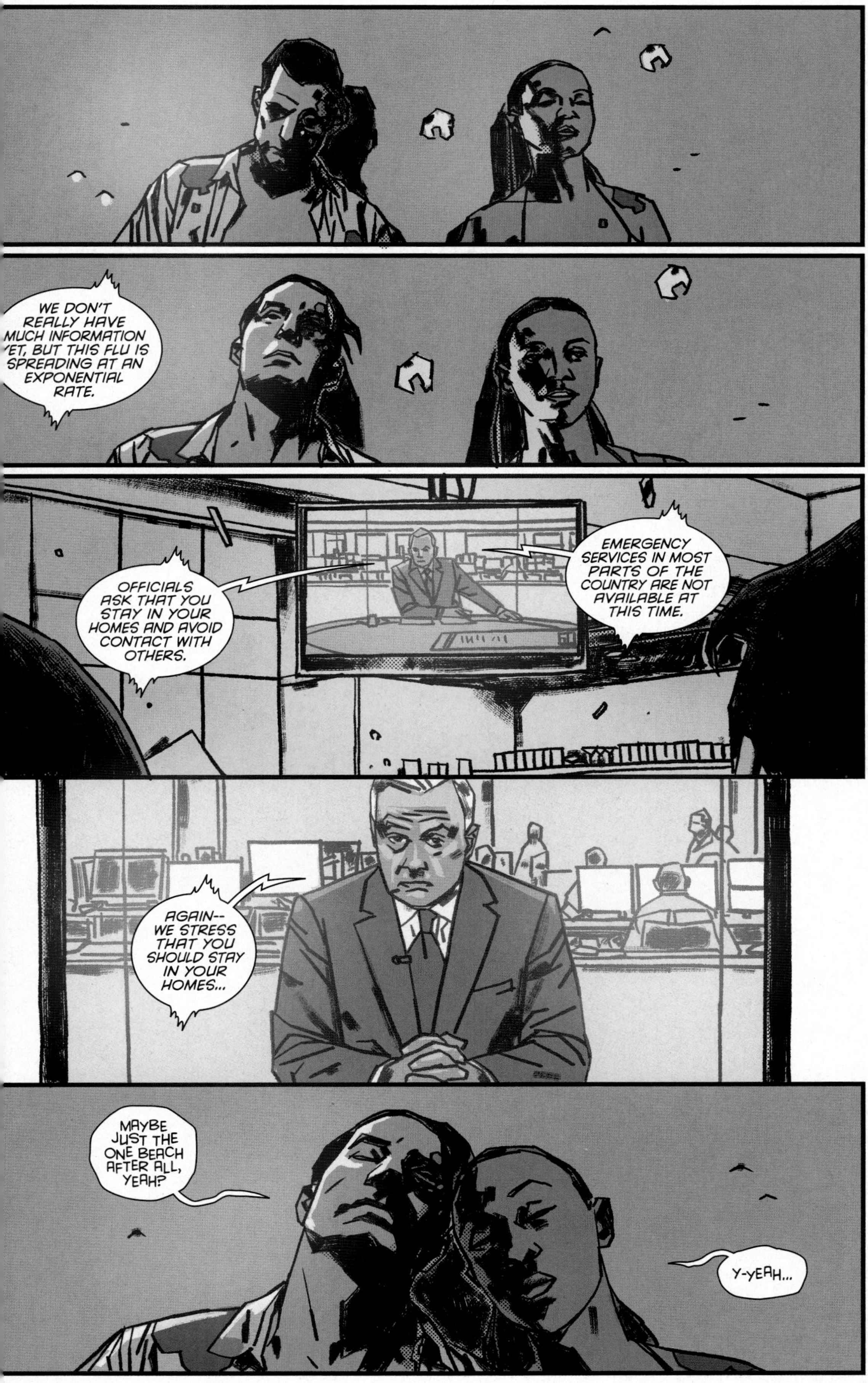
WE DON'T REALLY HAVE MUCH INFORMATION YET, BUT THIS FLU IS SPREADING AT AN EXPONENTIAL RATE.
OFFICIALS ASK THAT YOU STAY IN YOUR HOMES AND AVOID CONTACT WITH OTHERS.
EMERGENCY SERVICES IN MOST PARTS OF THE COUNTRY ARE NOT AVAILABLE AT THIS TIME.
AGAIN-- WE STRESS THAT YOU SHOULD STAY IN YOUR HOMES...
MAYBE JUST THE ONE BEACH AFTER ALL, YEAH?
Y-YEAH...

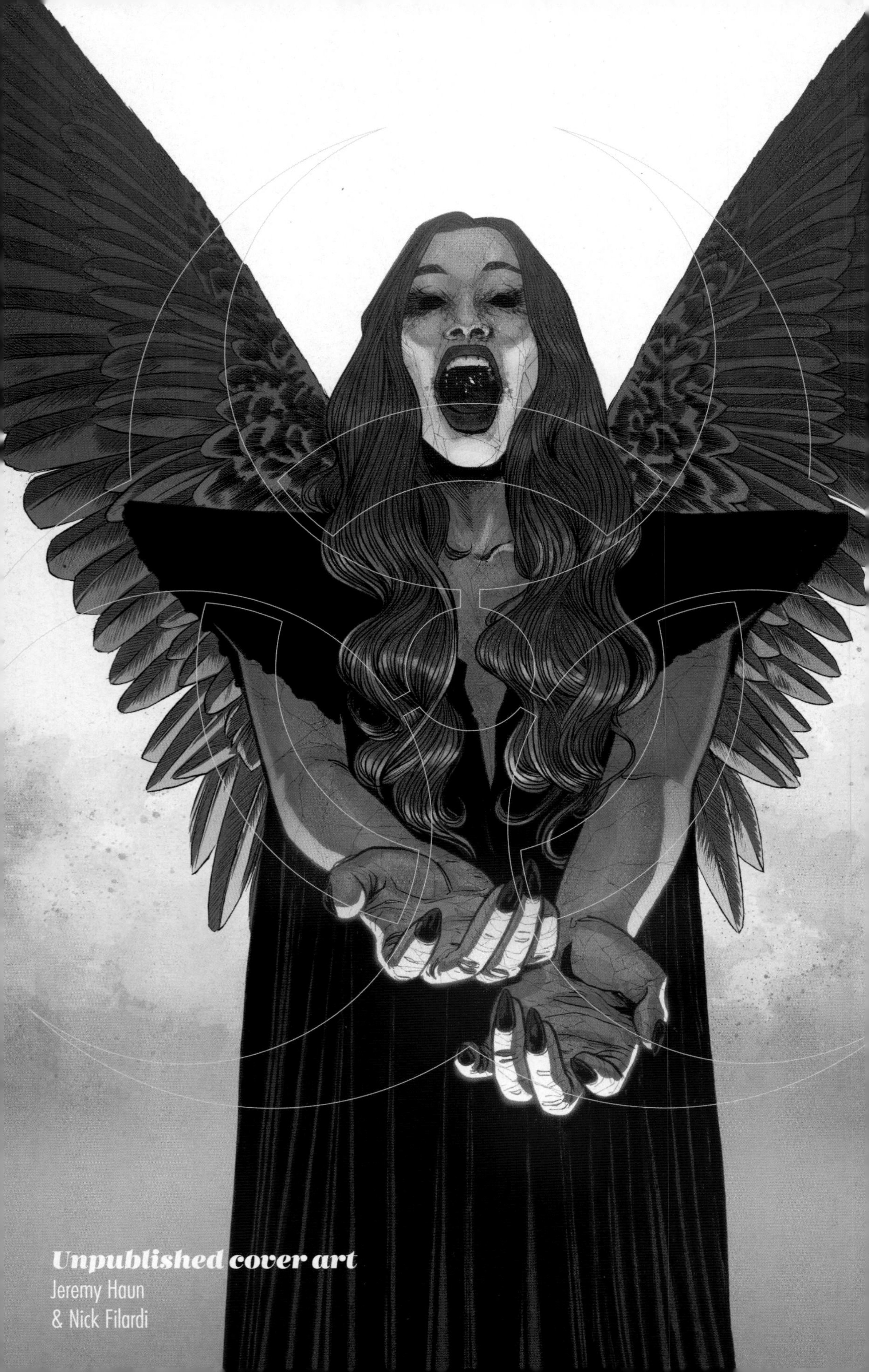

***Unpublished* cover art**
Jeremy Haun
& Nick Filardi

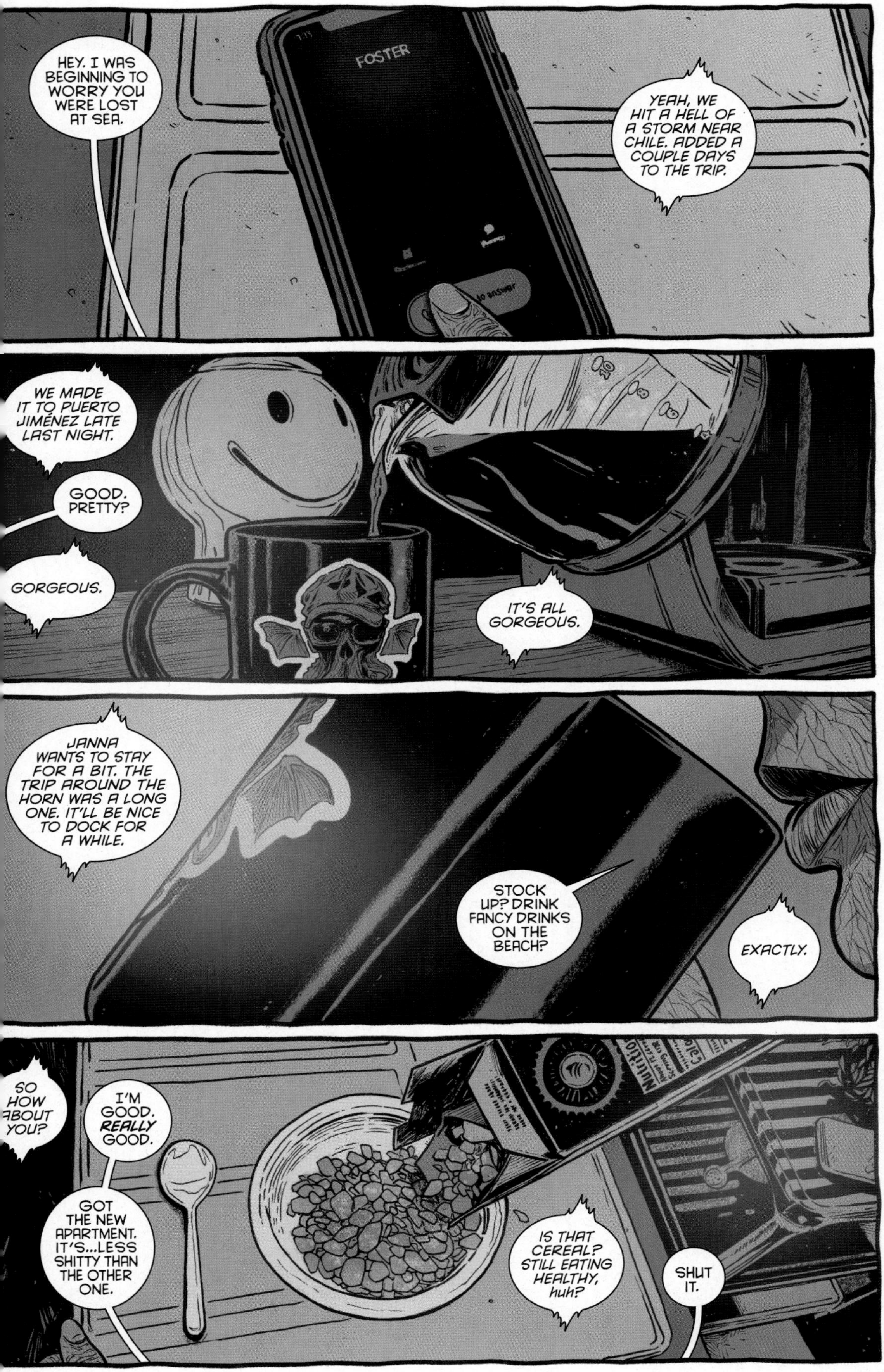

FOSTER
HEY. I WAS BEGINNING TO WORRY YOU WERE LOST AT SEA.
YEAH, WE HIT A HELL OF A STORM NEAR CHILE. ADDED A COUPLE DAYS TO THE TRIP.
WE MADE IT TO PUERTO JIMÉNEZ LATE LAST NIGHT.
GOOD. PRETTY?
GORGEOUS.
IT'S ALL GORGEOUS.
JANNA WANTS TO STAY FOR A BIT. THE TRIP AROUND THE HORN WAS A LONG ONE. IT'LL BE NICE TO DOCK FOR A WHILE.
STOCK UP? DRINK FANCY DRINKS ON THE BEACH?
EXACTLY.
SO HOW ABOUT YOU?
I'M GOOD. REALLY GOOD.
GOT THE NEW APARTMENT. IT'S...LESS SHITTY THAN THE OTHER ONE.
IS THAT CEREAL? STILL EATING HEALTHY, huh?
SHUT IT.

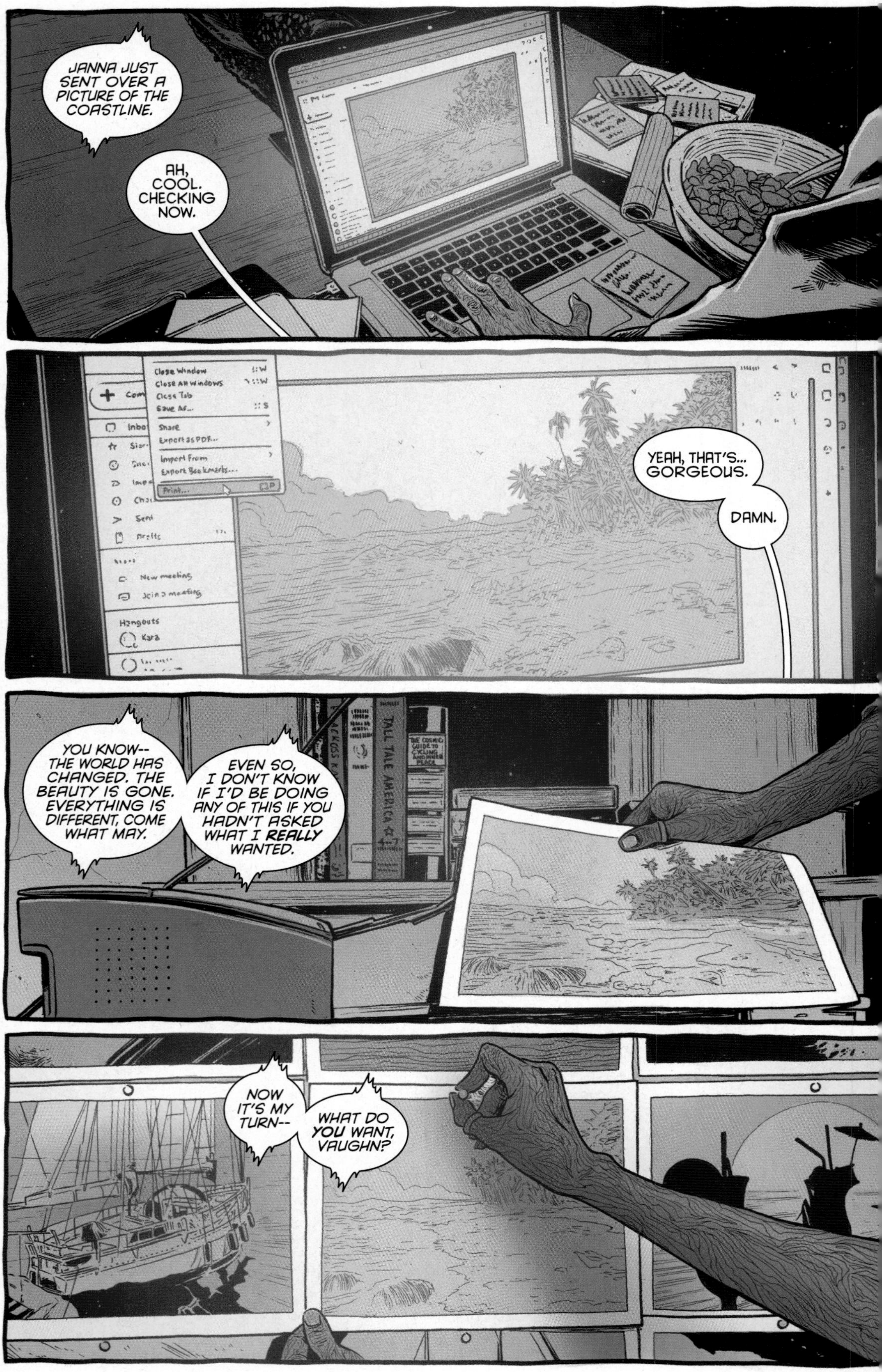
JANNA JUST SENT OVER A PICTURE OF THE COASTLINE.
AH, COOL. CHECKING NOW.
Close Window
Close All Windows
Close Tab
Save As...
Share
Export as PDF...
Import From
Export Bookmarks...
Print...
Inbox
Sent
Drafts
New meeting
Join a meeting
Hangouts
Kara
YEAH, THAT'S... GORGEOUS.
DAMN.
YOU KNOW-- THE WORLD HAS CHANGED. THE BEAUTY IS GONE. EVERYTHING IS DIFFERENT, COME WHAT MAY.
EVEN SO, I DON'T KNOW IF I'D BE DOING ANY OF THIS IF YOU HADN'T ASKED WHAT I REALLY WANTED.
TALL TALE AMERICA
THE COSMIC GUIDE TO CYCLING
NOW IT'S MY TURN--
WHAT DO YOU WANT, VAUGHN?

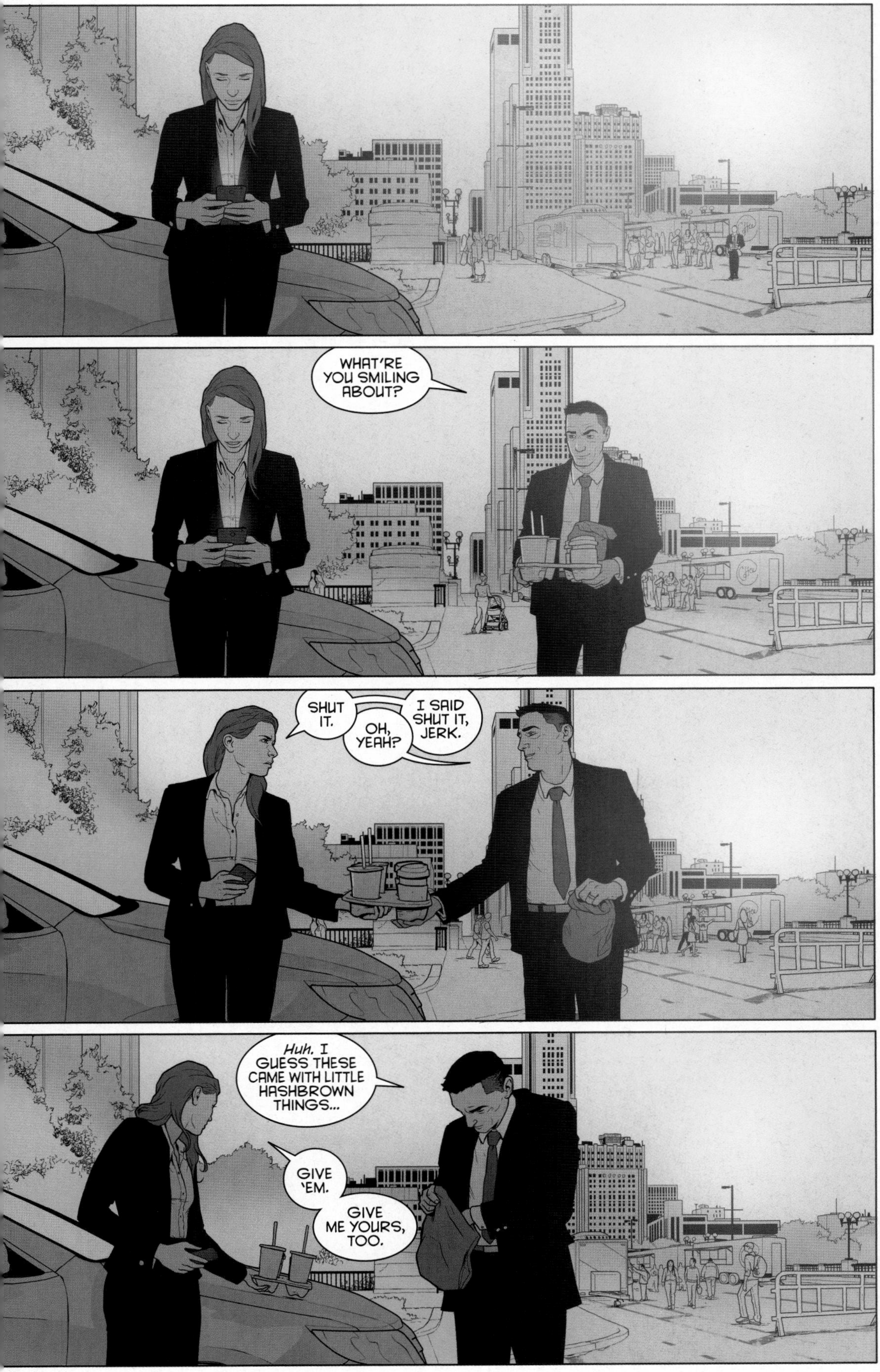
WHAT'RE YOU SMILING ABOUT?
SHUT IT.
OH, YEAH?
I SAID SHUT IT, JERK.
Huh. I GUESS THESE CAME WITH LITTLE HASHBROWN THINGS...
GIVE 'EM.
GIVE ME YOURS, TOO.

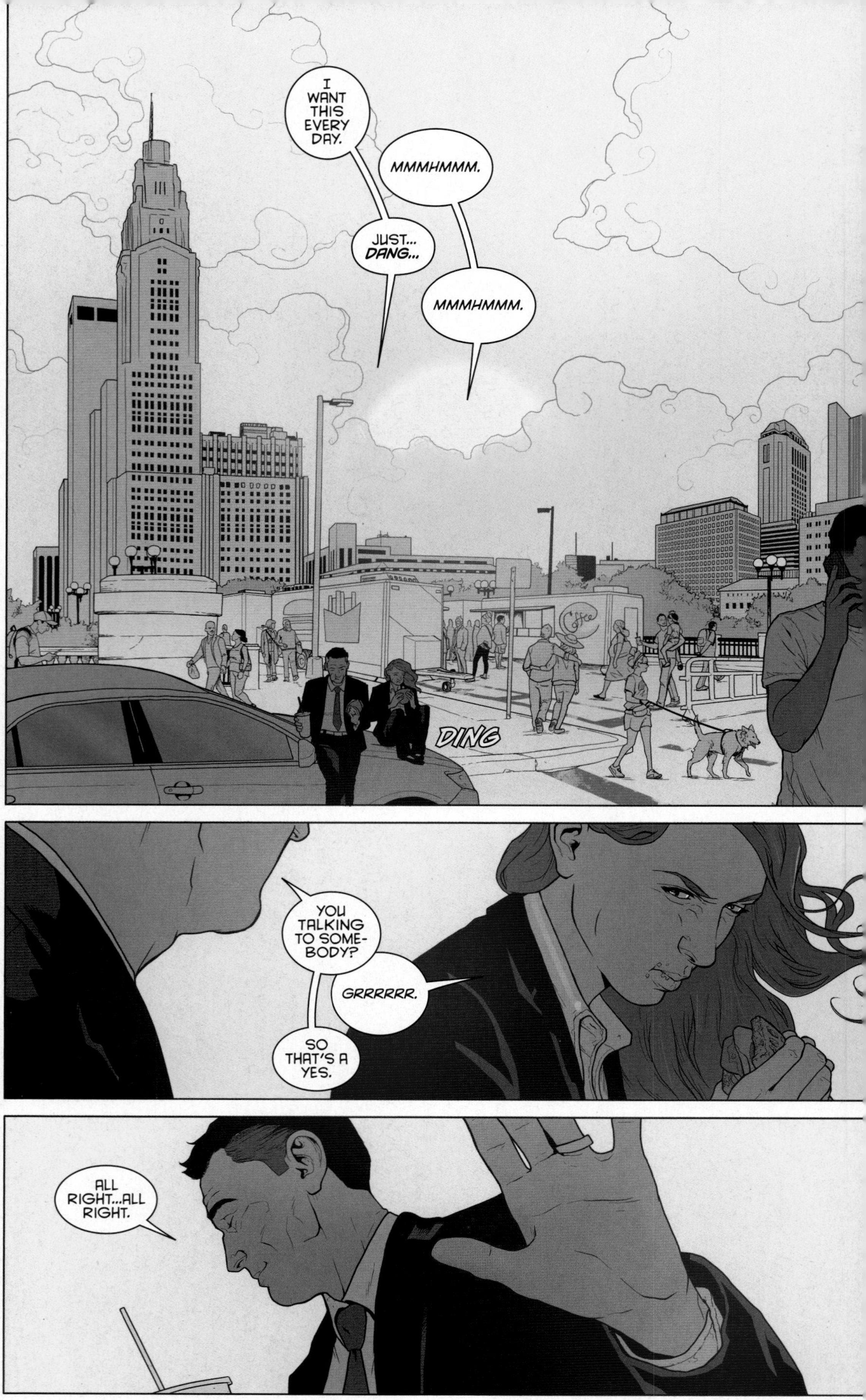
I WANT THIS EVERY DAY.
MMMHMMM.
JUST... DANG...
MMMHMMM.
DING
YOU TALKING TO SOME-BODY?
GRRRRRR.
SO THAT'S A YES.
ALL RIGHT...ALL RIGHT.

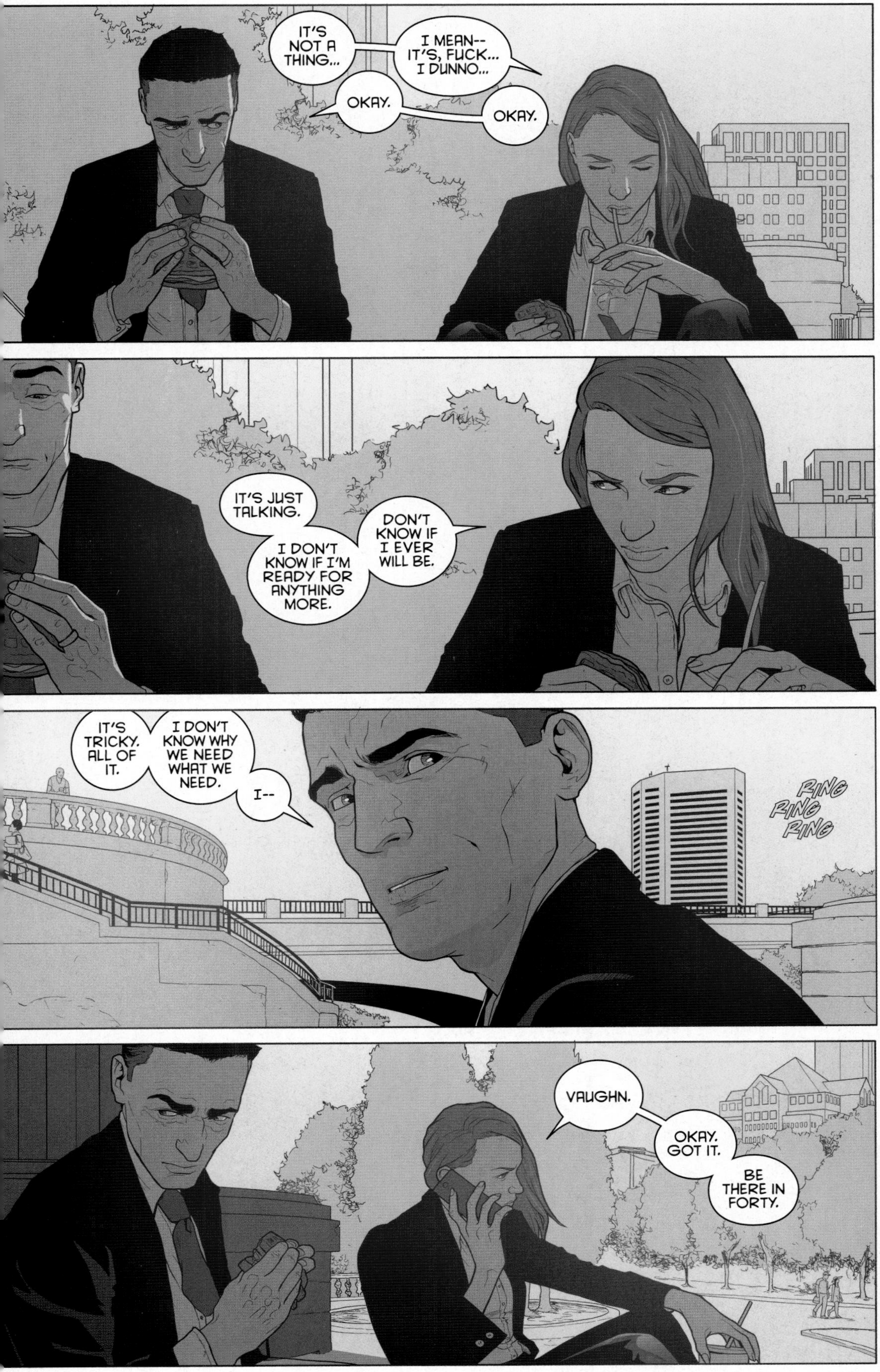
IT'S NOT A THING...
I MEAN-- IT'S, FUCK... I DUNNO...
OKAY.
OKAY.
IT'S JUST TALKING.
I DON'T KNOW IF I'M READY FOR ANYTHING MORE.
DON'T KNOW IF I EVER WILL BE.
IT'S TRICKY. ALL OF IT.
I DON'T KNOW WHY WE NEED WHAT WE NEED.
I--
RING RING RING
VAUGHN.
OKAY. GOT IT.
BE THERE IN FORTY.

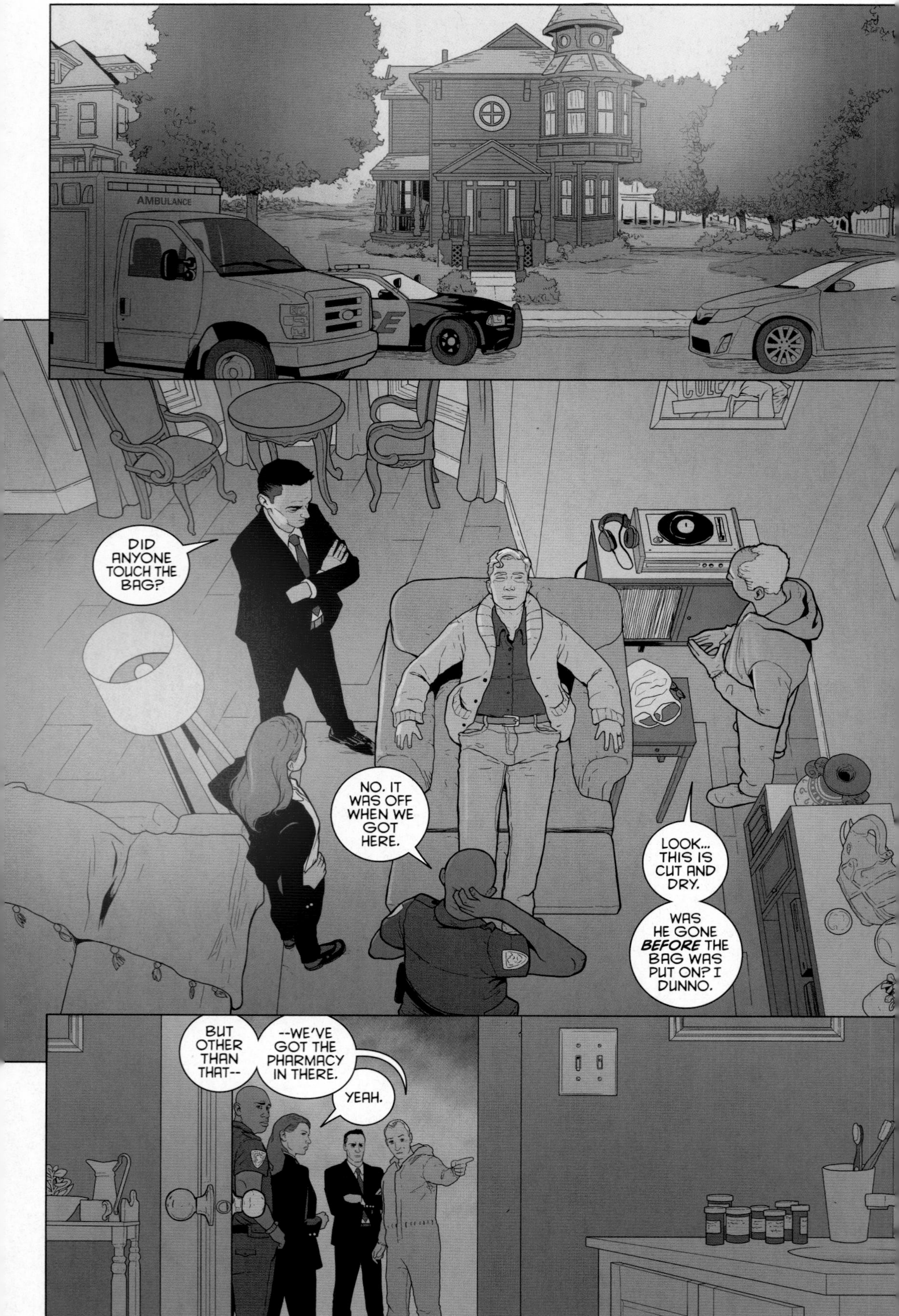

AMBULANCE
DID ANYONE TOUCH THE BAG?
NO. IT WAS OFF WHEN WE GOT HERE.
LOOK... THIS IS CUT AND DRY.
WAS HE GONE *BEFORE* THE BAG WAS PUT ON? I DUNNO.
BUT OTHER THAN THAT--
--WE'VE GOT THE PHARMACY IN THERE.
YEAH.

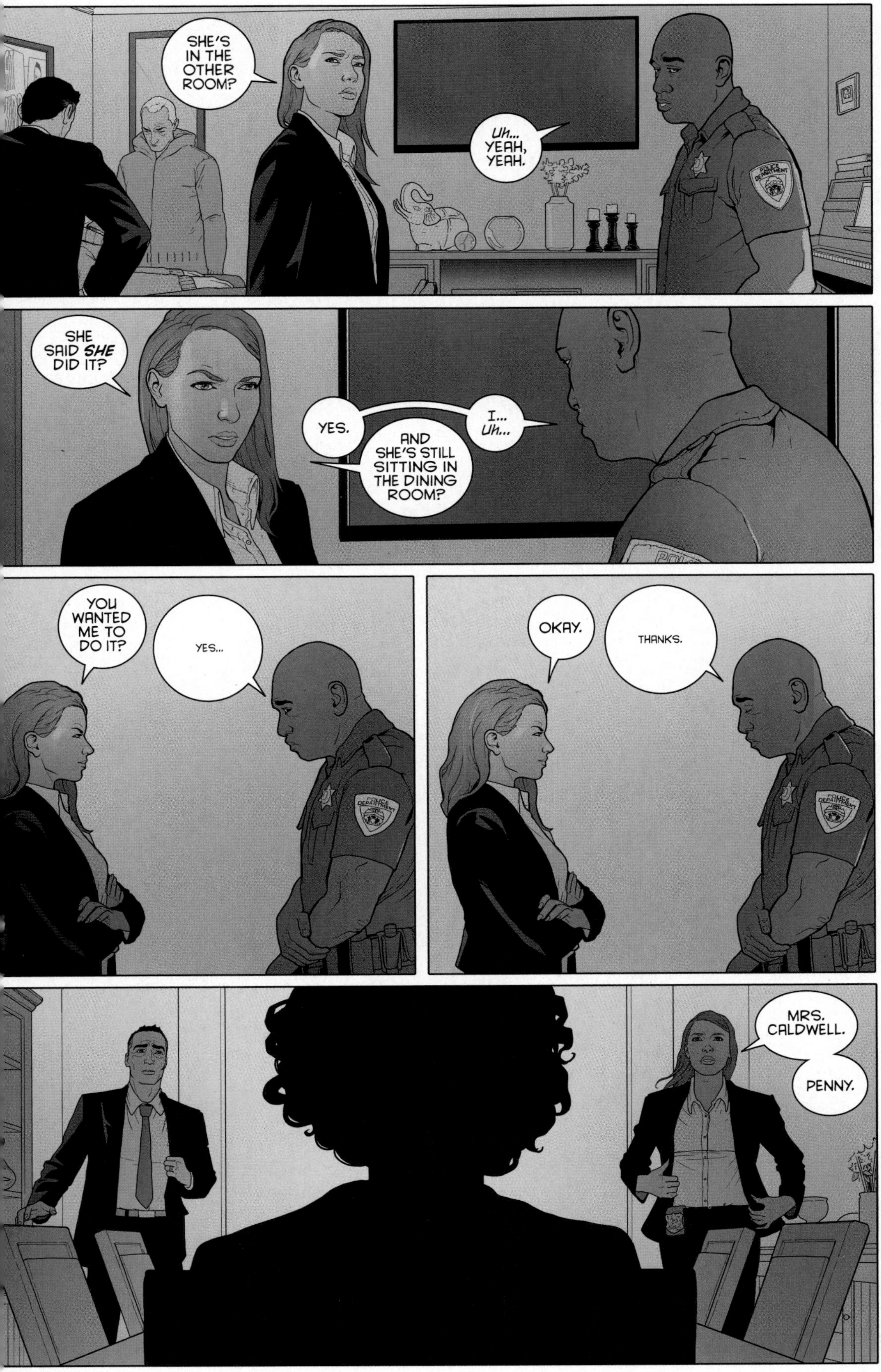
SHE'S IN THE OTHER ROOM?
Uh... YEAH, YEAH.
SHE SAID SHE DID IT?
I... Uh...
YES.
AND SHE'S STILL SITTING IN THE DINING ROOM?
YOU WANTED ME TO DO IT?
YES...
OKAY.
THANKS.
MRS. CALDWELL.
PENNY.

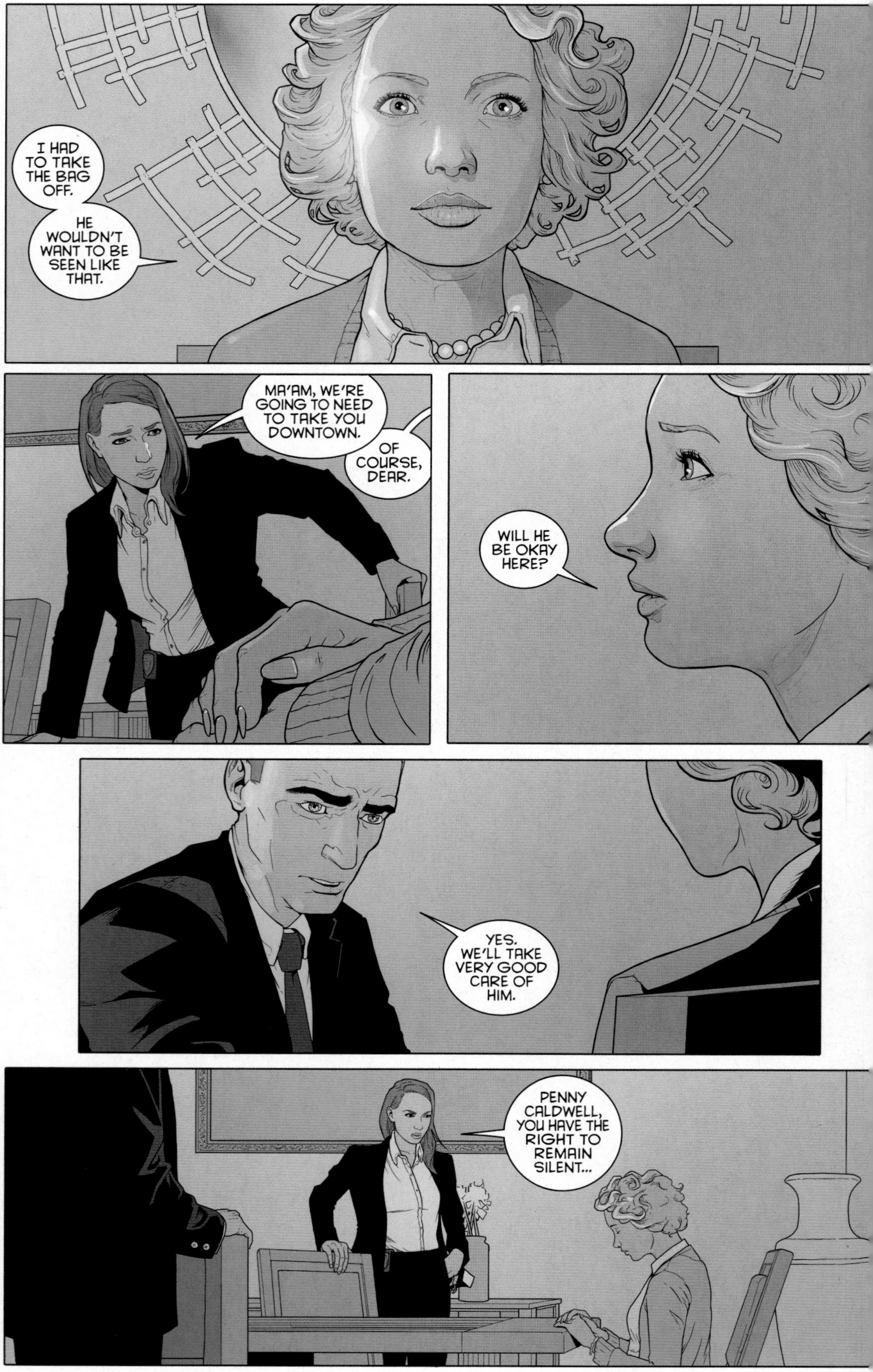
I HAD TO TAKE THE BAG OFF.
HE WOULDN'T WANT TO BE SEEN LIKE THAT.
MA'AM, WE'RE GOING TO NEED TO TAKE YOU DOWNTOWN.
OF COURSE, DEAR.
WILL HE BE OKAY HERE?
YES. WE'LL TAKE VERY GOOD CARE OF HIM.
PENNY CALDWELL, YOU HAVE THE RIGHT TO REMAIN SILENT...

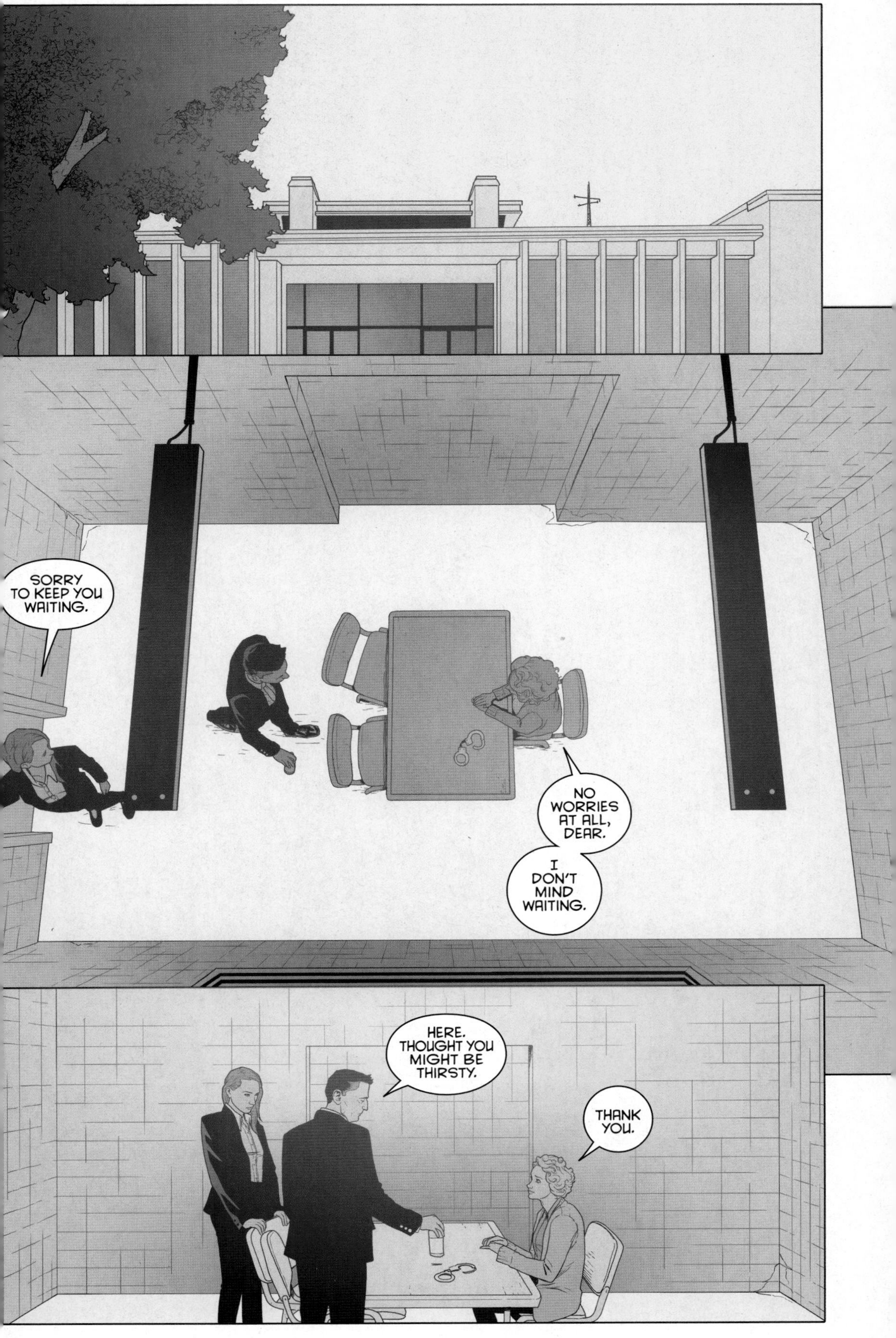
SORRY TO KEEP YOU WAITING.
NO WORRIES AT ALL, DEAR.
I DON'T MIND WAITING.
HERE. THOUGHT YOU MIGHT BE THIRSTY.
THANK YOU.

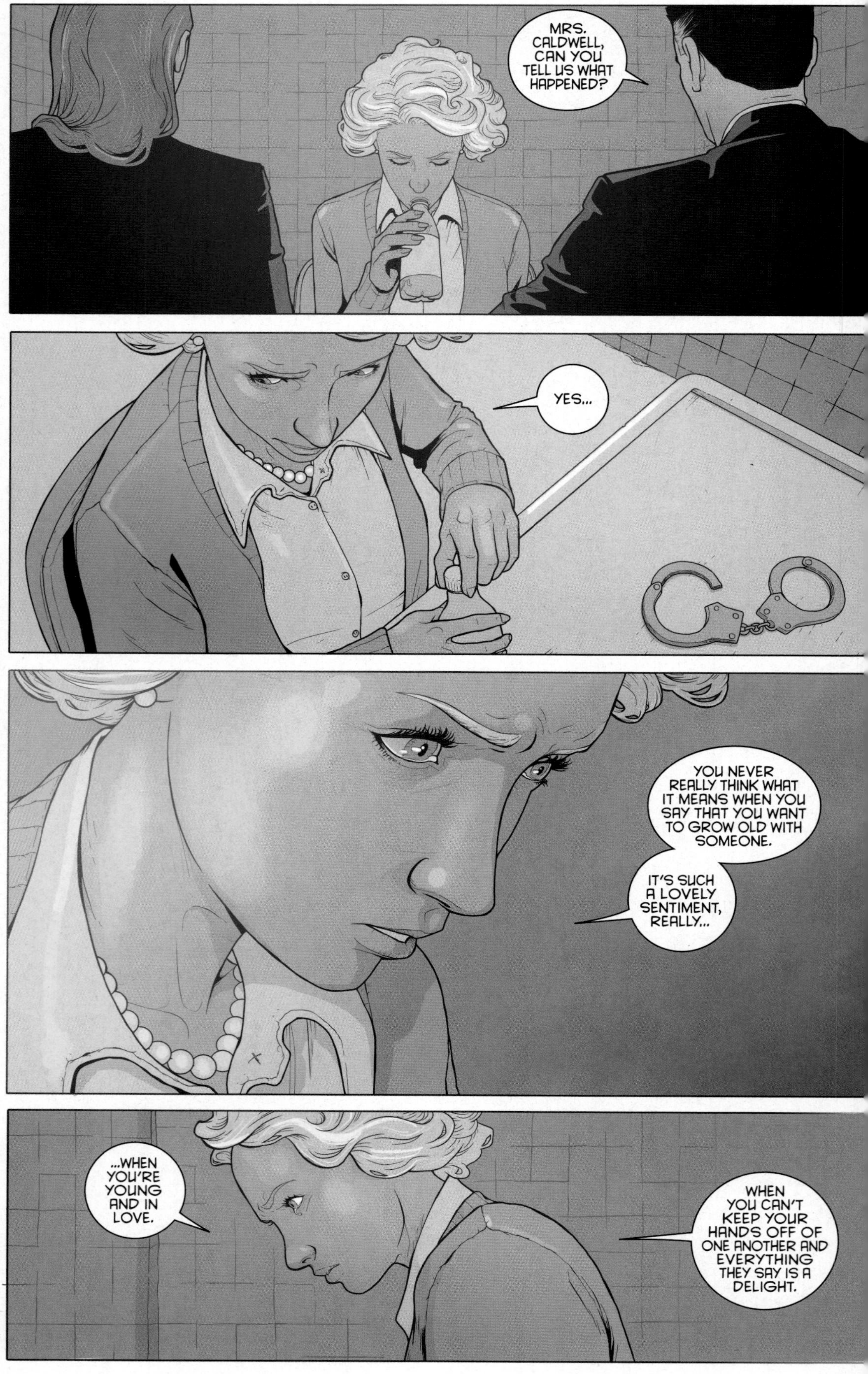
MRS. CALDWELL, CAN YOU TELL US WHAT HAPPENED?
YES...
YOU NEVER REALLY THINK WHAT IT MEANS WHEN YOU SAY THAT YOU WANT TO GROW OLD WITH SOMEONE.
IT'S SUCH A LOVELY SENTIMENT, REALLY...
...WHEN YOU'RE YOUNG AND IN LOVE.
WHEN YOU CAN'T KEEP YOUR HANDS OFF OF ONE ANOTHER AND EVERYTHING THEY SAY IS A DELIGHT.

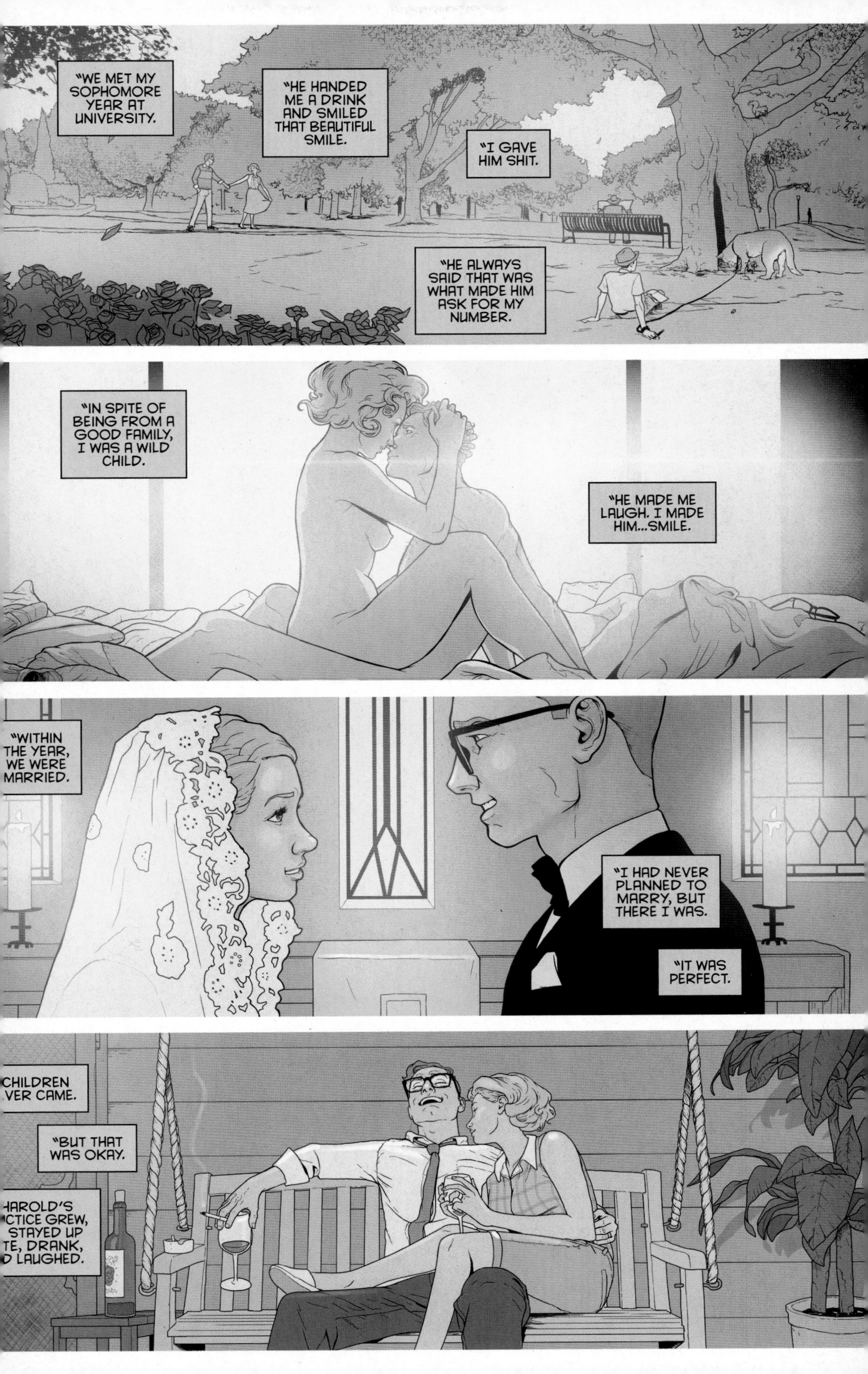
"WE MET MY SOPHOMORE YEAR AT UNIVERSITY.
"HE HANDED ME A DRINK AND SMILED THAT BEAUTIFUL SMILE.
"I GAVE HIM SHIT.
"HE ALWAYS SAID THAT WAS WHAT MADE HIM ASK FOR MY NUMBER.
"IN SPITE OF BEING FROM A GOOD FAMILY, I WAS A WILD CHILD.
"HE MADE ME LAUGH. I MADE HIM...SMILE.
"WITHIN THE YEAR, WE WERE MARRIED.
"I HAD NEVER PLANNED TO MARRY, BUT THERE I WAS.
"IT WAS PERFECT.
CHILDREN
VER CAME.
"BUT THAT WAS OKAY.
HAROLD'S
CTICE GREW,
STAYED UP
TE, DRANK,
D LAUGHED.

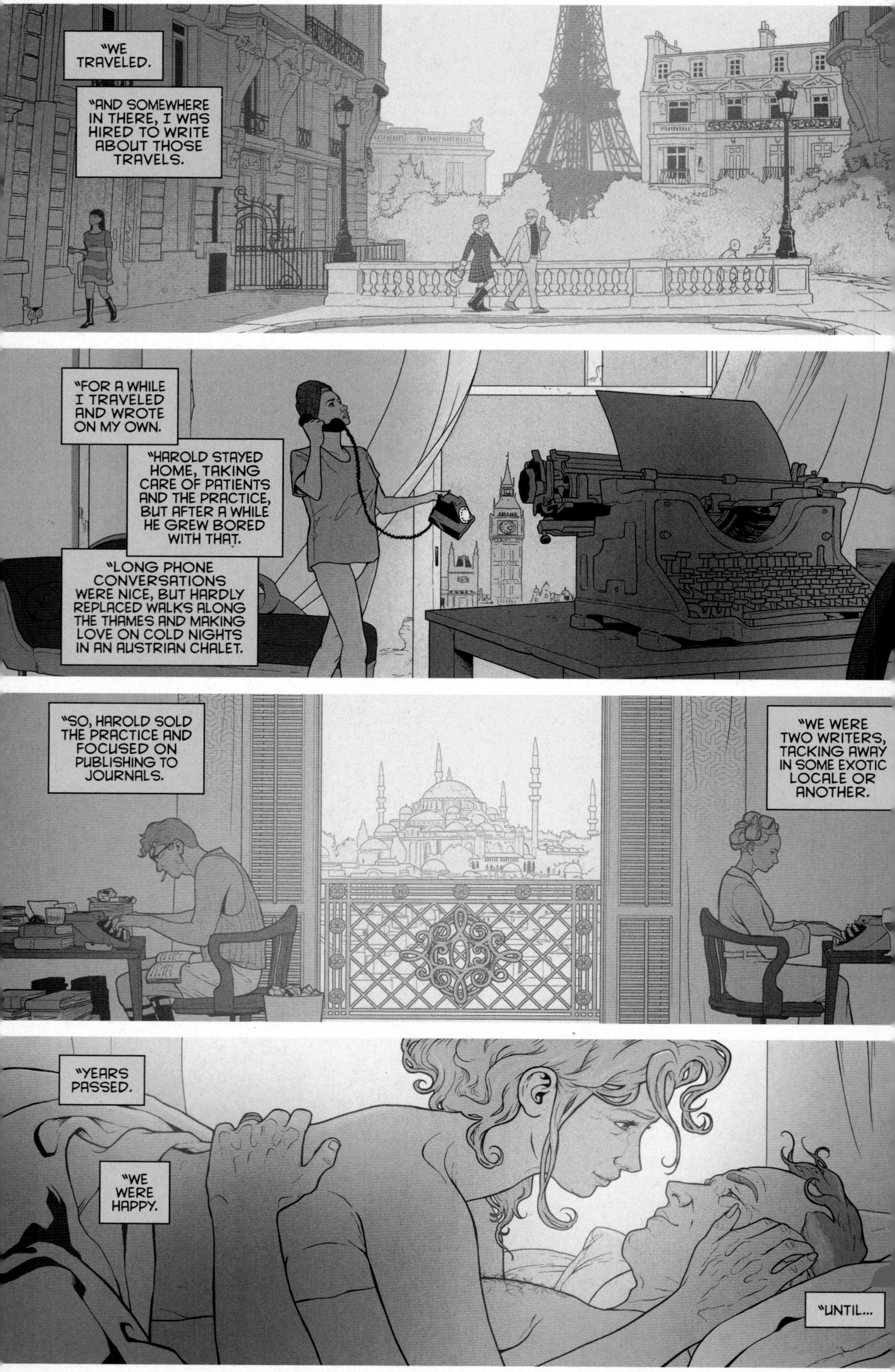
"WE TRAVELED.
"AND SOMEWHERE IN THERE, I WAS HIRED TO WRITE ABOUT THOSE TRAVELS.
"FOR A WHILE I TRAVELED AND WROTE ON MY OWN.
"HAROLD STAYED HOME, TAKING CARE OF PATIENTS AND THE PRACTICE, BUT AFTER A WHILE HE GREW BORED WITH THAT.
"LONG PHONE CONVERSATIONS WERE NICE, BUT HARDLY REPLACED WALKS ALONG THE THAMES AND MAKING LOVE ON COLD NIGHTS IN AN AUSTRIAN CHALET.
"SO, HAROLD SOLD THE PRACTICE AND FOCUSED ON PUBLISHING TO JOURNALS.
"WE WERE TWO WRITERS, TACKING AWAY IN SOME EXOTIC LOCALE OR ANOTHER.
"YEARS PASSED.
"WE WERE HAPPY.
"UNTIL...

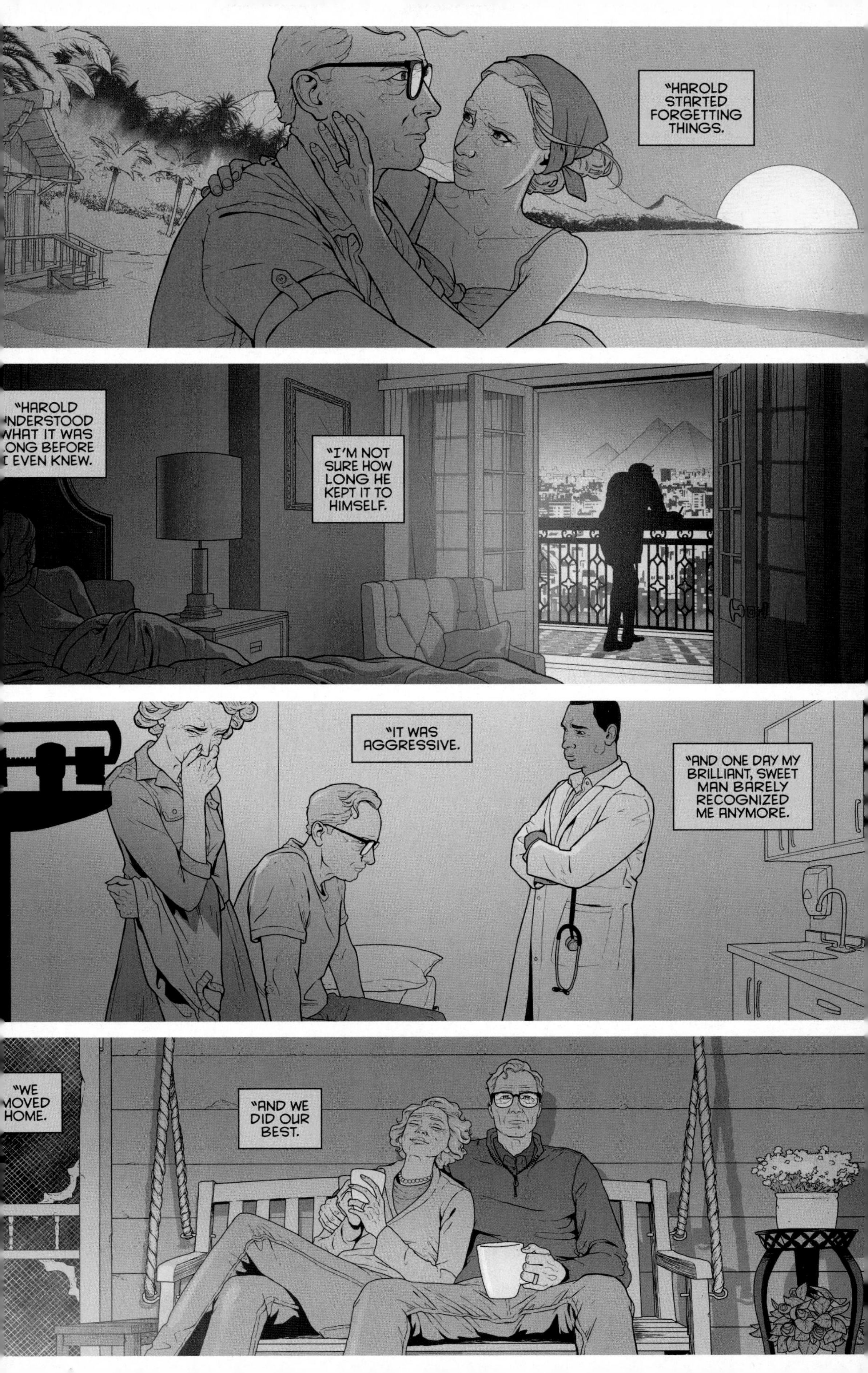
"HAROLD STARTED FORGETTING THINGS.
"HAROLD UNDERSTOOD WHAT IT WAS LONG BEFORE I EVEN KNEW.
"I'M NOT SURE HOW LONG HE KEPT IT TO HIMSELF.
"IT WAS AGGRESSIVE.
"AND ONE DAY MY BRILLIANT, SWEET MAN BARELY RECOGNIZED ME ANYMORE.
"WE MOVED HOME.
"AND WE DID OUR BEST.

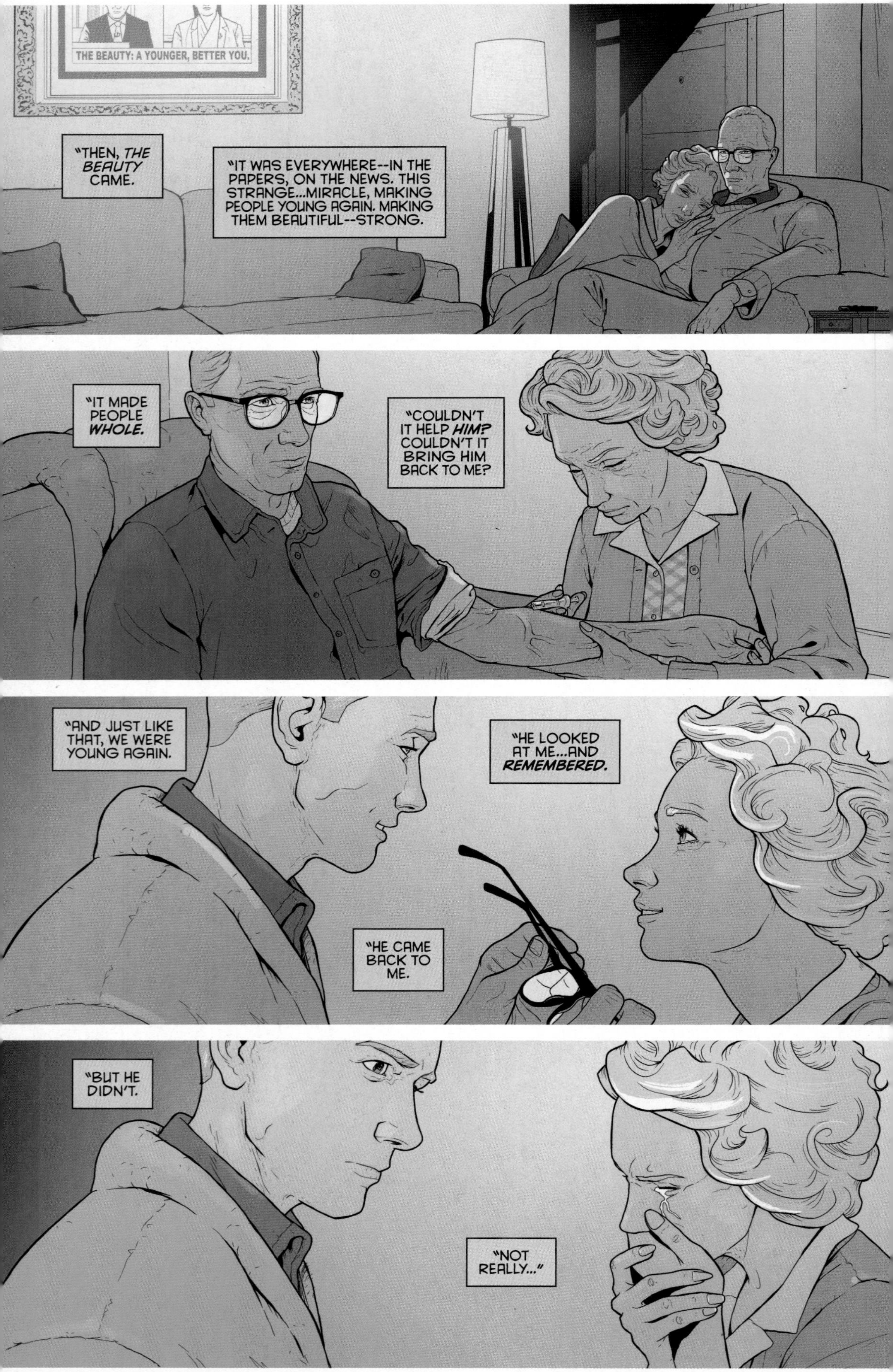
THE BEAUTY: A YOUNGER, BETTER YOU.
"THEN, THE BEAUTY CAME.
"IT WAS EVERYWHERE--IN THE PAPERS, ON THE NEWS. THIS STRANGE...MIRACLE, MAKING PEOPLE YOUNG AGAIN. MAKING THEM BEAUTIFUL--STRONG.
"IT MADE PEOPLE WHOLE.
"COULDN'T IT HELP HIM? COULDN'T IT BRING HIM BACK TO ME?
"AND JUST LIKE THAT, WE WERE YOUNG AGAIN.
"HE LOOKED AT ME...AND REMEMBERED.
"HE CAME BACK TO ME.
"BUT HE DIDN'T.
"NOT REALLY..."

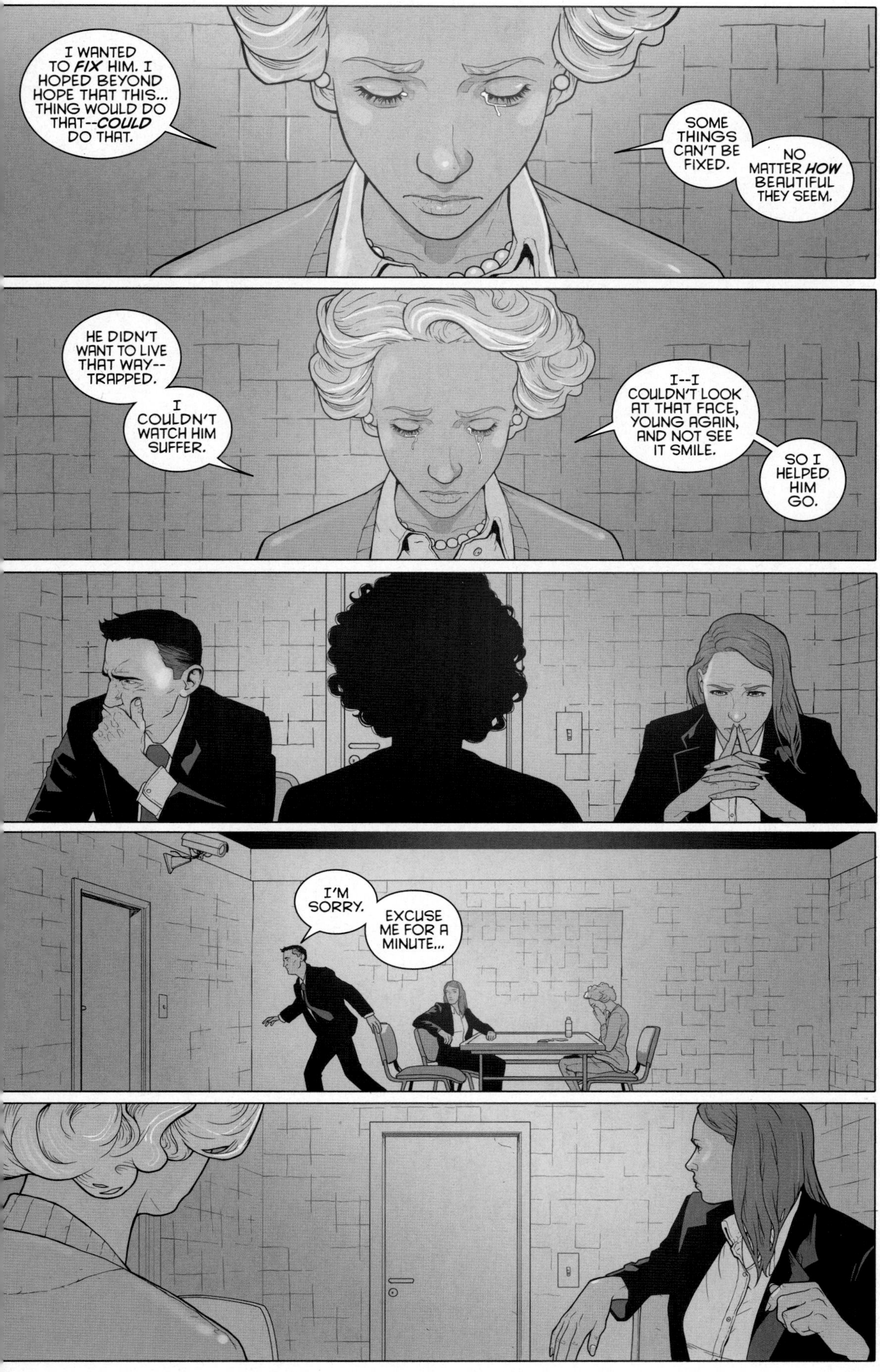
I WANTED TO **FIX** HIM. I HOPED BEYOND HOPE THAT THIS... THING WOULD DO THAT--**COULD** DO THAT.
SOME THINGS CAN'T BE FIXED.
NO MATTER **HOW** BEAUTIFUL THEY SEEM.
HE DIDN'T WANT TO LIVE THAT WAY-- TRAPPED.
I COULDN'T WATCH HIM SUFFER.
I--I COULDN'T LOOK AT THAT FACE, YOUNG AGAIN, AND NOT SEE IT SMILE.
SO I HELPED HIM GO.
I'M SORRY.
EXCUSE ME FOR A MINUTE...

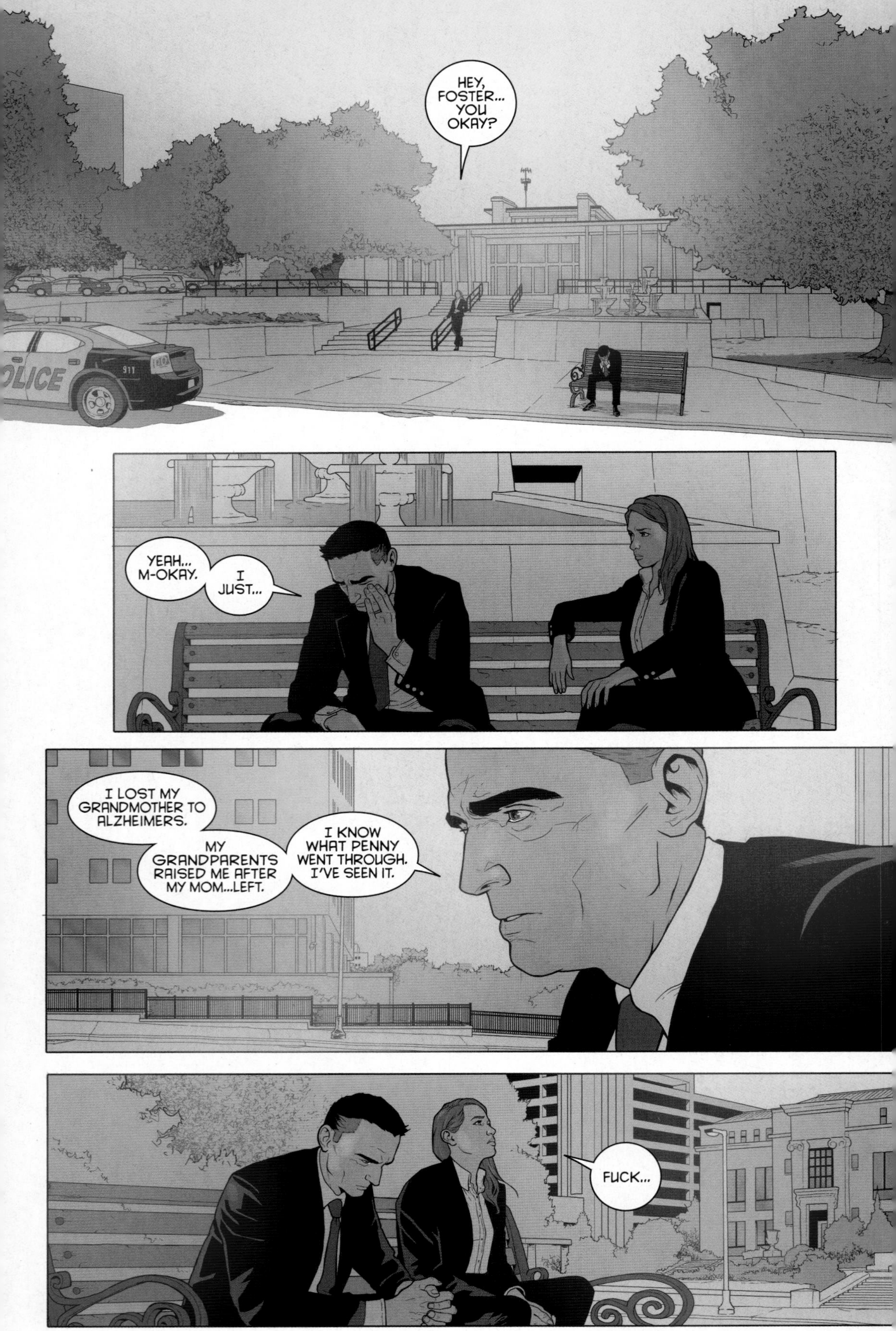
HEY, FOSTER... YOU OKAY?
POLICE
911
YEAH... M-OKAY.
I JUST...
I LOST MY GRANDMOTHER TO ALZHEIMERS.
MY GRANDPARENTS RAISED ME AFTER MY MOM...LEFT.
I KNOW WHAT PENNY WENT THROUGH. I'VE SEEN IT.
FUCK...

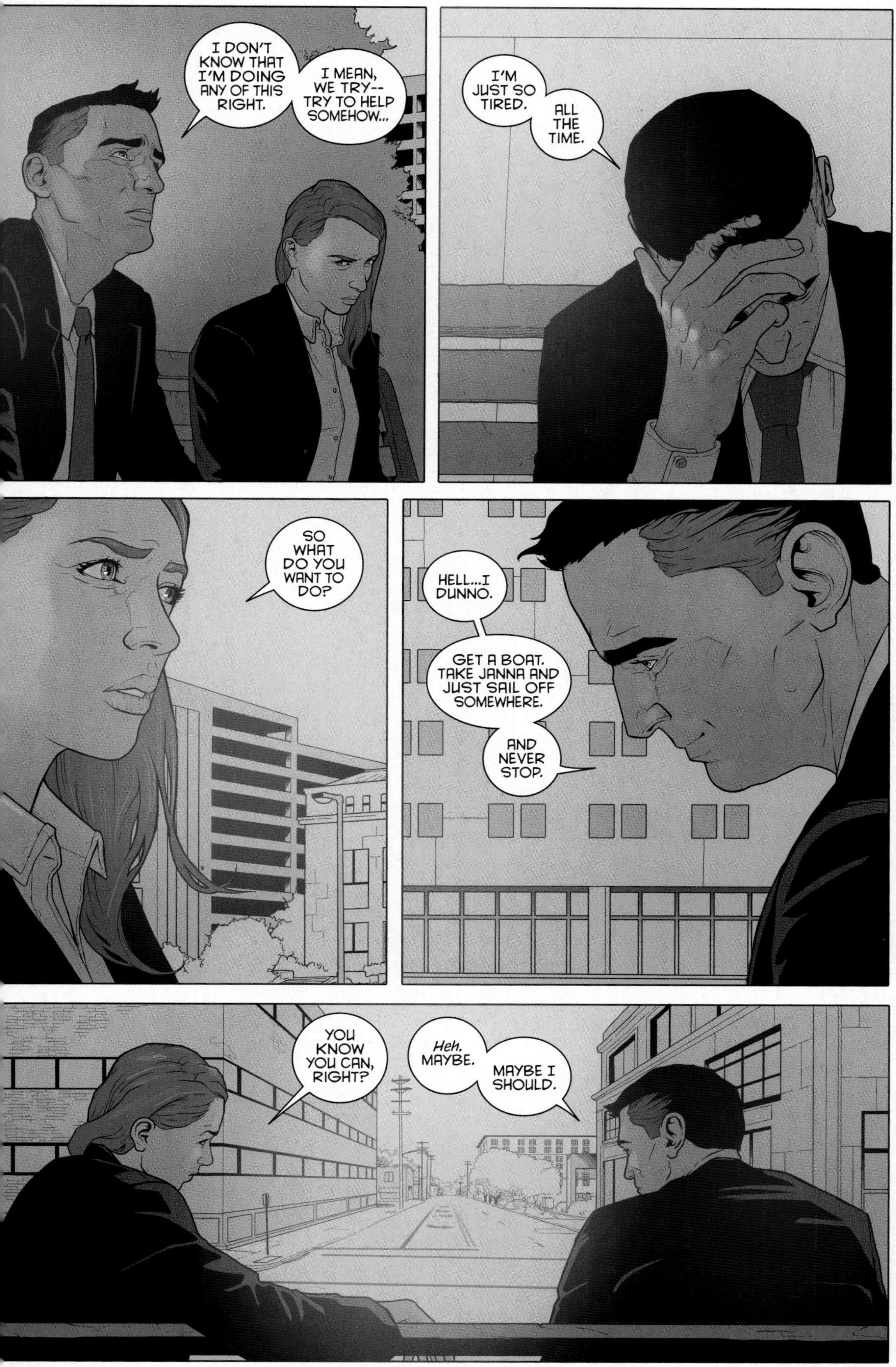
I DON'T KNOW THAT I'M DOING ANY OF THIS RIGHT.
I MEAN, WE TRY-- TRY TO HELP SOMEHOW...
I'M JUST SO TIRED.
ALL THE TIME.
SO WHAT DO YOU WANT TO DO?
HELL...I DUNNO.
GET A BOAT. TAKE JANNA AND JUST SAIL OFF SOMEWHERE.
AND NEVER STOP.
YOU KNOW YOU CAN, RIGHT?
Heh. MAYBE.
MAYBE I SHOULD.

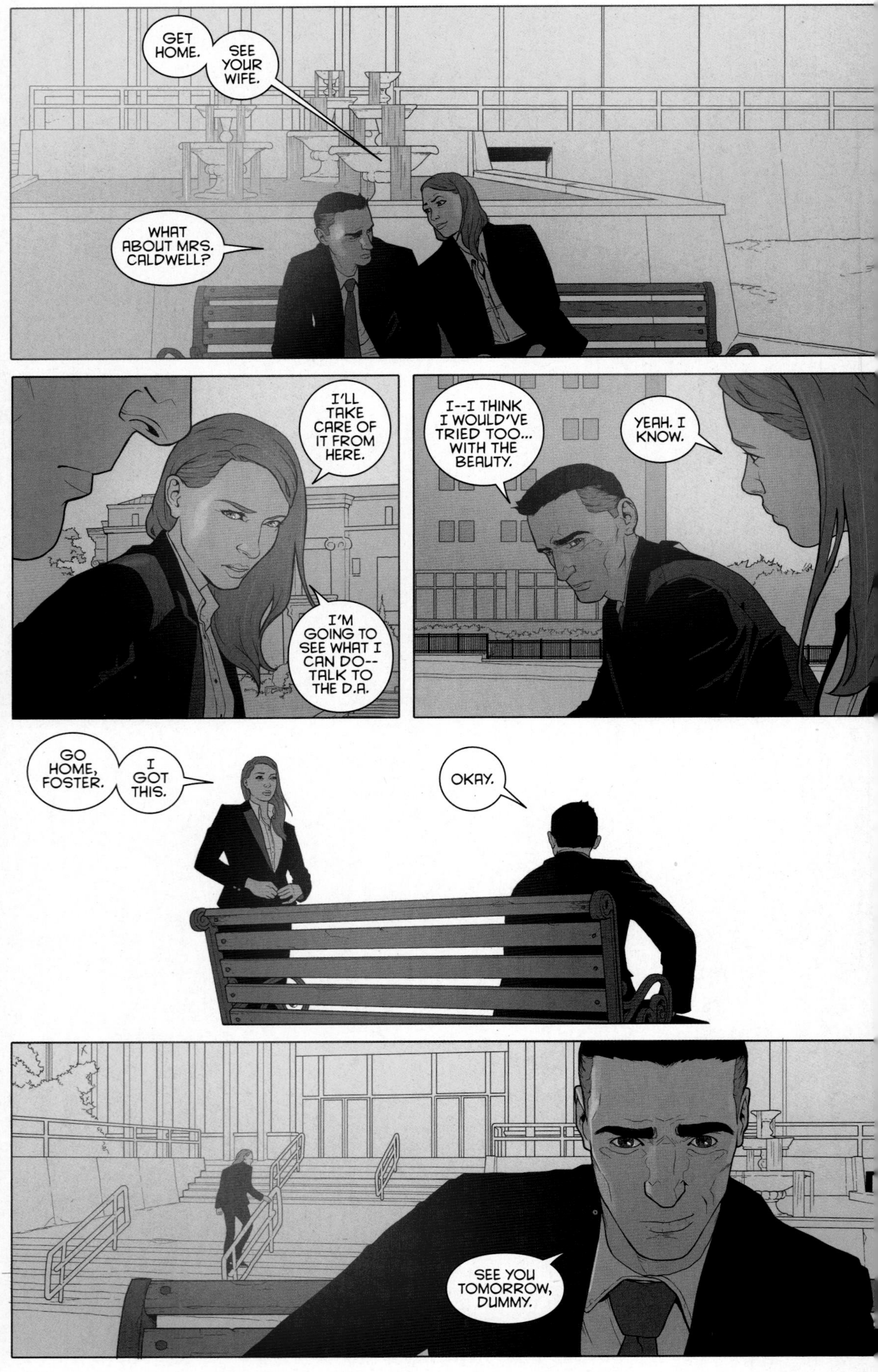
GET HOME.
SEE YOUR WIFE.
WHAT ABOUT MRS. CALDWELL?
I'LL TAKE CARE OF IT FROM HERE.
I'M GOING TO SEE WHAT I CAN DO-- TALK TO THE D.A.
I--I THINK I WOULD'VE TRIED TOO... WITH THE BEAUTY.
YEAH. I KNOW.
GO HOME, FOSTER.
I GOT THIS.
OKAY.
SEE YOU TOMORROW, DUMMY.

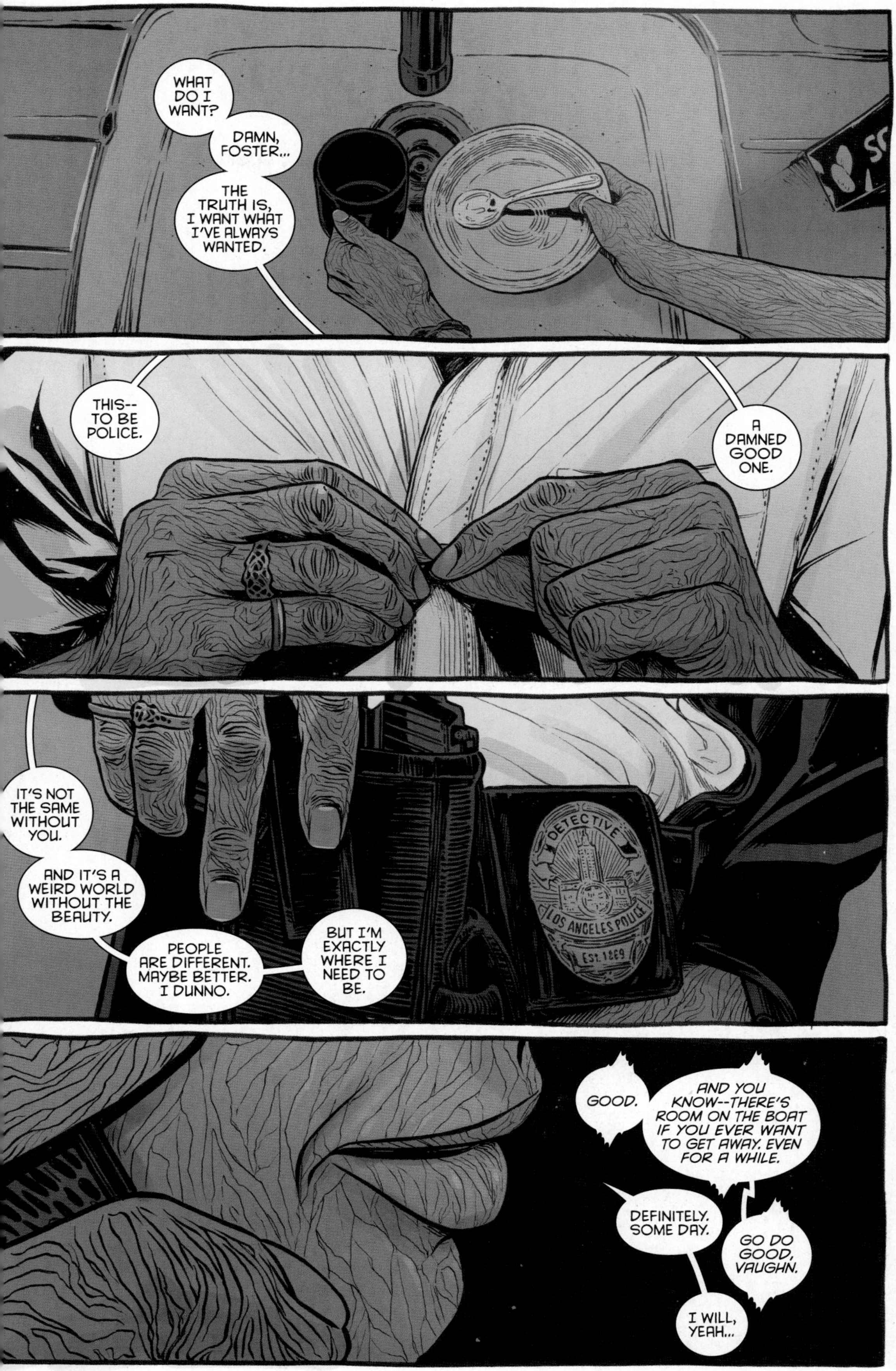

WHAT DO I WANT?
DAMN, FOSTER...
THE TRUTH IS, I WANT WHAT I'VE ALWAYS WANTED.
THIS-- TO BE POLICE.
A DAMNED GOOD ONE.
IT'S NOT THE SAME WITHOUT YOU.
AND IT'S A WEIRD WORLD WITHOUT THE BEAUTY.
PEOPLE ARE DIFFERENT. MAYBE BETTER. I DUNNO.
BUT I'M EXACTLY WHERE I NEED TO BE.
DETECTIVE
LOS ANGELES POLICE
EST. 1869
GOOD.
AND YOU KNOW--THERE'S ROOM ON THE BOAT IF YOU EVER WANT TO GET AWAY. EVEN FOR A WHILE.
DEFINITELY. SOME DAY.
GO DO GOOD, VAUGHN.
I WILL, YEAH...

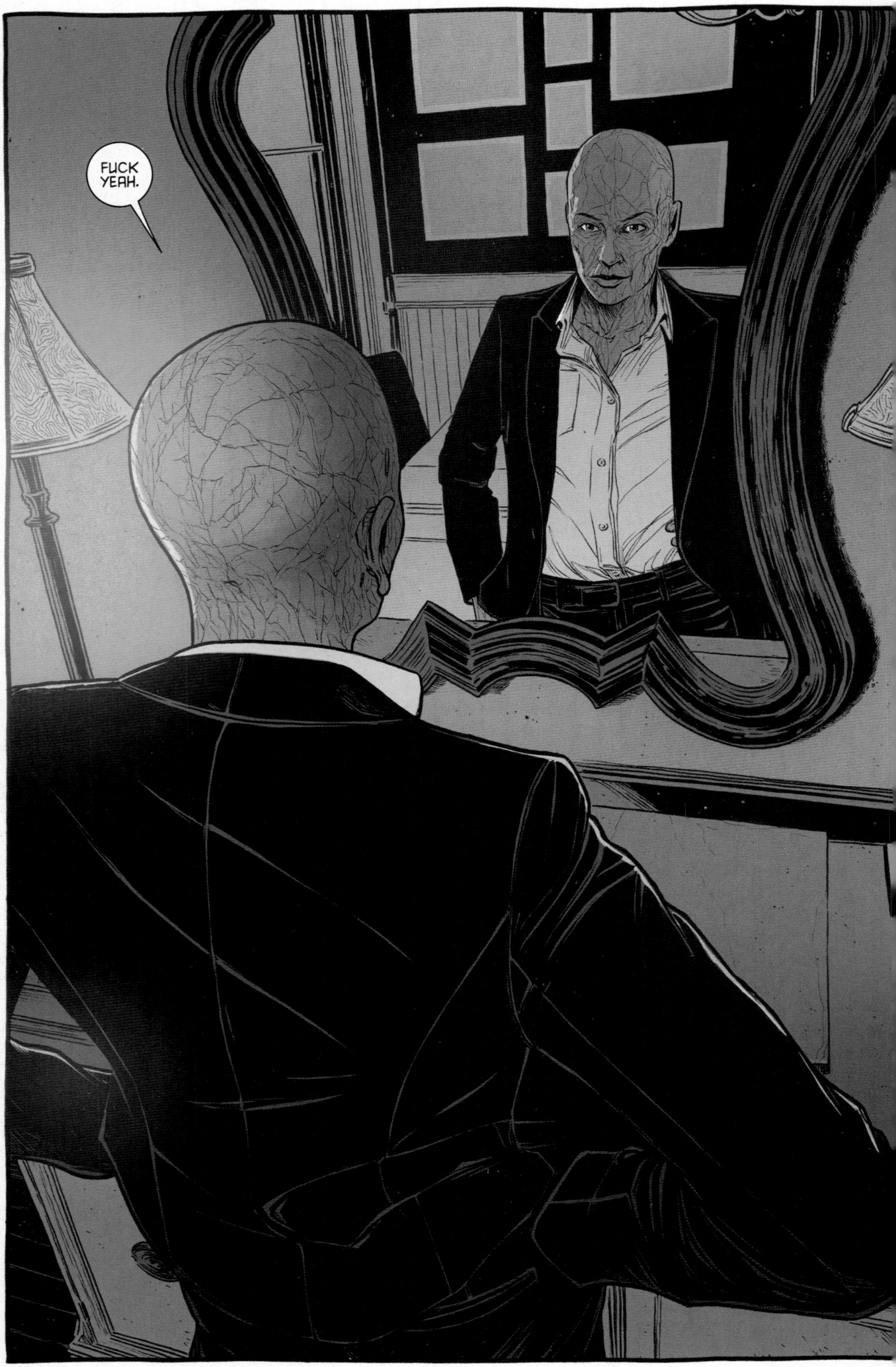
FUCK YEAH.

ISSUE #27
Cover B
Adam Gorham
& Hilary Jenkins

ISSUE #27
Cover A
Jeremy Haun
& Nick Filardi

ISSUE #28
Cover B
Thomas Nachlik
& Nick Filardi

ISSUE #28
Cover A
Jeremy Haun
& Nick Filardi

ISSUE #29
Cover A
Jeremy Haun
& Nick Filardi

ISSUE #29
Cover B
Greg Hinkle

ISSUE #30
Cover B
Jeremy Haun
& Nick Filardi

ISSUE #30
Cover A
Jeremy Haun
& Nick Filardi

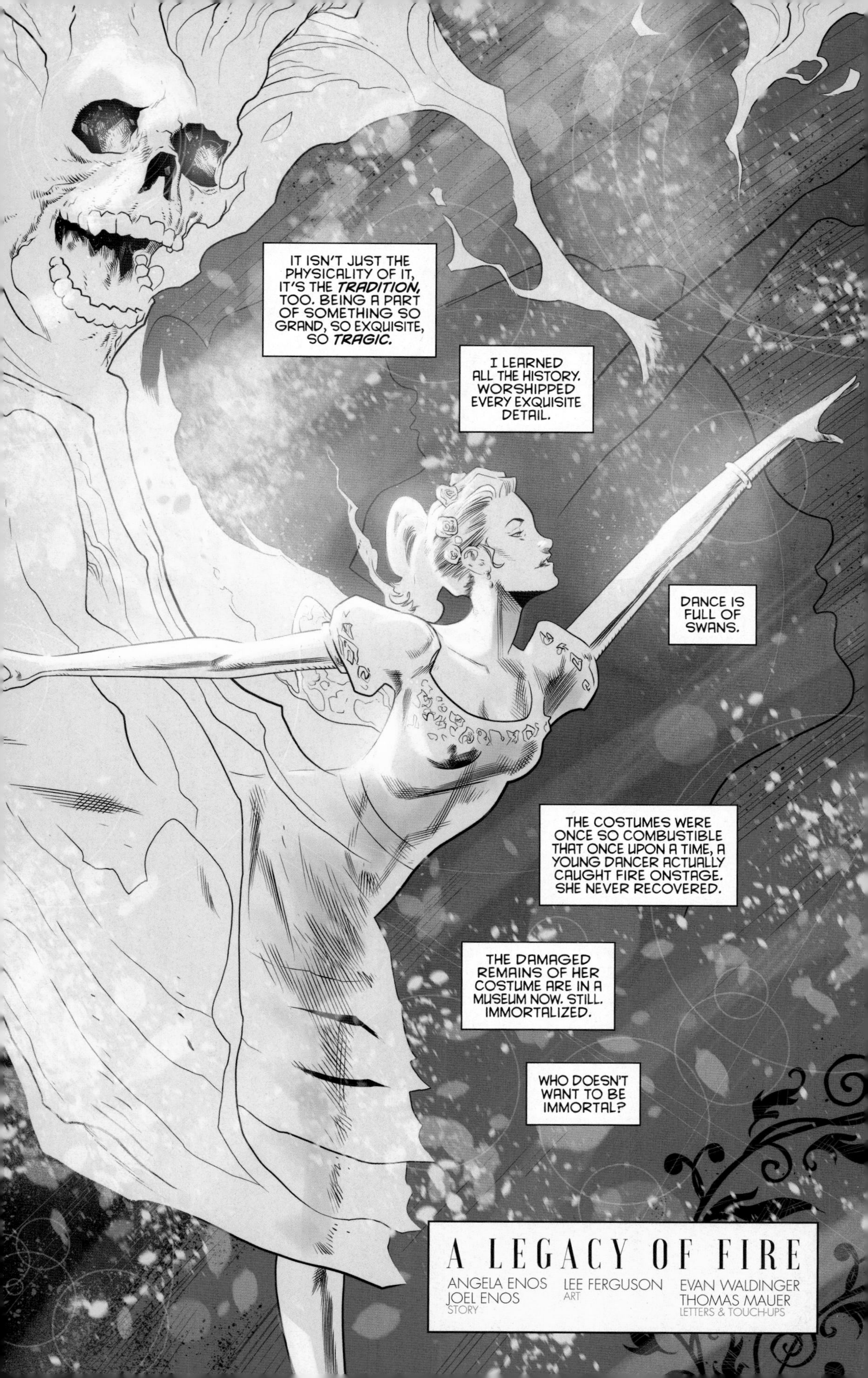
IT ISN'T JUST THE PHYSICALITY OF IT, IT'S THE *TRADITION,* TOO. BEING A PART OF SOMETHING SO GRAND, SO EXQUISITE, SO *TRAGIC.*
I LEARNED ALL THE HISTORY. WORSHIPPED EVERY EXQUISITE DETAIL.
DANCE IS FULL OF SWANS.
THE COSTUMES WERE ONCE SO COMBUSTIBLE THAT ONCE UPON A TIME, A YOUNG DANCER ACTUALLY CAUGHT FIRE ONSTAGE. SHE NEVER RECOVERED.
THE DAMAGED REMAINS OF HER COSTUME ARE IN A MUSEUM NOW. STILL. IMMORTALIZED.
WHO DOESN'T WANT TO BE IMMORTAL?
A LEGACY OF FIRE
ANGELA ENOS
JOEL ENOS
STORY
LEE FERGUSON
ART
EVAN WALDINGER
THOMAS MAUER
LETTERS & TOUCH-UPS

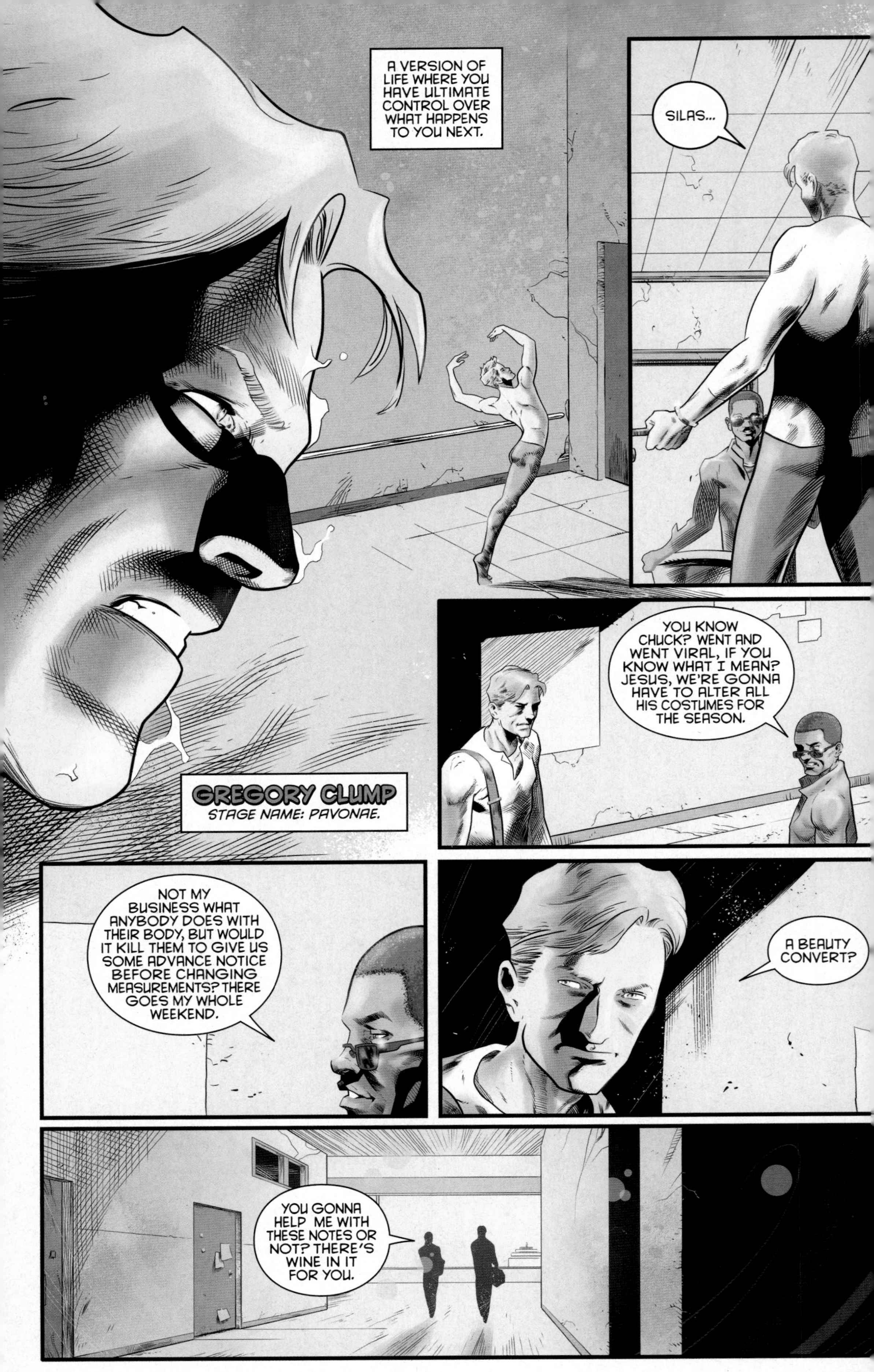
A VERSION OF LIFE WHERE YOU HAVE ULTIMATE CONTROL OVER WHAT HAPPENS TO YOU NEXT.
GREGORY CLUMP
STAGE NAME: PAVONAE.
SILAS...
YOU KNOW CHUCK? WENT AND WENT VIRAL, IF YOU KNOW WHAT I MEAN? JESUS, WE'RE GONNA HAVE TO ALTER ALL HIS COSTUMES FOR THE SEASON.
NOT MY BUSINESS WHAT ANYBODY DOES WITH THEIR BODY, BUT WOULD IT KILL THEM TO GIVE US SOME ADVANCE NOTICE BEFORE CHANGING MEASUREMENTS? THERE GOES MY WHOLE WEEKEND.
A BEAUTY CONVERT?
YOU GONNA HELP ME WITH THESE NOTES OR NOT? THERE'S WINE IN IT FOR YOU.

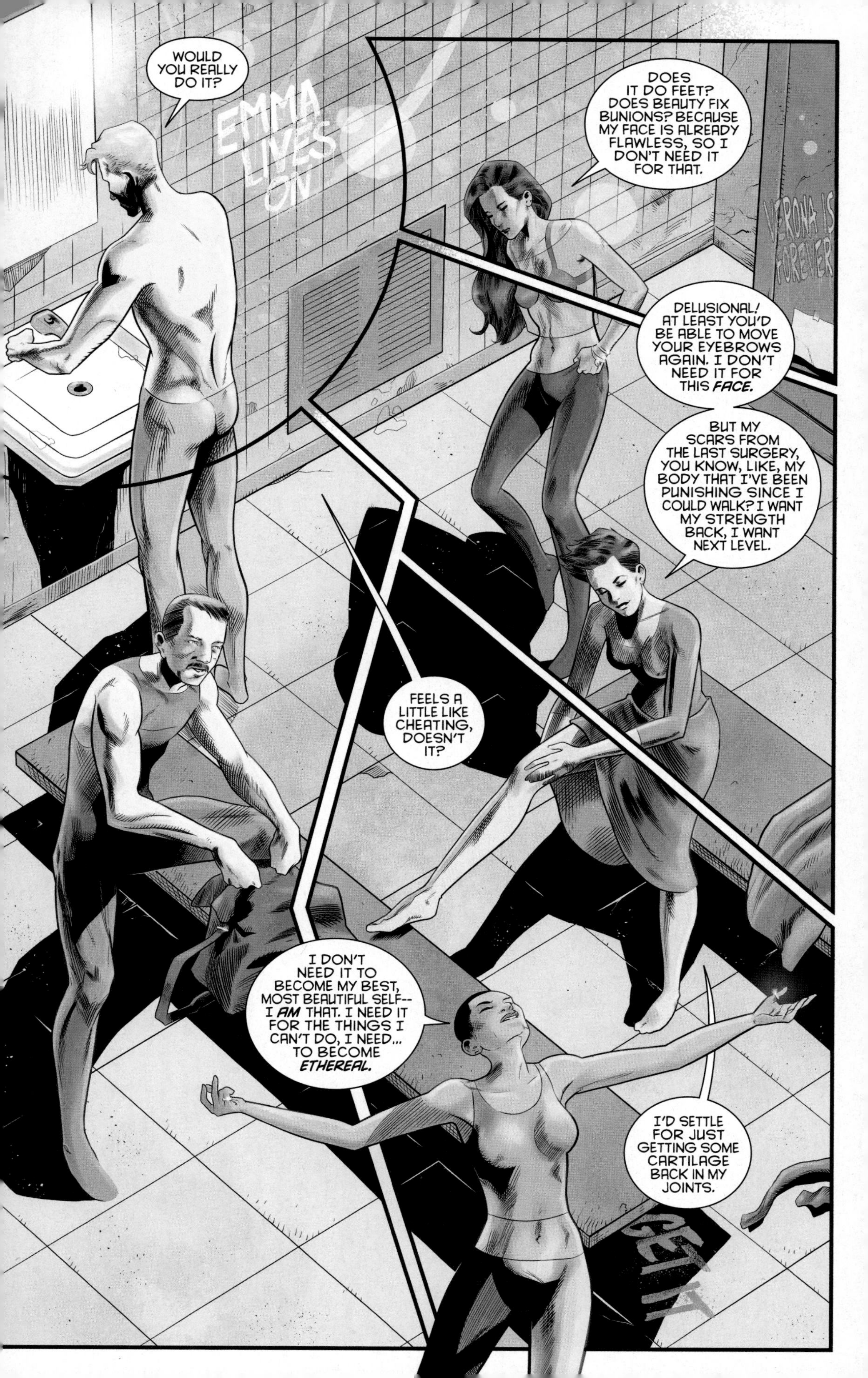
WOULD YOU REALLY DO IT?
EMMA LIVES ON
DOES IT DO FEET? DOES BEAUTY FIX BUNIONS? BECAUSE MY FACE IS ALREADY FLAWLESS, SO I DON'T NEED IT FOR THAT.
VERONA IS FOREVER
DELUSIONAL! AT LEAST YOU'D BE ABLE TO MOVE YOUR EYEBROWS AGAIN. I DON'T NEED IT FOR THIS FACE.
BUT MY SCARS FROM THE LAST SURGERY, YOU KNOW, LIKE, MY BODY THAT I'VE BEEN PUNISHING SINCE I COULD WALK? I WANT MY STRENGTH BACK, I WANT NEXT LEVEL.
FEELS A LITTLE LIKE CHEATING, DOESN'T IT?
I DON'T NEED IT TO BECOME MY BEST, MOST BEAUTIFUL SELF-- I AM THAT. I NEED IT FOR THE THINGS I CAN'T DO, I NEED... TO BECOME ETHEREAL.
I'D SETTLE FOR JUST GETTING SOME CARTILAGE BACK IN MY JOINTS.
GET IT

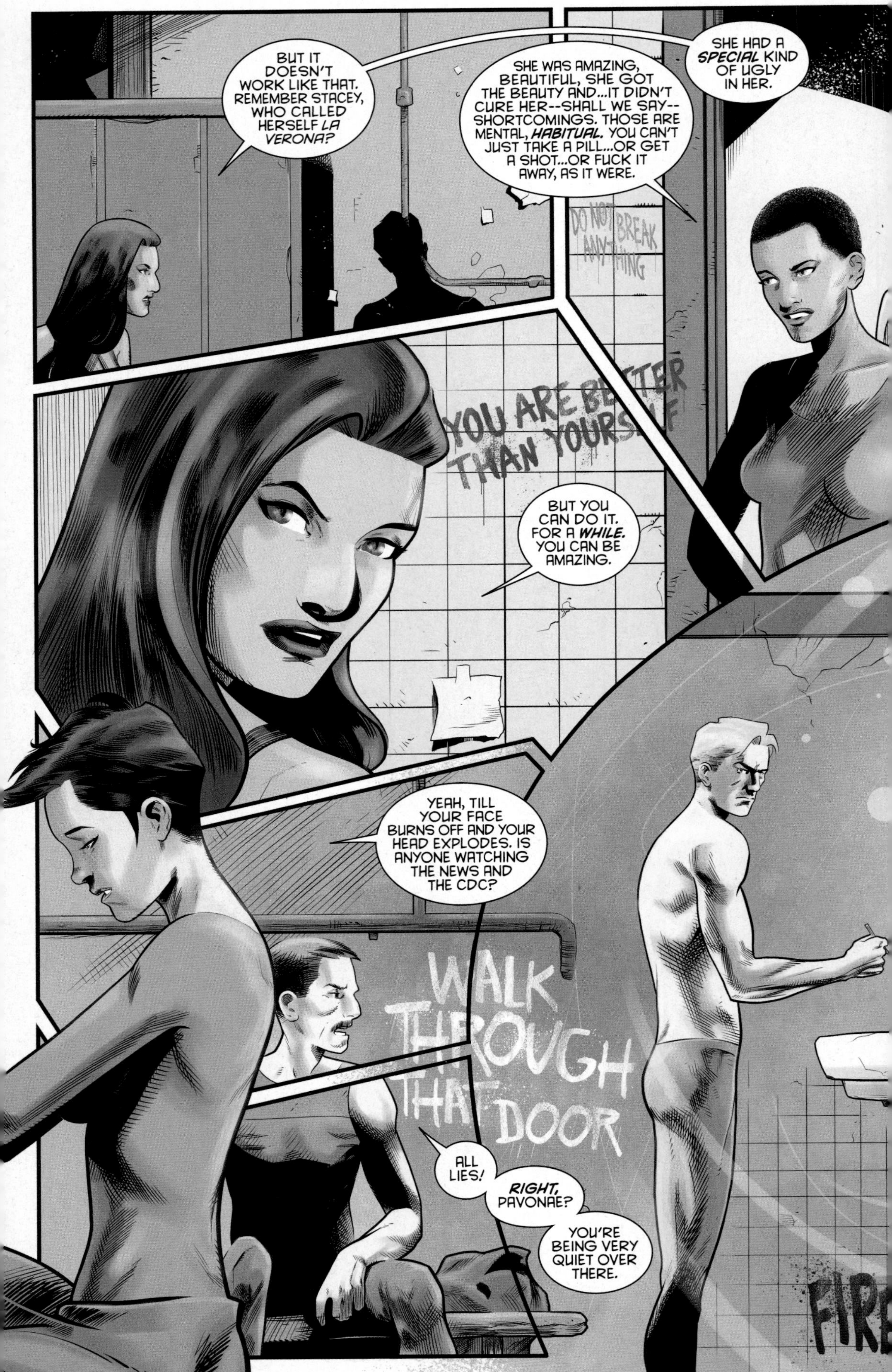
BUT IT DOESN'T WORK LIKE THAT. REMEMBER STACEY, WHO CALLED HERSELF *LA VERONA*?
SHE WAS AMAZING, BEAUTIFUL, SHE GOT THE BEAUTY AND...IT DIDN'T CURE HER--SHALL WE SAY--SHORTCOMINGS. THOSE ARE MENTAL, ***HABITUAL.*** YOU CAN'T JUST TAKE A PILL...OR GET A SHOT...OR FUCK IT AWAY, AS IT WERE.
SHE HAD A ***SPECIAL*** KIND OF UGLY IN HER.
DO NOT BREAK ANYTHING
YOU ARE BETTER THAN YOURSELF
BUT YOU CAN DO IT. FOR A ***WHILE.*** YOU CAN BE AMAZING.
YEAH, TILL YOUR FACE BURNS OFF AND YOUR HEAD EXPLODES. IS ANYONE WATCHING THE NEWS AND THE CDC?
WALK THROUGH THAT DOOR
ALL LIES!
RIGHT, PAVONAE?
YOU'RE BEING VERY QUIET OVER THERE.
FIRE

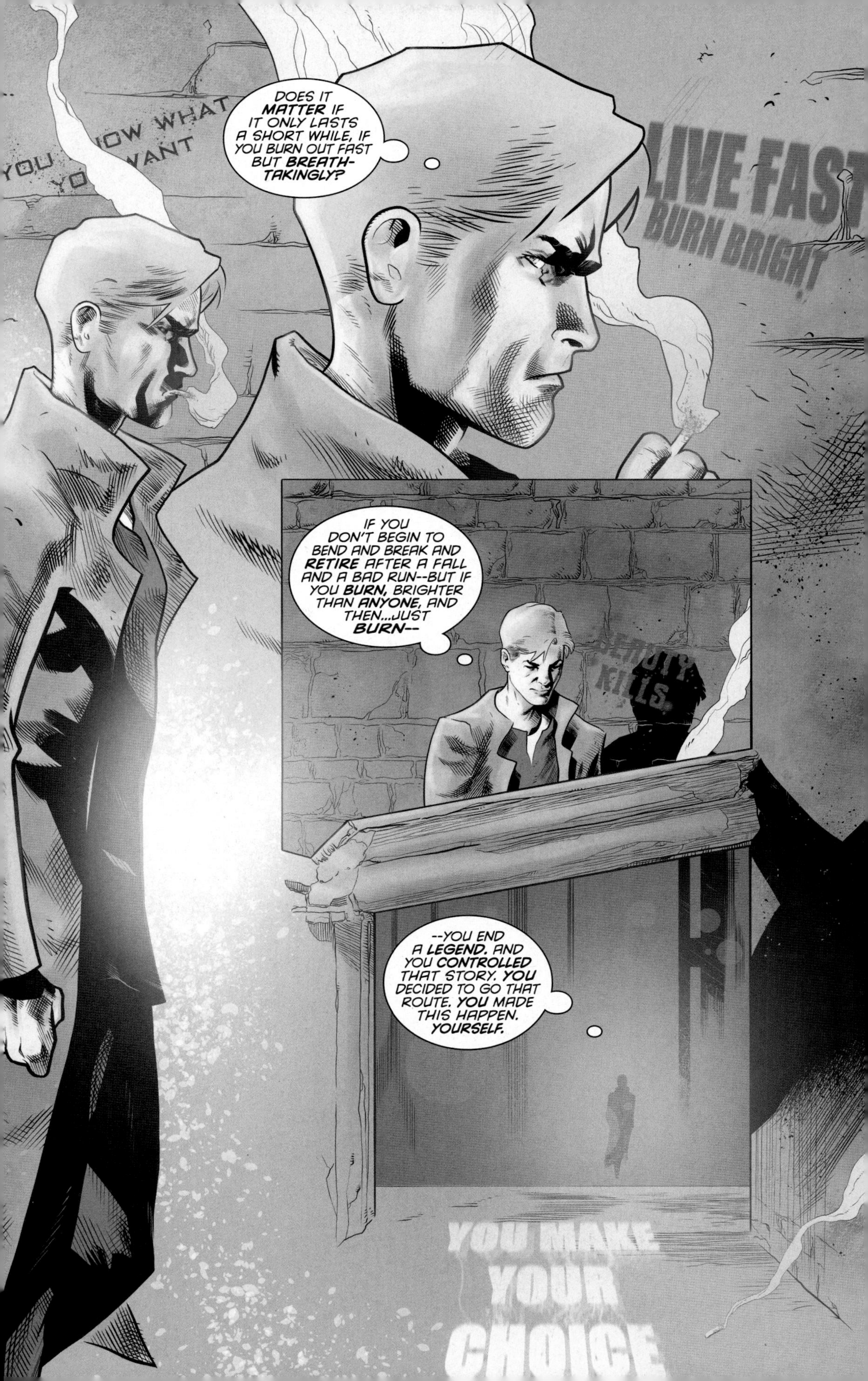
DOES IT MATTER IF IT ONLY LASTS A SHORT WHILE, IF YOU BURN OUT FAST BUT BREATH-TAKINGLY?
LIVE FAST BURN BRIGHT
IF YOU DON'T BEGIN TO BEND AND BREAK AND RETIRE AFTER A FALL AND A BAD RUN--BUT IF YOU BURN, BRIGHTER THAN ANYONE, AND THEN...JUST BURN--
--YOU END A LEGEND. AND YOU CONTROLLED THAT STORY. YOU DECIDED TO GO THAT ROUTE. YOU MADE THIS HAPPEN. YOURSELF.
YOU MAKE YOUR CHOICE

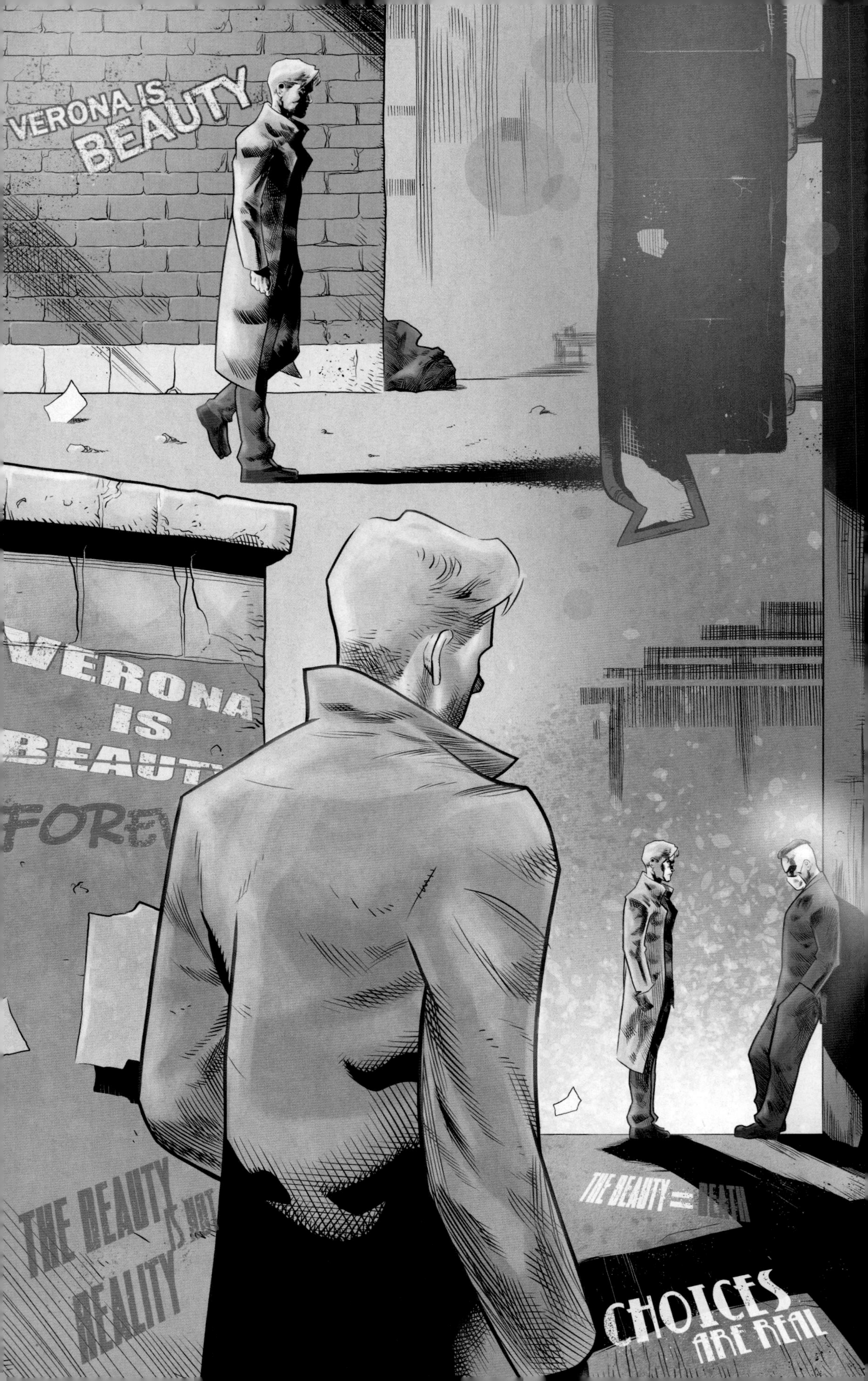

VERONA IS BEAUTY
VERONA IS BEAU
FORE
THE BEAUTY IS NOT REALITY
THE BEAUTY = DEATH
CHOICES ARE REAL

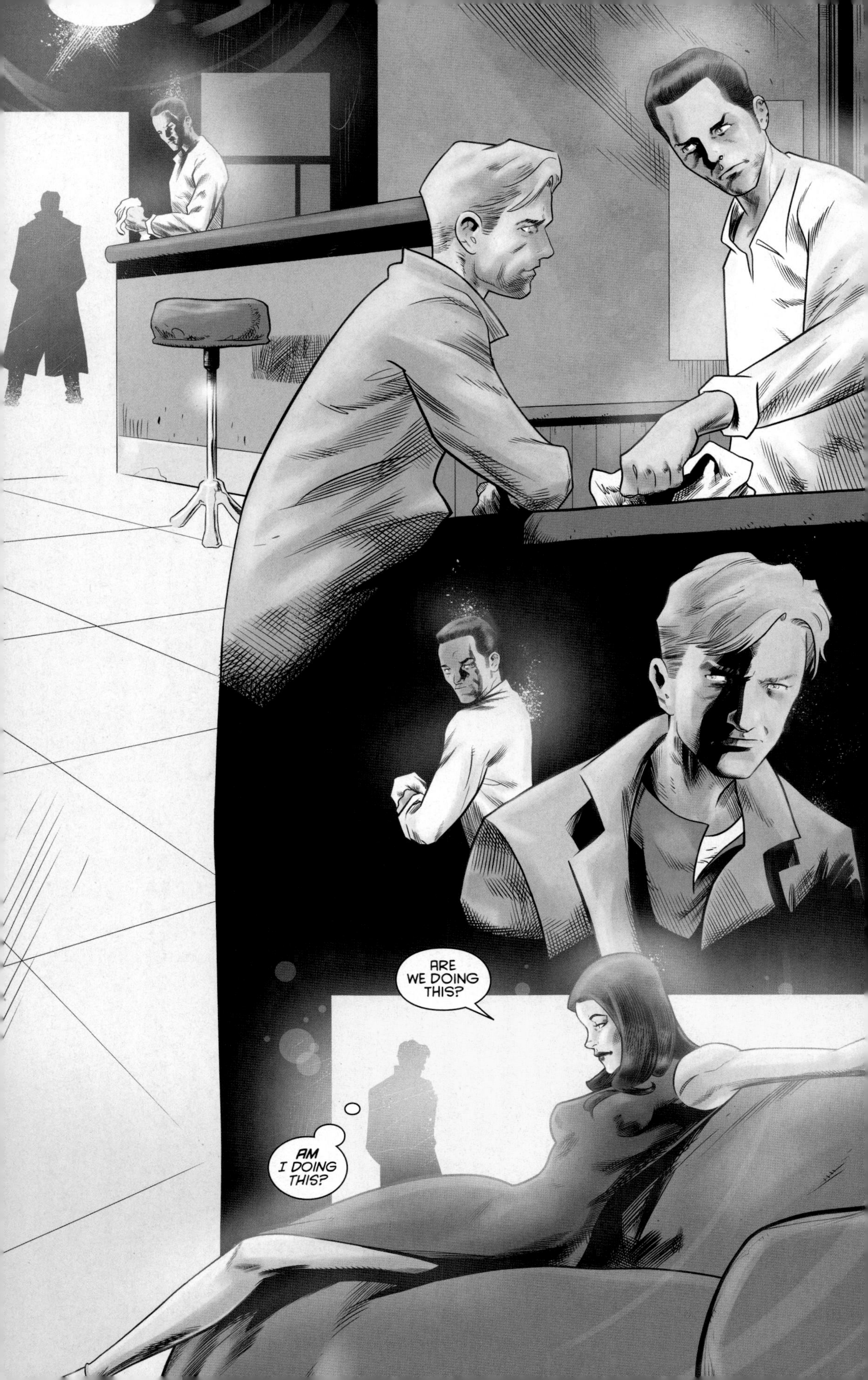
ARE WE DOING THIS?
AM I DOING THIS?

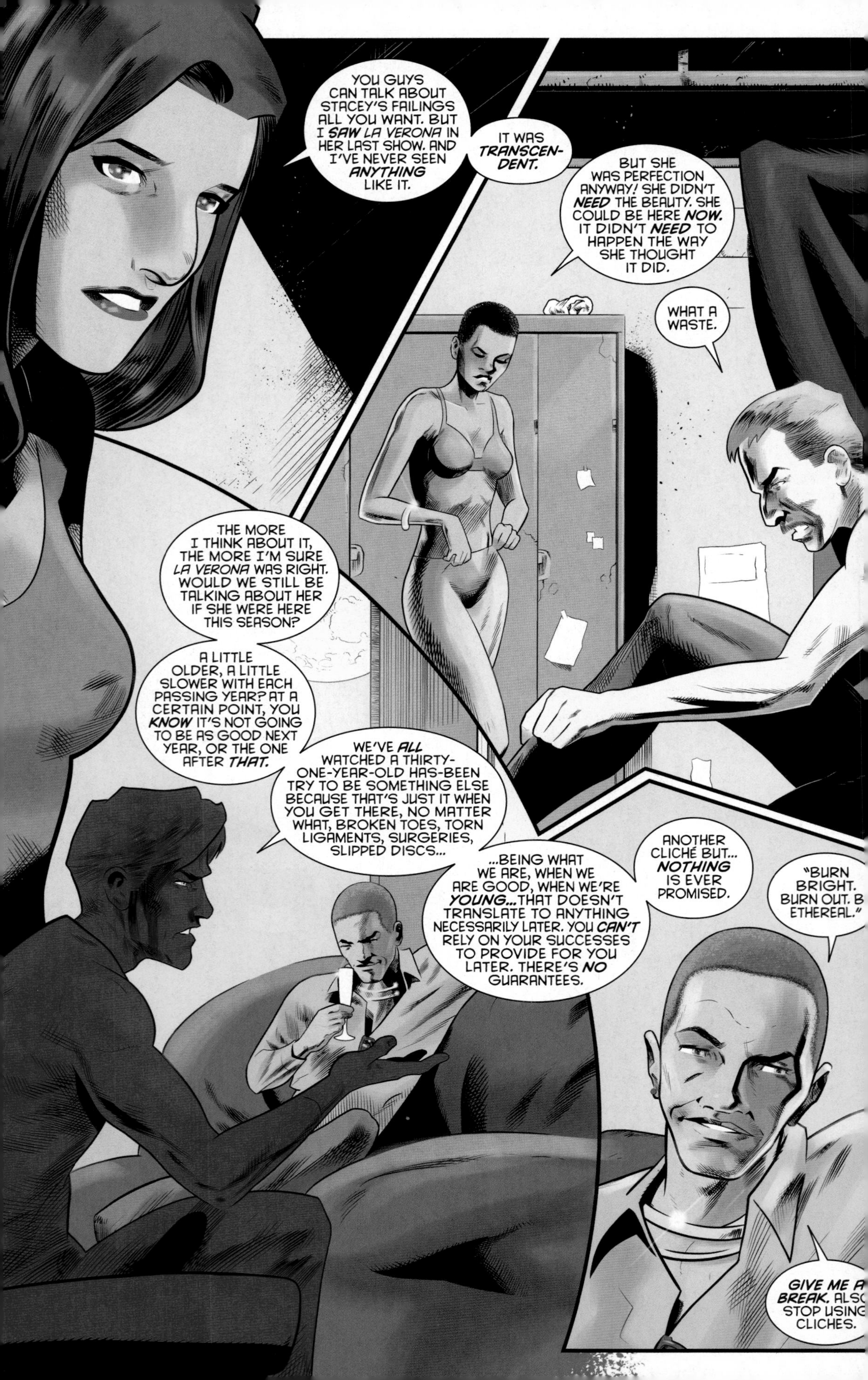

YOU GUYS CAN TALK ABOUT STACEY'S FAILINGS ALL YOU WANT. BUT I *SAW LA VERONA* IN HER LAST SHOW. AND I'VE NEVER SEEN *ANYTHING* LIKE IT.
IT WAS *TRANSCEN-DENT.*
BUT SHE WAS PERFECTION ANYWAY! SHE DIDN'T *NEED* THE BEAUTY. SHE COULD BE HERE *NOW.* IT DIDN'T *NEED* TO HAPPEN THE WAY SHE THOUGHT IT DID.
WHAT A WASTE.
THE MORE I THINK ABOUT IT, THE MORE I'M SURE *LA VERONA* WAS RIGHT. WOULD WE STILL BE TALKING ABOUT HER IF SHE WERE HERE THIS SEASON?
A LITTLE OLDER, A LITTLE SLOWER WITH EACH PASSING YEAR? AT A CERTAIN POINT, YOU *KNOW* IT'S NOT GOING TO BE AS GOOD NEXT YEAR, OR THE ONE AFTER *THAT.*
WE'VE *ALL* WATCHED A THIRTY-ONE-YEAR-OLD HAS-BEEN TRY TO BE SOMETHING ELSE BECAUSE THAT'S JUST IT WHEN YOU GET THERE, NO MATTER WHAT, BROKEN TOES, TORN LIGAMENTS, SURGERIES, SLIPPED DISCS...
...BEING WHAT WE ARE, WHEN WE ARE GOOD, WHEN WE'RE *YOUNG...* THAT DOESN'T TRANSLATE TO ANYTHING NECESSARILY LATER. YOU *CAN'T* RELY ON YOUR SUCCESSES TO PROVIDE FOR YOU LATER. THERE'S *NO* GUARANTEES.
ANOTHER CLICHÉ BUT... *NOTHING* IS EVER PROMISED.
"BURN BRIGHT. BURN OUT. B ETHEREAL."
GIVE ME A BREAK. ALSO STOP USING CLICHES.

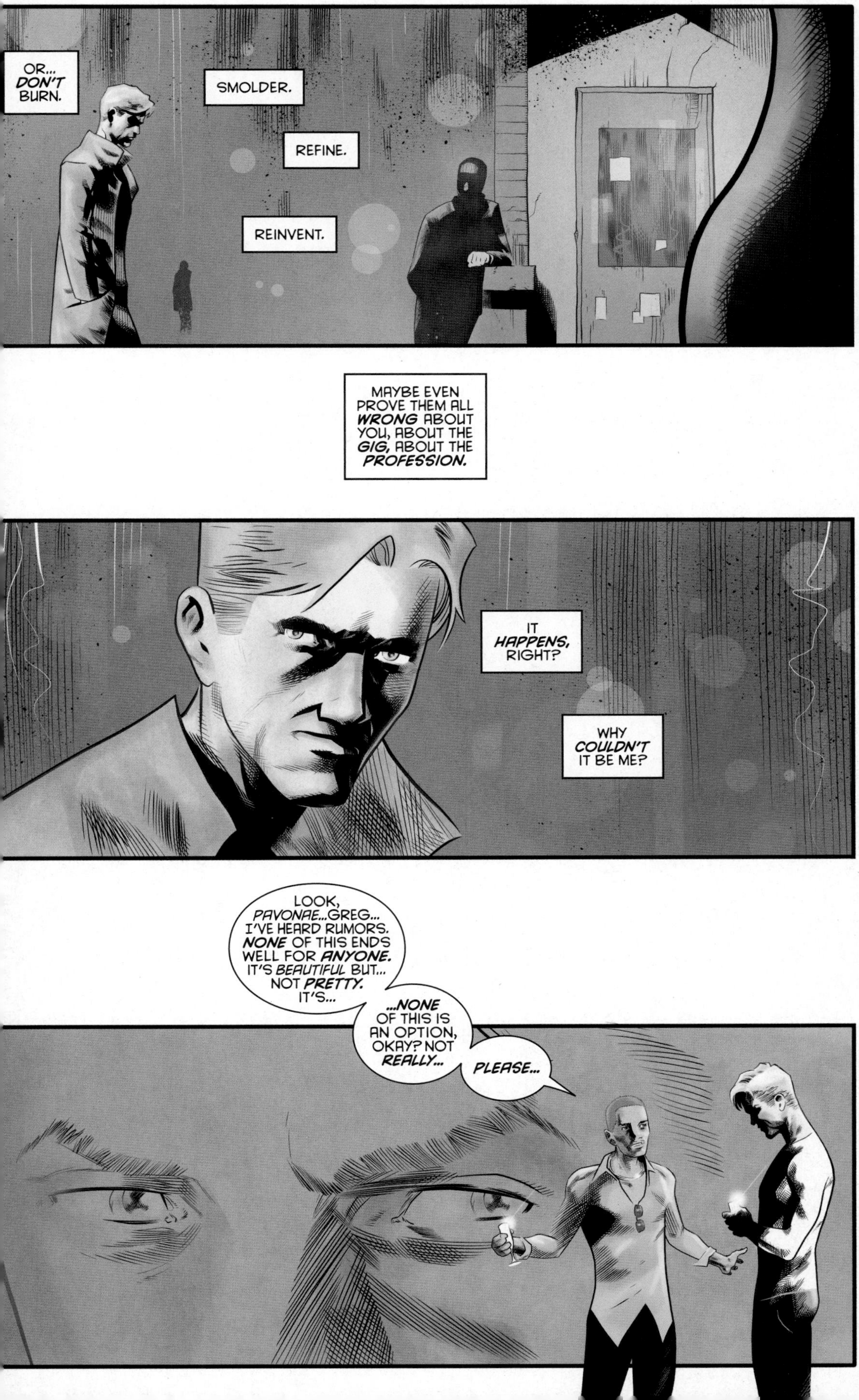
OR... DON'T BURN.
SMOLDER.
REFINE.
REINVENT.
MAYBE EVEN PROVE THEM ALL WRONG ABOUT YOU, ABOUT THE GIG, ABOUT THE PROFESSION.
IT HAPPENS, RIGHT?
WHY COULDN'T IT BE ME?
LOOK, PAVONAE...GREG... I'VE HEARD RUMORS. NONE OF THIS ENDS WELL FOR ANYONE. IT'S BEAUTIFUL BUT... NOT PRETTY. IT'S...
...NONE OF THIS IS AN OPTION, OKAY? NOT REALLY...
PLEASE...

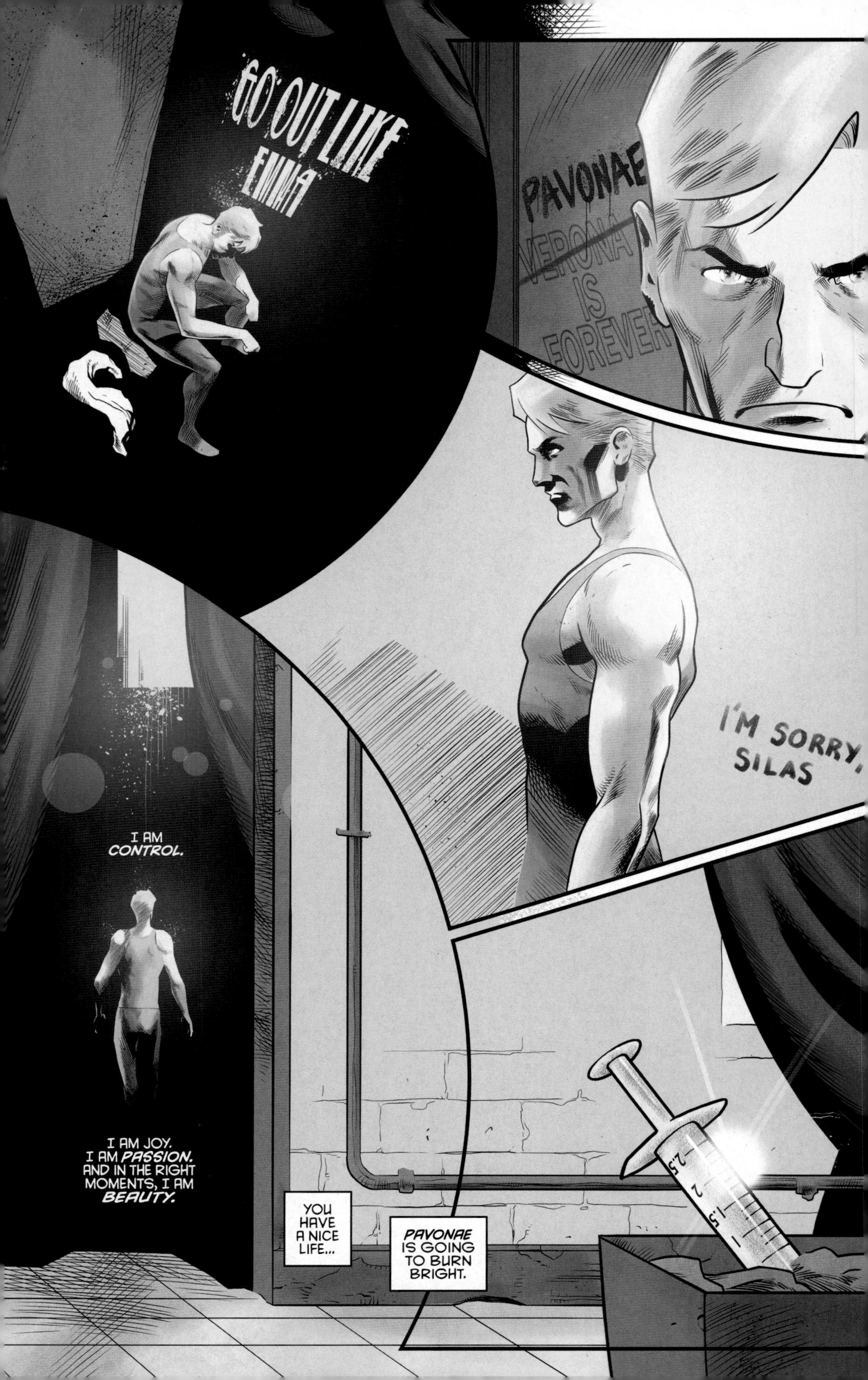
GO OUT LIKE EMMA
PAVONAE
VERONA IS FOREVER
I'M SORRY, SILAS
I AM CONTROL.
I AM JOY. I AM PASSION. AND IN THE RIGHT MOMENTS, I AM BEAUTY.
YOU HAVE A NICE LIFE...
PAVONAE IS GOING TO BURN BRIGHT.

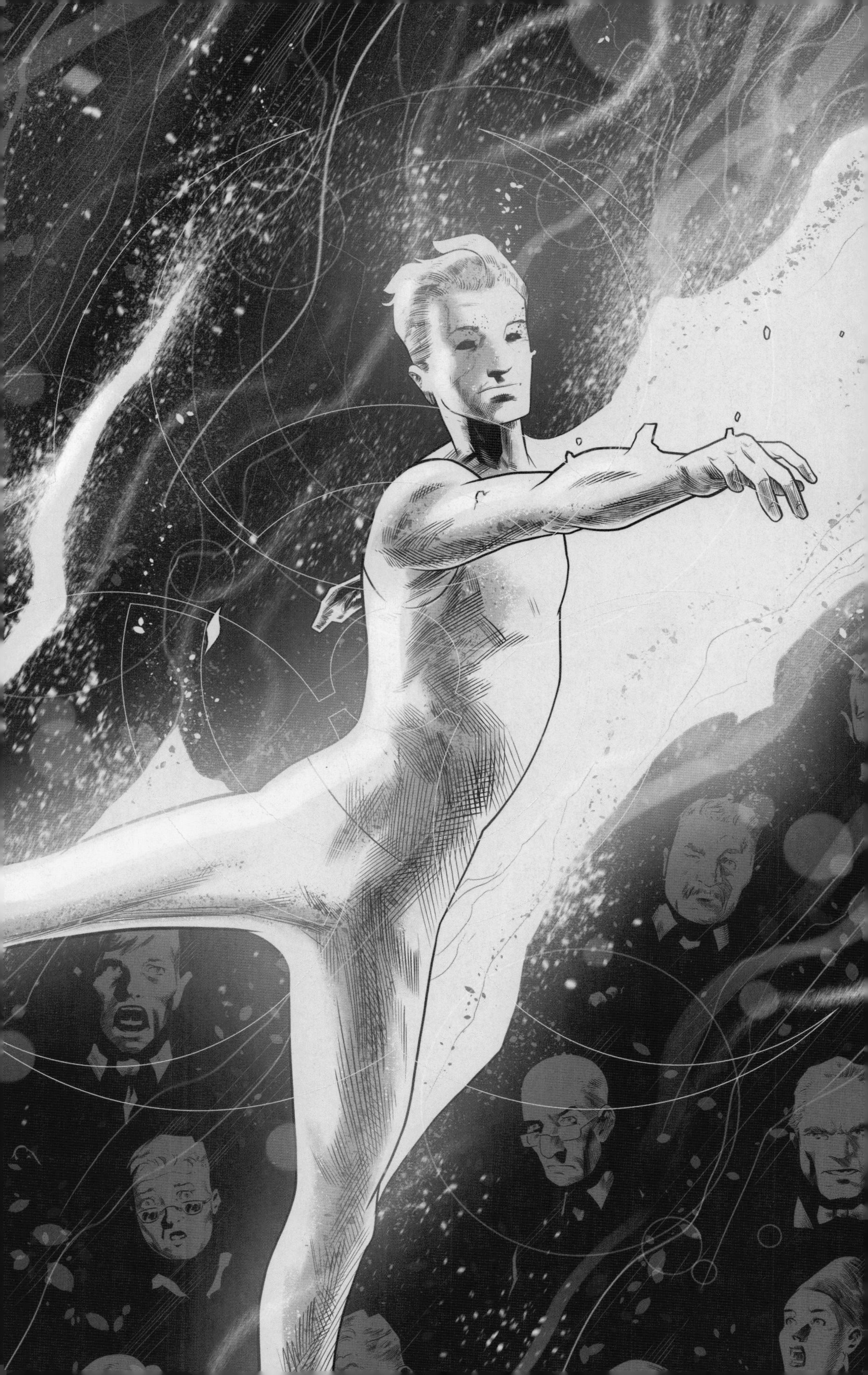

All good things...

...come to an end. Sure. That's part of it. But there's more.

This final volume of THE BEAUTY has been a long *long* time coming. There was no real planning for the series of twists and turns that brought us here. There *certainly* wasn't any way we could've seen a global pandemic hitting the stop button on all of our lives.

But here we are. Finally. And you know what? This is a *good* thing.

We're telling this last volume—this final little button—exactly the way we always wanted to. We've spent this arc looking at the world in the days leading up to issue one of the series. We're saying goodbye to Vaughn, Foster, Timo, Ezerae, and all the rest of this spanning cast right at the moment where we first met them.

We never had a lot to say about the world of THE BEAUTY after the cure. After all, this was a book examining the lengths we all go to in order to look a certain way.

The longer we sat with this story, though, the more we realized that there was just one thing we *needed* to say. We needed to visit Foster and Vaughn just one last time. So much of their partnership—their friendship—was figuring out who and what they wanted to be. Over the past couple of years, with everything going on in our world, that's something we've all had to examine. It was important for us to give a bit of a hint that Foster and Vaughn found what they wanted for themselves. We like that.

We'd like to take a moment and thank everyone who made this series possible...

To **Mike Huddleston**, **Brett Weldele**, **Stephen Green**, **Thomas Nachlik**, **Matt Dow Smith**, and **Danny Luckert** for their absolutely gorgeous interior art.

To **John Rauch**, **Nayoung Kim**, **Nick Filardi**, and **Brett Weldele** for their stunning color work.

To **Fonografiks** and **Thomas Mauer** for their design and lettering work. There's never enough love for what they do.

To **all of the brilliant cover artists** that helped this book jump off the shelves.

To **Image Comics**, whose staff has been fantastically supportive every step of the way.

And finally to **Joel Enos**. Editor doesn't really sum up what Joel brought to this book. He was a patient guiding hand and herder of cats. He was a friend—no—he's family.

Finally, we want to thank you for joining us on this weird wonderful journey. We couldn't have done this without you.

And that's it. Thirty issues. THE BEAUTY.

Well...maybe not "it" it.

After all...all good things never *really* end.

See you again soon.
—*Jeremy Haun & Jason A. Hurley*